BENNYTOWN

Matt Carter

OWL HOLLOW PRESS

Owl Hollow Press, LLC, Springville, UT 84663

Bennytown

Library of Congress Cataloging-in-Publication Data
Bennytown / M. Carter. — First edition.

Summary:
For nearly sixty years, Bennytown has been America's most exciting family theme park destination. But sixteen-year-old Noel Hallstrom is about to find out more about Bennytown's darkness than he ever wanted to know.

ISBN 978-1-945654-53-4 (paperback)
ISBN 978-1-945654-54-1 (e-book)
LCCN 2020937110

To Jeff G.,
Without you, this never would have happened.

ADAM
1989

"I believe in Bennytown," Adam sniffled.

You weren't supposed to cry at Bennytown, since it was a magical place where dreams come true. Bennytown was a themed wonderland of rides, shows, and fantastical worlds that let you escape from real life.

His parents and commercials repeated that to him on a regular basis, so it had to be the truth.

It didn't feel really magical right now, though.

Adam sat on the curb in Happy Hollow, whimpering and wiping away tears. Bits of vanilla ice cream and chocolate smeared his chin. He wanted to kick Shawn for ruining everything. Mommy and Daddy always took Shawn's side and barely listened to their other son. Even when Adam was right.

He wasn't supposed to cry, but he did anyway.

"I believe in Bennytown," he repeated.

Repeating the phrase helped ease the pain a little. The words had a power he found comforting, like saying he believed in Santa or the Easter Bunny. Unlike any of those mythical figures, these words had extra power because Bennytown was real.

Bennytown wasn't entirely as magical as he'd hoped, but it was pretty close. The rides he was tall enough to ride were amazing, the food was great, and walking through each of the themed lands was like walking into a movie.

Primordial World made it feel like dinosaurs still walked the earth.

Journey through Americana was a Western brought to life.

Island of Legends turned storybook characters like dragons, the minotaur and genies into a reality.

But they all paled in comparison to Happy Hollow.

Happy Hollow was like walking through all the best Dorian Studios cartoons. The rounded houses lined up all in a row with fluffy-looking edges. Ice cream and churro carts sat at every corner. Being the home to Benny & Friends made it even more perfect.

That was the greatest part.

The brightly clad costumes helped the performers appear identical to the characters in the cartoons, even if they didn't talk. They danced, hugged, and high-fived every time he approached them. Already, he had gotten the signatures of four characters in his autograph book. Flora Fox's was exciting, even though she was a girl.

They were amazing! Pictures would have been better, but he didn't get any of those. Mommy and Daddy were so focused on getting pictures of Shawn, that they forgot to take pictures of him.

His parents reprimanded Adam for complaining and reminded him that this day wasn't about him. After hearing for the third time that he should be grateful for the opportunity, he couldn't help feeling they were mad at him.

And because he didn't want anything messing up the big moment, the one he'd waited for since they got here, he didn't say anything.

Then Shawn had to mess it up anyway.

Adam pouted, looking at the big green house with the bigger green rabbit ears sticking out of the top. These ears were so much bigger than the Benny ears everyone else was wearing.

His parents should've been here to get him by now. Maybe they'd just taken Shawn home and left Adam behind because they were mad.

Angry as he was, that thought made him even sadder.

It was because of Shawn that they got to come to Bennytown.

Six months ago, just after his fifth birthday, Shawn started having headaches that wouldn't go away. The doctors said he had something called brain cancer, and that he might die. Though he'd never liked Shawn much, it still made Adam upset, especially because Mommy and Daddy started fighting so much after the trips to the hospital.

They fought, they went to doctors, and they started making everyone go to church three times a week. They hoped that if everyone prayed hard enough, a miracle would occur to save Shawn.

Something must've been right, since a miracle did come, though it wasn't the one Mommy and Daddy wanted.

Some people from this company called Make-A-Wish came to the house and promised to grant any wish that Shawn wanted (other than making him better).

Being a good American kid, Shawn wanted to visit Bennytown.

It was great. After a plane ride, a nice hotel, and passes to get to the front of the ride lines, there was even a special lunch with Benny the Bunny!

Adam couldn't wait to meet Benny.

While all the other Dorian Studios cartoon characters had great adventures and got into trouble, Benny knew how to solve every problem as the levelheaded leader. Usually, he worked things out while strumming a banjo on his front porch. When Benny talked or sang to the screen, Adam felt like he was talking only to him.

As a kid in desperate need of friends, Adam felt like Benny was his and his alone, and he wanted to keep it that way.

When the moment finally came for their big meal, Adam was excited.

His parents were more focused on Shawn, pushing him out in front and trying to distract Adam with a Benny the Bunny–shaped ice cream bar. He'd never had a treat so delicious, so utterly perfect that he ate it in a deliberate manner so he wouldn't defile Benny's face too quickly Though the ice cream was tasty, Adam wasn't that easily distracted. Despite their best efforts, Adam pushed his way in front of Shawn, so he'd be the first to see the real Benny.

He was everything Adam imagined.

Benny was so tall that his long ears almost touched the sky. He was every bit as round and fluffy as he appeared in the cartoons. With large, white-gloved hands, neon-green fur, and denim overalls with red patches on the knees, his familiar presence warmed Adam's heart. Despite big buck teeth, Benny's smile was friendly. Something felt wrong about the eyes since they were just white plastic circles with tiny black pupils that stared at nothing and everything all at once. It was an unsettling feeling, but it only briefly bothered Adam.

This was Benny, and Benny was home.

When Benny beckoned them to his side, Shawn chose that moment to ruin everything.

After a long, over-stimulating day, Shawn let loose with a wailing fit. After cringing away from the characters all day, he kicked and screamed as Benny drew close. Mommy and Daddy tried calming him, but he kicked Adam's ice cream bar, smashing it into Adam's face.

Hard chocolate chunks and vanilla ice cream dripped down Adam's chin and onto his favorite Thundercats t-shirt.

"YOU RUINED IT, YOU SHIT!" Adam yelled, slipping in one of Daddy's favorite cuss words and hitting his brother.

The next thing he knew, Mommy slapped Adam. Both parents were screaming at him to apologize and stop ruining Shawn's day.

Adam ran out of the room to clean up the mess, but he collapsed on the curb to cry. Waiting for his family to finish lunch, he tried to cheer himself up, even though it wasn't fair, and everything was Shawn's fault.

"I believe in Bennytown, I believe in Bennytown, ibelieveinbennytown…"

"Hey, kiddo," a friendly voice called out.

Adam turned. Behind him, the door to a house was opened a crack. The house was new and looked like an igloo, not like anything from any of the cartoons Adam knew. Signs on it said it was an exciting new attraction "COMING WINTER 1989."

White eyes peered out through the crack in the door.

"Me?"

The big round eyes nodded. Adam stood up and walked over to them.

"You look like you need a special friend," the cheerful voice said.

Sheepishly, Adam nodded.

"Well, I need a special friend, too. But people aren't supposed to see me yet. Can you keep a secret?"

Adam nodded again.

The door swung open and Adam entered.

His new friend was shaped like a pear, with a fat lower body getting smaller at the top. With a tiny head dwarfed by a bushy mustache and two long, pointed teeth, he looked similar to the other characters but was most certainly a new addition to the park. A colorful, flowered shirt covered his light purple skin and a pair of sunglasses sat on his forehead above his plastic white eyes.

"What's your name, kiddo?" the big guy asked through his unmoving mouth.

"Adam," Adam said, unable to meet his eyes.

"Well it's a pleasure to meetcha, Adam! I'm Wilbur Walrus! Wanna give me some flipper?" Wilbur asked, holding out a flat hand. Instinctively, Adam slapped it.

"Such a strong boy, totally awesome. Come, grab a seat! Let's getcha cleaned up and turn that frown upside down!" Wilbur waddled across the house and out of sight through a doorway.

Adam sat in an oversized chair that seemed to be carved from snow. Wilbur returned holding a towel. Grateful, Adam took it and wiped down his face.

"Whaddya think of ol' Wilbur's house?"

"It's neat," Adam said, casting his eyes around the white, icy looking room and settling his eyes on the floor.

Wilbur took a seat across from him and said, "Well I'm glad you think it's neat, but you shouldn't have seen it yet—it's not finished. But when it is, it'll be real cool. You can keep this secret, can'tcha?"

"Yes Wilbur, I can," Adam replied.

"Wonderful! So, ya wanna tell ol' Wilbur why you're cryin' when you could be having an exciting Bennytown day?"

Adam was hesitant, but then he let it all out.

Shawn and his cancer.

Mommy and Daddy.

What happened in Benny's house.

The more he talked, the better he felt, like Wilbur was just taking the sadness right out of him. When he was done telling his story, Wilbur clapped his flippers again.

"Well, why didn'tcha say so? Let's go meet Benny!"

"Really?" Adam asked, hopeful.

"I may not have a lot of friends yet, but Benny and I know each other very well. I got a rabbit hole in the back that'll take us right over there. Whaddya say?"

Adam smiled, nervous with excitement.

"Sure!"

"Totally awesome!" Wilbur exclaimed, hopping up and taking one of Adam's hands in his flippers. Though the flippers looked soft, the hand beneath squeezed tightly as it led Adam to the back of the house. Wilbur led him through a door marked

"BENNYTOWN FAMILY MEMBERS ONLY!" and into a stairwell.

The stairwell didn't look like the rest of the house, or a rabbit hole for that matter. A concrete tunnel with a wide, curving metal staircase lead underground, lit by buzzing fluorescents.

Adam followed without question, because Wilbur seemed cool and because he really wanted to meet Benny.

The hall at the end of the stairs was still bare concrete.

Adam was confused.

He was even more confused when the lights went out, and Wilbur let go of his hand.

"*Wilbur?*" he wailed, his voice echoing down the long hallway.

Adam reached out blindly. Wilbur had left him. Left him! No, Wilbur wouldn't leave him. Wilbur was his special friend, and friends didn't leave friends behind when they needed them. No sir, they—

Something in front of him growled, a deep, wet sound that rattled the floor itself.

Something big.

The words came to Adam, full of power and hope. "I believe in Bennytown, I believe in Bennytown…"

The air was full of a damp, gross smell that almost made Adam hurl. It smelled like Mr. Windy, their cat, after he went under their porch and died. When Adam found him, the bugs were crawling over his body and he didn't look like Mr. Windy anymore.

Adam was sure he heard the writhing sound of the feasting bugs hiding somewhere in that growl.

He turned to run from the growl and smacked into a wall, stumbling and falling down.

"I believe in Bennytown, I believe in Bennytown, I believe in Bennytown!" He repeated the phrase at a machine gun's pace, hoping their power would make this evil go away.

The growl still came for him. It would catch him, and there was nothing he could do.

The words meant nothing. Bennytown meant nothing.

He cried again, and then felt terrible.

You weren't supposed to cry at Bennytown.

"I'm sorry, Mommy! I'm sorry, Daddy! I'm sorry, Shawn! I want to go home! I'll do whatever you want! I'm sorry! I'm sorry! I don't want it, I don't want it, I don't—"

By the time Adam thought to scream, he found that not only was Wilbur pressing his body against his, but that Adam could no longer breathe for the plastic bag covering his face.

"Shhh, kiddo, or he'll catch you!" Wilbur whispered from behind, pulling Adam back by his favorite Thundercats shirt as he began to forcefully disrobe the boy.

Even in his fading consciousness, he knew this was still better than the *growl* catching him.

PART 1
ISN'T THAT EXCITING?

NOEL
2019

You think you know fear, but you don't.

Not really.

Not until you've interviewed for your first job.

Great way to start off my sixteenth birthday, huh?

I'm sitting in a clean, small room and trying not to shake too much from the nerves and the overpowered air conditioner, waiting for an interview to become Bennytown's newest food service employee. There are maybe six other applicants sitting in chairs along the same wall as me, and a secretary at the desk in front of us. Beyond her is a sea of cubicles where I can sense activity but see no one.

Of course, Benny's everywhere—on posters, in glass display cases featuring his merchandise and artifacts from some of his classic films, in a row of bobbleheads on the secretary's desk.

I hear his voice, playful and comforting in my head, singing all the songs from the cartoons I used to live for as a kid, and that makes me less nervous. But it's his white, staring eyes— staring into me, through me, and at nothing all—that put me on edge.

I wasn't expecting an audience, and I am *way* too nicely dressed for this.

Most of the people sitting around me are in t-shirts and jeans. One guy in a tank top has his only sleeves made of tattoos, while another girl wears cutoff shorts that won't be much of anything if they're cut off another half inch.

They look unprofessional, but they look comfortable.

Not like me.

I'm freshly showered and shaved (not that there's much to shave) with gel in my hair and wearing one of Dad's nice shirts and ties that doesn't fit properly. I'm nervous, overdressed, overprepared, and overtired (probably from being forcibly woken up at 6 a.m. on my birthday to interview for a job I don't really want that'll eat up the rest of a summer I *do* want), while the rest of the applicants look like they could care less.

But who knows? Maybe that's just what I need to get a job at Bennytown.

A well-dressed young man in a large pair of Buddy Holly glasses comes from the back office and speaks quietly to the secretary before looking up and scanning the room.

My heart turns to ice.

Only one of the other applicants looks up from her phone, briefly.

"Noel Hallstrom?" Buddy Holly Glasses says.

"Present!" My voice hitches as I reflexively raise my hand like I'm in class.

"Come with me." Buddy Holly Glasses smiles warmly.

He walks me into the back office, and gradually I calm down. Not because there are fewer Bennys (there aren't), but because everyone else is dressed similarly to me.

So maybe Dad was right about this after all.

"I'm Rufus," he says, guiding me down another hall of cubicles. "I'll be conducting your final interview. Would you like some water, soda, coffee maybe?"

"No thank you, I'm not thirsty," I say.

I really am thirsty, but I don't want anything in my hand that might spill and mess up my chances of getting this job.

I don't really want the job, but I want to *get* the job. I think. Is that messed up? It feels messed up.

There's less Benny in Rufus's office, but not by much, and there's a framed, painted portrait of Bennytown's smiling creator, Fletcher Dorian, that takes place of pride on the wall.

Dorian looks young and energetic, handsome and burly with his brilliant red beard and flannel shirt. He looks every bit the father figure all the shows and authorized biographies make him out to be, nothing like what the unauthorized biographies claim he looked like in his final years.

In the portrait, his hand rests on the shoulder of a smiling redheaded girl no more than four years old. Given the age, that must be his daughter, Caroline Dorian, who died probably not long after the painting was finished. It's sad, but if the bios are right and her death inspired her dad to make Bennytown… well, at least something great came of it.

"So, Mr. Hallstrom, if you're ready to begin, I must say, we are *very* impressed with you," Rufus says.

"You are?" I try not to sound too surprised.

"Yes, we are. You've got the clean-cut, *all-American* look that we want in our most visible family members. Despite your lack of work experience, you came prepared to take this interview seriously. And on top of that, you spelled everything correctly on your application *and* you were the only person we've had this week who got a perfect score on the math test. Like I said: *impressive*," he says.

That is surprising. The math test was fifteen basic addition and subtraction questions with a couple of multiplication word problems at the end to mix things up.

Score one for paying attention in sixth grade.

"Cool. I mean, *good.* I try," I say.

"No, you had it right with cool. We're all about *cool* around here," he says, smiling and checking his clipboard. "So, you're sixteen?"

"Sixteen, yes sir. Sixteen today."

"Really?" he asks, looking at my application in disbelief. "Sixteen today, isn't that exciting? Well, happy birthday! What are you doing here when you could be out partying?"

I've been asking myself the same question since I woke up.

"Well, I'll still have time after we're done here. Dad and I will go inside the park afterwards. He says if I get a job it'll be a celebration, and if I don't it'll be a consolation."

"Putting those Annual Passports of yours to good use, I see?" he says, all smiles.

"I… what?"

How does he know about those?

Why does he know about those?

He flips further through the clipboard. "One of the key factors we look for in any new potential family member is your love for Bennytown, and Annual Passport membership is one of the simplest metrics to determine it by. We see here that you and your father have been members of our Annual Passport program for a shade more than eight years now, totaling 373 visits."

I don't have an exact count, especially not from those first couple years which are a blur now, but it sounds close enough. "Something like that, I think, yes."

"No, it's exactly that. We keep very good records."

"I'm sure, I just meant—"

"It's all right, Noel."

"Yes, sir," I say.

"*Rufus*," he corrects.

"Yes, Rufus," I say.

"You know there's no reason to be nervous, right? Your attendance records are admirable, and many among our family started out like you: true fans of Bennytown looking to make their passion more a part of their lives," he says.

I don't think passion is the right word. I'm not quite sure what the right word would be. I'm also not sure if this is supposed to be an ordinary part of an interview or not. I don't think it is, based on all those online interview tips Dad made me read, but maybe it's more normal than it feels, and I'm just making too big a deal out of things because I'm nervous.

This *is* Bennytown, after all.

How bad could it be?

"Well, that's me," I half lie.

Rufus gets up from his desk, holding his hands behind his back and walking to the portrait of Mr. Dorian and Caroline. He looks at it with an almost religious reverence.

"When Fletcher Dorian built Bennytown, he wanted to create the ultimate adventure for the whole family. We aspire to cross-generational appeal with a focus on technological and psychological innovation that other parks can only dream of. When dreaming of this park, Mr. Dorian didn't just want to make a welcoming park for other families, but one for his own as well. Every employee, from the lowliest janitors to the park manager herself, is a member of that family. We love each other, we take care of each other, and we're very particular with whom we share that precious trust, especially while we prepare for this August's Sixtieth Birthday Celebration. This is a vital time for Bennytown, and if we're not careful when considering who to let into our family, we could be courting great danger," he says gravely.

I sit quietly in my chair, holding the handles, trying not to say or do anything that might be misinterpreted as a lack of enthusiasm or rudeness, trying to figure out how I'm supposed to respond to this.

"Tell me, Noel, do you believe in Bennytown?"

"Yes!" I exclaim.

"*Why?*" he presses me.

So many easy answers. By the way he's looking at me, I'm pretty sure this interview will be over if I choose an easy answer.

If I want out, this is the perfect opportunity. I can tell Dad that I wasn't what they were looking for and I can have a little more summer, a little more time hanging out with Olivia until school starts again.

But do I really want to blow this? This is *Bennytown*. If I have to get a job, even if it means hard work, I couldn't imagine a more fun place for one.

Why would I want to blow that?

"Because Bennytown was there for me during some really bad times," I say. "Mom died when I was seven and I… I don't know what happened to me, but I didn't talk for a long time. Dad tried everything to engage me for close to a year. He got us the Annual Passports and started taking me almost every day. After a few months, it was like something clicked, and I was back to my old self. Or close enough, I guess. I owe Bennytown, and I'd love to pay back some of the good it's done for me and everyone like me."

Rufus watches me silently, his eyes bright and huge behind his glasses. The room is cool, cold even, but I feel like I'm going to break out in a sweat.

The Bennys are watching me, Mr. Dorian in his portrait is watching me, and Caroline's watching me. There are eyes everywhere, judging me, seeing if I've got what it takes and waiting for me to lose my nerve and start screaming. I think I just might because now I want this more than I've wanted anything and…

And…

He daintily taps a few keys on his laptop.

"The job's yours if you want it. Just say the word, I hit Enter, and you're in the Bennytown family," he says.

"*Yes!*" I exclaim. Then, trying to get a better handle of myself, "Yes, I'd like the job! Thank you so much!"

"You're very welcome," he says, hitting Enter. A nearby printer comes to life, spitting out four pieces of paper. Reaching into a desk drawer, he pulls out a small spiral-bound booklet, puts it beneath the papers, and hands them to me.

"These are your availability forms and the binding non-disclosure agreement. Read them over carefully and sign them. The booklet is our C of C, D & E: our Code of Conduct, Dress & Ethics. You'll want to read that over by Thursday."

"Why Thursday?" I ask, the smallest lump forming in my throat.

Thursday is the Fourth of July. Olivia and I had plans.

"Because Thursday's orientation day! It'll be one of the busiest days of the year, so you'll get a really good look at what this park looks like at its peak. Isn't that exciting?" he says.

"Yeah, yeah it is," I say, trying not to let too much disappointment into my voice. I'm not looking forward to the conversation with Olivia, but I can hold off on that for now.

"I knew you'd think so. Did you bring your social security card? I'll need to make some copies of that for our files."

"Sure." I pull it from my wallet and hand it to him.

He looks it up and down, smiling broadly. "I'll be back in a jiff!"

I fill out the forms quickly, feeling even more disappointment at the availability form's message—WEEKENDS OFF CANNOT BE REQUESTED BETWEEN MAY AND SEPTEMBER WITHOUT DOCTOR'S NOTE—before starting on the long and very small-print non-disclosure agreement.

Rufus isn't back yet.

I should read this, but I can't hold back any longer as I slip the phone from my pocket and start texting.

Noel: I GOT IT!!!!!

Olivia: Yay! Celebrate?

I don't look forward to telling her we won't have the Fourth of July together, but I'll make it up to her. My earnings are supposed to go to my college fund and a car, but maybe I can keep some on the side to take her on nicer dates and—

The doorknob turns behind me. Quickly, I sign the non-disclosure agreement and stack all the papers on his desk.

Before sliding the phone back in my pocket, I type a quick final message.

Noel: Looking forward to it.

Without sitting down, Rufus looks at my papers and attaches them to his clipboard.

"Well, it seems we have everything in order!" he says, motioning for me to stand.

"Thanks," I say, putting out my hand to shake.

Still smiling, he shakes my hand.

I almost withdraw in fear. Something doesn't feel right, and when our hands part I understand why.

Most of the middle finger of his left hand is missing.

If he's offended by my retreat, he gives no sign as he puts a hand to his forehead theatrically. "I almost forgot!" Reaching into his jacket's breast pocket, he says, "I had to go looking in back for this, since I didn't know where we kept them. How silly of me!"

He rolls his eyes and pulls the button out.

I've seen (and worn) these before—large buttons to pin to your shirt for special Bennytown occasions, blank spaces filled in with Sharpie.

This one reads:

MY NAME IS **NOEL**

WISH ME A HAPPY BIRTHDAY

FOR TODAY ON **6/30** I AM **16!**

"Isn't that exciting?" he asks perkily.

"Yeah," I say as he pins the button to my shirt. I try not to look as he does it and focus on anything but his hands.

I don't want to be rude, and I definitely don't want to be weird.

Don't want to notice that the scars on the stump almost look like teeth marks.

"All done!" he exclaims, straightening the pin and brushing my shirt down. "Congratulations! I think you'll be an exciting member of the Bennytown family!"

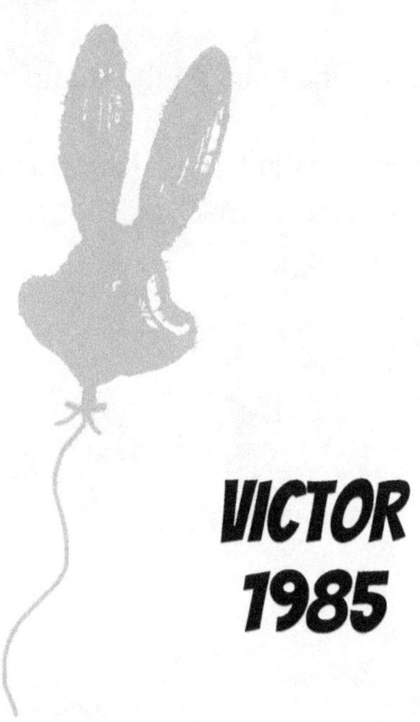

VICTOR
1985

Behind the scenes, the system of elevated escalators that connected the Upper and Lower Parks of Bennytown across hundreds of feet of hillside was called the "Stairway to Heaven." Although if you were riding the escalators down instead of up, most family members called them the "Stairway to Heck."

Victor never liked riding the Stairway to Heck at night, since it meant he'd done something to deserve a late shift. As a six-year veteran of the Bennytown family, he was usually afforded the desirable daytime shifts in the Upper Park.

Holding onto those shifts required not getting too many points in your file. Something that was not exactly easy if you had a social life. Once those points started adding up…

That wasn't to say evening shifts didn't have their own perks, too.

"So, you doin' anything after?" Victor asked.

As always, Marisol rolled her eyes. "Going home. Taking off my shoes. Spending a few minutes watching Diego sleep before passing out."

"Cool, cool. How old's the little guy?"

"Turns two on Saturday. And you really don't care, do you?"

"Of course, I care!" Victor protested.

"Nice try," Marisol said. "Next you're gonna try singin' for me again, and—"

"I sang one time! One time! And I wasn't that bad," Victor said, fondly remembering his crowd-pleasing rendition of "American Girl."

Well, it would've been crowd-pleasing if there'd been a crowd instead of just Marisol.

"You were worse than *that bad*. You frickin' mangled Tom Petty," Marisol laughed.

"Hey, hey, hey, nobody can mangle Tom Petty," Victor replied.

"You found a way," she said, amused.

They got off the first escalator, walking around the maintenance crews taking advantage of the Lower Park's emptiness to do some much needed work on the Stairway to Heaven before Bennytown's off-limits hours kicked in for everyone.

They walked across the large landing toward the second escalator, harassing the daytime janitors as they came off duty.

"Hey, heads up on the Safari Lodge! They had a few pukers 'round closing time, and Kathleen's on the warpath!" one of them shouted in passing.

"Where you fail, I succeed! Goodbye, day shift!" Victor teased.

When they got to the second set of escalators, Victor was annoyed. As was customary at the end of the day, three of the four escalators were going up to ferry people out of the park, while only one went down. The problem was, the only down escalator at the moment had a maintenance barricade at the top of it, which meant off-limits.

"I don't wanna take the stairs down," Marisol moaned.

Victor looked behind him down the escalator. Though this escalator was the longest on the Stairway to Heck, he could see the bottom just fine. No maintenance guys were working on it at the moment. They probably hadn't gotten started yet.

"We got pukers to clean up," Victor said, pulling the barricade to the side and waving Marisol toward the escalator like a gentleman holding a car door for a lady, even if he was no gentleman and Marisol was no lady. "I'll chance it."

"Me too," Marisol said, stepping aboard.

The escalator was louder than usual, sounding heavily of chains and grinding gears, but it held her just fine. Stepping aboard behind Marisol, he gripped the moving handrail tightly as the steps shuddered slightly beneath him.

It's about time maintenance got on these, Victor thought.

"So, I get why I get the lousy shifts, but you, you don't make sense," Victor said.

"Responsibility don't make sense?" Marisol asked.

"I get responsibility, but these shifts are punishment, and Management don't punish you," Victor said.

"I asked for these shifts," Marisol explained.

"Seriously?"

"Yeah."

"Why?"

"I need the money. I got family helping raise Diego, so we ain't hurting for food, but I don't wanna stay at Bennytown forever. I wanna go to college after I graduate, and that's gonna take money, so I take the lousy shifts," Marisol said.

"Don't leave much of a social life," Victor said, holding onto the handrail even tighter as the steps jerked again. Marisol stood, hands in her pockets, completely unconcerned.

"I don't need a social life. I need to graduate high school and go to college so I can get a good job and be an example for my son."

Victor saw an opening and took it. "Even if you don't need a social life, you might still want one, right?"

"I want a lot of things, but it don't mean I'm gonna get them," Marisol said.

"Well, lucky for you, I can provide a lot of things," Victor said smoothly.

Looking down at his pants, Marisol said, "Don't flatter yourself. I've heard the comestibles girls' stories."

"Oh, come on, they're not all bad," Victor protested.

"They got limericks and a skip-rope rhyme and everything," Marisol teased.

Putting a hand to his chest, Victor said, "Marisol, you're breaking my heart!"

They were almost at the bottom of the escalator. Marisol turned to face the approaching landing.

"First, that's not your heart that's broken. And second, don't call me Marisol," she said.

"Sorry, sorry," Victor said as the escalator steps reached the bottom and Marisol stepped off. "I'll—"

"NO, STOP, DON'T!" a maintenance man cried out, running toward them.

The flimsy metal plates covering the workings of the escalator gave way under Marisol's weight, dropping her into the powerful, turning gears. Maintenance men, who had been bent over and off to the side at the base of the escalator as they inspected the machinery, stumbled back with yells of alarm as Marisol thrashed and fought, trying to grab onto something as the gears were too strong and pulled her in screaming.

Blood and mangled bits of Marisol exploded all over the escalator, the maintenance men, and Victor. It was a contest to see who could scream the loudest.

Having fallen down from shock, Victor scrabbled backwards up the descending steps, trying not to look at the girl he'd just been hitting on while she got ground into chuck. He hoped he could crawl away fast enough so the stairs wouldn't drop him into the churning gears as well.

NOEL
2019

"**S**o, you can't say hell?"

"No."

"Or fuck?"

"If I can't say hell, I certainly can't say fuck."

"Or shit?"

"Still no."

"Or—"

"Whatever you were gonna say, Olivia, the answer's probably no."

"I was just gonna say re—"

"Like I said, no."

"Well what kind of job won't let you say fucking shit?" she asks.

"Bennytown," I say. "Any infractions on the C of C, D & E, especially using any of the *Poison Words*, add up to points. Earn enough points and there are punishments up to and including termination."

"You need to find a better job," she says.

"I like this one," I say.

"You don't know that yet," Olivia says.

"Are you gonna light the damn fireworks, or aren't you? Dad wants me home by ten," I say, impatient and wanting to change the subject.

"I'm lighting, I'm lighting," she says, spinning the wheel on her cheap lighter. She lights the fuse on the firework, then quickly brings the flame up to the cigarette she flips into her hand. She stands by the firework too long, and I fear it'll go off with her next to it, but after a quick puff of her cigarette, she runs toward me. She's at my side in time to watch the firework go off with a spinning burst of red and blue sparks, while the row of Roman candles rigged next to it go off one at a time.

"Pretty," I say.

"Very," she replies.

"I meant you," I say.

She gives her easy smile, the one that made me fall for her. "Smooth, Noel."

"I try," I say, pulling her in for a kiss. Though I hate the taste of tobacco, the closeness of her slender body to mine completely makes up for it.

I'm feeling warm, very warm, and I suddenly wish we were somewhere I could do something about it. The way Olivia's looking up at me, I know she's thinking the same.

"How did I get so lucky?" I ask.

"You know how to treat a girl better than Tommy?" Olivia teases.

"Glad to know that's all I've got going for me," I joke.

"Well, you're amazing and wonderful and sweet too, so that's something also, I'd say."

I smile, softly. "Good recovery."

"I thought so. But, seriously, you're still a better catch than him."

"Oh, by far," I acknowledge.

Almost empty, one of the candles falls over, sending its last fireball flying in our direction. Olivia dodges out of the way, shouting, "SON OF A BITCH!"

"Are you all right?" I ask. The fireball's a few feet from me and I stomp it out before it can become an actual fire.

Can't let anything get out of hand, now can we?

"I'm fine, I'm fine," she repeats, clearly not fine. Knowing how I react when she's not fine, she adds a joke. "How's my hair?"

"Sexy," I say, hoping to set her at ease.

"Thank God. Hey, son of a bitch!" Olivia says, snapping her fingers and pointing at me.

"What?" I say.

"Can you say son of a bitch?" she asks.

I laugh. "No, that one's still banned."

"You need to find a better job," Olivia repeats.

"Thanks," I say, rolling my eyes.

"But since you're only a free man for a few more hours, why don't we keep drinking and blowing more shit up?" she says, squeezing my hand.

Ladies and gentlemen, I present one of many reasons why I love Olivia Verne.

It's the evening of July 3rd, and my orientation starts tomorrow. Since I couldn't make any solid plans for the 4th, Olivia decided we could move up plans to tonight. Sure, the neighbors won't be happy, but with the mini-grill and hot dogs from my fridge, the beer that Olivia snuck from her stepdad, and the fireworks Dad bought, we've got a pretty good night ahead of us. As always, we're in the lot behind Olivia's house, empty enough for all sorts of fun and just over the town line so fireworks are legal.

I've known Olivia for two years now, ever since she was put in my homeroom class after she moved to our town with her mom and most recent stepdad. She wasn't as hot as a lot of the more popular girls in school, but she had that kind of confidence that still turned heads. My best friend at the time, Tommy, was more outgoing and better looking. He asked her out first even though he knew I had a crush on her. After Tommy broke her heart and moved away a few months later, I somehow screwed up the courage to ask her out.

A year and a half later, she's still the love of my life.

A warm summer night with her, hot dogs, beer, and fireworks… it really can't get any better than this.

"So, is there anything that you *can* say?" Olivia asks.

"I can say pretty much anything. Just nothing from the list." I haven't told her that the Poison Words list is about 300 words long and, in addition to cussing, it forbids saying the names of any competing parks, "death," "sad," and weirdly enough, "rubbish," "walrus," and "neon."

"I'm honestly more worried about the dress code. I mean, I don't have to worry about tattoos or earrings or facial hair or being pregnant or anything like that. Wearing a cleaned but not new uniform every day, something somebody else wore yesterday." I shudder.

"Yeah, like what if they were sick? Or maybe they even died in it?" Olivia proposes.

"People don't die at Bennytown," I say.

"People can die anywhere," she says.

"*Not* at Bennytown," I say, more insistent.

As always, when I get defensive of Bennytown, she rolls her eyes. "Fine, nobody dies at Bennytown. Benny's in line for sainthood because he farts puppies and cums rainbows."

She just waits there, smirking, knowing this'll start something. Even though it's where we shared our first kiss, she's always messed with Bennytown to get a rise out of me. As always, I want to shut her up, but nicely, and it's feeling increasingly hard to do so.

"Olivia," I say.

"*Noel*," she taunts back.

"Can you please—"

"I won't say sorry, but I'm fine to change the subject," she says, rooting through a paper bag and pulling out a couple cans of beer. This only postpones the argument, but I'm fine with that tonight.

"To freedom and long life," Olivia says.

"To us," I add, for lack of anything insightful.

We drink the shitty beer down because we don't have any other options.

Olivia picks up the bag of fireworks. "Now let's blow some shit up. You want loud, colorful, or destructive?"

"Why not all three?" I propose.

"I like the way you think!" Olivia pulls some odds and ends out of the bag and jams them into the ground, tying their fuses together and adding an extra-long fuse so we can light it at a distance.

Before she can light it, I pull Olivia close so I'm whispering into her ear through her long chestnut hair.

"Did you make it to the clinic?" I ask.

She smiles up at me, reaching into her pocket and revealing a few foil-wrapped condoms. "I grabbed four in case you felt particularly ambitious."

"I don't know if I feel *that* ambitious, but…"

"Well, it never hurts to plan ahead," she says.

"No, it doesn't," I say.

"Because you never know when you might die from a giant rabbit attack. Working there all the time, your odds of suffering that normally unlikely cause of death have increased exponentially. You know that, right?" she teases.

"*Bunny*. Benny the *Bunny*. Or *Hare* if you're referring to Dare, but no, no rabbits here," I correct her, laughing.

"Well, talk about splitting *hares*," she says, rolling her eyes.

"Funny. Cute," I say, sarcastic.

Olivia's eyes go wide, looking down. "Spider."

A large spider has climbed atop my shoe, slowly working its way toward the leg of my jeans. Its front legs play at the cuff, trying to find purchase.

"Kill it," Olivia whispers.

"Why?" I ask, laughing slightly. Olivia's pretty fearless normally, but spiders are one of the few things that terrify her. Slowly, I inch toward the paper grocery store bag of our supplies and tear a piece off. I work the spider onto the torn piece of paper, walk to the edge of the lot, and set it free.

"Better?" I ask.

"I'll never understand why you do that," she says, shuddering.

"Awww, come on, just let a spider be a spider," I say.

She's still shaking. "Let's not talk about spiders."

"Fine with me."

"So, we light these fireworks and then head back to your place?"

Knowing what that means, I snatch the lighter from her pocket and light the fuse.

"Sounds great to me," I say, kissing her and looking toward the fireworks, waiting for the explosion.

THE WEATHER FORECAST gave a 50-50 chance for scattered showers on the Fourth of July due to a tropical storm slamming Baja California. The morning started out all right, cloudy but otherwise normal heat and humidity. By the time we get to Bennytown, however, it's raining. Heavy, ugly raindrops that mirror my heavy, ugly mood.

Dad tries to lighten the tension by playing our favorite oldies station and talking a mile a minute, like that'll make me any less nervous.

"Didn't sleep well last night?" he asks.

That would be an understatement. Even without Olivia trying her level best to run through all the condoms, my sleep was iffy knowing that I'd be starting at Bennytown on the Fourth of July. Not even a stop by IHOP on the way over was enough to fully open my eyes after only a few hours of sleep.

Seeing the outline of Bennytown in the distance does have its usual effect. I'm less surly, a little more energized, and ready for orientation.

"I'll be fine," I say.

He laughs. "It's Olivia, right? Didn't think she could wear you out that much."

"DAD!" I exclaim, blushing. This only makes him laugh more.

Dad and I have had our fair share of issues, but he's always been one of my best friends. We laugh a lot and we hang out whenever I'm not with Olivia. I've heard his best stories ten times over and I still get a kick out of them most of the time. He did everything he could for me after Mom died, everything and more, and I don't know if I'll ever be able to fully repay him for his patience.

I guide him to the family member entrance around Bennytown's backstage, and he pulls up to the curb near a currently unused loading area.

"You have everything you need? Phone? Cash? Hat?" he asks.

"Yes, yes, and yes; I'll be fine, Dad," I say.

"Well, you know, it never hurts to be thorough."

"I know, Dad. Thanks." I unbuckle my seat belt. I want to get the hell out of here without making a scene, but I can't help it and throw my arms around Dad. He hugs back, then playfully pushes my shoulder.

"Come on, you don't want to be late," he says. I get out of the car, looking back at him.

"Text me if you get an idea when you're leaving," he says.

"I will," I say.

"And kid?"

"Yeah?"

"Knock 'em dead."

"I will!" I say, closing the door and watching him drive off. He waves to me before I realize that texting won't be an option.

As part of the C of C, D & E, we're to have our phones off at all times when in Bennytown. The thought sends an odd feeling of isolation to my gut, which only makes today feel even more foreboding.

I am alone.

I turn to the main Family Member Building, a glass and steel office tower with no hint of Bennytown charm to it. Fat raindrops roll down its surface like a giant's tears.

I close my eyes, ball my fists, and take a deep breath, dispelling stress.

Opening my eyes, I take a step forward and almost run into Benny the Bunny.

"I'm sorry, I'm so sorry! I didn't mean to—" I start to apologize before I realize it's not Benny.

Not the Benny you'd see wandering Bennytown, anyway.

Not my Benny.

The suit is bulky, like a radiation suit, with a face plate like a gas mask and an oxygen tank strapped to the back. Yet, it is undeniably intended to be Benny the Bunny. The skin of the suit is bright green and furry, and the mask is stylized to look almost like Benny's, with glowing white eyes, a mouth with big buck teeth, and two tall ears sticking straight up. It looks more bedraggled than it should, fur worn thin in some places and ears beginning to flop in the rain. It smells thickly of mildew and age, adding to the overpowering sense of wrongness that makes me want to look away yet leaves me unable to do anything but stare.

Not-Quite-Benny pays no attention to me, shuffling past, scooping a heavy white powder from a sack slung over its back and sprinkling it on the ground. Seeing this simple going-through-the-motions action of a person doing a boring job, the wrongness lifts from Benny, slightly, leaving me instead to try and figure its purpose.

An exterminator?

Extreme janitor?

(A monster?)

Whatever it is, it's just another Bennytown family member.

Walking to the Family Member Building, I look back briefly, watching the Not-Quite-Benny as it continues its strange, shuffling walk, spreading white powder as it goes.

Though Not-Quite-Benny feels fundamentally wrong, like something I wasn't meant to see, I'm calming down.

I'm joining the Bennytown family today.

I'm joining the Bennytown family today.

Feeling almost ready for this future, I step through the gates and prepare for orientation.

TAMMY
1958

There was an urgent radio call about another incident at Candy Mountain.

"Perfect. Bloody perfect," Tammy Zimbardo said, exiting her trailer and hopping on her bicycle.

Someone had attached bright pink streamers to her handlebars again. Normally she'd have torn them off immediately, but if the incident at Candy Mountain was as bad as they claimed…

She left them flapping in the breeze as she cycled across what would one day be Bennytown.

After two months of active construction (after another month of razing the ruins of the Japanese internment camp that previously occupied the hill), it was only an ugly lot at the top of a hill with a number of skeletal frames that would be turned into buildings and rides.

In a year's time, it'd be the greatest themed attraction in the world, full of love and children's laughter for generations to come, if you believed in Fletcher Dorian's vision.

Though she sometimes had her doubts, Tammy believed in Bennytown.

More than that, she believed in Fletcher Dorian.

Two years ago, she'd been twenty-two years old and fresh out of university with dreams of becoming an engineer and building a better tomorrow. It didn't matter that everyone told her she was mad, that nobody would trust a woman to build anything. They always felt obliged to tell her that she was pretty and smart and could easily find a good husband. If she truly felt daring, a decent clerical job would help her pass the time.

She wanted to prove them wrong.

A year of doors slammed in her face (or, worse, suggestions that there were other things she could do to encourage her hiring) almost broke her spirit.

Then she met Fletcher Dorian.

She hadn't held out much hope for her meeting with Dorian. He was, after all, a children's entertainer and one of the richest men in the world. There was no way he'd be interested in hiring her, but never one to break an appointment (and figuring she'd still get a free holiday in America), she met with him.

Their interview was only supposed to be ten minutes. It lasted just shy of two and a half hours.

In that time, she became certain of three things:

First, that Fletcher Dorian was mad.

Second, that he might also be a genius.

Third, that he was her big shot.

A large, vibrant ginger with a charming sense of humor and seemingly endless energy, he outlined his dream for Bennytown as being the greatest building project ever undertaken by mankind since the Great Wall of China. He'd shown her some preliminary designs and asked how she would improve them. She considered him for a moment, wondering if it was best to give her suggestions with the timidity that most men expected.

Taking a gamble, she bet on brutal honesty, admitting that while his ideas were innovative, they could be improved upon.

That honesty was how she'd become one of his "Bengineers," his collection of engineers, scientists, artists, psychologists, and other free thinkers he claimed would change the world.

While glad for the job, she initially thought her new position was a stunt. Did Dorian Fletcher want to prove himself a true maverick by hiring a woman? Of the twenty-five initial Bengineers hired, nearly half were women and a third non-white.

Fletcher Dorian said he wanted the best of the best, and he meant it.

Given his plans for Bennytown, he'd need the best.

Tammy dodged her bicycle deftly through work crews and heavy construction equipment, eventually reaching the Candy Mountain build site. For the moment, it was merely an ugly superstructure of twisted girders that had only recently begun reaching for the sky. When finished, it would look like a mountain of confectionary even taller than its actual hundred feet thanks to forced perspective tricks. It would be home to two of Bennytown's most thrilling rides, as well as concealing a number of complicated machines Dorian said would be the true "heart of the park."

When he told her what they were really for, she had thought him mad. When she looked further into his designs and his research and found that much of that madness made sense, she vowed to do everything to make Dorian's dream possible.

Now, the site was a gathering of terrified workmen. One lay on the ground, grabbing his eyes and screaming.

Dorian knelt beside him, rubbing the man's shoulder comfortingly. "It's all right, Lou. I've sent for Dr. Ziegler, and he'll get you to a hospital lickety-split! Everything will be taken care of."

Recently, Dr. Ziegler's alcoholism led to the accidental killing or maiming of as many workmen as he'd saved. This was something that Tammy thought politic not to mention.

In between screams, through sheer force of will, the workman said, "Thank you, Mr. Dorian."

Dorian noticed Tammy's arrival and stood up, brushing off his hands to shake hers. "Ms. Zimbardo. Thank you for coming so promptly."

"What happened?" she asked, angling to get a view of the downed man.

Dorian grabbed her by the shoulder, not unkindly, and took her away from the scene. "If you wish to sleep tonight, you won't want to see this."

"What happened?" she repeated, more forcefully.

"Lou Chan, one heckuva guy, had an accident with an acetylene torch," Dorian said.

Multiple bizarre accidents during construction typically caused her to react dramatically and ended with Dorian's admonishment. More than anything, this time she surprised herself by not being terribly surprised. "We'll give the other workmen the rest of the day off, paid, and have them back first thing tomorrow morning."

"Sensible. I've already sent for Dr. Cohen from Psych to make sure the others are all right," Dorian said.

As always, Fletcher Dorian was two steps ahead.

"Excuse me. That's not what happened, sir." A meek workman had come out of the crowd who stood a respectful distance from Dorian and took his moment to speak with great gravity.

"No? Juan Martinez, isn't it?" Dorian said.

"Yes sir," Martinez said, unable to meet Dorian's gaze.

"What happened?" Tammy asked.

"We were working along the foundation, Lou and me, when the ground collapsed under us. Found some kind of room down there. Lou went in to look. Then he came out, real calm like, picked up the torch and, and… he took it to his eyes, and—"

Dorian cut him off. "Show us."

Martinez led them into the center of the Candy Mountain superstructure, to a spot of ground that formed a neat little pit leading into darkness.

Looking in curiously, Dorian said, "Can I trust you'll be discreet on this matter, Mr. Martinez?"

"Yes, sir," Martinez replied.

"Also, may I borrow the flashlight from your belt?" Dorian asked. Martinez complied and Dorian waved him away. "That will be all."

"Thank you, sir," Martinez said, glad to run exit the site.

"Do you really think he'll keep quiet? The workmen have proven themselves proficient gossipers," Tammy said.

"Would you rather I fire him? Ruin the lives of two families?" Dorian proposed.

Thinking briefly, Tammy said, "It'd be better to have him on our side and silent than on the outside and leaking this to the press."

"My thinking exactly." Dorian knelt down by the hole and turned on the flashlight. The dark chamber beneath was hard to make out, but a lot of the architecture had a medieval look to it.

"An old Spanish mission. Likely sunken from an earthquake or two," Dorian said, completely unsurprised.

"You knew about this before we started building, didn't you?" Tammy asked.

As usual, Dorian didn't look surprised that she was the only person who spoke to him this way. "Of course."

"And when were you planning on telling me?" Tammy asked.

"Now's as good a time as any, I'd wager," Dorian said, looking down into the ruins with a dreamy, far-off gaze. "I'm coming, Caroline," he whispered.

Dorian got like this sometimes, and Tammy had become used to letting him come back to himself before continuing the conversation. Given the urgency, though, she didn't let him wait as long this time.

"I'll have a team survey the area and fill it in with concrete in three days," Tammy said, in damage control mode.

Stroking his beard, Dorian quickly said, "No. Have a survey team map it out, but do what you can to keep the ruins intact. Can that be done?"

The easy answer would've been no. Like all of Southern California, the build site was seismically active, and the system of "Rabbit Hole" tunnels they were digging into the hillside wouldn't make Bennytown any more stable. The sheer weight of Candy Mountain on top of these and the sunken mission would most likely be dangerous already.

She answered confidently. "It might slow construction by a month or so, but we'll make it work."

"Excellent," Dorian said, calmly sliding down into the hole and landing in the chamber.

"Up for exploring some darkness with me?" Dorian called up cheerfully.

Unhesitatingly, Tammy slid in after him.

NOEL
2019

The third floor is bustling with activity when I arrive, with close to a hundred people milling around and waiting for their orientation rooms to be available.

When I find the sign pointing out the various rooms, I understand the confusion.

ORIENTATION SESSIONS:

ENVIRONMENTAL SITUATION ENGINEERS - ROOM 302
COMESTIBLE SERVICE SPECIALISTS - ROOM 304
ENTERTAINMENT EXPERIENCE AGENTS (VIGOROUS) - ROOM 305

After wandering around and listening in on conversations, I finally translate these job descriptions to janitors/gardeners, food service, and ride operators, respectively. I line myself up outside of Room 304.

God only knows where prospective Radiation Suit Bennys have to line up.

Pulling to the edge of the group, I pretend to focus on a bulletin board with fliers announcing the family member talent show, "The 19th Annual Dinosaur Lagoon Rubber Duck Rally," and some discount coupons to a nearby carwash so I don't have to talk to anyone. I'm too tired and wired to go out of my way to make friends.

I don't mind being alone with my nervous excitement today. For now, I'll stay focused on my job and let people approach me.

Nobody bothers me, and soon enough we're called into our orientation rooms. At the door, we're told to turn off our phones and fill out a nametag sticker. Slapping the sticker onto my chest, I slide into the orientation room.

Like any good classroom, the seats in back fill up first, but I grab a seat up front.

Our orientation leader says with all smiles, "Hello everyone! Welcome to the Bennytown family! Isn't that exciting? My name is Lynette, and I believe in Bennytown!" The very short woman seems stuffed into a business suit two sizes small.

There are some murmurs, even some scattered applause.

Her smile turns into a mock scowl as she puts her hands on her hips. "Now that's not the Bennytown spirit, is it? I know it's early, and this is orientation day, but as dedicated Bennytown family members, let's give this the good old Bennytown try. Come on, lemme see some smiles, and repeat after me! *I believe in Bennytown!*"

Like kids being forced to recite the Pledge of Allegiance, we all repeat, "*I believe in Bennytown!*"

I put on my best smile and expect that to be the end of the exchange. Instead, Lynette goes from desk to desk, inspecting each of us. She passes me by quickly, nodding approvingly.

She snaps a ruler sharply on one desk.

Lynette's voice is acid and sickly sweet. "Young lady, that's *not* a smile, that's a snigger, and I will have no sniggers in my orientation room! Nor will I tolerate gum chewing!"

She lifts the ruler, so the end touches the girl's bottom lip. "Spit."

Dutifully and more than a little afraid, the girl spits the gum onto the tip of the ruler.

All smiles again, Lynette says, "Very good," and continues through the rest of the classroom, idly tapping desks with her ruler with the gum still stuck to the tip. Finished, she drops her ruler in a trashcan at the front of the class.

"Now, before we get to your park tours, we have a short film to share with a truly special surprise at the end. Isn't that exciting?"

This time the room is nearly thunderous with applause and cheers.

"Very good! So much better! Now pay very close attention; there will be a test!"

This gets some laughs from the audience until she says, "No talking during the movie!"

The lights dim, and a projector lights up the wall behind Lynette.

The orientation film is a basic introduction to Bennytown and its history, from its opening in 1959 all the way to the present day. The film appears to be about four years old based on the featured attractions, and absolutely filled to the brim with smiles. The video showcases the seven lands full of smiling guests, smiling costumed characters, and most importantly, smiling Bennytown family members.

The film ends with music swelling to accompany a montage of janitors, comestibles workers, ride operators, office personnel, and even president of Dorian Studios, Nicolas Dorian, all saying, "*I believe in Bennytown!*"

When we just have a blank, bright white screen in front of us, Lynette speaks again.

"Now, remember when I said we'd have a truly special surprise for you at the end? Well, what we have is an extraordinary *second* short film. One month before his death in 1993, our beloved founder and father, Fletcher Dorian, although very ill, recorded a message to all future family members. The man was a visionary and a saint, a talented artist, engineer, magician, war hero, and Olympic athlete. His influence and spirit can still be felt in Bennytown in every attraction, guest, and family member. As you are now a part of his family, you will be privy to this special, secret film. Isn't that exciting?"

More cheers and applause. I don't know how much longer we can keep this energy up.

Lynette starts the film. As soon as we see Mr. Dorian sitting in a chair in the back garden of his estate, there are several gasps and a girl sitting right behind me yelps in fear, loud enough that Lynette marches her outside.

I'm too transfixed by the screen because there's been no official report about what killed Fletcher Dorian. The popular explanation is that he contracted a rare and vicious wasting disease on one of his many global adventures. I don't believe any more about the rumors that his head was cryogenically frozen. Seeing this video, I'd say there may be some truth to them.

Gone is the healthy Mr. Dorian from Rufus's painting. In his place is a pale, gaunt figure with thin lips pulled back in a rictus grin over large dentures. Heavy sunglasses cover his eyes, and a wide hat shields his scalp. His skin, hanging off his bones, is almost cartoonishly pale with makeup, while his nose and visible left ear seem the wrong shape and color for his face. He still has his shock of red hair and bushy beard, but they appear glued on. He tents his hands beneath his chin, but the fingers are bony and gnarled, pulled tightly into the hands at impossible angles.

He was only seventy-four when this was filmed.

When he speaks, his voice sounds like an ancient tomb being opened, a rush of stagnant air followed by a voice that's both shrill and raspy, nothing like the voices he did for Snapper Gator, Brutus the Bear, and Benny the Bunny.

"Welcome to the Bennytown family. Though I will be long dead when you see this, know that I will always be proud of my family. No matter what happens, I will always be a part of Bennytown, watching and—"

The film leaps in a clumsy edit, one of Dorian's helpers suddenly darting out of frame.

This isn't the only time this happens.

"Each and every one of you is now a member of my family and a representative of Bennytown and its ideals. You'll be the first and the last thing every guest sees. You'll shape their experience and help them create memories that will last for a lifetime."

His voice crackled with fear as he said, "It is your duty to protect them from themselves and each other. After all, Bennytown is meant to be a place where the innocent can run free, and the guil—"

"Bennytown is a sacred place, and membership in our family makes you a part of a special, holy order. Follow the tenets of this order, and you'll find rewards everlasting. Defy or hurt the family in any way, and—"

"Once again, thank you one and all for joining the Bennytown family. I trust each of you will use your unique talents and experiences to build a brighter future and ensure your own immortality in this park. Now, isn't *that* exciting?"

As abruptly as it started, the old video ends and the lights of the room come back on.

Lynette stands at the front of the room, daubing her eyes with a tissue. "Such a beautiful, inspirational man. Now, about that test I promised?"

She motions for us to look down at our desks. On each of them is a test and a pen she must've snuck in during the movie.

There really is a test?

THE TEST WASN'T as bad as I'd worried. It had questions on everything from when various rides were opened, to "Poison

Words" listed in the C of C, D & E and questions like what color t-shirt was worn by the guide in the Kingdom of the Robots section of the orientation film.

After collecting our papers, Lynette fed them into a machine for grading. Those of us who scored lower than 90% were sent to another room for guided orientation, while those who scored higher were sent out into Bennytown for "Independent Orientation."

I was one of only six people to fall into that latter category, which was great since Independent Orientation turned out to be pretty sweet. We were given food vouchers, front-of-the-line passes, and a checklist of every ride and show in Bennytown. We were to get on every ride and watch every show so we could to explain them to guests, familiarize ourselves with the locations of first aid stations and restrooms, and sample as much of the park's food as possible. At 6 p.m., we were to meet back at the Family Member Building to give a report and receive instructions regarding our first real day of work.

With the exception of the no cell phones rule, it sounds like a great way to earn my first day of wages.

I don't need the checklist to know everything Bennytown has to offer. Happily, I accept the front-of-the-line passes and free food. Using my near-photographic memory of the park, I start making my circuit.

Not counting the Road to Adventure at the front of the park and Bennytown Plaza just outside, Bennytown consists of seven themed lands. At the top of the hill is the Upper Park. Branching off from a hub at the end of the Road to Adventure are the Candy Mountain, Island of Legends, Primordial World, Journey through Americana, and Kingdom of the Robots lands. The Lower Park at the bottom of the hill has Happy Hollow and Creepy Corner and is connected to the Upper Park by both the longest system of escalators in the world and the Sky Buckets gondolas.

Knowing that most crowds congregate near the entrance at the Upper Park at the beginning of the day, I head down to the Lower Park first, hitting every ride in about an hour, and even getting a cardboard framed picture of me high-fiving Benny in his Happy Hollow home. It cost a pretty penny, but I think it'll prove my dedication during my day's report.

The heat and lack of sleep get to me quickly, so I decide to cross off another ride from the list by taking the Sky Buckets from Happy Hollow to the Kingdom of the Robots. Bright blue sky breaks through the blotchy clouds, so it feels like a fine day for this ride.

Since I was little, the Buckets always scared and fascinated me. Small, brightly colored gondolas elevate about sixty feet off the ground by a thin steel cable and a set of rickety-looking towers. Every time I ride them, they feel seconds away from crumbling apart.

After a few minutes, the ride starts to make me claustrophobic and nervous, so I close my eyes and listen to the soothing music filtering through the bucket's speakers, broken up by the occasional message in Benny's jolly voice.

"Hi, I'm Benny the Bunny! Please, for your safety, keep your hands and feet in the bucket at all times! ¡Hola, soy Benito el Conejito! ¡Por favor, para su seguridad, mantenga las manos y los pies en el cubo en todo momento!"

Feeling more comfortable, I open my eyes and look at the small sign above my head.

MAXIMUM OCCUPANCY: 0 PEOPLE

All right, so someone graffitied over the real number. I know the sign is supposed to read "4 PEOPLE," so I'm not worried.

As if to confirm this, a bucket holding at least five kids wearing Benny ears passes me at the halfway point, going downhill. They're screaming and cheering and rocking their bucket violently. One kid appears to be hanging halfway out. He bobs a Benny ears balloon in his hand, laughing and screaming. After bobbing it too heavily, it escapes. The balloon lazily floats into the sky, leaving the wailing child reaching after it, unaware that if he reaches any farther, he's going to tip himself out of his bucket to splat on the ground.

I'm all too glad to leave the bucket when I reach the Kingdom of the Robots.

I grab a Coke from a nearby cart and relax for a moment at a large, gear-shaped table. Staring at a twenty-foot-tall robot statue I wonder when the park will turn on the misters.

I want to text Olivia since I know she wants to hear from me. I can't help feeling conflicted over potentially betraying the "no cell phones" rule even if I'm not officially on duty.

Finally, the temptation is too powerful, and I pull out my phone.

I'm about to turn it on when I hear the kid.

Though turned away from me, I can tell that he's short and pudgy, wearing oversized sneakers and an old Thundercats t-shirt. He's kicking the crap out of an overturned trash can, garbage spilled around him.

People keep walking by him, lost in fantasy or just wanting to ignore this little shit vandalizing Bennytown.

My Bennytown.

My family.

Even from here, something looks wrong with his head, like something is covering his hair. I should worry, but anger wins out. I get up and walk up behind him. I want to tell him a lot of things, but just wind up asking, "Are you lost? Do you need help finding your parents?"

Bringing parents in should scare any kid into stopping.

Then he turns to face me, and I take a step back.

He has a plastic bag over his face. It looks tight, so tight that it's pulling almost into his mouth. He shouldn't be able to breathe. The upside-down face of Stumbles the Clown Dog and a vintage Bennytown logo covers his face.

Cocking his head and hissing at me, the boy runs off and disappears into the crowd.

"*Abandon all hope, ye who enter here,*" a voice says behind me.

"What?" I ask, turning to meet the voice.

The girl is maybe one or two years older than me and has a black, braided ponytail that goes almost to her waist. She wears the drab, dark-green uniform of a park janitor, wheeling around a trash can and wielding a long stick with a small grasping claw at the end to pick up garbage. The look on her face is somewhere between tired and amused.

Her nametag simply reads GARCIA.

"You're new here, right? Bright-eyed and bushy-tailed, you can't wait for the adventure to start as you join the Bennytown family? Noel?" she says, nodding at my nametag.

"What's wrong with that?" I ask.

"I've seen you around. Passport holder, right? Always thought you had a stick up your… behind. But maybe that's just optimism, and I've forgotten what it looks like," she says. She clearly wants to use different words, but knows better than to mess with the C of C, D & E.

"I've never seen you before," I admit.

"Why would you? Nobody notices the janitors. But we notice *everything*. Every piece of garbage, every dirty secret that nobody wants to see. Like that Sack Head Kid," she says.

"You've seen him before?"

"Him and others like him, yeah. I keep telling the higher-ups that's what they get when they put character faces on bags. Some kid'll put it over their head, but do they listen?" She snorts.

"That's… awful," I say, watching my words.

"There's a lot of awful here. A lot of good, too. Besides, if you work here long enough, you get some unique souvenirs."

She unzips a pouch on her belt and shows me a collection of glass eyes.

"You found all those?"

"Most. Traded for some," she admits.

"Shouldn't those go to Lost & Found?"

She shrugs. "They lost 'em, I found 'em."

Though I don't entirely trust her philosophy, I think I like Garcia.

She looks me up and down. "What department you in? Rides? Retail? Comestibles?"

"Comestibles, yeah," I say.

"Want a tip?" she asks.

"Sure."

"Ask for a job indoors. If they put you in one of the carts, pasty as you are, you're gonna roast in five minutes and they'll never want you back," she says.

Since I hate getting sunburned, I say, "Thanks, I'll see what I can do."

"Don't *see what you can do*, make it happen. 'Cause if you don't go after what you want, you'll be one of the sad sacks stuck in the same job for thirty-two years wondering why you've had the same job for thirty-two years," she says.

She's assertive—more assertive than I am, and even though she's stuck as a janitor, her advice sounds good.

"I'll do it, then. After my orientation's finished," I say.

"Wicked," she says, looking at her watch. "I gotta get back to work. What time does your orientation end?"

"6:00," I say.

"Cool. If you wanna see what Bennytown's really about, meet me by the Fletcher Dorian statue at 6:15. I'll take you on my own quick private tour and show you some *real* behind the scenes secrets. There's stuff they'll *never* tell you on any other tour."

The offer's tempting. I want to make a good impression, and I don't want to be one of the sad sacks Garcia's talking about. If I'm going to work here, I want to make the most of it. I want to rise in the ranks as high as I can and make as much as I can to save for college, like Dad wants. I also want to save some extra for myself so I can buy a car and have some real freedom, like Olivia wants.

"I'll have to let my dad and my girlfriend know, but that sounds great," I say.

"See you then," Garcia says with a wink.

NEITHER OLIVIA NOR DAD are very happy with me when I say I'm sticking around a bit longer to hang out with some people I met at orientation. Maybe I should've lied, but the opportunity to get a private insider tour of Bennytown is too good to ignore.

Once I've finished dropping off my orientation paperwork at the Family Member Building, I've got a few minutes to kill. I spend them walking up and down the Road to Adventure. With the crowds at end of the day on the Fourth of July, it's less walking and more wading through shoulder-to-shoulder crowds. The mannequins in the windows of the shops along the Road to Adventure look vaguely creepy, with blank staring faces and slightly too wide smiles. Olivia refuses to look at them, and even I have a hard time believing one of them won't turn to me and say, "I believe in Bennytown!"

With a few minutes to spare, I make my way to the hub, where the five Upper Park lands break off. At the center of the hub is a ten-foot-tall bronze statue of Fletcher Dorian walking hand in hand with Benny the Bunny. This Benny is barely the size of a child, looking up at Fletcher Dorian with eyes that might as well be religious in their reverence.

I can't help but look at him in much the same way. This is the *real* Fletcher Dorian, not the withered corpse they propped up long enough to shoot that orientation video. This statue is of a man filled with a dream for all in Bennytown has to offer.

"Hey."

Garcia's behind me, still dressed in her uniform though now free of her cart.

"Hey back," I say.

She cocks her head, beckoning me to follow her.

"Where are we goin'?" I ask.

"A little bit of everywhere, but first stop's Candy Mountain." She leads me under the colorful archway to a land that, for as much as I love it, never fails to stir dark memories.

Bright and colorful, this was the first land for kids in Bennytown before they built Happy Hollow. The titular feature is naturally Candy Mountain itself, and the two rides built into it: Candy Mountain Swirler and Candy Mountain Mine Carts. While the Swirler is a fun thrill ride simulating a mild, looping toboggan ride down the surface of the Mountain from the peak to the base, the Mine Carts seem more sinister.

On one of the first trips to Bennytown I can remember, back when Mom was still alive, I was traumatized by the Mine Carts. At five years old, I was feeling adventurous and wanting to tackle one of the Candy Mountain rides. Dad was cautious, but Mom was always more adventurous and took me on the Mine Carts, a trip through a colorful set of tunnels where robotic candy miners sing their cheerful mining song.

However, as the ride goes on, their song grows ominous, warning about the Candy Troll deep within the mine. Their jaunty song becomes downright frightening, with the miners holding onto each other and shuddering as they realize they've accidentally broken open the Candy Troll's lair.

On that first ride, I nearly lost it at the story alone.

It only got worse.

When we got to the lair with the robotic Candy Troll standing above us, the ride broke down. It was only for three or four minutes, but it felt like an eternity. The looping song playing while the Candy Troll threatened to eat us and pick his teeth with our bones filled me with terror.

I lost it, but Mom held my hand and told me in her most soothing voice, "The Candy Troll's just pretend, and pretend can't hurt. It's all right, sweetie. Benny will take care of you."

Eleven years later, the ride is now a favorite, but to this day I can't help but close my eyes in the lair of the rather silly-looking Candy Troll or get a twinge of irrational fear whenever I see Candy Mountain up close. It's a small twinge, barely enough to even make me remember my freak-out, but I doubt it will ever leave me.

Quietly, as if we're not supposed to be here, she guides me to a dark corner toward the Mountain's rear next to one of the boarding stations for the Candy Mountain Swirler. A hot pink door, with the words "BENNYTOWN FAMILY MEMBERS ONLY!" painted jauntily on it, blends seamlessly into the base of the mountain.

Garcia unlocks the door and waves me inside.

I follow her into an anonymous white stairwell where I'm greeted by the sight of a glass box with a fire ax and hose. Steps leading up and down pass near the deafening hum of heavy machines that power the inner workings of the Candy Mountain rides. An electrical charge fills the air that makes the hair on my arms stand up, almost like the static you feel riding down a plastic tube slide on a dry, summer day. The air smells of ozone and industrial grease, and I relax.

The Candy Troll's just pretend.

Garcia guides me up what must be a couple dozen flights of twisting metal stairs. She's damn fast and in great shape. Though I'm wheezing and coughing after the first few flights, adrenaline from this new adventure won't let me lose her.

Finally, at what must be the dozenth anonymous door on the dozenth anonymous landing, Garcia stops. She knocks on the door and waits. After a minute of silence, she cracks it open, looks inside, then waves me in.

We must be close to the top of Candy Mountain and I'm not sure what I'm expecting when I step inside the expansive chamber Garcia led us to, but a sports court isn't it.

Garcia explains, "Jai alai—"

I interrupt her, my voice full of wonder. "Fletcher Dorian's favorite game."

The chamber is filled with jai alai equipment, rows of benches along the edges, a refrigerator, some ancient arcade cabinets, and even a few racks of character costumes including one Benny the Bunny outfit. Although it is much quieter than the stairwell, I can still feel the hum of the heavy machines beneath my feet.

"A-plus," Garcia says, impressed. "Welcome to the Candy Mountain climbers and maintenance staff break room. Fletcher Dorian had it put in as a hideaway where he could play jai alai with the family."

"I've heard about this, but I thought it was an urban legend," I say, gawking at the room.

"Chances are that whatever legends you've heard about Bennytown are true," Garcia says cryptically. She makes a beeline for one of the racks of character costumes against the wall. She parts the costumes to reveal a ladder, then immediately starts to climb. I follow her, squeezing between the furry costumes, up another twenty-foot climb. The journey ends at a hatch that opens to fresh, late afternoon light.

Standing on the platform at the top, I'm overwhelmed by a sense of awe as I look down on Bennytown. Standing on a ten-foot by ten-foot landing that looks like an oversized red-and-white-striped mint, we are more than one hundred feet in the air. Spread out beneath us, I can perfectly see the five lands of the Upper Park, all of them looking like children's toys. The Road to Adventure, the artery of the park, stands out sharply as a single, unwaveringly straight black line. The crowds look like thick trails of ants.

It's a view I never in my life would've thought I'd be lucky enough to see.

"Thank you," I say, holding back tears of awe.

"No problem," Garcia says, grabbing my arm to steady my shaking legs. "Bennytown's an amazing place. I can tell you so many stories about this place, things no one's ever heard. Stories that'll make you laugh, make you cry, make you go to bed clutching at your blanket and calling for your mommy. They might shatter some illusions, but they'll make you a well-prepared Bennytown family member. You wanna hear 'em? You wanna see where they happened?"

I love Bennytown, and I want to stay loving Bennytown, and what she promises might take that away. But I can't ignore that her promise holds a certain power. From up here, looking down on Bennytown with this god's eye view, I find it so easy to want to know, to *see* every hidden secret in the park. Knowing all the details will help me protect and stay a member of the Bennytown family forever.

I meet Garcia's dark eyes and say, "Tell me everything."

BARBARA
1976

Nearly the entire hill under Bennytown was hollowed out with a system of tunnels and subterranean chambers Fletcher Dorian dubbed "Rabbit Holes." Though primarily designed as a quick transportation route that allowed mechanics, janitors, and security invisible access to any part of Bennytown, many of the larger chambers held machinery vital to the functioning of the park's more complex rides. Hidden storage rooms and Bengineer laboratories carved so deep into the hill that few knew what truly happened in them.

In one of these Rabbit Holes beneath Journey through Americana was the break room for Bennytown's costumed characters. It wasn't nearly as nice as the break rooms the other park performers had since it smelled heavily of body odor and half of it was taken up by disembodied costume parts. Since there were only about thirty full-time costumed characters on staff at Bennytown and only about half of them worked at any given moment, it was never as full as any of the other break rooms.

Also, it included the most bitchin' sound system and record collection, so it was easily the best break room in Bennytown.

"Think they could've made these suits any heavier?" Barbara asked, sitting down at one of the lunch tables opposite a sleeping Terry Tortoise and tugging at the head of her Mary Annette costume's oversized, wooden-looking puppet head.

Standing behind her, Oren helped her pull the head off. "You can have it light, or you can have it cool, but you can't have both."

Barbara tried to blow a sweat-streaked lock of hair out of her eyes. It refused to move.

"Would you help me here?" she asked.

"Sure," Oren said, pushing the hair aside and helping her remove her oversized gloves. "So, did you brownbag it, or do you want me to make a commissary run?"

"I brownbagged it, but I'm really craving a commissary run if it wouldn't be too much trouble. I know it's hot out, but I desperately need a warm meal," Barbara said.

"Your wish, my command. I think they've got a special today on pastrami," Oren said.

"Get me one of those and I'll love you forever," she said.

He smiled at her awkwardly. "I'll, uh, I'll be back in ten."

Almost as an afterthought, he put her Mary Annette head up on the racks with all the other heads, pointing outward so they were facing the lunch tables.

Oren was her Skinner, the slang term for character assistants who helped them into, but more importantly out of, their costumes. While most of the costumed characters were tiny women since they could handle the heat better, the Skinners were typically lumberjack-looking guys strong enough to haul all the parts around.

He'd probably seen her naked more often than her boyfriend. Lately, Barbara noticed that Oren wanted to be more than just her Skinner. With how she'd been fighting with her boyfriend over the last few weeks, she was considering it. Oren wasn't a looker, but she could talk with him.

The speakers above her crackled to life. After a few seconds, the opening notes to "Love Rollercoaster" filled the break room.

"Now that's what I'm talking about," Barbara said.

"I knew you'd dig on that," Marvin said, shuffling out of the backroom wearing only a sheen of sweat and the lower half of his Brutus the Bear costume. Since Brutus the Bear was the largest and fattest Bennytown character, it was the reason why Marvin was the only man inside a character suit. In contrast to the tubby suit, Marvin was a lean, muscular man. A bandanna held down his impressive afro, but it threatened to pop out with the slightest misstep.

Shuffling, he grabbed a seat between Barbara and the sleeping Terry.

"She still out?" Marvin asked.

"Yeah," Barbara said.

"If she's out any longer, I'm thinkin' of pranking her. You want in?" Marvin suggested.

An unspoken rule existed that if you were caught sleeping in your suit, any other character could mess with you. Usually simple pranks ensued such as covering up eyeholes with Post-Its or hiding cloves of garlic inside the head of the suit which often improved the smell As Bennytown's resident prank master, Marvin took greatest pride for the time that he removed a sleeping Dare the Hare's head, redecorated the inside to look like an aquarium, and put it back on the Dare actress's head before she woke up.

"I could be down for that," Barbara said. "It'd be easier with a Skinner—"

"We can swing it," Marvin said, fanning himself off.

"Cooling unit not working in your suit?" Barbara asked. The in-suit cooling units were a new Bengineer innovation, but they caused as many problems as they solved.

"Workin' just fine. But, they're what, at least another twenty pounds?" Marvin said.

"At least."

"They keep it cold."

"Really cold," Barbara amended, shivering.

"Yeah, but I'm still sweatin' like you wouldn't believe from the lifting."

"Those NASA guys don't know spit, do they?"

"NASA guys?" Marvin asked, eyebrow raised.

Barbara smiled. She excelled at intrapark gossip and loved to tantalize. "Grapevine says they got a couple new Bengineers, one from NASA and the other a Soviet defector. Some of their spacesuit ideas influenced our new costumes. The cooling units are experimental."

"Needs work," Marvin said.

"You wanna send that suggestion up the line?"

"Heck no, but I'd love to hear more gossip."

Barbara would've loved to gossip; she knew so many people in so many places that her grapevine covered almost all of Bennytown. With her boyfriend working construction at the Happy Hollow expansion, she could've gone on at length about changes that'd soon be coming to the park, but there was something she wanted more now.

"Let's get Terry first," Barbara suggested mischievously.

"A woman after my own heart," Marvin said, hopping to his cartoony feet.

As stealthily as two partially clad costumed people, the pair shuffled behind the sleeping Terry and worked at the edges of her costume head.

Barbara knew something was off as soon as she touched the costume. The head barely budged. Even though they were usually on the verge of just falling off, this one seemed stuck tight. With a prank on the mind, she pulled with all her strength when Marvin suggested it.

When they finally popped the head off, they were greeted with a blast of super-cooled steam. The cold and noxious air made them both cough violently.

In a strange, crazed part of her mind, Barbara was glad she was coughing.

Coughing meant she wasn't screaming at the frozen solid head of the woman in the Terry Tortoise suit. Terry's face was contorted in a look of agony, tears stretching down as icicles on her cheeks.

"Guess they still need to work out the kinks on those cooling units," Barbara said. Her voice sounded dreamy and far away.

When realization and understanding slowly dawned on her, she looked down at her suit with horror. Violently, she tore at her suit as if it were a parasite feasting on her flesh. She was desperate to not become a flesh popsicle as well. In her haste, she bumped into Terry Tortoise, knocking her to the floor.

Although the human head didn't shatter completely, the skin and flesh shattered, exposing the pale bone of the skull beneath. It reminded Barbara of biting the crispy chocolate shell off a Benny the Bunny ice cream bar.

Only with that realization did Barbara scream.

NOEL
2019

"So you're off at 9:00?"

"Yes, Dad."

"Not 9:30? Not 9:45? Just 9:00?"

"Yes, Dad," I repeat. "It'll still take me about fifteen minutes to get to the Family Member Building and get changed and ready for pickup."

"You're not taking any more unscheduled side tours?" he asks half joking.

"No, no more side tours, I promise," I say. Trying to turn it into a joke, I add, "You know, if I had my own car—"

Dad smiles, not taking his eyes off the road. "Yeah, get some money together, pass your driver's test and then we'll talk."

Every time I bring up my own car, that's the answer I receive. I guess it is better than a complete refusal.

I have room to negotiate.

Having a car means freedom. A car means being able to take care of Olivia for once. Olivia's six months older than me and has been driving me around the entire time. I want to show her that I can contribute my fair share to this relationship.

That I'm willing to do what I can to pull my weight. That I can be strong, not in the muscly way that any guy can pull off, but the mental strength of someone who can provide.

She likes strong, even though I don't know if I've ever been that way.

Dad pulls around the loading area by the Family Member Building, and I get the impression that I'm gonna get used to this curb until I wind up getting that car.

"First day," he says, tousling my hair. "You're gonna do great."

"Any first day of work advice?" I ask him.

"Don't kill anyone."

I roll my eyes. "I think you can do better than that."

"Okay, okay," he says, clearing his throat. "Son: Don't. Fuck. Up."

"Dad!"

"Well, it *is* good advice."

"I got a smartass for a dad," I say.

"Yeah, well I got a smartass for a kid," Dad says. Thoughtful, he adds, "Don't worry so much. I meant it when I said you're gonna do great."

I'll do great.

After how well orientation went, I'm actually beginning to believe that.

THE WARDROBE DEPARTMENT is an expansive concrete chamber in the Family Member Building's basement that seems to go on forever. It's laid out like a massive dry cleaner with dozens of mechanical, spinning racks that move thousands of blue plastic wardrobe bags into position.

After retrieving mine, I go to the changing rooms to dress.

Striped blue shirt, khaki pants, belt, and a Bennytown baseball cap.

The clothes seem clean, and any holes are expertly sewn up, but Garcia explained that none of the uniform pieces are exclusive to any one family member. Anything we wear was probably worn by someone else yesterday, which makes me particularly glad I wore an undershirt today. They don't fit perfectly, but they're comfortable, and I'm happy that I don't have to wash my own uniform. A small plastic pouch at the top of the bag holds my nametag, and when I pin it to my chest, I feel like an official Bennytown family member.

My street clothes go back into the bag and back on the rack. After that, I'm on the elevator up to the Comestible Services department office.

Every second of the ride, I'm crossing my fingers for an indoor job. I'd listened to Garcia and put in a request so I wouldn't have to work out in the sun immediately after my Independent Orientation, but whether they'd grant that request wasn't up to me.

Still crossing my fingers, I listen as the man behind the desk determines my fate.

He says, "You're working Ice Cream Villa in Candy Mountain."

Though I feel a twinge of fear, gratitude for working indoors helps me manage to reply with a firm "Thanks!"

Heading into Bennytown's backstage area, I check my phone and find I'm half an hour early. I feel like skipping with glee for how well this day's going.

And then I hear a noise that seems out of place.

The mewling of kittens followed by laughter.

Curious, I walk around the side of a shipping container and pause when I hear the kitten sounds again. A young woman is wearing the khaki shorts, vest, and hat of one of the animal trainers from the Teddy Roosevelt's Wildlife Adventures show, curly blond hair spilling down her back.

Her nametag reads, "Lorraine."

A man in another radiation suit that looks like a bright purple Brutus the Bear kneels down beside her, watching as three kittens eat from a bowl of cream.

"KI-YY," the man laughs as a kitten rubs up against the thick fingers of his suit's hand. His garbled words are barely understandable, like he can't quite form words.

"Cuties, aren't they?" Lorraine asks in a light Australian accent, looking at me and smiling. She's cute in an outdoorsy sort of way, if you ignore the massive, mangled scar on the left side of her neck.

"These little guys can't be more than two months old. Makes you wonder where their mum is, doesn't it?" Lorraine asks.

"KI-YY," Radiation Suit Brutus repeats.

Behind me, a voice booms, "I've found him. Sector two. Send everyone you've got."

A bald, middle-aged man walks calmly past me toward Brutus and Lorraine. Wearing a black business suit with sunglasses and an earpiece, he looks like a Secret Service agent.

"Hello, Brutus. You know you're not supposed to be back here," he says soothingly, a hand inside his jacket pocket.

Radiation Suit Brutus stands, shaking slightly in his massive suit. "KI-YY?"

"No, not even for stray kitties. You know what you're supposed to do, right?"

"Sawk?" Brutus says.

"Yes, you're supposed to salt," Secret Service says. Then, without turning, he says to me, "Kid, you're gonna want to get out of here."

Amused, Lorraine stands up, approaching Secret Service. "Awww, come on, he just wants to have a li'l fun with a li'l pussy. Ease up on him and I'll let you see my li'l pussy."

Conspiratorially, she tips a wink at me. "You too, if you'd like."

Jokingly, at least I hope it's jokingly, she moves to unbutton her shorts.

I back away. "What? No! I have to get to work!"

"Awww, have a sense of adventure!" she teases.

Secret Service walks past her without paying attention, and suddenly we're surrounded. There's another man dressed identically to him and four tourists: two college students and a middle-aged Japanese couple. Calmly, with hands up, they surround Brutus and guide him away, maintaining their distance as if he's a wild animal that could strike. Although I have a hard time imagining that with the way he's loudly sobbing.

"They're fast today," she says from behind me.

"Hey, Garcia," I say.

"Hey back," she says.

"What… who were those people?"

"The guys in suits?" She leans on her clawed stick like a cane. "Park private security are here to take care of the real problems. The tourists are Daywalkers—plainclothes security. They mingle with the crowd, looking like anyone else, having fun, smiling, and reporting any potential crimes or breaches of park morality."

The security group and Brutus are gone.

"What're the radiation suit characters for?"

Garcia considers this. "The Redeemers? Another story for another time. Now get moving, you don't wanna be late."

Redeemers. It's a word that stops me in my tracks, a secret of Bennytown's that Garcia hadn't already shared on our tour but one that tantalizes my curiosity. Garcia's smirk says she knows exactly what she's doing to me, and that she's right about me not wanting to be late.

"Thanks," I say, running off.

"Don't mention it. See you around," she calls.

"Count on it!" I exclaim.

I can be annoyed with Garcia later. Right now, I need to not screw up my first day.

I race to the main Bennytown family member entrance, hidden between a couple shops on the Road to Adventure. On either side of the entrance ornate signs read:

REMEMBER!

PAST THIS POINT YOU REPRESENT BENNYTOWN! BE WHO FLETCHER DORIAN WOULD WANT YOU TO BE!

ISN'T THAT EXCITING?

WARNING: FOR YOUR OWN SAFETY, DO NOT FOR ANY REASON OCCUPY BENNYTOWN BETWEEN 11:30 P.M. & 4:30 A.M.!

Taking a deep breath, I step into the wide working world of Bennytown.

Only a very quiet voice in the back of my mind wonders where Lorraine went.

"WE NEED NEW meat before the Birthday. Glad to see you look meaty," JK says.

JK is not the manager of Ice Cream Villa, nor is he the Lead, a Bennytown supervisor. He's the Assistant Lead on duty when I get there, and he's training me.

He's blond and muscular, so it's no surprise to find out that he was a high school football player about seven years ago. He acts like he never got over it.

I wish someone else was training me.

"First thing you gotta remember is ya can't steal," he says, pointing out the cameras and at a framed photo on the wall of Fletcher Dorian and Caroline. "Eyes and ears everywhere. NOT

THAT WE'D WANT TO STEAL, RIGHT? WE BELIEVE IN BENNYTOWN!"

"Of course not," I say. Our other family members, too busy at the registers or pouring soft serve, pay him no attention.

"Right. Good kid. Second thing you gotta remember. If you wanna swear, learn some replacement words. I recommend carp, shed, bell, flip, and mudskipper. Third, respect the hot fudge, that shed's like napalm. Fourth, if a teen girl offers to show her boobs in exchange for ice cream, she only gets a small cone, single flavor."

"That's—what?"

"Fifth, you like rap?"

"Uh—"

"Good!" he says, smiling and clapping me on the back. With his free hand, he pulls a business card from his front shirt pocket and slips it into mine. "Download my album, give it five stars and we'll have a good time. Five stars? You look like the kinda guy who gives five stars. You don't look like a mudskipper. He doesn't look like a mudskipper, does he, Cara?"

The girl at the nearest register pushes past us and grabs a waffle cone. "I don't care what he looks like. We're getting slammed, so shut the bell up and get him working!"

"In a minute," JK says, guiding me into the cramped backroom of Ice Cream Villa. It's located behind the humming soft serve machines and filled with supplies, industrial sinks, and a small alcove featuring an ancient filing cabinet overflowing with paperwork. A short hallway just off this room leads to the full restaurant that occupies the other side of this building, Miners' Favorite Pizza. The smell from the ovens is mouthwatering.

Reaching for the rack above a small steel table, he pulls down a slightly dented metal lockbox. "Sixth. From clock in to clock out, your phone goes in here."

Dutifully, I drop my phone in the box. He slides it back up on the shelf and guides me back up front.

"Seventh—"

The park background music takes on a particularly jaunty, instrumental Western theme. I recognize it as a song from *Showdown at Pony Ranch*, a Dorian Studios movie they let fall into obscurity over the years due to its unflattering portrayals of Native Americans. Considering how much they've tried to bury it, I'm surprised to hear it.

Almost as surprised as I am at what happens next.

"PONY PARTY!" someone up front yells.

JK's smile fades, slightly. "Hold that thought and stay right here."

JK darts for the door leading outside and quickly locks it, checks it, and ducks inside Miners' Favorite Pizza.

I edge around one of the soft serve machines. All of my Ice Cream Villa family members stay at their stations, working and checking people out through the line at an impressively accelerated pace, their eyes dancing nervously.

"What's a Pony Party?" I ask.

Cara looks at me between the machines like I'm an idiot. "Potential active shooter or terrorist incident; real thoughts and prayers kinda stuff. We get these about once every two weeks or so. Music goes on, we stay on alert but keep working. When the music goes off, it means security has handled it."

The cold fear that shot up my spine at "potential active shooter or terrorist incident" doesn't go away with the casualness of her words. My eyes drift to the guests outside, wandering around or impatiently standing in line.

"What about them?" I ask.

Cara shrugs. "Management doesn't want them to worry, so they don't say a word unless things get serious. Just sit tight, these don't usually last long. Usually, it's just bullshed; there's no way a killer'd get in here unless Bennytown wanted it."

After a few seconds, the music changes to something more cheerful, more familiar. My fellow family members relax.

JK comes back from Miners' Favorite Pizza.

"Nothing like a Pony Party to wake you up!" he laughs, trying to look as far from pale and sweaty as possible and failing abysmally. "So, ready to rock, New Meat?"

"Uh, yeah?" I say, trying to wrap my head around what just happened.

"No complaints, Noel? I like no complaints. You'll do fine here. Rafael! Close your register and show new meat here the ropes."

"I've got a line, can't you do it?" Rafael points outside. The people in his line look hot and irritable.

"I'm on break. I'll help you close out your line, though," JK says, ambling outside.

Rafael grumbles, looking like he wants to take it out on me for a second before reconsidering. "Welcome to Ice Cream Villa."

Once JK closes his line down and wanders off to wherever it is JK wanders off to on a break, Rafael trains me. I know he wants to get back to opening his window again, but he's doing a better training job than JK, so I don't mind. Given that we're a soft serve ice cream place with three flavors, two different cones, a small handful of toppings, and only three sundaes, there's not much to learn. After Rafael thinks I've got what it takes to be an acceptable ice cream pourer, he opens up the line and I'm working as a runner for the four people on register.

After that, things are a blur of ice cream runner errands, which rapidly takes my mind off the Pony Party. The sweaty line bakes in the sun and becomes less pleasant as they lose their patience. Ice Cream Villa is air-conditioned but has terribly cramped quarters, barely room for two people to stand next to each other. I'm darting through everyone, trying not to slip as I get the right orders to the right people.

My feet and lower back start aching after only two hours.

By my fourth hour, I've been covered with whipped cream, hot fudge, and so much unfrozen soft serve mix that I wonder if my shoes will ever stop being sticky.

JK comes in to "help" periodically and though he knows what he's doing, he'd clearly rather be anywhere else.

By dinnertime the floor is slick with soft serve mix and the water we use to wash it down the drain. Everyone else is used to this and are as light on their feet as dancers. Every time I turn around, I nearly fall over. Hopefully, I'll pick up their grace sooner rather than later.

Dinner's a welcome reprieve. I take my food vouchers to the family member commissary and enjoy a hot meal. The other family members in the commissary tend to stick among their own particular cliques, marking off territory. Ride operators and entertainers seem to be the popular ones with retail just a step beneath them. The half-dressed costumed characters appear to be the weird loners, tired and burned out by the heat. While the janitors are on the bottom, the comestibles are just a step above them.

Just one big, happy family.

Dinner is too brief, and soon I'm back in Ice Cream Villa. This time I'm in charge of a cash register, fielding orders and making ice cream. I have to make sure I remember every button on the digital display.

By this time of the day, the customers are even more irritable. At one point, JK gets into an argument with a couple of hippie-looking types at his window. I wondered if there was a time portal since the girl has a daisy painted on her cheek. Both of them are complaining about how Fletcher Dorian owned large amounts of stock in DOW Chemical and Monsanto and must have been directly responsible for the use of Agent Orange during the Vietnam War. Seeing them irritate JK is fun, but I'm happier they didn't come to my window.

Finally, 8:00 pm rolls around, and we close up shop. I'm sticky and smell terrible, while my legs and back are screaming. Somehow, I survived my first day.

When it comes time to count my register out with JK, I'm fairly confident my change and receipts will add up perfectly.

When I tell JK this, he looks at me smugly and says, "Yeah, let's see about that. Get me one of the count-out sheets from the filing cabinet."

"What do they look like?" I ask.

"Count-out sheets. Third drawer. You can't miss 'em," he says.

I don't think anyone's gone through this filing cabinet in years. It is near-bursting with old family member records and blank forms of every type other than count-out sheets.

Finally, I find a small stack of papers that seems likely and pull them free. Stuck to them is a colorful, empty file folder. As I am placing it back in the drawer, I glance at it and smile.

Printed on the folder is a picture of Benny and his friends from the late '80s, terrible fashions and all. The gang's all there: Benny the Bunny, Flora Fox, Brutus the Bear, Dare the Hare, Terry Tortoise, Snapper Gator, Pedro Parrot, Mary Annette and Stumbles the Clown Dog and...

Who's that?

In the back, just barely staring over the rest of the crowd, is a smiling walrus in a Hawaiian shirt.

Remember the Poison Words list?

"What's taking you? Do I gotta come over and do this myself?"

"Sorry, just looking at some ancient history," I say, showing him the folder.

"Yeah, it's old, I get it. You find the forms?" JK asks.

There's probably a lot of better people I could ask, but I'm tired, and he's here, and, well, I'm kinda curious.

"Who's this guy?" I ask JK, pointing at the walrus.

He looks at the folder for a second, bored. Then he does a double-take that'd be fit for a cartoon and snatches it from my hands.

"Nice, where'd you get that?"

"In the cabinet," I say.

He hides it in the crook of his arm. "I gotta look through that cabinet more, and *you*, Noel, you're new meat, but you're officially my lucky charm."

He counts me out with gusto, and when I prove to be three cents short, he adds a few pennies from someone else's register to make sure I keep my perfect day.

"Great job, Noel," he says, pulling his phone from the lockbox. "Keep an eye on the place. I gotta make a call."

Keep an eye on the place?

Does he really want me to watch the whole restaurant and all our other family members?

Seriously?

My heart starts pounding, and I want to ask him what he means, but he's gone before I mention it.

What the hell just happened?

THOUGH BENNYTOWN'S OPEN for a little while longer, I'm ready to leave when my shift is over at 9. My body feels like a giant bruise, I smell bad, and I'm ready to go to sleep.

Surviving my first day feels like an accomplishment.

I walk backstage to the Family Member Building, hearing the low mewls of stray cats running in the darkness. The evening fireworks over Candy Mountain crackle behind me, adding bursts of colored light to the dark.

When I'm sure I'm alone, I turn on my phone and make a call.

"Hey Dad, it's me."

"Hey, Noel! You done for the day?" Dad asks.

"Yeah, I just got off shift."

"Ready for me to pick you up?"

"Yeah, I just need to change."

"Okay, I'll meet you where I dropped you off?"

"Sure, meet you there soon, Dad."

"I'm so proud of you. Your mom would be too."

Dad says this for pretty much anything I do, but it still hits me with force.

"Thanks," I say, choking up slightly.

"I love ya. See you soon."

"Love you too. Bye."

When I hang up, I'm more emotional from the phone call with Dad than I expected. Needing a change of pace, I call the one voice I've wanted to hear all day.

It rings once, then voicemail picks up. *"Hey, this is Olivia. Don't know why you're calling when you can text, but, whatever. You know what to do."*

Of course, she'd have it charging now.

Wonderful.

"Hey, Olivia, I was hoping to hear your voice, but… call me? I just… I need someone—"

I hang up quickly, sliding the phone into my pocket the moment I see the figure walking out of the darkness. With another burst of fireworks, I see the large, round costume of Terry Tortoise, with her backward baseball cap and perpetual smile. In moments, she's in darkness again, and I keep walking to the Family Member Building.

During next burst of fireworks as we pass within inches of each other, I mean to smile and nod, but then I get a better look at her. Steam pours from her mouth, like someone filled it with dry ice. Moving jerkily like the suit lacks joints, she sounds like she's sobbing.

The better part of me wants to see if she's all right.

The tired part of me propels me forward with my head down.

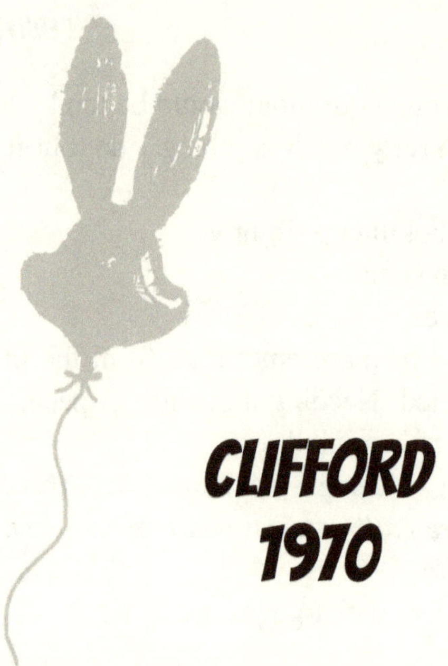

CLIFFORD
1970

The hippies were everywhere, a seething mob of unwashed flesh and anger.

Management let them in because Bennytown "welcomed everyone."

And what did Bennytown get in return?

A *goshdarn* riot brewing in Journey through Americana on the day of Bennytown's eleventh birthday.

Clifford knew trouble was brewing when he saw the five hundred kids shouting un-American slogans.

"Buncha commie assholes, spittin' on the graves of our brave boys," Wendell, one of Clifford's officers, said.

"Language, Wend," Clifford said. While he normally didn't care what his men said, Clifford believed in Bennytown and its rules.

"Sorry, boss."

"It's all right, Wend. Stuff happens. Just don't let it happen too much," Clifford said.

They wore riot gear developed by the Bengineers to be state of the art with clear plastic shields covered with Benny the Bunny's face and sculpted helmets with clear plastic face plates that looked like Benny & Friends. They made his men look ridiculous, but like Mr. Dorian said, the riot uniforms didn't upset any of the proper guests when they'd been forced to evacuate this land.

The improper guests, though…

"Mr. Tally?"

Turning around, Clifford was face-to-face with Fletcher Dorian himself. As ever, he was surrounded by his dark-suited security personnel, blank faces behind sunglasses.

"Mr. Tally," Dorian said, shaking Clifford's hand firmly.

"Mr. Dorian," Clifford responded nervously.

Sensing his tension, Dorian smiled. "Similar to your service days, isn't it?"

"Oh, uh, yes sir," Clifford said. Searching for some adequate small talk with his younger boss, he continued, "And yours?"

"I never saw much of this back in the OSS, but I've seen my share of ruckus," Dorian said knowingly.

"I see," Clifford said, lacking anything better to say. He'd fought two wars, one across France and Germany, the other in Korea, and never flinched. After one brief exchange with the man up top, he was nervous as a schoolboy.

"Any progress with dispersal?" Dorian asked.

Glad to be getting back to business, Clifford replied, "No sir."

"Any cameras?"

"None that aren't ours. Some of the rabble-rousers called in news crews, but my men on perimeter kept them out."

"Good. Good. I want to take care of this peacefully and quietly, if possible," Dorian said. "Do you have a bullhorn?"

One of Clifford's men handed one to Dorian. Bravely, he jumped onto a planter behind the skirmish line and spoke through the bullhorn.

"Hello, Bennytown guests! My name is Fletcher Dorian, and I'd really like us all to be friends! I know you're upset and want someone to listen to your grievances! Well, I want to be that someone! Calmly disperse, have your leaders identify themselves, and I'll speak to them personally so we can open a dialogue!"

The crowd was momentarily quiet. Clifford saw the wave of recognition and confusion spread through the formerly angry mob as the man they came to protest changed to a confidant before their eyes. Many of them grew up being entertained by this man and remembered that kinship. There was a moment, brief though it was, when Clifford even thought Dorian would sway them.

Then a light bulb hit Fletcher Dorian, shattering against his jaw. Surprised, he fell off the planter into a tangled sprawl. He got to his feet quickly, dazed and bleeding from his scalp, and then fell back down.

"NO MORE DEAD BABIES!" one of the protestors shouted. Greasy and cackling, he was no doubt counting on the support of the rest of the mob to back him up.

The group of onlookers didn't react though.

Instead, they looked at the heckler silently.

The calm propelled Clifford into the crowd. Storming through the skirmish line, he pulled out his baton as he went. The bulb thrower pulled the wrist of a blond woman and disappeared into the crowd.

Another of the hippies stepped between Clifford and the couple.

With a flick of his arm, Clifford dropped the longhair with a heavy baton hit to the skull.

The screaming began.

The skirmish line ran forward, yelling as they viciously avenged their fallen king, beating the hippie mob to the ground while adding planters, benches, and boots to their arsenal. The rioters tried to run, shattering shop windows in Journey through Americana while attempting to open new escape routes.

Clifford forced his way through the melee, searching for Bulb Thrower and his girl.

In moments, he spotted them running on the sidewalk, trying to dodge the barricades set up along the passage to Primordial World.

Clifford pounced, slamming his shield between their joined hands. Bulb Thrower fell against the curb, while the girl stumbled and bounced violently off a lamppost.

Gasping, she fell onto her back and grabbed her already swelling throat, trying to take in air.

"Oh god, Jeannie! Jeannie! *Jeannie!*" Bulb Thrower screamed as he cradled her head. Her pitiful, watery eyes dropped tears that streaked the daisy painted on her cheek.

When she stopped trying to take in breath, Bulb Thrower looked up at Clifford angrily. "You killed her. You killed her, you FUCKING PIG!" he yelled, tears falling into his ratty little beard.

Feeling more alive than he had in years, Clifford raised his baton high.

"Language!"

NOEL
2019

I live for hot showers these days.

Every night after work, I stand under the hot water scrubbing the day away. I wash away the sticky, tar-like spots of hot fudge, the chemical dyes of the strawberry syrup, and the rotten milk stench of the soft serve mix. I can clean the mess, but the smell lingers on my body.

After four days, I feel like I'm improving. Despite sore muscles, stink, and time away from Olivia, I'm unbelievably content. Silly as it might sound, I feel a satisfaction with my job I never expected, like I'm doing something great.

For myself.

For my future.

For *Bennytown*.

After I dry myself with a towel, I pull on my boxers and tank top and open the door, letting the steam out.

Olivia is sitting at her computer. Her mom and stepdad trust us, so we basically have our own little apartment to ourselves. It feels like my own little home away from home.

I like it when she welcomes me home wearing her jacket and pretty much nothing else.

Her eyes dart over to me, briefly, but I don't distract her from one plugged-in earbud.

"This rap album's a piece of shit," she says.

"Don't tell me you bought JK's album," I say, running a hand through my still-wet hair.

"Fuck no! Ewww! I found it on a pirate site. After seeing that card, I had to know."

Half of JK's card had his contact information, while the other half showed him wearing sunglasses while flashing a thumbs-up with a look I doubt was ever cool.

"You wanna hear some?" she asks.

"Not really."

"Wanna do something else?" she proposes, swiveling her chair toward me provocatively.

For a moment, I very much want to.

Then I see the damn letterman's jacket.

After stealing it from an ex-boyfriend, she likes to wear it constantly because she says it is comfortable. She knows I don't like it as a reminder of old boyfriends and refuses to listen to my protests.

I've stopped arguing, but it doesn't mean I have to like it, either.

"Let me cool down some first," I say, propping out on her bed, staring up at the posters she's taped to the ceiling.

"No problem." She turns off the computer and crawls onto the bed next to me. I put my arm around her, but the jacket feels rough.

I need to get her a new jacket once I get paid.

*A jacket from **me**.*

"Are you okay?" she asks.

"Yeah. Just tired," I mumble, which is mostly the truth.

"Sorry. If it makes you feel better, I've found something about your walrus," she says.

This *does* sound interesting. Ever since JK went nuts over that folder, I've been trying to find details about this walrus character. I asked other Ice Cream Villa people to see if they knew anything, but they were clueless, or at least pretended to be.

Then I got a reprimand for using a Poison Word, and I stopped asking.

Either someone told, or JK was right about there being ears everywhere.

"What'd you find?" I ask.

"Nothing," she says.

"That's not something."

"I found no real information, but there are a lot of rumors floating around," she says.

"Rumors?"

"Rumors you're not gonna like," she says.

"Why?"

"Because they deal with a lot of the crazy stories."

"What kind of stories?"

The kinds of stories Garcia told me?

"Stories of all the deep, dark secrets of Bennytown and Dorian Studios. Lawsuits, labor strife, human rights violations, deaths…"

I shake my head. "People don't die at Bennytown."

"Do you know why? It's park policy to not declare anyone dead until they've been taken offsite."

Garcia told me that, but it made more sense when Olivia repeated the information.

"But—"

"There are verifiable reports of thirty-six deaths over fifty years."

"It's not *that* many," I say.

"Forty-two if you count the parking lot and structure. Forty-five if you count the employee areas too."

"Family members, not employees," I correct her.

"Whatever," she says.

Though the idea of that many people dying in Bennytown strikes me as insanity, I have to find some reasonable explanation.

"Millions of people go through Bennytown every year, so there's bound to be a heart attack here or there," I say. The explanation feels right to me.

She continues as if I hadn't spoken. "These are just the *reported* deaths. Bennytown has likely hushed up way more. And these numbers don't include the injuries or disappearances. Or that riot. I've read theories the death number might be as high as—"

"And the walrus?" I ask, wanting to get back on track.

She sighs, knowing she's not going to change my feelings about Bennytown. It's one of the things I wish we never fought about, but somehow it always pops up in conversation. I know she likes the place well enough, since, for fuck's sake, we wouldn't have gotten together without Bennytown. But she doesn't love it as much as I do, not like a real fan or family member would.

I know she's upset, so I follow up with, "Please?" I shoot her my most sympathetic, cartoonishly pleading eyes.

She grumbles, "You're lucky I love you."

"I know."

"You should."

"So, about that nothing that's something?" I ask.

She relents. "Try searching for Bennytown and walrus together and you'll find nothing. Or you'll find blank pages where information has been removed. I asked around on some 'Dorian Truth' subreddits, and I heard about a new Bennytown character in the late '80s called Wilbur Walrus. After a big media blitz and all sorts of merchandising, he disappeared one day out of nowhere. Every reference to him was eliminated and a recall was issued on all sold merchandise with his depiction. Bennytown has been buying any piece that makes it up for auction for big money. Dorian Studios used their power to remove any mention of the walrus anywhere. About an hour after I started asking, my posts got deleted."

"What happened to him?" I ask.

She's annoyed but answers. "Some say the actor who played him was involved with the alleged child disappearances in the early '90s. Others say that he just went nuts, stole the costume and ran. Whatever the reason, Bennytown's been trying to erase him ever since."

"Huh," I say. I have a hard time picturing someone from the Bennytown family doing anything like that. I know there are bound to be some eccentrics, but they're not criminals.

"Huh? That's all you gotta say?" she asks, amused.

"What would you like me to say?"

"I don't want you to say anything," she rolls on top of me, kissing me. Her breath smells like cigarette smoke and gum. "I don't want to talk about Bennytown anymore. I've got you for the night, and I want your undivided attention."

I'm briefly distracted by the idea of finding something walrus related and trading it in for big bucks.

When she removes the jacket, my undivided attention is hers.

FOR THE NEXT week, she can't hold my attention because work is an absolute madhouse. My schedule is all over the place, working mornings and nights randomly, but always when the crowds are heaviest.

I've come to like mornings the most. People tend to be optimistic and excited for their day ahead.

Afternoons on the other hand are a different story. People are tired. Hot. Dehydrated. They get mean. Real mean.

JK's hippie enemies have stopped by my window to yell at me twice.

There have been three more Pony Parties. As far as I know, none of them amounted to much. After the second one, I began ignoring them.

A couple of dads got into a fistfight at the next window after one accidentally cut in line. Making it a family affair, the winning dad encouraged his kids to hit the fallen dad.

Too often I've seen people order our biggest sundaes, stuffing their fat faces, and get off the Candy Mountain Swirler with their sundae all over the shirts. I don't know what disgusts me more: the people puking or when they get back in line to order more ice cream.

The lingering, unseasonable humidity has caused many people to be wheeled off on stretchers with heatstroke. The air conditioning in Ice Cream Villa has electrical problems when it's overtaxed, which is all the time. Vickers Flickers are what the other family members call these glitches. I try to stay hydrated, but I'm soaked through with sweat by the end of the day.

The other family members seem to be all right, but they cycle through so fast that I don't get much time to get to know anyone. JK doesn't count because I sure don't want to befriend him. About the closest thing I've got to a friend here is Garcia. I can never find her on my own, but I stumble across her often enough. She doesn't judge me for saving up for a car or college, and she's always good for stories and gossip.

I'm getting paid, but not as much as I want. And I keep hoping I'll stumble upon more walrus paraphernalia. I've searched through the filing cabinet after my shift and found nothing.

With random days off, I still manage to squeeze in some time with Olivia and Dad. After a date night with Olivia, she begs for more of my time. All I can do is apologize.

When sleep comes after a tiring day of work, I dream of Bennytown. I hear the whirring noises of ice cream machines and registers, the constant flow of customers, and the same three songs that play on the loudspeakers at all times on a constant loop.

Benny, of course, is the star of most of these dreams.

Despite all the frustrations that come with the job, for the first time in my life, I feel like I'm really a part of something bigger than myself. Often, I find myself thinking about what I can do to help Bennytown now that I'm part of the family. These thoughts seem to consume me when I'm awake.

This is my new normal, and I *like* it.

I believe in Bennytown.

I see a long future here that will help me make something of my life. Make something of *myself* and be the kind of perfect man for Olivia.

I've started down the path that will take me all the way to graduation. And that safe and easy path might've even been easy to stay on if JK hadn't dropped the strawberry syrup.

TROY
2008

Shussett High's Grad Nite was gonna kick ass.

Along with a few dozen other Southern California high schools, SH won a lottery draw to have Grad Nite at Bennytown. From 7:00–11:00 p.m., the park would be theirs. They could ride rides, take pictures with the characters, and celebrate.

As long as you could afford admission.

"I don't think we should be doing this, man," Bryce said as they sneaked along the outer wrought iron fence of Bennytown's Lower Park.

"Let me do the thinking. Then you won't have nothing to worry about," Troy said.

Bryce eyed Troy skeptically for a moment, then said, "'Kay."

They reached a large wrought iron gate with the face of Benny the Bunny carved into it and "BENNYTOWN" across the top. During the day it was a tourist attraction, not nearly as famous as the front gates or Candy Mountain, but you still saw a lot of pictures of people posing in front of it on Myspace. At night, it was so poorly lit that it seemed capable of casting shadows in the dark. To make matters worse, it looked like a cage.

There was a section of fence low enough for someone to get over with a boost. Decorative spikes lined the top, not that sharp-looking, but dangerous enough if you landed on them wrong.

That's why they'd brought the blankets.

Troy and Bryce couldn't afford to get into to Grad Nite, but this was hardly an obstacle for these two. They'd use the blankets to hop the fence, hide out until Grad Nite the following night, and walk out with their class like goddamn rock stars.

Assuming Bryce could hold up his end of the bargain.

"You're sure we won't get caught?" Bryce asked.

"Yeah. You know Snopes?"

"He in fifth period English?"

For a question that stupid, Troy slapped Bryce upside the head. "No, asshat, the website."

"That hurt, man," Bryce said, rubbing the back of his head.

"Snopes is the site that tells you which urban legends are true or not. While you can't trust every bad thing they say about President Bush because of all their liberal agenda bullshit, their info on Bennytown is solid. And one of the best little-known secrets is that this park's completely empty from 11:30 to 4:30 every night."

"Completely? Every night?" Bryce asked.

"Yup. Not even security sticks around. That's why tonight's our night if we wanna do this without gettin' caught."

"Why's it empty?"

Troy shrugged, taking a blanket from Bryce and tossing it on top of the fence. It landed easily on the spikes. Troy tossed a second blanket right on top.

"Come on, gimme a boost," Troy said.

Bryce obliged, helping Troy struggle on top of the fence. He swung one leg over so that he could straddle a space between two of the spikes. It wasn't comfortable, with one spike poking uncomfortably close to his dick, but he could support Bryce's weight from here.

"Come on, let's do this," Troy said, reaching down.

"You hear that?" Bryce asked, looking over his shoulder.

"Hear what?"

"Someone's coming!" Bryce exclaimed, running away.

"Bryce! You fuck!" Troy yelled after him.

Troy couldn't see or hear anyone coming. This was just like Bryce, always jumping at shadows. If he didn't have a car, they probably wouldn't have been friends, and… and…

Bryce had the car.

"BRYCE! FUCK!" Troy yelled.

He thought it over. He could follow Bryce, but what'd that accomplish? He'd made it this far, and there was no way he was gonna miss Grad Nite.

Something brushed against his leg inside the park. Something soft and fluffy, like a stuffed animal. It rubbed up against him experimentally at first, almost a caress, before wrapping itself slowly around his ankle.

"The fuck?" Troy muttered.

Someone inside Bennytown was grabbing him.

No, several someones.

The soft caresses turned into powerful yanks that threatened to pull him off the fence. The dominant hands that had him were soft and furry, but the others were cold and dry, scratching as they pulled at the exposed flesh of his leg.

He wasn't really sure it was people he was looking at. The inside of Bennytown was pitch black, but the hands that came from the black almost glowed gray. There were dozens of them, pushing past each other and grabbing for him. Some of them were human, some were the muted, fluffy hands of costumed characters, and some of them were so truly inhuman, so completely and utterly alien, it chipped at Troy's sanity just looking at them.

The darkness wasn't darkness, though.

It was whispers.

(The Voice of the Park.)

Sad, angry, giddy whispers grabbed at him, wanting him for their own terrible purposes, to be one with them. He considered joining them to end the madness. Just listening for a few seconds tore the last bits of his sanity apart.

He decided not to move, though. Not when a powerful hand grabbed his left leg. This hand, larger and softer than any of the clammy hands grabbing at his right leg, closed around his ankle and yanked him off, dropping him outside Bennytown's fence.

Sanity returning a fragment at a time, Troy stared at his savior.

It was Stumbles the Clown Dog, only not. The suit was bulky, almost a suit of armor, with a face that looked halfway between Stumbles and an oversized gas mask. Gray hands reached for Stumbles through the fence and gates, whispering dark promises.

Stumbles reached behind his back to an overstuffed pack of tools and pulled out a pair of cattle prods. One in each hand, he shoved the weapons against the bars. Showers of sparks forced the hands back inside.

Stumbles turned to Troy and hollered in a strangled voice, "GOOO! RUUU! GOOO!!!"

Stumbles turned back to the hands. A pawful of white powder thrown at ghostly crowd elicited a chorus of terrible screams.

Troy sprinted without thinking, unmindful of Grad Nite, or that half his hair had fallen out while the rest turned white. He didn't notice that he was bleeding heavily from the feet and ankles where the hands and Stumbles grabbed at him.

The only thing he could think about was what hid beneath those dark whispers.

NOEL
2019

I'm at the end of another late shift with JK and Stu, a tempo-rary transfer. The late summer clouds have become a late summer thunderstorm, and Bennytown is closing early due to the rain and wind.

I'm counting out my register in back, trying not to listen as they clean up front.

"So, she's a virgin, or she used to be. I'm not sure which, but you know how—OH SHED!"

I hear a sloshing noise and then the loud thump of some-thing heavy hitting the floor. I barely notice until Stu, hands covered in bright red, comes around the wall of ice cream ma-chines.

"Can you give us a little help, kid?"

The front room of Ice Cream Villa looks like a murder sce-ne. The floor is covered in red, spatters cover the white walls. Lying in the middle of the mess, JK has his back arched over a broken drum of strawberry syrup and looks like someone ripped him in half.

He looks at me, bleary-eyed, smiling crookedly.

"Don't worry, I'm alive," he says.

I wasn't worried is what I want to say. What I actually say is, "Need help?"

"No!" JK exclaims as Stu helps him to his feet. "Don't touch me! You'll get this shed everywhere. I need you... I need you to run an errand."

I shouldn't be running an errand, not with ten minutes left on my shift.

Olivia's picking me up tonight, and I have the day off tomorrow. I don't want to miss a minute of spending all day with her. At the same time, I want to prove that I'm a hardworking family member.

"What do you need?" I ask.

Wobbly, JK walks to the back, picking the store phone from its cradle and dialing a quick set of numbers.

"Yo, Joaquin. You know that solid you owe me? Need a drum of syrup. Strawberry. Uh huh. Uh huh. Okay, for attitude like that, it's two drums, and don't let me hear anything about inventory numbers not matching up! Okay? Cool. And did you put in that good word for me with Gina? No, I don't care what she thinks of me. Okay, see ya."

"Errand?" I ask, looking at him with increasing unease.

"Need you to make a run downstairs to the Happy Hollow Frosty Hut. Take the dolly and pick up two drums of strawberry syrup from their Assistant Lead, Joaquin. Then head to the Sky Buckets, ask for their Lead, Jenna. Take the bucket back here, and you're home free."

I can think of a bunch of things I don't like about this idea. Like why does it have to be me or why do I have to take the Sky Buckets even though I know you can't take the dolly on the Stairway to Heaven and the elevators take forever. In the end I know I'm going to do this anyway, so I take the dolly and run.

It's raining, the drops fat and hot. The dolly squeaks in front of me, shockingly loud now that Bennytown's ambient music has turned off. A few workers are cleaning up for the night, but this end of the park is mostly abandoned.

The Stairway to Heck is turned off when I get there, so I descend carefully, glad for the glass roof that protects me from the rain. The escalator steps are hard and angled with metal teeth on the corners. When I was little, I thought the teeth were real, ready to bite down on feet if you didn't pay attention.

I make it down the first escalator.

Then the second.

Halfway there.

The third escalator is the longest, looking like a black cut has opened in the earth before me. Carefully and quickly, I bound down the steps.

Halfway down, Benny starts laughing over the speakers with a mechanical, staticky roar. His voice mingles with what sounds like a man whistling. The steps shake beneath me as the escalator jolts downward, twisting me off balance. The dolly flies from my hands, tumbling end over end down the moving steps. My arms reach out wildly for purchase, and I grab one of the rubber handrails, slowing my fall, but not stopping it.

I land on my back, upside down with the wind knocked out of me. I try to ignore the stabbing pain from the steps while Benny interviews Flora Fox about her upcoming movie over the loudspeakers.

The voices are shrill and the pain rings in my ears so loudly that I don't realize there's a humming sound coming from the bottom of the escalator.

The dolly lies at the edge of the disappearing final steps, tumbled and with a gouge in one of its wheels and a yellow sticker I've never noticed on the bottom of its scoop. In front of the dolly, I'm staring straight at the escalator's base with welcoming spikes ready to swallow my hat, my scalp, and my face. I can picture the flesh being peeled from my bones. I try to claw my way out of my sprawl, but my hands are slick from sweat and rain. My fingers can't find anything to grip on the polished escalator sides. The motor is getting louder while the grinding vibrates the steps beneath me.

Wordlessly, I cry out, attempting to twist and fight my way free.

Instantly, the steps jolt to a stop as Benny's voice turns silent.

Stupidly, I start laughing, a twisted, hitching laugh of pure joy at my escape.

Just another Vickers Flicker.

On my feet, I finally get a glimpse at the sticker on the bottom of the dolly.

It's a yellow smiley face with the words "HAVE A NICE DAY" wrapped around it.

"Flip off," I tell the sticker, unable to stop laughing nervously.

WHATEVER JK'S GOT on Joaquin has to be pretty bad, because Joaquin grimaces at me like I personally ran over his dog as I pick up the syrup drums.

Just get these upstairs and then it will time to go home to Olivia.

Jenna at the Happy Hollow Sky Buckets station is anxious to lock down the ride for the night. She doesn't want to send another body through, but she places a call into the station up top and says there's one last straggler coming through.

Though the fit is tight and awkward while working the dolly with the two five-gallon syrup drums into the moving bucket, I manage to squeeze on before it takes off.

It's too late before I realize that I didn't consider the weather when agreeing to this errand.

The bucket rocks violently in the wind. Fat raindrops soak me, and I have to grip the stacked drums of syrup to keep them from tipping over and breaking open.

"Hi, I'm Benny the Bunny! Please, for your safety, keep your hands and feet in the bucket at all times! ¡Hola, soy Benito

el Conejito! ¡Por favor, para su seguridad, mantenga las manos y los pies en el cubo en todo momento!"

I know winds on the hill can get pretty severe, but I've seen these buckets take a beating and make it to the top just fine. Then again, I also remember watching a story on the news about the fire department rescuing people from the buckets after a breakdown.

You're gonna be fine. Gonna make it to the top and see Olivia.

A crack of lightning breaks across the sky, while deafening thunder fills the inside of the bucket. Curious, I look behind me toward the Lower Park and see only a few dim lights from the businesses as well as the fluorescent trail of lines of the Stairway to Heaven.

A particularly strong gust of wind rocks me nearly out of my seat. Sprawling, I look up and see a familiar sight.

MAXIMUM OCCUPANCY: 0 PEOPLE

You're gonna be fine. Gonna make it to the top and see Olivia.

Another strong gust of wind almost tips the dolly into the door. I grab it to ensure it doesn't spill out. I pull with all my might, leaning into it, steadying the dolly as the wind calms briefly.

I try not to be the kid who was scared of the Sky Buckets. I'm a working *man* now. I can't just lose it when stuff like this happens.

As the bucket rocks slightly, there's a heavy thumping sound of metal overhead, and I know I've reached the halfway point tower, even if it's too dark to see.

You're gonna be fine. Gonna make it to the top and—

With a shuddering jolt, the bucket rocks to a stop.

"Hi, I'm Benny the Bunny! Please, for your safety, keep your hands and feet in the bucket at all times! ¡Hola, soy Benito

el Conejito! ¡Por favor, para su seguridad, mantenga las manos y los pies en el cubo en todo momento!"

Just my luck. It doesn't take a lot to stop the Sky Buckets, usually someone in a wheelchair getting off or on. I've no idea why the Sky Buckets have stopped, but I'm gonna be late. With my phone in the lockbox, I won't be able to tell Olivia.

Or call for help if the Candy Troll comes for me.

"Stop it," I tell myself, shaking my head.

All I can do is wait for them to fix the problem. I hope to hell that Olivia's still waiting and that JK's not too ticked at me because Jenna couldn't get me up top fast enough.

Looking ahead, I see the faint glow of each bucket above me swaying in the wind. Any moment now, I'll arrive at the Upper Park station, unload this syrup, and then I'll be in a warm car with a warm body beside me.

One by one, the lights of the buckets flicker out above me.

Then beneath me.

And finally, the power in my bucket cuts out. Benny silences in the middle of a sentence about being sure to pick up a Bennytown T-shirt or collectible (and refillable for a nominal cost) sipper cup before leaving the park.

My heartbeat quickens.

They couldn't forget me.

They made a call.

JK's waiting for me.

Olivia's waiting for me.

Someone must know where I am. When they realize they made a mistake, I'll be fine.

The Candy Troll can't find me here.

I start counting the seconds. A minute passes.

Then two.

Then five.

Nothing. No motors gear up and Benny's voice doesn't crackle over the speakers to apologize for the delay. Just the sounds of the rain, the wind, and the creaking of the steel cables above me as they try their best to hold the Sky Buckets up in this vicious summer storm.

After a few minutes have passed, I try to stay strong, but I'm starting to lose it.

Darkness is all I can see in any direction. I see shadowy, moving shapes I know to be buckets around me and maybe an outline of the escalators but nothing in complete detail.

I am abandoned.

No, no, no. I can NOT be abandoned. Somebody has to know I'm here. Somebody will look for me. Any second now. Any second…

I grip the railing and scream, "HEEEEEEEEEEY! HEEEEEEEEEEEEEEEEELP!"

My cries are pitiful against the wind and the rain. I doubt anyone can hear me from thirty feet away, let alone from the distance of the station. Despite that, I'm too scared to stop screaming.

Someone *has* to hear.

I scream again.

This time there's a scream back.

Not a person. Not an animal.

I don't know what.

It's low, mechanical and almost organic. Only something large can make a sound like that.

Briefly, I hope that it's the motors starting up, ready to pull me to safety.

I'm not that lucky.

And maybe it's a good thing I'm stuck here. There's something about that scream I don't like, something that reaches into the furthest, most primitive recesses of my brain and tells me that whatever made that noise is hungry.

The wind picks up, and the steel cables above me creak and groan in protest.

A bolt of lightning flashes close enough to light up the sky. It's so bright it burns my eyes, and the thunder sounds like the whole world is exploding around me. With spots and stars in my eyes, I wonder if I'm going blind, as the electricity in my bucket turns on again. The light is dull and yellow, flickering, and the speaker briefly comes to life. The voice whispers right into my ear.

"Hi, I'm Benny the Bunny! If you are thinking about jumping, please hit someone when you land. ¡Hola, soy Benito el Conejito! Si usted está pensando en saltar, por favor, golpear a alguien cuando aterriza."

I stifle another scream.

I didn't hear that.

When I was little, right after Mom died, I saw and heard things that weren't there. Sometimes, I blacked out and went somewhere else. This experience reminded me of those times. I remembered when Dad brought me to Bennytown, to show me that there was good in the world and that—

Another bolt of lightning flashes. I look towards the buckets opposite me to avoid the after glare. In the buckets meant to be going down, I see a group of people.

Three people look at me. Unconcerned, one of them even waves.

They're not stuck here too. I'd have seen them before. They're just in my head.

Another bolt. In the bucket above me, I see the walrus, fluffy and smiling in his bright Hawaiian shirt. He stares at me with empty, white eyes that look like ping-pong balls with black circles drawn on them. He waves lightly before the light in his bucket goes out.

Another bolt. Screams. The bucket with the tourists breaks free from its cable. They crash to the ground, screaming for God and family with a thin wail of pain and despair. That wail will be mine if I stay in this storm any longer.

This is all in my head.

All in my head.

Allinmyhead.

allinmyhead

Darkness envelops me again. I close my eyes, but it doesn't make anything go away. I'm still here, the wind is still violently rocking my bucket, and I'm still trying to hold onto a dolly carrying two heavy jugs of strawberry syrup, making sure they don't tip over.

I hear that large, far-off scream again, though it's larger and much less far-off now.

(allinmyhead)

There are other sounds beneath me. Some animal and some human talk in tones I know I don't want to hear. Before I can cut them out entirely, I hear them on my bucket's speaker.

Children's voices, soft and pleading.

"I don't want it."

"Please. I don't want it."

"I didn't mean to."

"I'm sorry. Please don't."

"I won't tell, swear!"

"Please, I don't want to."

I cry out, blindly, but my cry doesn't bring help from Dad or Olivia or God. Instead, there's a thudding sound beneath me like something heavy hitting the bottom of my bucket. I hear a scraping, grabbing, and twisting. The mechanical roar tears through the night, much closer than before. The sound is so loud beneath me that it feels like the end of the world and the end of me. I wonder what can make a noise like that, what could reach that high, and in my madness, I'm struck by a great, dark certainty. I've wanted to deny this from the first moment I heard the scream on top of the hill but no longer can.

It's the Candy Troll.

It dug itself out of its Candy Mountain lair to come for me because I escaped before. It's ready to strip my flesh and melt me into taffy. The troll will drag me beneath the Mountain to a place of madness.

I collapse to the bottom of the bucket, wailing for this storm to end. I call for Mom. It's been nine years since I saw her die. I know she can't help me, but I want her here with me.

Another crack of lightning shakes the Sky Buckets.

I close my eyes, wishing to be anywhere else.

And then I feel a presence near me. Someone big and furry who'll never hurt me, even with his lifeless, staring eyes.

But the smell. The godawful smell of charred flesh and wet rot. It's overpowering and reminds me of my Mom during her last moments. The stench is sickening enough to tempt me to jump.

Benny's big, fluffy paw is on my shoulder, damp and squeezing me tightly.

Mom's voice. So close and so clean she might as well be sitting next to me, even though she can't be, can she? But I want her here so much, I want to believe what she's saying so much that I can't help but listen.

"It's all right, sweetie. Benny will take care of you."

PART 2
GHOST STORIES

NOEL
2019

Light and movement in a far-off place. Vague and undefined. Shadows dancing in the light, slowly coming into focus. The voices seem far away.

"Not another one."

"Look at all the blood."

"That's not blood. Looks like strawberry syrup from one of the ice cream shops."

"He looks dead. If there's another body, you know what Management'll do?"

"He's not dead. Look, he's moving. He probably just went through the Dark Park."

One of the shadows bends down, a hand on my shoulder, rocking me.

"Hey kid, you alive?"

I open my eyes blearily. I'm still curled up at the bottom of my Sky Bucket. Everything around me is sticky and red, but not filled with blood. The two janitors gaze at me with concern. When I reach out a hand to them, they step back, startled. The younger one heads for a doctor while the older one stays to comfort me.

He doesn't need to tell me that everything will be alright.

I know already.

I feel so great that I'm laughing. Laughing joyfully, I laugh until he backs farther into the station. He crosses himself and mutters in Spanish.

And why wouldn't I be laughing?

I'm in Bennytown.

Isn't that exciting?

IT TOOK THEM nearly twenty minutes to get me out of the Bucket. The spilled strawberry syrup solidified into a solid, inch-thick covering of the floor, fusing me and the dolly to it. They scraped me off before carting me back to the Family Member Building on a stretcher.

In the infirmary, I was given a positive bill of health, despite maintaining a curled up position in the bucket all night. Dressed in my street clothes after showering off most of the syrup, I'm sitting alone in a waiting room. I know from experience I'll smell of strawberries for days.

The room is a white box: white walls, white floor, white ceiling, white door. The chairs and table are stainless steel while security cameras line the ceiling. If it weren't for the posters of Benny the Bunny on the walls (always him smiling, his eyes twinkling judgmentally down at me, each printed with him saying something like "Have A Happy Day!" or "Isn't That Exciting?"), this room would look like a pretty standard interrogation room.

That doesn't change the fact that it *is* an interrogation room. And that is why I'm terrified.

I know the worst of last night was *allinmyhead*. It's been years since anything like that's happened, but something about that storm must have broken something in me. I thought I was past seeing…and hearing…

It wasn't real.

Still, I feel like I'm in serious trouble. I probably broke all sorts of rules, and I never delivered the syrup. With the points on my file from asking about the walrus, I know they'll be upset. I'm sure they are going to fire me. Then, Dad will be angry with me, and Olivia won't want to spend time with a loser. What kind of future will I have after being fired from my first job? A good job *at Bennytown* after only a few weeks? Just when I was starting to get comfortable, too.

Before I know it, tears are pouring down my cheeks. My life is over.

I rock back and forth in a ball, trying to hold it together. Someone is going to come in here soon and they're not going to want to see me crying.

Someone is at the door.

Instantly I straighten myself out, wiping my face, wanting to look like I've been sitting here calmly the whole time.

A woman in a Secret Service uniform enters. Her features are harsh yet sympathetic, though her sunglasses make her hard to read.

She sits at the chair opposite me and slides my phone across the table to me before speaking. "Hello, Noel. My name is Cassidy. *I believe in Bennytown.*"

"*I believe in Bennytown,*" I repeat, mechanically.

"Did you want any water?"

"No," I mutter.

"Very well. Before we go further, I want to note that your father is downstairs waiting for you while we finish up. This is just a routine sit-down as we try to get to the bottom of what happened. I have a few questions I'd like you to answer, and then you'll be on your way."

Before she can say anything else, the words pour from my mouth. "I was just doing what I was told. JK spilled the syrup, so he sent me down to pick up more. He *told* me to take the Sky Buckets up, so I did, but then I got stuck. And then…"

And then what? Tell her everything you saw? Everything you heard?

"…and then, then I was here all night. Please… please don't fire me. I was just doing what I was told. *I believe in Bennytown!*"

She smiles. "Your job is in no danger, Noel."

"It isn't?" Relief floods through me like a drug.

"No. Thank you for your candor. We've determined the facts of this incident from security feeds. JK and the Leads working the Sky Buckets will be disciplined appropriately for their involvement in your unintentional false imprisonment."

"Then why am I here?" I ask, timid.

"I was sent here by the Psychology Department to ask you a few questions about your experience. Are you all right to answer a few questions?" I notice one hand on the table while she keeps the other in her jacket. She's tense, like I might attack if she says the wrong thing.

She's not a psychologist. After Mom died when I disappeared into my head for a while, Dad sent me to a lot of psychologists. Most of them made a token effort to appear sympathetic. I saw the lies in their eyes, but they were professional enough to at least pretend they cared.

Cassidy doesn't even pretend to be sympathetic.

I focus on Benny's eyes on the posters over her shoulder, knowing he'll take care of me.

"Sure," I say.

"Very well. First question: how are you feeling?" she asks.

"Tired. Sore."

"Scared?" she proposes.

"Not anymore."

"No headaches? Ringing in the ears? Funny tastes in your mouth?"

"Not unless you call strawberry funny."

Her smile twitches upward slightly. "Do you feel like you're not quite yourself? That you're being followed, or that you're more than you were before you spent the night in the bucket?"

"What?" I ask.

"Common side-effects from traumatic isolation. We're just trying to be thorough."

"No."

"Did you witness anything you would consider out of the ordinary?"

"Like what?"

"Did you hear anything strange? See anything that didn't belong?"

I don't want to think about what happened last night any more than I have to. I saw plenty out of the ordinary, and that wouldn't even be the tip of the iceberg. If I say yes, she'll think I'm crazy. They'll think I've lost it and fire me, just when they say I'm home free.

I'm not unstable and not crazy. Not all the time, at least. I was once, and maybe I can feel the madness creep in sometimes, but I'm better now. Do I tell her that? Do I tell her any of this?

"No," I finally say. "I got scared, I fell asleep, I woke up, and that was it."

She knows I'm lying as much as I do but says nothing.

Slowly, she stands, motioning for me to do the same.

"Thank you for your assistance, Noel. As of right now, you are on a three-day block of paid administrative leave," she says.

"I can work!" I exclaim, trying not to look weak.

"That's non-negotiable. We need you to rest and recuperate. And when that leave is up, we'll need you to report to the Comestible Services office for reassignment," she says.

"Reassignment?" I ask, suddenly terrified.

"Relax, Noel, this is a good thing," she says, putting a hand on my shoulder. "You've shown remarkable growth as a Bennytown family member, and we want to reward that. We'll find something more suited to your dedication and intellect than Ice

Cream Villa. Something that'll really give you a chance to shine. Isn't *that* exciting?"

A chance to shine.

More beautiful words couldn't have been spoken at this moment.

BY THE TIME I'm home, my night in the bucket feels far away, like a bad dream. I know it happened, and I don't think I'll ever entirely forget what I think I saw, but the feelings it stirred are no stronger than the memory of a badly stubbed toe.

It may sound mental, but I want to see what they have in mind for me back at Bennytown. If I'm going to go through something as bad as my night in the Sky Buckets, at least I could get something good out of it, and if Cassidy was right about my reassignment giving me a chance to shine, it sounds like it might be a really good opportunity.

Since I can't go back to work right away, I decide time with Olivia is the next best thing. She was supposed to pick me up the night before and was probably pissed when I didn't show. Maybe she even got worried. Eager for the chance to share my story, I text her to meet me for lunch at our favorite In-N-Out.

When I arrive, Olivia's already ordered. She casually waves me over. After giving her a quick kiss, I slide into the booth opposite her.

"Thanks," I say, looking over the food hungrily.

"No problem. What the fuck happened last night? I texted and called. When you never showed up, I figured your battery must've died and you got a ride, so I went home. You should've tried to reach me somehow. After sitting out there forever, I felt like an idiot when one of those security guys told me to move," she huffs.

I know this look means she's annoyed with me.

Time to flip the script.

"Dad didn't pick me up last night," I say.

"He didn't?" She looks less concerned than irritated, which deeply annoys me.

I can still salvage this.

"Not really. You're not gonna believe me, but have I got a story for you…"

It took me most of the morning to figure out what version I wanted to tell. Ultimately, I decided on a comedy of errors leading to my brave tale of survival. A miscommunication leaving me hanging overnight from a Sky Bucket while a wild storm raged around me, dodging heavy rain and lightning bolts.

Sounding far from brave when I admit to falling asleep at the bottom of the bucket, I decide to throw in some truth as well.

I expect her to be enthralled.

Finally, Olivia starts to look concerned. "They left you there, and they didn't even apologize? Those fucks!"

"Hey, they apologized," I say. It's hard to remember word for word what Cassidy said, but I think there was an apology in there somewhere.

"You gonna sue them?" Olivia asks.

"What? Why?" I ask.

"You better bring this up to your union rep. You do have a union, don't you?" Olivia asks.

"No, Bennytown doesn't have unions, but I don't think you're getting the big picture. They're moving me to a much better position, probably with better pay and hours," I say.

"So, they're bribing you?" she asks.

"They're not bribing me, they're—"

"That doesn't matter. You should leave. What they're doing isn't righ—"

"*Look, enough, all right?*" I exclaim, pounding the table. She looks at me, shocked, and for a second all eyes in the restaurant are on me before returning to their burgers.

I'm embarrassed by the attention, but I won't let Olivia talk over me about this.

"Noel?" she peers warily at my face.

I try to stay calm. Gripping the table and choosing my words very slowly, I manage it, mostly.

"I don't think you understand what's going on. This is my job. A job that I love. It's giving me a future, building experience, and helping me to save money. The better I am at being a Bennytown family member, a family I very much like being part of, the better a future I can ensure for myself. For *us*," I say.

She looks at me, a bit fearfully. I don't think I've ever raised my voice at her like this. I should feel ashamed for how I've handled the situation. Maybe I am, a little, but she doesn't get what it's like to have these kind of responsibilities and this kind of potential.

Maybe she never will.

But she's still my girlfriend.

Grabbing and devouring a handful of fries, I force a smile that soon becomes real enough on its own.

"Now, come on. I have three days off, and I wouldn't want to spend them with anyone else," I say, playfully touching her foot with mine. She smiles, nervously.

"So, what do you wanna do?" I ask.

LLOYD
1959

Bennytown's opening day was in two weeks on August 6th, a Thursday. If it wasn't an utter failure, Fletcher Dorian's "theme park" fantasy was bound to make him rich beyond measure.

The newspapers called it "Dorian's Folly."

The pulp tabloids had much nastier names for it.

Whatever it really was, Lloyd Carentan meant to be the first to find out.

A shrewd, wiry little man, Lloyd excelled at his job as a tabloid freelancer. Few people were better at getting into places illegally than him. The security perimeter around Bennytown was thorough, and the average looky-loos who wanted a sneak peek never got close to seeing what was inside.

Lloyd wasn't just any looky-loo.

Finding the right empty stretch of wall at the right time of night had led to an easy, dark entry into Bennytown. From there he had the run of the place. Maintenance men, electricians and janitors were all rushing around working on last-minute touch-ups. The place was dark enough to avoid all of them.

Whenever he was certain he was alone, Lloyd took pictures with his well-used Nikon SLR and worked out text in his head.

Bennytown is a glossed-up temple to American jingoism with elements of fantasy and science fiction. In an attempt to create some sense of cultural relevance, the prognosticators who have called this noble experiment "Dorian's Folly" have greatly underestimated the depth of failure on display. Mark my words, "Dorian's Lament" will prove far more apt. If my warning hasn't been enough to steer you away from this tacky menagerie, visit at your own risk.

There was one thing Lloyd knew about people. He noticed everyone secretly wanted to see those they admired fail. Whether or not Bennytown failed didn't matter one bit to Lloyd as long as he got his article printed before the park opened. The checks would clear, and then he would be in the clear.

Now if only—

"The hell?" Lloyd muttered.

From out of the darkness, two figures were barely visible on the moonless night. A man in a tux and a woman in a nice evening gown were both wearing green wooden masks carved to look like stylized versions of the park's titular mascot. Silently, they walked farther into Bennytown's darkness. Hiding by a façade, Lloyd kept his eyes open and watched as a handful of similarly dressed figures emerged. Some carried lit torches, while the largest among them pushed wheelbarrows full of lumber.

A misspent youth full of reading *The Vault of Horror* and *Tales from the Crypt* told him something very bad was about to happen, or maybe was already happening. He thought for a moment that he ought to put a lot of distance between himself and these strange people, but the reporter's instinct kicked into overdrive.

Following them toward the base of Candy Mountain, he hid behind a decorative planter shaped like a giant gumdrop. He paused to take mental notes of bizarre strangers.

There were nearly forty people dressed to the nines and wearing wooden Benny masks, as well as people dressed in disturbingly life-like costumes of Benny the Bunny, Flora Fox, and Dare the Hare. Dare held an ancient, leather-bound tome in his large paws that filled Lloyd with inexplicable dread. A few of the men piled lumber into a teepee-shaped structure until the stack reached about six feet high. Once they were finished, a young woman poured gasoline onto it.

Finally, a burly man carrying a torch came before the group. Over his tuxedo he wore a dark robe with strange symbols sewn into it. Once the woman with the gas can finished, the man threw his torch into the bonfire. It went up with a muffled thump, illuminating the entire circle of frightening figures.

The figure in the robe began to address the crowd, his voice too low for Lloyd to hear clearly. Something about it was familiar, so familiar he was tempted to approach. Only the comics of his youth held him back, knowing what happened to people who got too close to dark rituals. Of course that's what this had to be. Some dark ritual being held on the eve of Dorian's project's culmination.

Now that was a story, wasn't it?

At once, on cue from their leader, the assembled figures shouted, "I BELIEVE IN BENNYTOWN!"

The words were simple, but they sent a sick thrill up Lloyd's spine. Rumors spread of movers and shakers belonging to secret societies and cults, but nothing seemed stranger than the Masons.

Nothing like this. This was too good to be true.

The man in the robe gave a speech as animated as a Southern preacher at a revival meeting. The crowd broke into cheers. Lloyd would have joined them, for all the freaky ammunition they were offering him. No one would believe a word of what he was watching, but he didn't care. He'd write the story and he'd shout it to the world until everyone heard.

The robed man waved for one of the costumed characters. Dare the Hare handed him the leather bound tome. The robed man put a hand on his fluffy shoulder. By the way he gripped Dare's shoulder, Lloyd immediately understood that Dare was being chastised, maybe even punished. He hung his enormous fluffy head, its immovable face cheerful in spite of the person inside clearly being upset.

Unbeknownst to Dare, two large security officers flanked him. Lloyd was struck with a sudden memory of watching a scary movie as a child, wanting to scream at the people on screen. All the other kids in the theatre would talk to the on-screen characters, but Lloyd caught himself before going that far. As a child, he felt great pride in being able to separate the real from the unreal. Even as he felt a sense of unease at the large men flanking Dare, there was no way anything would actually happen. This was pageantry. Rich people enacting their dance for some stupid, unknown purpose.

Even when the guards seized Dare's arms, Lloyd remained quiet. Not a peep escaped his mouth when a third guard sneaked behind the prisoner with a sledgehammer and broke the squealing, screaming Dare's arms and legs.

"For Bennytown to function, it must feed!" the robed figure roared.

"I BELIEVE IN BENNYTOWN!" the crowd shouted again.

The guards threw the broken, screaming Dare into the fire. His screams, muted by the heavy fur of his suit, continued for a surprisingly long time. His thrashing went on even longer than that.

"MS. ZIMBARDO! START THE MACHINE!" the robed man yelled.

A hum turned into a clunking roar as a great machine hidden within the Candy Mountain came to life. Reading from the tome, the robed man began to chant in an ancient, eldritch language that sounded like Latin, but definitively wasn't. The sounds were more guttural and chopped.

Part of Lloyd finally realized the danger and propelled his body forward.

He got two steps before running into a security guard standing right behind him. The masked guard grabbed Lloyd in a chokehold and dragged him to the assembled group by the bonfire. The robed man turned his head to Lloyd, briefly, but kept reading until the humming roar of the machine within the mountain grew deafening.

Then silence.

A certainty overcame Lloyd that this was no longer the world he knew. He would've screamed if it weren't for the chokehold.

Giving the tome to Flora Fox, the robed man walked over to Lloyd.

The guard dropped him at their feet. With as much righteous indignation as he could manage, Lloyd brushed himself off and said, "My name is Lloyd Carentan! People know where I am! I'm a—"

The eyes. The eyes behind the robed man's wooden mask were achingly familiar.

Too familiar.

"Fletcher Dorian," Lloyd said softly.

Dorian considered him with unblinking eyes, then in a compassionate voice asked, "Do you believe in Bennytown?"

Shocked by the sheer strangeness of the question, Lloyd responded, "No."

He knew at once that it was the wrong thing to say by the way Dorian slumped, sighing. The fire seemed to burn even hotter, that strange feeling in the air tingling. Lloyd could hear voices that didn't belong to anyone present. Voices that told him it was too late.

Lloyd didn't want it to be too late. He was a survivor with a silver tongue, and he was known to say or do whatever it took to get out of sticky situations. He was willing to do whatever Dorian wanted to escape this mess. Lloyd built his life on a pile of lies, and one more wouldn't be more than a drop in a very large pond.

He could've charmed his way out of this if Dorian had not spoken first.

"Pity," Dorian said, waving over the guard with the sledgehammer.

NOEL
2019

In the regular world, I'd look silly wearing my new uniform of a pith helmet, button-up white shirt, and khaki cargo vest and shorts.

But I'm not in that world.

I'm back in Bennytown after three days of administrative leave spent with Olivia and Dad. Currently, I am walking down the stairs alongside the Stairway to Heaven to the Lower Park.

After my talk with Cassidy, I thought of a number of possibilities of what they might do with me next.

Assistant Lead in a different restaurant? Possible, but Cassidy's cryptic hints suggested more.

Up me to retail or ride operator? There's a fair chance.

Server at the Green Door Society? Yeah, that's probably not gonna happen.

A whole lot of possibilities, each as improbable as the next, filtered through my mind. Seeing this costume in my uniform bag almost led to a happy dance on the spot.

This costume means I'm working at Pedro Parrot's Safari Lodge.

There are two Bennytown restaurants considered "elite" because they require phoning in reservations in advance or using the in-park exclusive app. Both serve the best food in the park, contain beautifully themed decor, and have a memorable meal-and-show experience. If you want classy, you go to Independence Hall in Journey through Americana, but if you want fun, you go to Pedro Parrot's Safari Lodge in Happy Hollow.

I haven't found much need for Happy Hollow since I was little. The cartoonish surroundings are made to look like Benny's hometown. Each of his friend's houses contain a mini-experience, full of special effects to keep the kids in line entertained until they get to meet the costumed character at the end. The three rides here are designed for little kids, and usually I only pass through to get to my favorite land, Creepy Corner. Dad and I have a long-standing tradition of going to the Safari Lodge for my birthday.

I've made a lot of good memories in there and am excited to make more.

Two stories of bamboo, palm fronds, and tikis greet me when I walk up to the Lodge. With nearly an hour before Bennytown opens, the animatronic elephant at the entrance that playfully heckles guests is motionless, its blank eyes staring off into nothingness.

Having no idea where the family member entrance is, I enter through the front door, taking in the familiar jungle décor.

The restaurant floor is arranged in a horseshoe shape, with two floors of curving booths angled so that all can see the animatronic stage show in the middle, currently hidden by a red curtain. There are animatronic monkeys, parrots, and insects scattered throughout the trees with a number of other surprises hidden for intrepid explorers.

Each booth has a trophy, a large animatronic head of Benny or one of his friends mounted on a plaque. The trophies take guest's food orders and provide jokes and advertisements during downtime in the show. Walking closer to the stage, I recognize a few dozen mounted heads of my favorite childhood characters staring back at me.

Well, at least they'd be staring out at me if their eyes were open.

"Son of a gun!" a voice calls out.

A wet scrub brush falls from above, landing at my feet.

"Little help?" she asks. Garcia leans over the second-floor railing, smiling at me.

"Sure," I say, grabbing her brush and climbing one of the curving staircases at the edge of the room to her.

"You're making your way up in the world," she says, eying my uniform.

"You too," I say.

She shrugs. "I go where I'm needed."

The booth she's cleaning desperately needs her attention, judging by the foot-tall words painted across the table.

NO MORE
BITING IN
THE DARK
PARK PLEASE?

Scrubbing it down, she muses, "Park security searches every guest before they enter, confiscating anything they think suspicious, and still we get this."

"Could be worse?" I propose.

"It has been. At least whoever did this didn't take a dump on the table first."

"Seriously?"

"Seriously. You'd be amazed what people do after hours. Ride operators get drunk and race through the rides with the lights out. A group of mechanics once got busted taking bets on stray cat fights, which was probably for the best since that meant they didn't get caught cooking meth inside Candy Mountain."

"Seriously?"

"You gotta stop asking me if I'm serious. I'm always serious. Except when I'm not," she says, finally scrubbing away a full word from the table.

I take some comfort in the certainty that she's just messing with me, because gambling on animal fights and meth labs... well, that could never happen at Bennytown.

"And that's not even talkin' about the sex. Work here long enough, you're gonna get laid," she says, smiling nostalgically.

"I don't need to work here for that," I say, trying not to notice how cute Garcia is when she smiles.

"Right. *Olivia*," she says, pronouncing her name like a Poison Word. "You know, keeping yourself tied down means you're gonna miss out on a lot of fun."

"I have plenty of fun, thanks," I say.

"But you could have *more*. You're not a bad looking kid, not *great*, but not bad, and the Bennytown family's a *really* close family—like, *Alabama* close. When the lights go out, you can't go more than fifty feet without stumbling on a couple-few people finding a dark corner to have some fun in."

"I've worked plenty of nights. Never seen anything like that," I interrupt.

She shrugs again. "You just don't know where to look."

Change the subject, just change the subject.

"Have you...?"

"Oh yeah. I've *Run the Seven* twice now. A girl's gotta find her fun somehow, right?"

"You don't have anyone outside?"

"I used to," Garcia says with a nostalgic sigh. Her smile, so casual and easy most of the time, flickers and almost burns out. After a split second, she brightens, "Give it enough time and you'll understand. You start to work so much, you'll never see who you want outside. Then you'll start wondering why you even bother when Bennytown hires a smorgasbord of the most delicious people around, and you'll *Run the Seven*."

Her cynicism, normally so fun, grates me now. Maybe she's had some bad experiences, but she doesn't know what I share with Olivia.

Not that doing something with Olivia here isn't worth dreaming about. If only I could sneak her into some dark corner.

"Can I help you, hon?"

The Southern-accented voice comes from the first floor. A big woman in her mid-sixties with enormous hair is dressed in a more professional-looking explorer's costume than mine. Her hands are on her hips, expectant.

Startled, I grab for my pith helmet. "Hi! I'm supposed to start here today?"

"Really? Poor kid. Well, come on down and I'll give you the five-dollar tour of Hell before we put you to work," she says.

Her fearless use of a Poison Word startles me even more.

Garcia waves me off. "I got it here. And be nice to Kathleen. She goes way back, knows more about Bennytown than just about anyone, and she's more bark than bite. Usually."

"Usually," I repeat.

"Hey, you're in the big leagues now. There's gonna be some biting," Garcia scoffs.

FIRST ON THE agenda, Kathleen hands me a plastic Bennytown sack with six rubber duckies inside.

"What are these for?" I ask.

"The 19th Annual Dinosaur Lagoon Rubber Duck Rally's coming up. You heard of it?"

"Yeah," I say.

Family members can pitch in two dollars to buy rubber duckies to decorate and race around Dinosaur Lagoon before Bennytown opens, with prizes going to the winners.

Wanting to hold onto all my cash, I haven't considered putting anything toward it, though it was all JK could talk about in the days leading to

(allinmyhead)

"Comestibles used to kick some serious rubber ass, and Pedro's had two wins back in the day. For the past seven years, the Bengineers have been the Lords of the Lagoon. They cheat, but since they're the big boys behind the scenes, nobody questions 'em. So, this year, Pedro's is gonna show 'em the what-for. I bought a hundred fifty of these bad boys, six for every regular, and we're gonna kick their Bengineering asses. We plan to split the prizes. If we lose, I'll spring for a cake. If we win, pizza. Sound good?"

"Sounds great," I say.

"Good, now decorate 'em however ya like in Sharpie, and no vampires, okay? Girls 'round here got into that sexy vampire shit a few years back and I am *sick* and *tired* of all those sparkly little shits floatin' around." She readjusts her large, blond hairdo. "So, why'd you get sent here?"

How do I answer that?

"I'm a hard worker, I guess?"

"Yeah, *bullshit*. This restaurant's the place they send people to apologize when something goes wrong and they don't wanna take responsibility."

There's a lot about Kathleen that should upset me, from her pushiness to her fearlessness of the Poison Words to the way her hair doesn't seem to move with the rest of her head, but there's something about her that I just trust.

So, I give her the short version.

Occasionally nodding, she's quiet for most of the story. About halfway through, when I'm talking about the storm and the dark, I swear something changes in her face. It's not quite scared, I don't think Kathleen does scared, but it's in the same family.

"You stayed overnight, and nothing bad happened?" she asks.

Why does everyone keep asking me that?

"No."

"Uh huh," she says, skeptical. I wonder if she'll keep pushing me, or if she'll keep me at arm's length. Maybe I've done something terrible by being dishonest to her.

"Well, lemme assign you a locker, and I'll show you the ropes. Don't fuck up too much and we might even be friends," she says.

I'M NOT SURE why Kathleen calls Pedro Parrot's Safari Lodge "Hell," because compared to Ice Cream Villa, it's practically Heaven. Not only is it clean and spacious, but we relax in the back and shoot the breeze when we're not needed on the floor.

When we *are* needed, the restaurant works like a well-oiled machine.

Guests come in, greeters check their reservation and seat them.

If they haven't ordered in advance, they read the digital menu beneath their table's trophy. Once they're ready, the animatronic head takes the order, which then shoots directly to the kitchen.

While they're distracted by the animatronic stage show that lasts for fifteen minutes on the half hour, the kitchen preps their food. There are six distinct shows on random rotations unless someone paid for the special birthday package, which keeps things from getting too repetitive.

I deliver food and drinks to my assigned tables when ready. Every so often I make my rounds to see if people need refills and answer questions about the show.

The guests provide their payment information when they make the reservation, so I don't have to handle credit cards or a register. When guests leave, a team of runners sterilizes the table and removes all the dishes.

If people make their reservation time, they're in and out in an average of forty-one minutes, according to Kathleen.

In comparison to my old position, I don't smell, the guests are relaxed and cooled by air-conditioning, and I spend most of my time off my feet. Even with her blunt attitude, Kathleen's a big improvement over JK. She cracks the whip on us, but everyone here adores her for being fair and friendly by Management standards.

One of the green lights at my station flashes, the speaker blaring to life with a tinny voice piped in from one of my tables trying to speak over a crying child.

"Can someone come out front to help us?" the voice asks.

"Certainly, sir, I'll be right out!" I respond cheerfully, heading to the main floor.

In the middle of a show, Pedro and his band of jungle friends rock out to their reworded covers of the hit songs from six years ago. Most of the animatronics awkwardly pantomime playing their instruments in their safari gear, while the monkeys, birds, and insects hidden in the faux jungle join them, hooting and squawking.

As I make my way around the stage to my section, Mary Annette descends from the ceiling on her mock marionette cables, sexily crooning some pop ballad. Scantily clad and cartoonishly proportioned, there's not a boy alive who didn't hit premature puberty watching one of her cartoons.

Walking past her, I swear she winks at me. I know it's programmed into the show and I was at the right place at the right time. Still, I become uncomfortably aware of what Garcia was talking about earlier.

Walking swiftly, I reach my section.

Since this is my first day, I'm only covering three booths at the edge of the horseshoe. The fourth one in my section is unlit and cut off by a green cordon. They're cheap seats, but they've kept me busy all day.

The call was to the third booth from the edge. There's a Midwestern-looking family with three kids. The youngest, a girl no more than four, is crying and struggling her way out of the booth while her mother holds her back.

"I don't want it!" the little girl protests.

(allinyourhead)

The dad's angry. "My daughter heard something strange coming from our head—"

"The tusks wanna gobble me!" she proclaims, looking at me with terror in her eyes.

The father continues, "And we want another table."

Kathleen didn't teach me the protocol for this. "Well, sir, the seating is assigned…"

"Look, I paid a lot to get us in here and I don't want my kid bothered by something that's *your* problem. There's an empty booth next to us. How about you just move us there and we continue not complaining to your manager?" he says, never once breaking his angry smile.

"Let me talk to my Lead," I say, never breaking my smile either.

"You do that," he says, smug.

As soon as I reach the back, I run to search for Kathleen. She's lending a hand in the kitchen, seasoning a batch of fries. She smiles when she notices me, amused, and checks the clock. "Three hours before you got your first problem booth. You're havin' a good first day."

I give her a quick rundown on the situation while she continues lending a hand in the kitchen, even throwing out the father's suggestion of moving them to the cordoned off booth.

"No can do, hon'. That table's reserved for a VIP who can be a bit unpredictable," she says, unclipping the tablet from her belt and checking a map of the restaurant. "I'll send Carlos to move 'em to a table that just got freed up in Melissa's section. Head back to storage and grab a cordon to block off the table. I'll get a tech to look at the head and make sure it's not cussin' again. If we got another goddamn hacker…"

"And that's it?" I ask.

Putting her hands on her hips again, she asks, "I don't know, *is* that it?"

I think for a second, then say, "Maybe we should sweeten the pot? Send them an extra appetizer on the house for their inconvenience?"

Kathleen nods, impressed. "Smart kid. I already comped them some carrot cake. When it arrives at the end of the meal, compliments of Management, they'll be so happy they'll forget what happened. They probably won't even mind that they hate carrot cake."

They're not the only ones, and I let it show. Kathleen laughs.

"We make good carrot cake here! Not only is it cheap, but it's Benny's favorite. Kids'll eat anything if a cartoon bunny tells them to. Now scoot, you got booths!"

I walk away, satisfied, looking for the storage room.

"And Noel?" she calls after me. "Nicely done."

Yeah, this day couldn't get any better.

I find the storage room and retrieve one of the green cordons. By the time I'm back on the floor, the family has already moved, while the little girl looks so entranced by the stage show she's probably already forgotten what happened.

At the table, I'm about to cordon it off when curiosity gets the better of me.

I slide into the booth to get a better look at the trophy.

Snapper Gator's bright eyes are staring off into space. His teeth are pretty sharp, but I don't know if I'd call them tusks like the little girl. Looking closer, I spot two gouges in the wood beneath Snapper's trophy, about eight inches apart and maybe a quarter of an inch deep. I run my finger over them, feeling the years of varnish that have covered the gouges but not erased them.

It looks like something with tusks used to be mounted here. A walrus?

With a mechanical click, Snapper's eyes lock onto me. His lower jaw starts stuttering and jittering, no sounds coming out as the head turns slightly to face me. When the music of the stage show ends and the audience claps, I finally hear the hissing, urgent whisper coming from Snapper's mechanized lips.

"Isn't it exciting to be Wilbur's special friend?"

(allinmyhead)

I close my eyes tight. When I open them, Snapper stares off into space again.

Quickly, I slide out of the booth, cordon it off, and get back to work.

KURI
2001

Only two weeks after the Towers fell, the shock of what happened started to wear off a little, just in time for the shock of how the world was changing to set in.

As a ride operator at Dinosaur Lagoon in Primordial World, Kuri had worked at Bennytown for more than four years. It wasn't the job she preferred, since driving sedately paced boats around the Lagoon while joking about aging animatronic dinosaurs put her in the hot sun more than she would have liked, but the pay was good. Being able to speak fluent Japanese only boosted that pay further, as it made her uniquely qualified to host private tour groups. Typical tourist problems aside, it was a pretty sweet gig.

That was before the Towers fell. Now, with warnings that Bennytown and other theme parks were potential terrorist targets, the park looked like a police state from the outside. The roads leading to Bennytown were lined with concrete freeway dividers, there were metal detectors in front of the ticket booths, and every vehicle going into the parking structures was subject to search. Security, including a small National Guard detail, were omnipresent at Bennytown Plaza, but remained nearly invisible in-park.

The worst part wasn't how Bennytown had changed, but how management expected the employees to change. As ambassadors of the Dorian Studios brand, they were expected to look as happy as they had ever been before the tragedy. People looked to Bennytown for happiness and hope, and the personal feelings of Bennytown family members could not interfere with that. Even if those family members were suffering because they had lost people in the attacks.

Not only that, family members were suddenly trained to be frontline security personnel. They were taught to look for suspicious behavior and learned how to deal with potentially dangerous situations.

Kuri considered quitting. As a loyal family member, even thinking about this tore at her heart. Bennytown helped pay her way through college but having to plaster a smile on her face at all times felt disrespectful. At times, she felt like her life was silently falling apart since she couldn't express her true emotions.

Instead of picturing the bodies being pulled out of the wreckage, she switched her focus to saving lives in the park. So far, she hadn't seen anything, which wasn't surprising with the thorough security checkpoints. Staying alert for the possibility of future danger kept her going.

If she hadn't been on guard, she wouldn't have noticed the nervous woman waiting to board the boat that morning. The mousy, little woman was middle-aged and only about five feet tall. Kuri bet the woman was only a hundred pounds soaking wet. The guest wore a Bennytown t-shirt and carried a cheap, knockoff Bennytown backpack. Clutching the bag to her chest fearfully, the woman's eyes darted back and forth through the crowd. Doubts started growing in Kuri's mind about the woman's shifty behavior.

While the woman waited in line, Kuri smiled and stepped off her boat. Forcing a look of calm serenity onto her face, she approached one of the techs who launched the boats.

"We've got a suspicious character in line, Ramon. Call security," Kuri said without breaking her smile.

Ramon looked toward where she cocked her head. "Don't look suspicious to me."

"She's on edge," Kuri said.

"Everybody's on edge these days," Ramon replied.

"Are you calling security, or will I have to?" Kuri threatened.

"I'm doing it, I'm doing it, keep your undies on," he grumbled.

Kuri waited until he actually pulled up his walkie before she slowly approached the woman. She wasn't sure what she meant to do, but Ramon's doubt made her want to be certain before security swarmed the place.

The woman in line didn't notice anything amiss as she unzipped the backpack to peek inside. From this distance, Kuri only caught a brief glimpse of the contents of the bag. It was enough to make Kuri's blood run cold.

Plastic bag.

White powder.

Anthrax.

The news reported mail attacks with anthrax in the weeks after the Towers fell. Could terrorists be here in Bennytown?

The line was packed. Security wouldn't have time to get here if the powder was unleashed. Kuri knew that only she was close enough to react in time, so she took her chance.

Darting through the crowd, she hooked one arm through one of the backpack's straps and wrenched it away from the woman. The guest squawked in surprise and tugged on the remaining strap. Kuri hadn't anticipated a struggle. In her mind, she imagined grabbing the strap and pulling the pack away from the woman victoriously. It wasn't supposed to be a tug-of-war with this tiny, surprisingly strong villain. And there definitely weren't supposed to be any video cameras pointed toward her maneuver.

The woman fought and hissed, kicking at Kuri's shins, but Kuri didn't surrender her hold.

The bag wasn't built to withstand this fight and its cheap plastic and even cheaper stitching gave way. Ripping in half, the contents sprayed all over. The white powder was actually a thin gravel, chalky and tasting of char.

In that moment, Kuri saw her life flash before her eyes.

After a heartbeat, the woman slapped her repeatedly. "That was my son, my son, my son. You fucking bitch!" the mother cried, tears streaking the white powder down her face.

In that instant, it all made sense to Kuri. She'd heard tales of people smuggling their children's ashes into Bennytown, but she never thought they were true. Her heart soared, and she couldn't help but laugh at the realization that she wasn't going to die from anthrax poisoning.

Kuri took a deep, steadying breath. Choking for a second on the dust, Kuri doubled over and vomited once she realized what covered her body and filled her lungs.

NOEL
2019

Even if what happened in the Sky Buckets was all in my head, the events that took place on the Stairway to Heck were real. After my fall, I gave those escalators space for a time. Thankfully, there is a set of actual stairs running alongside the escalator's zig-zagging path down the hill. Even though the steps are long and kind of torture in summer, I try to convince myself it will be good cardio.

Garcia's joined me on the walk down today. After some small talk, I want to pick her brain about the experience I had with the Snapper trophy.

"So, you're saying you know nothing about... Tusks?" I ask, avoiding Poison Words.

"There has to be better stuff to talk about, right?" she says.

"Yeah? Like more death, destruction and debauchery?" I ask, naming her three favorite conversation topics, more or less in order.

"No, there's more to Bennytown than that. Like fun," she says.

"Of course. It's Bennytown," I say.

"No, I mean, *real* fun. I'm throwing a party here tomorrow night with some buddies of mine. We will sneak in a few beers after hours. We can hide and play around a little. You know, fun?"

"Is it safe to come to the park after hours?" I ask.

"If you know how to be safe," she raises her eyebrows knowingly.

Wanting to fit in even if I'm not a partier, I say, "Sounds cool."

"Come with us then?"

I meant to spend my day off tomorrow with Olivia, but she's been pretty unavailable the past few days. Since she hasn't confirmed anything for tomorrow, I say, "Sure."

"Cool. Eleven o'clock, Creepy Corner, I'll find you," she says.

Eleven. That's pretty late, but I can probably talk Dad into it.

"Cool. Looking forward to it," I say.

"Nice."

"So… Tusks?" I'm not going to let this go.

"Nothing I haven't already told you." She sighs.

"Come on, you know everything that happens here," I try to goad her pride.

"*Why* do you want to know about Tusks?"

"I dunno. I heard about the suit going missing, and I thought maybe I could pick up a couple bucks if I found it." That's all I'm going to tell her about what I need to know.

She looks at me like I'm crazy before bursting out laughing.

"What!" I exclaim.

"I'm sorry, but that's a good one," she laughs.

"I can be a pretty good detective," I say.

"I'm sure, I'm sure, it's just that people have gone all over Bennytown for decades trying to claim the $40,000 bounty on that suit. I don't see how you could do better, no offense."

"Wait, $40,000?" I ask.

JK told me walrus stuff went for good money, but not that much money.

That's enough to make my dreams come true.

That's a car. That's a college education.

That's respect.

"Yeah," she says.

"*And* they think it's still here?" I ask.

"They *know* it. Ever since the mid-80s, Bennytown's included tracking devices in all of the character costumes to prevent theft. If it were ever to leave, people would know."

"So, it's still here?" I ask again, hopeful.

"Maybe. They probably incinerated it, but it could be hiding somewhere. Don't waste your time. You're back to school soon. And you got a girlfriend. You're not gonna have time to go hunting down Rabbit Holes."

"But if I find it, it'll be worth it. If I can find it before the Sixtieth Birthday, it might even be worth more than that, right?" I say.

She shakes her head. "Your funeral."

WE'RE SHORT-STAFFED TODAY, since two people are out sick. Another two guys have Dodgers tickets, so they took half-days. While we've got a couple floaters from Independence Hall, I've been busting tail over my five tables.

Over the last several days I've mastered the art of table serving and everything else in between. I haven't seen anything bizarre like what happened with the Snapper trophy. The other family members enjoy my company, and I'm making a good impression on Kathleen. She tells me that this energy and dedication won't last, but that she'll enjoy it until I break down.

My tables are on the second floor today, almost in the middle of the horseshoe. Running up and down the stairs with trays of drinks and food can be precarious, but I haven't dropped anything yet.

On a trip back to the kitchen, I see someone sitting at the dark, cordoned-off booth.

The silhouette is so round that I think for a moment it's a character. When I get closer, it's clearly a man. He's got a camera strung around his neck and is wearing a faded green shirt over his obese frame. A cheap pith helmet from the gift shop sits askew on his head.

And he's crying.

This big, blubbery man with a pinched, baby face adorned with a tiny, blond mustache, waxed so the points curl upwards, is sitting there crying, occasionally muttering something in German before crying some more. He doesn't mind the darkness of his booth and ignores the raucous stage show. Instead, he's just crying in his private, cordoned-off booth, alone.

I normally don't deal with criers, but as a Bennytown family member it's my duty to make sure that everyone's having as fun a day as possible.

I approach him, slowly, and I get the strangest feeling. It's similar to the feeling that I had in the Sky Bucket and in the Snapper booth. This increasingly tangible sense that tells me I should just walk away and focus on my job. Something strikes me about his face, beyond the profound sadness. In a way, he looks so flush he's almost purple. Everything in me screams to back away from this pitiful man. Part of me tells me that he's someone, some*thing* I should avoid, but I can't leave him, can I?

My pace slows, and I'm ready to listen to that flight instinct when a hand grips my shoulder.

"You see him, don't you?" Kathleen asks, letting go of me. Her eyes are intense and curious, but she otherwise keeps a calm-looking façade.

"Who is he?" I ask.

"That's Fritz. He's a regular," she says slowly, evenly. "Mostly he just sits there and cries. Sometimes for a few minutes, sometimes for a few hours."

"He's a passport holder?" I ask.

She looks at me as if choosing her words carefully. "Something like that. Just leave him alone, and he'll disappear soon."

"Okay," I say, though it's hard not to look in his direction.

Gently, Kathleen guides me into the back of the restaurant. She adjusts her massive blond hair and takes on an "I'm not mad at you, but…" stance.

I get the impression I might've asked one question too many.

"Look, you know by now there's a lotta things in this park that're a bit out of the ordinary. Fritz there is one of 'em, understand?"

"Yes," I say meekly like when Mom lectured me.

"Good. Now we've got a real VIP coming in soon. Since your station's got a free booth, I'm assigning 'em to you. I can count on you, right?"

"Yes, ma'am!" I reply brightly, going to my station to wait.

After a few quick calls, my VIP order comes in.

<u>1 ICE TEA</u>
<u>2 WATER</u>
<u>EXTRA NAPKINS</u>

It's hardly the most compelling order, but if they want an iced tea, two glasses of water, and extra napkins, I'll deliver.

After I check myself in the mirror to make sure I'm presentable for a VIP, I grab the tray of drinks and napkins. Heading back out onto the floor and up the stairs, I try to keep cool, like it's any other customer.

This charade lasts until I see her.

IN MY LIFE, I've fallen in love at first sight three times.

The first was Gabby Wheelwright in first grade. She was pretty to a six-year-old's eyes, and I courted her in the usual delicate way of six-year-old boys, mostly by calling her names and pushing her. If Mom had not died the next year, I probably would have continued the chase.

The second was Taylor Swift. Yeah, I know she's a celebrity, but as a ten-year-old I was convinced it was meant to be. If I just had a chance to let her know my feelings, she'd reconsider the age difference and we could live happily ever after.

I never claimed to be a smart ten-year-old.

The third… wasn't Olivia.

No, the third time was Kelly Marie Carpenter.

I was eleven on the first day of middle school. She'd come from another elementary school in town, so I'd never seen her before, and I was head over heels at first glance. Not only was she the prettiest girl in school by far, for some inexplicable reason she was also really nice to me as well, even when she didn't have to be.

Once, I screwed up the courage and asked her out. In her defense, she turned me down in the nicest way possible.

It took having Olivia in my life to finally figure out the difference between infatuation and love. Now I realize the importance of starting something on the basis of mutual friendship and care rather than having a relationship based on physical attraction. I'm lucky because Olivia is both beautiful and one of the greatest people I know.

With Olivia in my life, I thought I'd never experience the gut wrenching sensation again.

Until this table, because the fourth time is sitting at it.

She's barely older than me with curly red hair and a very slight tan, the kind that some redheads get before they burn. She's in good shape, but still fills out her low-cut top and tight designer jeans. Her eyes are hidden by a pair of sunglasses that cost probably more than Dad's car, while her full lips are curved in a disinterested smile as she splits her attention between the stage and her phone.

An unlabeled bouquet of flowers lies on the table in front of her.

Maybe love is too strong an emotion in this situation, and maybe it's just some confused animal instinct. Despite Olivia, I feel an overwhelming urge to impress this girl.

Before I can make my move, I notice the two intimidating Secret Service guys sitting with her. One gets up to stop me.

"I'll take it from here," he says.

The girl sighs, loudly. "Oh, come on, Gareth. *He's* trying to do his job, and *I'm* trying to have fun. You're getting in the way of both. Stop it."

There's zero threat to her tone, but Gareth backs down unhesitatingly. I know she's considering my pride when she says that.

I hand them their drinks. "Thank you for coming to Pedro Parrot's Safari Lodge, my name is Noel. If you need anything, just press the button beneath the trophy and I'll be here to help."

"Thank you, Noel," the girl says, distracted by a joke Brutus the Bear made onstage.

The other Secret Service, Not-Gareth, looks at me. "Noel *Hallstrom*?"

"Yes, sir?" I say.

He taps his earpiece, whispering something before nodding. "Continue with your duties."

"What he means is, *thank you*, Noel. Isn't that right boys?" she asks.

Gareth and Not-Gareth mechanically and simultaneously say, "Thank you, Noel."

I'd be more hung up on the strangeness of Not-Gareth knowing my name if it weren't for the fact that it means *she* remembers my name.

I walk down the stairs slowly, looking back every so often in case she needs anything. I pick up my pace when I reach the first floor, heading back to my station.

"What do you think of your VIP?" Kathleen asks when I pass her.

I try to play it casual. "She's all right. Why does she have park private security?"

Kathleen smirks. "You're shittin' me, right?"

"No," I say.

"You don't recognize her?"

"No," I repeat.

"That's Elle Dorian," she says.

"Oh, shed!" I exclaim as it all clicks into place.

Elle Dorian. Granddaughter of Fletcher Dorian. Heiress to the Dorian Studios fortune, second only to her father Nicolas Dorian. Child star of more than two dozen Dorian Studios live-action hits long before she looked like this.

No wonder Kathleen thinks I should've recognized her.

"She givin' you any trouble?" Kathleen asks. "She's always been somethin' of a hellraiser; takes after her mom. Problem is she's a hellraiser we gotta treat nice, ya know?"

"She's fine, and I'll treat her nice, I swear."

"See that you do. But don't neglect your other tables, either, ya hear?"

"Have I ever?"

Kathleen smiles. "Not so far. And don't give me reason to think you might change."

Since I really respect Kathleen and don't want to let her down, I know I won't make any mistakes.

That doesn't mean I won't give Elle's table a little extra attention. Though all my tables keep me busy, I take time to see if her table needs anything when I pass by. Dutifully, I pour refills and bring out appetizers, trying to make casual banter when given the opportunity, which isn't easy given Gareth and Not-Gareth.

And Olivia.

Right, and Olivia.

The tray of food for Elle's table is finally ready. Gareth and Not-Gareth have ordered chicken clubs while a pasta and shrimp dish waits for Elle. Hurriedly, I bring it onto the floor.

In the quiet between shows, I clearly hear the sound of a man crying.

I look at the darkened booth, but Fritz is gone.

"It's all your fault." The crier darts in front of me and I recognize JK. He's a mess with clothes unkempt, hair in tangles, and several days' worth of stubble. He's also crying like a baby.

"It's all your fault," he whimpers, his breath reeking of cheap liquor.

"What?"

"We were *family*, and family watches out for family!"

"I don't know what you're talking about, but I have this—"

"No!" he exclaims, putting a hand on my chest. "You said it was my fault! But you shoulda covered so they wouldn't fire me! What kind of shed thing is that to do to family?"

Not only am I terrified of him, but I feel a pressing need to get this food to Elle's table.

"You got fired?" I ask.

"Yeah," he blubbers, looking at me for pity or reassurance.

"Good riddance," I scoff.

He looks crushed, but I don't feel any pity for him after spending the night in the Sky Bucket. Twisting the knife feels especially good right now.

I step around him and make my way upstairs to Elle's table. She blasts me with a genuine smile as I set down her pasta.

Another show starts up below us, and I raise my voice to ask the next question. "Is there anything else I can get you?"

Between bites of shrimp, Elle says, "No, thank you." Suddenly, her eyes go wide.

JK is barreling toward me.

Thinking fast, I step out of his way.

Not-Gareth stands up in a flash and grabs JK. The smaller and less-trained man fights hard, flinging himself against the railing. Reflexively, Gareth pushes Elle deeper into the booth for safety, her eyes bulging in surprise.

JK hits Not-Gareth just right and tips the giant over the railing. Not-Gareth catches JK's sleeve, and they both tumble over the railing together. The two men flail end over end as they land in a heap right in front of the stage. Glancing over the railing, I see them, barely moving but still swinging at each other.

Calmly, Gareth leaps over the railing and lands on his feet by the scuffle.

Looking around, I expect to see everyone recording this with their phones. Everyone is so absorbed in the show that they barely noticed the three men falling two stories.

Turning back around, I notice Elle has turned a strange shade of purple. Her hands beat at the booth and scratch at her throat.

Choking.

I grab Elle by the wrist, yanking her from the booth before spinning her around so I can wrap my arms around her stomach. Just above the bellybutton, I perform the Heimlich maneuver, forcing her against me hard enough to send her sunglasses flying. Her hands paw at me, trying to find purchase.

Then, with a sick, wet sound, the piece of shrimp lodged in her throat explodes from her mouth and sails over the railing. Exhausted, my legs give out from under me, and we collapse onto the floor.

Gasping for breath and coughing grotesquely, she says, "Thanks."

Her moist lips seem close enough to kiss. Her watery, red eyes are a beautiful shade of green.

"No problem," I say.

Uncomfortably aware of how close my hands are to her breasts I unwrap myself from her.

"What's happened?" Kathleen asks, suddenly standing over us.

"I think we need a doctor," I say.

"On it," Kathleen says, running back downstairs. I keep expecting a crowd of people to be staring at us, but it seems the show has everyone hypnotized.

Trying to think of something funny to ease the tension, I ask, "Can I interest you in anything from the dessert menu?"

It must have been the right thing to say, because Elle suddenly can't stop laughing.

ERIN
1990

The character break room beneath Happy Hollow was crowded with nearly every character performer and Skinner present. It was normally impossible to get this many in one place at the same time, but desperate times called for desperate measures.

"We need to talk about Dewey," Jeanine said, wearing her full Benny the Bunny costume except for the head. The others grumbled in agreement.

"None of these disappearances happened until he got here," Linda noted, wearing little save for her tank top and Flora the Fox's legs.

"Alleged disappearances," one of the Skinners said.

"It's Bennytown. They're disappearances," Oren said. As the most senior person in the character department, people usually listened to him.

Erin had to speak up since she worked directly with Dewey. She might not have had the seniority or a strong voice, but she felt protective of Dewey.

"Look, guys, let's talk this over," Erin said, trying to raise her meek voice above the din. She caught Oren's gaze, and he quieted the others down.

Erin continued, "I know Dewey's an oddball, but he's a good guy. I've worked in the igloo for six months now, and I haven't seen anything inappropriate. He's great with kids, and, I mean… he's Wilbur the friggin' Walrus! Why would he do anything bad?"

"The most accomplished freaks are good at keeping it quiet," Jeanine said.

"But do you have proof?" Erin shot back.

"We'll find some. He can't have hidden what he's done completely," Jeanine said.

"Five kids missing. Maybe even six," Oren agreed. "He's getting away with it because Bennytown's blinding everyone to what's happening. Maybe we're the only ones who can see it. And that means we're the only ones who can do anything about it."

The rest of the group rumbled in assent.

"Are you gonna form a lynch mob?" Erin asked.

"Not if we don't have to," Jeanine said, rubbing the bridge of her nose with one of her great Benny the Bunny paws. "Look, the rest of the family thinks we're a bunch of wackos. We're on our own, and if we don't take care of the problem, who will?"

It was madness. The park, the stress, the disappearances—it was getting to everyone.

"I'm out of here," Erin said, getting up from the table.

Oren stepped in her way.

"You're warning him, aren't you?" Jeanine said.

"No," Erin lied.

"If you're not with us on this, you're against us. You know that, right?" Jeanine said.

Erin looked to Oren. The Skinner might've had a kind face once, but not anymore.

"Please, let me go," she said.

Begrudgingly, Oren stepped out of her way and let her pass.

Erin couldn't believe she'd ever respected the people in there. She might be only an attendant who helped characters get from place to place without tripping, but when she first joined the family eight months ago, they'd welcomed her with open arms. Even though it was a tense time to join, especially with all the abduction rumors, she felt more welcome here than she ever had in her own poor excuse for a family.

Especially with Dewey.

He was an oddity as a forty-something, slightly pudgy man. He was the opposite of the young female dancers who made up most of the characters. Outside of the costume, he was shy and more than a little awkward, but he had a sweet side and an odd sense of humor that never failed to make Erin laugh. She looked to him as a bigger brother, and maybe this blinded her to some of his less endearing traits. At his core, she was still certain that he was a decent man.

She navigated the Lower Park Rabbit Holes until she found Dewey's dressing room. Erin was not certain what she wanted to say, not with the threat of the other workers, but she had to say something. To do something. He was her friend, after all.

And he was talking to someone.

She heard voices through the door. One of them belonged to Dewey while the other murmured softly like a child.

"They just don't understand me," Dewey complained.

"We still like you," the other voice spoke in strange tones.

To Erin, it sounded like a multitude of voices, twisted together.

"You're the only ones that do," Dewey said. "That's why I love you so much; you always know how to make me smile."

"We like making you smile too."

"You know what would make Wilbur really smile?" Dewey asked.

"No," Erin whispered.

It couldn't be. She should have known. If she had sensed something or done something earlier, this wouldn't be happening. Dewey was a lot of things, but he wasn't a monster.

She raised her hand to knock on his door and to interrupt what was really going on. She had to see why Dewey really brought children down into the Rabbit Holes despite every rule against it. But the door was barred to her.

There were more voices in the room. Unnatural voices. Whining, scared, twisted, angry voices. Dozens of voices were speaking over each other and with each other. The voices rose in volume and power when joined in legion. There was no way that these were real children's voices. The sound was only a mockery that made Erin sick to her stomach. *Was it the voice of the park?*

The door started to vibrate, and the hall grew colder, darker.

A light blew out nearby, another Vickers Flicker, and another farther down the hall shortly after.

Erin ran back for the break room.

NOEL
2019

Somehow, I've never been in a Rabbit Hole before this moment. Comestibles workers have no reason to be in these hidden tunnels, but I'd always hoped I'd see them sooner or later.

Just not like this.

In a Rabbit Hole security complex under the Upper Park, I notice a sign above the main entrance proudly labelling this place "The Zoo." While lacking a lot of Bennytown charm, the walls are painted in cheerful pastel colors, decorated with Benny & Friends posters, and a centralized oil painting of Fletcher Dorian and Caroline. This main room looks like a stereotypical TV show police station, with a dozen desks and a row of heavy metal doors along one wall that look like holding cells.

Security Officer Knight sits across from me wearing a traditional pale blue Bennytown security uniform. He's been good-naturedly questioning me over the past half hour about what happened during the confrontation with JK and Elle's Secret Service guys.

He's nice, a helluva lot nicer than Cassidy after my night in the—

(allinmyhead)

After the third reiteration of my story without any changes, I'm antsy to get back to work. Kathleen's covering my tables, and I don't want her to get upset for taking too long.

Right around the time we are finishing up, one of the metal doors along the wall swings open. JK, flanked by two Secret Service, is escorted out. He's bloody and bruised with a muzzle covering his mouth. With his hands zip-tied behind his back, he's surprisingly sedate, shuffling his feet slowly with glassy eyes.

"What'll happen to him?" I ask.

Knight says, "Not my problem. A family member way above my pay grade wants to make him an example, which won't make me lose any sleep."

Management wants to make an example of him?
Good.

"So, can I get back to work?" I ask.

"Almost…" He trails off.

"What?" I can see the tables piling up and poor Kathleen running herself crazy.

"Young Miss Dorian's down the hall in medical getting the once-over, and she wants to talk to you," he says.

Oh.

I guess if Elle Dorian wants to talk to me, Kathleen'll understand me being late.

I follow the signs down the long, twisting Rabbit Holes toward the medical ward, getting out of the way of passing maintenance crews and janitors on their golf carts and bicycles. Occasionally, I hear the hissing of pipes or the rumble of the park above me. The tunnels are an efficient way of getting around but are confusingly inconsistent. Some are large enough to accommodate a few lanes worth of golf carts side by side, while others are barely wide enough to fit two people shoulder to shoulder.

Bennytown's arteries and veins. You can almost feel them pulsing, can't you?

My mind is playing tricks on me. Sound carries in odd ways down here and voices seem to slither around me. I know I'm just hearing people doing their jobs. I know those whispers aren't following me. Whispers like that would be…

(allinmyhead)

When I reach the medical ward, I'm glad to focus on something else. The waiting room looks similar to any major hospital, except for the posters featuring Dare the Hare dressed up as a doctor and handing out sage advice.

DOCTOR DARE SAYS, "REMEMBER: JUST BECAUSE YOU CAN EAT IT DOESN'T MEAN YOU SHOULD!"

DOCTOR DARE SAYS, "BE VIGILANT OF RIDERS' RESTRAINTS, OR ELSE!"

DOCTOR DARE SAYS, "REPORT ALL WORKPLACE INJURIES TO YOUR BENNYTOWN REPRESENTATIVE FIRST!"

Doctor Dare on the posters isn't as warm and cuddly as his cartoon counterpart and appears stern as he encourages proper workplace safety. Blood covers his scrubs in some of the posters depicting more dangerous accidents.

The man at the desk sends me down another long hallway, past modern hospital rooms and trauma facilities to a small triage room with a doorway flanked by Gareth and Not-Gareth.

Elle argues with someone over a landline phone while a couple of doctors fusses over her.

"No, Daddy, I'm fine. *I'm fine.* No, don't gas up the jet. I almost choked on a piece of shrimp, it's not like I'm dodging assassins or anything like last summer. Daddy, it's *Milan,* and it's your anniversary. Stay, enjoy yourself. I'm being well taken care of." She sees me and smiles.

"Here, let Doctor Taliaferro tell you that everything'll be fine soon. If you fly out here before you both are done celebrating your anniversary, I'll talk Mom into divorcing you again. Kisses!" she exclaims with a laugh, tossing the phone to the nearest doctor. She grabs her flowers from her bed and sprints toward me.

She grabs me by the wrist and shouts, "Come on!"

Before I know what's happening, we're sprinting past Gareth and Not-Gareth. A millisecond after the surprise, they're hot on our heels, but we stay just out of their reach. Elle's laughing. I'm laughing too, because this is quite probably the most insane thing I've ever done in my life.

When we reach the waiting room, Elle swings a wheelchair in front of Gareth and Not-Gareth.

Gareth leaps over it with the dexterity of an Olympian.

Not-Gareth isn't as nimble. He stumbles over it, rolling into Gareth with enough speed to knock him down.

Elle pulls me into the hall and through the twists and turns of the Rabbit Holes until I'm thoroughly lost. When we have some distance between us and Medical, she pauses to listen. Through the echoing hallway, we hear Gareth and Not-Gareth arguing, before picking a direction and running away from us.

Breathing heavily, she says, "Thanks. Any other family member would've turned me over to my nannies."

"No problem," I say. Suddenly I'm aware that we are still holding hands, so I let go.

"I've been dodging guys like them since I was five. Every time I think I've got all their tricks down, Daddy hires a new set. He likes to keep me on my toes."

"Why do you need them? I mean, you're here…"

She scoffs. "Because 'It's a dangerous world, and we can't risk the last of Dorian's bloodline.' I'm supposed to take over daddy's empire after he's gone. It wouldn't be appropriate to let me have a little fun now and then. Not with the glory of the Sixtieth Birthday around the corner, *heavens* no."

I'm stuck between gawking at her beauty and realizing this is probably the most I'll ever talk to someone as famous as her. My conflicted silence stretches between us awkwardly.

Feeling the need to say something that doesn't conflict with the Poison Words, I choke out a reply. "That stinks."

She eyes me, smiling almost sweetly. "Sorry to make you an accessory."

"Sorry I got you involved with JK," I say.

"Don't worry about it, since we've had our eye on him for a while. He was bound to get into our redemption program sooner or later."

"Redemption program?"

Something about that sounds familiar.

"It's necessary for repeat rule-breakers. We like to give them an opportunity to make it up to the family they've betrayed."

The very thought of JK coming back to work here after what he pulled today makes my blood boil.

"Some people don't deserve redemption," I grumble.

She sizes me up for a long minute. "Walk with me? I need to give my statement at the Zoo, but I'd like a moment of your time first."

"Sure," I say.

She holds the bouquet of flowers with reverence, almost like a talisman of great religious importance. Her expensive purse bounces against the Rabbit Hole wall periodically, gaining new scuff marks. However, she grasps the cheap grocery store bouquet like her life depends on it.

"I want to thank you for saving my life," she says.

"Oh, don't worry about it. Anyone would've done it," I say.

"They might, but I bet they would be smug about it. After all, they saved the fabulously wealthy, famous, beautiful, and did I mention *humble*, heiress of the Dorian Studios fortune," she says, her voice laced with sarcasm. "But you're not humble-bragging or turning the conversation around to a reward. You're just letting me ramble."

Briefly, she touches my arm, and I'm reminded of Olivia. I tell myself not to read too much into this whole scenario. Maybe she's just naturally affectionate and is used to having her pick of guys. I bet she's not trying to send me any signals. I know I should be grateful for Olivia, but why do I want Elle frickin' Dorian to stay here and continue this affectionate behavior?

"Again, it's my pleasure," I say with a blush.

"Now that I've awkwardly told you about how glad I am that you're not asking for a reward, I did want to offer you something in gratitude," she says.

"You don't have to—"

"But I *want* to," she says firmly. "Have you ever heard of the Green Door Society?"

The Green Door Society is one of the worst-kept secrets among Bennytown fans. It's a hidden social club in Journey through Americana for Bennytown's elite to rub elbows with corporate moguls, politicians, and celebrities. Membership is rumored to require a six-figure annual fee, and there's an average waiting list of about ten years unless you are an invited guest. Photography or any other recording device is strictly forbidden. What goes on in there is strictly speculation and legend. Five presidents (Johnson, Nixon, Reagan, Clinton, and Trump) have allegedly boasted membership cards, and it's rumored to be the go-to wedding destination for quiet, celebrity weddings.

So, yeah, you can say I've heard about the Green Door Society.

"A little," I reply.

"As thanks, I'd like to invite you and a guest to join me for lunch at the Green Door Society this Thursday."

I almost screech out an immediate acceptance, but I make myself calm down enough to think things through. A beautiful woman and my sorta boss just invited me to lunch at one of the most exclusive restaurants on Earth.

I'd be a fool to reject such an offer. Right?

Then reality hits me.

Begrudgingly, I say, "I don't think I can. I've got a shift."

"Really?" she says, crossing her arms and raising an eyebrow. "Really?"

"Really," I confirm.

Rolling her eyes, she says, "I *think* I can get your schedule rearranged."

Maybe my smile's too large, but I say, "Yeah, that'll be great!"

"Good," she says, squeezing my hand.

Two invitations to private park functions in one day? You're coming up in the world, Noel.

The tunnel ends at a large metal door with a massive lock. She pulls out a single, delicate key from a chain hanging around her neck. She uses it to open the door into a large, seven-sided chamber with a well-lit bronze statue in the center. Fletcher Dorian, beaming and proud, holds a smiling little girl on his shoulder. Dozens of lit candles surround the statue.

Elle sets her flowers next to a plaque at the base and whispers as if a prayer, "*I believe in Bennytown.*"

I quietly repeat after her before taking a look at the plaque at the statue's base.

CAROLINE DORIAN

1950 - 1955

"YOUR LOSS BRINGS A GRIEF UNFATHOMABLE, BUT
GIVES US PURPOSE IN THIS GREAT UNDERTAKING."

"That little girl is my Aunt Caroline. Grandpa built this place for her after she died at such a young age. My daddy was born after her death and grew up in her shadow. Daddy complains about how Grandpa ignored his achievements and was consumed with memories of the dead girl. I don't think Daddy realizes he now does the same thing to me," Elle says.

I am overwhelmed by the heartbreaking story, so I don't say anything.

"Despite Daddy's jealousy, he knows family traditions must be upheld. Sometimes, I think he hates her a little," Elle continues, motioning to the flowers.

Lamely, I answer, "I didn't know she had a memorial here."

"Few do. People would be uncomfortable knowing there's a little girl's crypt hidden in the heart of Bennytown," Elle says.

"You mean…" I gape at the statue's base, not wanting to believe a body is buried in there. And I definitely don't want to think about how similar this statue is to the Fletcher Dorian statue at the end of the Road to Adventure. The statue that was erected shortly after his death.

"Grandpa may have been strange, but he made all this for love. Haven't you ever done something crazy for love?" she asks.

"More times than I can count," I admit. "And for what it's worth, I don't think it's crazy. I think it's a beautiful gesture. The park is her eternal playground."

She glances at me with a worried expression, but then breaks into a smile. "I'm glad you understand. Not everyone is so considerate. Can you please keep it a secret?"

"My lips are sealed."

"Good," she says, kissing me on the cheek.

This is becoming the greatest day of my life.

JILL
1999

arning signs were posted by the lines for all the rides. They said things like:

Benny Says Do Not Ride This Attraction If:
You might be pregnant
You have heart problems
You have photosensitive epilepsy
You suffer from back or neck problems
You suffer from motion sickness, claustrophobia,
vertigo or paranoia

After going on a few rides with some girls from her cheer squad, Jill was pretty sure the signs were only there to make the rides appear to be dangerous. Jill wasn't a thrill seeker, but there was no way she'd let the other girls on the squad know. Whatever big, bad rides they rode in Bennytown, she'd join them and come back for more.

At first, she'd been able to pull it off.

Candy Mountain Swirler? Piece of cake.

Mine Carts? No problem.

Fall of Atlantis? Easy as pie.

After lunch, when they'd gone on Dino Safari 3D Adventure in Primordial World, she started to understand the signs. The ride itself was an intense motion simulator of a time machine flying through a world of dinosaurs. The movement made her stomach queasy. With the 3D glasses thrown in for good measure, Jill's head started to spin after a minute.

After two minutes, the spinning became a headache and nausea.

By the time the ride was over, Jill was ready to puke her guts out.

She impressed herself by holding it the whole way out the ride's exit. She couldn't let the others see her weakness, especially after she fought to avoid getting cut. There was no way she was going to miss the state finals that had the special exhibition at Bennytown Plaza. She was performing later today, and she was not making a mess out of her freshly dry-cleaned, mostly white uniform.

Running daintily, she held one hand on her stomach and another over her mouth. She was swift enough to fly past the crowds yet careful enough to not lose her Benny ears hat. Following the signs through the faux-jungles of Primordial World, she raced toward the bathroom.

There was an "Out of Order" sign on the door. In desperation, she grabbed the handle and twisted. Predictably, it was firmly locked.

Stomach turning, ready to unload at any moment, she frantically worked the handle. She hoped beyond hope that it would magically open in order for her to maintain her dignity.

This was Bennytown and a place of miracles. It was the kind of place where a princess like her wouldn't have to suffer embarrassing situations.

A painful shot of static jolted her hand away from the handle, as the door swung open. It was an odd miracle she was willing to accept given the circumstances.

The massive bathroom, lined with dozens of stalls and sinks, was pitch black. There was enough light coming in through the crack at the bottom of the door, so she fumbled her way over to a stall, swung its door open, bent over, and vomited into the toilet. Her body nearly turned itself inside-out, but she felt a lot better when she finished.

Smoothing down her uniform, she realized she knelt in a shallow puddle of water. In fact, the entire floor seemed to be a puddle.

"Fucking great," she said, wondering how her knee socks would look onstage. Maybe one of the others brought an extra pair. They better have. She'd made it this far, and she wasn't going to be humiliated by something so ridiculous.

The lights flickered on, shocking her eyes and jolting her backwards.

When they went out again, her eyes filled with faint after-images.

She stumbled to her feet as the lights flashed on and then off again, then one by one flickered to life, and one by one went out. Just as the hand dryers roared to life, an entire row of motion sensor-activated sinks exploded full jets of water while steam filled the mirrors.

Over the noise and confusion, she heard a man whistling.

"Hello?" she called out. "Who's there?"

At once, everything went dark again, so Jill fumbled through the blackness.

"*Stop it! This isn't funny!*" she yelled, voice quavering.

The man whistled again, not far-off.

Jill whirled around, hoping to see him and wanting to confront the jackass that was trying to scare her. There was nothing but pitch blackness in every direction.

Briefly, she felt fingers brush against her hair. Reaching up, she felt no hand.

This was not the time to feel woozy or sick. It was time to run. It was time to get outside and be surrounded by people. But where was outside?

As her eyes adjusted, she saw the faint white lines of daylight streaming through the doors. Slowly, feet splashing through the water, she made her way for the exit.

"Hey girly. Wanna be young and pretty fer-ever?" a dry, raspy voice chuckled only inches from her ear.

Jill screamed and tried to run. This action only made her slip on the water, and she fell down hard on the linoleum.

He was close and smelled of copper and burning flesh. His heavy steps slammed against the floor without making a splash. Jill felt her hair rising. Not from gooseflesh or that instinctive bristling from fear, but this was more like the world's worst case of static cling. Her hair floated above her head, and the short little hairs on her arms started to glow as electricity arced between them. Her mouth tasted of rust, and stars popped before her eyes.

A man appeared in front of her out of thin air. He was just a large black shape in the dark, given form only by the blue glow of the sparking electricity around him. As he moved toward her, sinks and hand dryers popped and exploded. Lights flickered above him, but never long enough to show his true face.

The glimpses she caught of his grinning, malevolent face in the darkness were more than enough horror for one lifetime. Possibly seven or eight lifetimes, but who was counting anymore?

She wanted to run, to scream, to put as much distance between her and this damned bathroom as possible. Before she could move an inch, electricity coursed through her body to ensure she never had to worry again.

NOEL
2019

Creepy Corner has always been my favorite land in Bennytown, probably because it was the first place I remember being tall enough to go on the "big kid" rides. Though horror themed, it's always had that perpetual warmth and friendliness that the rest of Bennytown radiates, skewing more toward perpetual Halloween than splatter movie on the fright scale.

I've always wondered what it looks like at night.

The Lower Park is empty except for a few stray janitors and maintenance workers hurrying to leave. No one pays me any mind as I walk across Happy Hollow to Creepy Corner.

I check my phone and find no new messages from either Dad or Olivia. Dad dropped me off, a little disgruntled at the late hour but happy enough that I was making friends. He was even happier that one of them was driving me back. Olivia has been difficult to get in contact with lately. She blames family obligations, but I know it's because of me. Maybe I messed things up after my night in the Sky Buckets, and I have apologized to her about it. I'll need to do some more apologizing, I guess.

I'm not going to think about that tonight. I just want to have fun.

Have fun and search for walrus intel.

The Creepy Corner entrance is marked by stone arch, with the land's name imprinted on it in Gothic lettering. Two iron gates greet me that should be locked since it's afterhours, but one of them is open slightly. As I approach, a rusty creaking startles me.

"Don't worry, it's not real," Garcia says, stepping out from behind the arch and pointing to the speaker making more rusty sound effects. I've never seen my friend out of her uniform. Although her clothes and hair are a bit retro, she looks good cleaned up.

Garcia motions me through the gate. I'm suddenly aware that I haven't spent any time with her outside of a professional setting, and I'm really not quite sure what I'm supposed to do.

It's been a long time since I've had a new friend.

She breaks the awkward silence. "So, I've gotta warn you."

"About what?" I ask.

"We're gonna meet some of my friends. They're good people, but they've been here a while and it's made them go a little crazy."

"How crazy?"

"Not like strip-your-face-off-and-wear-it-around-while-dancing-in-front-of-a-mirror crazy, but don't be surprised by anything they do."

"Thanks for the safety tip," I say.

"No problem. By night's end, I'm sure you'll be asking for more than one warning," she says cryptically.

She leads me to a large, decorative mausoleum behind a souvenir shop. Sliding open a hidden panel on one side, we descend a curving metal staircase.

I pause before I follow her. Something doesn't feel right about this.

"I thought all the Rabbit Holes were in the hill and Upper Park," I say.

"No one uses these ones anymore. A lot of them collapsed during the Northridge Quake in '94. Every Lower Park Rabbit Hole was abandoned, which is great news for us."

"Why's that?"

"You'll see," she says, leading the way down.

Taking a deep breath, I follow her.

These Rabbit Holes lack the pastel paint jobs of the upper ones. It is just bare concrete marked with dark stains from water and rust. Numerous deep cracks line the walls as far as I can see in the dark.

While descending the stairs, I try to pull out my phone for light, but Garcia quickly puts a hand on my wrist.

"Don't," she says.

"Why?" I ask. "I can barely see a flipping thing down here."

"You can say fuck now if you want to. They can't hear you here."

"That didn't answer my question."

"Say fuck first," she says.

"No!" I reply.

"Well, it was worth a try." Garcia laughs.

"Why can't I use my phone?"

"Soon," she says, guiding me by the hand the rest of the way down the stairs. When we reach a concrete landing with a shallow puddle at its base, she lets go of me. Soon, I glimpse a flash of light from a lighter, brilliant in the dark. She lights a lantern and holds it high, illuminating a long, dark tunnel. The light of the lantern is dim and yellow, pitiful in this overpowering blackness.

"Come on," she says. Hesitantly, I follow.

The tunnel is labyrinthine, with many hidden chambers and stairways branching off from it. Earthquake damage is everywhere. Cracks in the ceiling let in grasping roots that dangle almost all the way to the floor. There are a few points where the walls have broken inward, letting earth in, but Garcia guides me past these obstacles silently. Some sections are so full of dirt and rubble that we have to really squeeze through them, while other branching paths are completely impassable.

After one of these squeeze-through sections, we come across a recessed fluorescent lamp in the ceiling, still flickering and buzzing intermittently. With a grave look on her face, Garcia points to the light.

"There are a lot of legends about ghosts in this park," she says dramatically.

With the way she's trying to hide a smirk, I know we've entered story time.

"Oh?" I say, amused.

Garcia continues, "Bennytown's always been one of the most haunted places in California. All the ghost hunters check out the Queen Mary, the Winchester House or Alcatraz. But this place has got 'em all beat. Ghosts are everywhere in Bennytown. And the deeper down you go underneath the park, the more they appear, especially at night. Everybody's got their own story…"

"Do they, now?" I prompt.

"So many, and everyone'll tell you they know the real reason why the spirits infest this park. Personally, I don't believe in most of them; too many people telling too many stories, but on a night as dark as this, with all the people who've died here…"

There's a gentle teasing in her voice. When I realize she's just messing with me and telling me campfire stories, the more I relax.

"It's dark because we're underground," I say.

"Are you gonna let me tell the story or not? Because I can stop," she says, annoyed.

"Fine, sorry, continue."

"Anyway, deaths, dark night, creepy atmosphere. You ruined my pace, but I forgive you," she says with a laugh. "Now we get to what I wanted to tell you about, which is the Vickers Flickers."

She motions toward the light.

"You've seen Vickers Flickers before? Random malfunctions and electrical stutters?"

"I have," I confirm.

"Have you ever been curious as to why they're called that?"

"I'm curious now."

"Just remember what they say about curiosity and cats," she says, guiding me down the tunnel. I don't know if it's the tone of her voice or the actual tunnel, but I swear it's just gotten darker in here. "Once upon a time, there was a maintenance man named Wallace Vickers. He had a darling wife, the world's most beautiful twin baby girls, and an ideal job as a Bennytown family member. Everybody loved the man. He was the kind of guy you could just as easily go drinking or to church with, the kind of guy who knew a little of everything about everything and was always whistling a tune from his heart. Everyone who knew him said he was an utter sweetheart who'd never consider hurting a fly. Until one day he started hearing and seeing impossible things."

I shudder for dramatic effect but can't shake a cold feeling. Whether I want it to or not, the story's affecting me, and with building anticipation, I'm getting a mighty case of the willies.

(allinmyhead)

She doesn't notice. "They say his work got erratic, and he became more hostile. He made a lot of friends who protected him, kept him on the job even after he lashed out at a few guests, but he was on thin ice. One day he came to work with a crowbar and started smashing up the animatronics in Journey through Americana's old Wonders of Nikola Tesla show. He did a lot of damage, and even killed a security guard who tried to stop him. Afterwards, he lodged the crowbar in a Tesla coil and pretty much exploded from the voltage."

Garcia sighs. "After such a tragic incident, the police went to his home, only to find that Wallace Vickers had gotten in some crowbar practice on his wife and daughters first."

My stomach feels like someone's just squeezed it. "Did they…"

Garcia nods. "You wanna know the worst part?"

"No," I whisper.

"Too bad," she continues. "On the wall over the bodies of his family, he wrote in blood, 'I WON'T LET THE DARK PARK GET THEM.' Creepy, right?"

"Yeah," I agree, shuddering.

She leads me to a corner. "Everyone thought that'd be the end of it, especially after they replaced the ruined show with one about Edison. Ever since, there have been strange occurrences in Bennytown that nobody, not even the almighty Bengineers, can figure out. Things'll shut down for no obvious reason or work when they're not supposed to. Like that light back there. Sometimes, they say you'll hear strange whistles coming out of speakers, and they call it the ghost of Wallace Vickers."

As if on cue, a low whistle echoes through the hall.

"Did you hear that?" Garcia asks.

"Yeah," I reply.

"Stay here," Garcia says.

"Why stay here? Why can't I come with you? Why can't…" I trail off, not wanting to ask her why we can't just run. Even I know that would make me look like a coward.

"Don't worry. I got this," she says confidently, walking around the corner ahead.

When she rounds the corner, I can still hear her footsteps—until they stop.

"What the, that can't—*Noel, run!*" she screams.

The light from her lantern drops to the floor with a heavy clatter.

"Garcia?" I call out. I want to run. I should run and never look back, but Garcia is my friend, and friends don't leave friends like this. I want to think that Garcia's just had an accident. Maybe I can help her, but people don't yell for you to run when they've had an accident, do they? "*Garcia?!*"

She doesn't answer me. Once again, I hear that low whistling sound.

It's not real, it's not real, it can't be real, ghosts can't be real, it's all in my head, all in my head, allinmy-

A white, fluttering shape emerges from the gloom carrying the lantern. It runs right at me, wailing like a damned soul. The shock of surprise is short lived when I truly take in what's before me. With my heart beating at a normal pace again, it takes everything I have not to burst out laughing.

When the shape stops in front of me, thrashing and screaming, I raise a hand and fake a casual wave. "Hey, what's up?"

"*You're not scared?*" it bellows.

"Not anymore," I say.

"Not even a little?" Its bellow softens to a whine.

"Maybe just a little," I chuckle.

"Awww, come on," the ghost says, pulling off its sheet to reveal a gawky Korean boy with glasses. "We put a lot of work into this."

As the lantern brightens, Garcia turns the corner. "A sheet ghost? Really, Jimmy, that's the best you got? I wanna scare the shit out of him, and you use a sheet ghost?"

"You try scrounging something better around here!" he exclaims. "I mean, if I saw a ghost down here, even one with a sheet, *I'd* be scared."

"Yeah, Jimmy, we know," Garcia says, shaking her head, then patting me on the shoulders. "Well, come on, let's get out of this Hole and introduce you to the others."

Trying not to sound too sarcastic, I say, "Sounds like this will be a treat."

THE RABBIT HOLE ends in a storage room hidden near the loading area of Escape from Briarthorne Manor. The area is designed to look like a garage at an old Victorian estate that's fallen on bad times. Right now, the creepiest part is the emptiness. Normally, this loading area is full of almost a hundred people. At this moment, there are just four waiting for us in a room dimly lit by dozens of false candelabras with tiny, glimmering light bulbs.

A tall, lean girl with black pigtails sits on top of a turnstile, snapping bubblegum, watching a shorter girl with curly blond hair and a tall black man making out. Another girl with messily chopped red hair, a tight tank top with Benny's face, cutoff jeans, and a cowboy hat smokes a cigarette, idly watching us as we enter.

"Hail, hail, the gang's all here!" Jimmy announces, raising his arms dramatically.

"Did the ghost work?" Pigtails asks, snapping her gum.

"No," Jimmy replies dejectedly.

"Toldja." Cowboy Hat flicks her cigarette onto the ground.

"Yeah, yeah, but with these new kids it's always worth a shot," Pigtails says, rolling off the turnstile. She performs a lazy cartwheel before landing in front of us. Curtsying with her short skirt, she holds out a hand to me.

"Monica," she says.

"Noel," I say.

"Pleased to make yer acquaintance, Noel," she eyes me up and down while working her gum. "Not as cute as you said, Garcia. Still cute. But not *that* cute."

"Don't mind her," Garcia says. "She's picky."

"It's called standards. Jolene here ain't got no standards and look what happened to her!" Monica says.

"Fuck you," Cowboy Hat replies, flipping the bird.

"Maybe later if you ask nice," Monica jokes.

"Whatever," Garcia pushes past them and leads me to the making out couple.

"And these two…" she says, pulling them apart with difficulty. "Are Lorraine and Lance. Lorraine and Lance, this is Noel."

"Hey," Lance says simply.

"Hey," I say.

"We've met already, actually," Lorraine replies, smirking. Her street clothes cover up the vicious scar on her neck, but it's the girl with the Australian accent who offered to show me her pussy on my first day of work. The discomfort of that memory is not made any easier when she saunters over and gives Garcia a long, lingering kiss.

When she parts, Lorraine looks at me. "Sorry, didn't mean to leave you out."

Before I know what's happening, her arms are wrapped around my neck and she's kissing me. She's not too forceful and tastes faintly of candy. For an instant, it's easy to forget pretty much everything.

And then I do remember.

Where I am.

Who I am.

Olivia.

And the kiss suddenly tastes rotten. Like something from a garbage can escaped and is trying to crawl into my mouth.

Before I can recoil, she lets go, winking at me.

"Can we keep him?" Lorraine whispers.

"Only if we're good," Garcia says at room volume. "And *only* if we don't scare him off!"

"We promised we'd be good," Lance says, raising his hand. *"I believe in Bennytown."*

The others raise their hands and repeat, *"I believe in Bennytown."*

Lorraine's officially the only girl outside of Olivia I've ever kissed.

I shake my head to clear my thoughts and force a confused smile. I write everything that just happened off as just another quirk of the family working this park.

Taking a deep breath, I ready myself to make some new friends.

After some real introductions, I find that Jimmy's a ride operator out of Island of Legends, Lorraine's an animal trainer at Journey through Americana, and Lance and Monica are dancers who occasionally moonlight as costumed characters. Jolene seems to be a civilian, but she is as much a family member as the rest.

Once the ice is broken and we all start talking, they seem normal enough. Jimmy and Monica are working their way through college, and Lance took this job to help his little sister do the same. They welcome me without any pretense or prodding and seem as interested in me as I am in them.

Like family.

"Now, I know you're all excited to be here, especially on the eve of our all-important SIXTIETH BIRTHDAY OF BENNYTOWN!" Lance roars.

The others laugh sarcastically, clapping half-heartedly. They're about the least excited people I've ever seen for the Birthday.

Lance continues, "But now that we're all together *and* we've got a new prospective member of the Bennytown Cool Kids Club, it's time we got down to business."

"Cool Kids Club?" I whisper to Garcia.

"Roll with it," she whispers back.

"Tonight, ladies and gents, we're having ourselves a lights-out relay race," Lance says, sitting dramatically on a turnstile and lighting a flashlight beneath his chin. "The ride before you is pitch black. In teams of three, you'll run through one at a time. You'll have to use your wits and memory of the track to survive. The team with the shortest time between its three runners, wins."

"Wins what?" Jimmy asks.

"Does it matter? You just win. Winning isn't good enough?"

"Not for Jimmy here," Lorraine says. Jimmy sticks out his tongue.

I do a quick count. "There's seven of us."

"Yeah, Jolene, being the only civilian, has graciously volunteered to referee," Lance says.

"Graciously *my ass*," Jolene huffs. "New kid stole my spot and you know it."

"Sorry," I say.

"Ah, don't let it eat your ass or nothin'. Just promise me we'll have us some fun later," she challenges, her voice husky.

"We'll see," I say, noncommittally.

Lance continues, "Are we gonna race or what?"

Glad to be back on task, I let the thrill of the challenge pump me up.

I know the layout of this ride like the back of my hand. The ride vehicle's path is pretty wide, so I shouldn't have to worry about running into anything. As long as I stay out of the track itself and don't get my feet stuck in it…

Long straight stretch down the Great Hall, sharp left through the catacombs, slight curve to the right, through the observatory, zig-zag left through the laboratory, the torture chamber, past the fake-out crashed ride vehicle, then up the ramp to the dead bride's room, through the study and the playroom, down the second ramp, through the swamp, then home free.

It won't be the same without the 3-D screens and animatronic effects, but I'm confident.

We draw for teams. I get Lance and Lorraine, while Jimmy, Monica and Garcia make up the other team. Jolene twirls her hat around on one finger.

"Make sure to be careful in there and watch your step. Take a bad tumble and you're apt to break your neck," Lorraine says.

"I'll be careful," I say.

"Good, because there's a million ways you can die in this park, and we'd prefer it if you didn't find way number one million and one," Lorraine says.

"A million ways?" I ask, skeptical.

"At least," Lorraine says.

"Yeah, like being thrown off a coaster," Jolene suggests.

"Getting broken in half by a robot is my favorite," Lance says.

"Or savaged by a falcon," Lorraine says.

"Or frozen by a faulty costume cooling unit. *That's* a fun one," Monica jokes.

"Yeah, yeah, amateurs. Best way to bite it in Bennytown is having your head kicked off by a guest's foot hanging off a roller coaster," Jimmy says.

The others give him a look that says they can't top him.

"That really happened?" I ask.

"Oh yeah. In the Fall of Atlantis," Jimmy explains. The Island of Legends ride is an indoor, hanging roller coaster over animatronic dioramas of Atlantis sinking.

He says, "Guest loses a hat and goes nuts on the ride Lead, so the Lead sends in a new meat worker to go looking for it. New meat doesn't look both ways when picking up the hat, and fast-moving-low-hanging foot met face. New meat got his head punted something like fifty feet, guest got a broken leg, and a nice payoff for their trouble. I'm pretty sure when they found his head it looked something like this."

Jimmy pulls a twisted face. For a fraction of a second, I see him being the one with his head getting punted off, blood pouring from the ragged stump of his ruined neck.

(allinmyhead)

The next second, he's back laughing with the others.

Nervously I joke, "Yeah, yeah, I get it. I'll be careful."

"Good, because if you die in there, it's Garcia's job to clean all of you up," Jimmy says.

"Ass," Garcia says.

Jolene pulls a stopwatch from her pocket and collects our flashlights. As soon as Jimmy takes the starting line, she raises her hat over her head.

"All right! On your mark… get set… *go!*" she yells, waving him off.

When it's running, the ride takes about three minutes to wend its way through the massive show building and all its set pieces. I know it has to be longer on foot, especially in the dark.

When Jimmy comes through the ride's end with a triumphant whoop, Jolene declares a time of 6:02.

Garcia goes through next and takes a little longer with a time of 7:16. She's laughing when she comes out, although she seems shaken up.

"Are you okay?" I whisper to her as Jolene sends Monica through.

"I'm fine," Garcia answers quickly.

"What is it?" I ask.

She hesitates. "Just gave myself a case of the heebie-jeebies."

"Maybe it was the ghost of Wallace Vickers?" I propose in a creepy voice.

"Fuck off," she laughs, still a little nervous.

If Garcia looked a little shaken from her run through, Monica looks petrified when she exits the tunnel. She's shaking and checking over her shoulder repeatedly.

"Nine minutes, thirty-six seconds! Monica makes a grand team total of twenty-two minutes, fifty-four seconds!" Jolene pronounces like a game show host.

Before my team decides on a running order, Jolene passes over my buzzing phone.

I check the reminder I set to get a ride home.

I look around the group. "Hey, guys, can one of you give me a ride later?"

Garcia explains, "We all got early shifts tomorrow. Usually, we crash in one of the Rabbit Holes and stay the night. Always room for one more."

I think for only a second before agreeing and shoot Dad a quick text to explain. He won't like it, but I'm having too much fun to care.

After that, we settle on a team order. Lorraine will go first, Lance is second because he is the fastest, and I know the ride the best so I'm last.

With Jolene still keeping time and the other team jeering us on, we start our run.

Lorraine sprints into the darkness and takes long enough that we start wondering if she'll need a rescue party. At 10:32, she exits even though she swears it must have been half that time.

Making up for lost time, Lance sprints through at 6:30 on the dot.

I do the math quickly in my head. In order to win, I need a time of 5:52 or less.

I can do this. I can do this.

"Come on, Noel, you got this!" Lance cheers as I take my place on the starting line. Even the other team, though still razzing us, claps for me. It almost feels like we've been friends for a long time, even though I only met them tonight.

I don't want to let them down.

Jolene yells, "*Go!*"

I'm off like a shot.

After leaving the garage, the hall turns sharply to the right. All at once I'm dropped into darkness deeper than I've ever experienced. Rationally, I know this building has no real windows, but it's still a shock to the system to see the black of true darkness.

Straight shot down the Great Hall...

Feeling the track beside my ankle, I take off down the Great Hall. If the ride was operating, windows with projections of a stormy night would be on either side of me. Usually, blowers flick the curtains toward the ride vehicle while suits of armor lean in menacingly. At the end of the hall, a round window waits where the red eyes of Lord Briarthorne materialize. A spooky voice declares that he'll have our souls, before sending us careening wildly out of control.

Now, I just see black, hearing only my footsteps echoing dully off the walls.

With arms out in front of me, I finally hit the wall at the end. My heart is pounding. I half expect Lord Briarthorne to cackle at me, but it's just the darkness playing tricks.

(allinmyhead)

Sharp left through the catacombs...

The wet air smells of chlorine from the inactive water features in the catacombs. Dozens of inactive animatronic skeletons seem to reach out at me in that darkness. I touch the rail beside my foot, feeling comfort from it.

I'm through the observatory and the laboratory before I hear it.

Something big is moving behind me.

(allinmyhead)

"Very funny, guys." My voice sounds pitiful in the darkness.

From far away, I hear the sound of breathing.

(allinmyhead)

I pick up my pace. The curves in the track tell me I'm just past the torture chamber.

Blinding light flashes before my eyes. A car horn blares in my ears. Flames roar around me.

This isn't happening now. This happened a long time ago.

Mom isn't dying again.

This isn't real, this isn't real, this...

(allinmyhead)

Lights flash on for a moment to highlight a fake ride vehicle, crashed into a wall. Just a fake-out scare halfway through the ride to show riders that they're luckier than those who came before them. The bent and broken skeletons inside, some wearing hats from rival theme parks, look at me dumbly.

It's a joke. A cruel joke. One they can't know hurts me deeply.

Or is it the ghost of Wallace Vickers come for you?

As quickly as it came on, the lights cut out, and I'm blinder than before. My eyes see a photo negative of the crashed car while my ears ring with the sound of a blaring horn.

And now I'm certain something's behind me.

I'm running on instinct.

I want to hide.

I have to hide.

But I can't hide, because I can't see.

Running up the ramp, I flee past the most horrifying rooms in the house that are invisible to me. I slide down the ramp and through an archway meant to be the house's false exit. I'm running into everything in my path and stumbling over the track more times than I count. Somehow, I keep my feet as I keep running. I smell the rich, damp chlorine smell of the swamp, and then I see the light, the literal light at the end of the tunnel, and I just sprint for it.

I LET THE darkness get to me, and I choked.

I beat Lance's time, barely, but it wasn't enough to win. This cloud of defeat surrounds me the rest of the night, and I can't shake this awful feeling that I let my team down.

The winners are crowned after much bowing and speechgiving on Jimmy's part. We descend back into the Rabbit Holes to their "crash pad."

Like the rest of the Lower Park Rabbit Holes, the pad is a concrete box with water stains and no lights. The place seems comfortable with lanterns, a couple old couches and mattresses, a mini-fridge, and an ancient boom box the size of a coffee table.

The music, pot, and alcohol start flowing. There's dancing, laughing, and people making out, and it soon doesn't matter that I let my team down. It barely registers that I'm disobeying about half the C of C, D & E. For a little while, I feel bad that Olivia isn't here. Then I realize that she wouldn't be able to have fun like real Bennytown family members, so I push her to the back of my mind.

Before too long, I start to slow down. Remembering that I have a shift tomorrow morning, the exhaustion hits me.

Suddenly, I need some space and stumble into the hallway. The air is still stuffy here, but cooler. I can almost trick myself into thinking I'm outdoors. My head spins slightly from the beer, and I'm having a hard time keeping my feet.

"You know it's not safe to be around here at night alone, right?"

Jolene's leaning on the wall opposite me. The glow of a joint illuminates her face as she inhales, and she looks especially luscious in the dark. She passes the joint to me, and I take a hit.

"Because of the ghosts?" I giggle, once the coughing stops.

"Among other reasons." She leaves this hanging, like I'm supposed to ask a follow-up question. Although I'm enjoying myself, I'm too tired to care about their ghost talk tonight.

I ask, "So, you're not a family member?"

"No."

"Then how are you even here?"

She takes the joint back, then takes another hit. "You ever been in a shit relationship?"

"I…" I'm surprised when I almost say yes. Olivia may not get my obsession with Bennytown, but we love each other. We'd never do anything to hurt each other, not on purpose at least.

"No," I finally say.

"My last boyfriend, Bogart, was fire to my ice. We were crazy opposites who drove each other nuts but also fucked like crazy people. Too much crazy got to be too crazy. When I called it off, he got even crazier. We were in a bad place when I ended things, and he did something terrible. When she saw what a mess I was, Garcia took me under her wing. Taught me that I got more to offer than what he could bring outta me. I'll never escape the bastard, but I got a home here. That's better than spending your life with someone who doesn't get you, right?"

Again, Olivia's name lands on the tip of my tongue, but I hold it back before it can escape.

"Sounds like he was a jerk. You don't break someone's heart at Bennytown," I mumble the best words I can string together with my head swimming.

She laughs a barking laugh, then crosses the hall and leans next to me. "You're wasted!"

"Am not!" I feebly protest.

Smirking, she takes my right hand in both of hers.

"What are you doing?" I ask.

"You took my spot in the race and you promised me we'd have some fun."

"I never actually promised anything," I clarify.

She pouts, turning my hand over to look at my palm. "What, you don't wanna have *fun*?"

"I like fun, but… I got a girlfriend, all right?"

"Yeah, but where is she? I don't see her here."

"That doesn't—"

"And she don't like you having fun?"

"She does, but—"

"But what? Don't you like me?"

"Yes, but—"

She places my palm against her breast, squeezing my hand, forcing me to cup her. It feels good, like it ought to the way she fills out this thin shirt, but I can't enjoy it, and I don't think it's even just because of Olivia. I'm dizzy and more buzzed than I meant to get, and acutely aware that I'm underground, in a labyrinth of dangerous tunnels I can't find my way out of alone.

What was it the joker said to the thief?

"What, come on, have some fun," she says.

"This isn't right," I say.

"Oh, come on, it's not cheating if it's through clothes."

"That's not—"

"Ugh, fine. If that doesn't lighten you up, maybe this will," she says, pushing my hand across her stomach and down to her, oh god, her cutoffs are unbuttoned. Why didn't I notice her cutoffs are unbuttoned? I need to get out of here. Not down the tunnels, not in the dark, but maybe to the others. Would they just laugh if they heard what happened? And how do I get away without hurting her?

And now she has me touching her in a way I've only ever touched Olivia before. It's through a thin layer of panties. I start to panic again.

"Just relax. Have fun. There are panties in the way, so it's not cheating." She grinds against my hand, closing her eyes and biting her lip. One of her hands drifts over to the bulge in my pants, rubbing me in a way that feels confusingly good.

"See? You're having fun," she says between groans.

I don't want this, but my body doesn't agree with me. My fingers move almost of their own accord. Her stroking even feels good through my pants.

"Just don't think about her. Okay? You're just having fun, and she doesn't have to find out. Relax," Jolene says.

I want to relax and make myself believe that Jolene's right. Olivia never has to find out about this harmless fun, but I'm so confused. Feeling trapped, I'm being made to finger a girl I just met while she jacks me through my pants. Maybe it's the weed combined with the liquor mixed with the fear and the exhaustion, but I can't move, and I'm enjoying it even while I'm not enjoying it.

For a split second, Jolene's no longer beside me. Replacing her is a twisted, rotten corpse, another Bennytown ghost. Her mangled cheeks show nothing but teeth as she leers at me. Dark, viscous fluid leaks from her crushed eye sockets. Suddenly she's even wetter than she was when she started, but not because of what I'm doing. She turned into a corpse, and I'm digging a hole in the flesh of her inner thighs.

I want to vomit and to scream. Where can I run? I don't know where I am, I don't know these people. I don't know anything but the horror before my eyes, and the feeling of my gore-soaked fingers.

And then she's Jolene again, shuddering heavily and collapsing to the floor with a groan, letting go of my hand and my pants.

Giggling to herself, she says, "If only Bogart could see me, he'd shit himself!"

I stumble back into the crash pad, hoping for a place to calm down, but I'm wrong.

The others continued the party without us, but they've decided to do it without most of their clothes. The mattress pile is a writhing mass of increasingly naked flesh. Jimmy is making out with Monica, while Lance is with Garcia. Lorraine fills in wherever she feels like it.

Coming up for air, Garcia cocks her head, inviting me over.

I shake my head.

Your loss, she mouths.

Think of Olivia. Think of Olivia. This is wrong. But, they are my friends and they just want to have fun. Think of Olivia, think of how much fun we would have here.

And suddenly, the plan makes sense. It'll take a little doing, but I can throw it together. Maybe soon.

Collapsing onto a nearby couch, I ignore what's going on around me and pass out into an uneasy slumber.

PENNY
1998

Penny spent the last hour shadowing the couple. As a Day-walker, her duty was to search and remove any troublemakers from Bennytown.

If they went peacefully, after a nice conversation backstage, she'd have them escorted to the front of the park.

If they didn't behave, then they were removed to the Zoo, where they were no longer her problem. If the couple continued their current behavior, Penny was sure they'd wind up in the Zoo.

Although they hadn't done anything illegal yet, they were clearly high on something. They were jittery, inappropriate and all over each other. Taking disgusting pictures up against statues or costumed characters, the guy had the nerve to grab one of Mary Annette's big fake hooters, though he was hardly the first. When they lingered a long time in gift shops, the girl looked longingly at the jewelry but hadn't stolen anything yet. Penny knew she would try to grab something by day's end.

Every half hour, usually after a ride, they started some screaming match, only to make out and continue walking the park afterwards.

I left Langley for this? Penny thought.

The thought came more often now that she had been here for a year. Bennytown's incentives package impressed her more than anything the government had to offer, especially under this Philanderer-in-Chief. If it meant following tweekers every day for the rest of her life, Penny didn't know if she could take it much longer.

Just get enough in the nest egg so Luke doesn't have any student loan debt, and you can retire comfortably. Another year, two tops.

The couple roamed the Island of Legends' statue garden. They took stupid picture after stupid picture at each statue until they got to the land's tasteful recreation of the Birth of Venus. Out of nowhere, the man turned around, locked eyes onto Penny and zoomed toward her.

The people she tailed weren't usually on the lookout for suspicious, old ladies. Penny tried to escape, but the man caught up to her.

"Hey, lady, can I ask you somethin'?" he asked.

"What can I do for you, young man?" Penny responded, adding an extra hint of doddering to her voice.

He thrust his cheap disposable camera into her hands. "Can you take a picture of us by the naked clam babe? I'm gonna propose to my chick."

Now ain't he a winner, Penny thought.

Still, the request was earnest enough. Since the couple wore buttons on their shirts saying, "THIS IS MY 1ST VISIT!" Penny decided to cut Romeo some slack.

Walking up to the girl by the statue of Venus, he got down on one knee and pulled a small box from his pocket, presenting it to her. Penny obligingly took a picture.

"Hey, babe, so, let's get married, right?" he said.

Shakespeare couldn't have said it better himself.

The girl looked at him for a while, then burst out laughing. "God, no!"

Still laughing, she walked away. For posterity, Penny took another picture.

The boy snatched the camera back and ran after the girl without a word. Penny waited to follow them until some distance separated them.

She'd seen a lot of proposals at Bennytown. Nine times out of ten they were successful and touchingly, beautiful.

The other one time out of ten was unpredictable. Usually the poor brokenhearted schlubs left Bennytown. If they were desperate to get their money's worth, they stayed in the park with their date as if their life hadn't just gone up in flames.

Sometimes the situation turned to violence. Penny witnessed guys beating on their girlfriends. One psycho flung his girl into Dinosaur Lagoon, and then jumped in to make sure she didn't come up.

So far, Penny didn't have a good enough read on this couple to know how far things would go. She bet on a bad outcome.

The couple hopped into the line for Candy Mountain Swirler, dropping out of sight.

Penny tapped her earpiece. "Need some Daywalkers at Candy Mountain Swirler, got an imminent domestic and need backup."

She bought a Churro Raft at Ice Cream Villa and took a seat, enjoying the snack while keeping an eye on the ride's exit. Going by the digital display in front of the ride, the lovely couple would be in line for at least half an hour. That was plenty of time to get everyone in place.

Within minutes of her call, other Daywalkers appeared in the crowd. Montoya and Dorn pushed a baby stroller and watched Benny the Bunny dancing at a meet-and-greet area. Serkov, with his long white beard and cane, strolled slowly past the Yi twins as they argued loudly about some basketball game.

Per protocol, they were on an observe-and-report basis. They kept an eye on the perpetrators and refrained from interfering. Unless something happened.

In the background, they heard a woman screaming. That was nothing out of the ordinary, since people screamed on even the most sedate Bennytown rides. The Candy Mountain Swirler was no exception.

The problem with this scream was that it kept getting louder.

As Penny looked up, she watched the girl come careening down the side of Candy Mountain. Bouncing off of a jutting decorative candy cane and pinwheeling, the poor girl slammed into the ground by Penny's feet with a wet splat.

Covered in the young woman's blood, Penny froze in shock. Somehow the broken girl was still alive. Despite her head being cracked open with brains spilling out and being surrounded by a lake of blood, the woman still clung to life. Her mouth bobbed open and close like a fish, silently hissing through a blood-filled throat. Her bulging, ruined eyes searched for comfort and finally locked onto Penny's face.

Then the girl fell still.

As people started to notice, Penny gathered her wits enough to call for a containment team while the other Daywalkers created a perimeter.

When she knelt down and got a good look at the woman, Penny recognized her from the marriage proposal just minutes earlier. The white trash clothes, the cowboy hat, the button on her chest.

MY NAME IS **JOLENE BEAUREGARD**
TODAY IS MY FIRST VISIT TO BENNYTOWN!
ISN'T THAT EXCITING?

NOEL
2019

It's been a good day so far. Not just a good day, but a *great* day.

Even though my night in the Rabbit Holes with the others was strange, my head has been clearer ever since. Everything makes sense, and I know what I want in life.

I have good friends, a good job, and a great future.

To top it off, even the weather's fantastic. The weather this morning is cool and dry, which is a nice change from the regular humidity. It's the perfect weather for walking Bennytown with my girlfriend.

Olivia's dressed to the nines for our meal at the Green Door Society. Even though Bennytown doesn't open for another hour and a half, I got her a special pass to join me at the family members only function for my first ever Rubber Duck Rally.

At this hour, most of the few hundred people look like they need coffee.

Since I'm riding high on life and Bennytown, I don't need anything extra today. I'm trying not to think about Jolene and focusing on the beautiful day.

Most of the watchers lean against the railings around one side of Dinosaur Lagoon. People like me who are familiar with the layout jockey for positions on the second floor of the ride's queue building. This spot gives a better view of the jungle and the placid lagoon water. A few costumed characters dressed as Benny & Friends, as well as a few land-appropriate dinosaur costumes, entertain the crowd. I look around for Garcia or any of the others to introduce to Olivia. Aside from some family members from the Safari Lodge, I don't see anyone I know.

Serenely, Olivia smiles up at me.

"So it's a *little* fun, right?" I ask.

"A little fun, yeah," she agrees. "When you promised some off-hours fun, I was expecting something a little more provocative. Like a virgin sacrifice or a cult orgy."

(Jolene)

"Nah, that comes later," I joke, although it doesn't feel very funny.

She raises an eyebrow, then laughs.

It's good to see her laughing again. Things have been tense between us for a while, and they got worse after I brought up this Green Door Society idea. I've been trying to make it up to her because I want today to be perfect. I know today will fix everything.

We'll watch the race, wander around a little until lunch, then we'll go to the Green Door Society, meet Elle, have lunch, and I'll spirit her away for a private "rendezvous."

Then she'll remember how I feel about her, and things will be back to normal.

I still don't know how to feel about the party in the Rabbit Holes. Everything that happened in there is on me, and I'll have to carry the guilt with me until my dying day. As long as I make things right with Olivia today, I think I can move forward with my life.

Part of me wonders what it would have been like to join them. What would it have been like to completely let go? How incredible would it have been? How *crazy* would it have been?

Would I lose all self-respect because I'd betrayed Olivia? Or for another, harder to define reason?

(Don't forget what you saw in the dark!)

I force that thought born of drugs and scary stories told in darkness to the back of my mind. The night of the party was dark and strange, but it helped me realize that today would be the ideal day to seduce Olivia at Bennytown. If I couldn't find a better dark corner, their crash pad would work perfectly.

Thank you, Garcia.

If I can carry out this master plan, then everything will be back on track, creating a balance between my work and home lives.

A woman from Human Resources announces the start of the rally over the loudspeaker. Dramatically, she holds the first large plastic tub of rubber duckies over her head and pours it into the water.

The crowd goes nuts.

We watch for a while as HR people spill tub after tub into the water, thousands of bright yellow rubber duckies begin floating down the lagoon.

"How long do you think it'll take?" Olivia asks.

"I have no idea. Fifteen minutes, maybe?" I guess.

"Cool," she says, staring down at the water.

"I'm glad you came today," I say.

"Why wouldn't I?" she asks, eyes never leaving the water.

"I know I've been stupid lately, and sometimes I've made bad choices," I say.

Her eyes drift to me, then back to the water. "Keep going."

"I want us to work. But I'm also not giving up on everything I've made here. I shouldn't have to," I say. She doesn't say anything, so I continue, "I just want to know that you'll support me in what I want to do like I'd support you in whatever you want to do."

"Within reason, yes," she says. "But Bennytown's become your obsession. I don't want you to have to choose between me and Bennytown, because I'm not sure which you'd pick."

I take her in my arms and plant a kiss on her lips. "I'd pick you. No question."

"Promise?" she asks.

"Promise," I say, kissing her smile. "Though I'd prefer it if I could pick both of you."

She rolls her eyes at me. "Calling Tommy back is looking better every day."

I'd give her a comeback, but someone's tapping my shoulder. I break apart from Olivia long enough to see Kathleen with a disgruntled look on her face, hair slightly askew.

"Kathleen! Hey, glad to see you. This is—"

"Olivia, I know," Kathleen says. "Can I have a word, Noel?"

"Sure," I say.

"In private?"

"Awww, come on, we fought for the good spots to see the ducks." I'm trying to keep the moment light. By the look on her face, I know that what Kathleen wants to talk about is anything but light.

Kathleen licks her lips, nervous. "Look, I've had a few people call in sick today. I need you on shift."

"What?" I ask.

"Yeah, I need you to work. I know it's last minute, but—"

"But I got a deferral," I say. "From up top."

"And I understand this, which is why I'm asking you, as a personal favor, to *please* help out for a shift."

This isn't her usual, forceful way of asking. It's almost like she's begging me.

I respect Kathleen almost as much as I respect Dad. She's an adult who's treated me fairly. And she certainly hasn't treated me like a kid like everyone else. Normally I'd listen to anything she's got to say.

"I'm sorry. I really can't," I say, looking down at Olivia. "This is a special occasion."

Kathleen sighs, quickly scrawling something on the back of a business card and forcing it into my hand.

"My cell. If you change your mind." Kathleen looks like she wants to say more but turns on her heels and forces her way through the crowd instead.

"Thanks," Olivia says, smiling broadly.

"No problem," I say. "Because today *is* a special occasion. We're here. We're happy. And we're gonna have a free lunch at one of the most exclusive restaurants on earth."

"Fuck yeah," Olivia says.

I wince. "Do you really have to, you know, say that here?"

Olivia looks at me like she thinks I'm joking. When she can tell I'm not, she says, "Really?"

I know I've said something wrong. "Can we pretend that I maybe didn't say that?"

"You can pretend whatever you want, but it doesn't change anything." Olivia sounds more amused than anything else. Phew. She cranes her neck to see if any ducks have made their way around the bend.

"Anything yet?" I ask.

"Nothing yet, but soon, I think."

Curious, I sneak a look at the business card Kathleen slipped me. She put a message right above her number.

THESE PEOPLE ARE DANGEROUS

WHEN YOU NEED HELP, CALL ME

PEDRO PARROT'S DIDN'T win, but at least Kathleen'll be happy the Bengineers didn't win either, once she stops being so dramatic.

This year's top prize went to some guy in maintenance with a Lakers-themed rubber ducky that looks like something chewed on it. A duck from the Safari Lodge was in the Top 20, so we should get some gift cards.

After the rally, Olivia and I hang around Bennytown Plaza waiting for the park to open to the public. After my talk with Kathleen and our brief disagreement on language, things are a little cooler between Olivia and me than I'd like. I try pointing out one of the salt-spreading radiation suit characters to her. This one is made to look like Snapper Gator, but before I can point him out, he disappears into a Rabbit Hole.

Olivia rarely dresses up, and she looks especially hot in the slinky green over-the-shoulder dress she's wearing. Elle didn't give me a dress code for today, so I'm hoping I don't look like a complete idiot in my interview outfit.

When the time comes, we reenter the park and make our way to Journey through Americana. Walking down the simulated small-town street, we see more bald eagle statues, flage, stars and stripes than you think could exist in one place. Its buildings are a mongrel mishmash of American eras. Independence Hall is next to an old west street which sits beside a disco with music pouring out the doors. Every other era in between is represented by a ride, gift shop, or semi-tasteful food cart.

Following the directions Elle gave me, we find the red door on the post office right behind Independence Hall and knock three times. A slot opens at about eye height, and I pass our reservation card through.

A Secret Service guard wearing a tux opens the door and quickly motions us down a short hallway. Closing and locking the outer door, he guides us to another door. This one is green and ornately carved with bizarre, ancient, interlocking designs. On this door, he knocks four times.

The carved designs shift and twist until they seem to come alive. When I remind myself of the skill of the Bengineers. I know it's just some exceptional mechanical trickery.

The wooden door swings open silently, revealing an up-ward-curving, green-carpeted staircase. A finely dressed hostess who could easily be a runway model greets us.

"Mr. Hallstrom and Miss Verne? Please, come this way; Ms. Dorian has been expecting you," she says, leading us up the stairs.

"They don't go light on ceremony here, do they?" Olivia whispers.

"Doesn't seem so," I chuckle.

"The *second* someone busts out a dagger and asks me to get naked, I'm bailing."

"But what if it's me?" I ask, feigning hurt. Olivia laughs.

Along the curving staircase are framed black-and-white pictures from different eras. Many people in tuxes and gowns are wearing Benny the Bunny masks. These aren't the cheap plastic masks they sell in the gift shops but seem carved out of wood. The empty looking eyes are weirdly angular.

The captions read things like:

BENGINEERS' NEW YEAR'S EVE GALA - 1975

OLYMPICS PARTY - USA WINS! - 1984

NEW RECRUITS - 2012

With the exception of the fashions, I have a hard time telling them apart. All show nearly identical poses with mystery people raising glasses in a toast to the camera.

At the top of the stairs is a room that is equal parts museum and elegant restaurant. Immaculate tables, lush carpets, and polished wooden walls are lined with framed pictures, vintage posters and maps, and glass cases full of artifacts from Bennytown's early years. Smaller, private chambers branch off from the main room.

Aside from the staff, we appear to be the only ones here.

"Cool, huh?" I whisper.

"It's getting there," Olivia admits.

The hostess leads us to one of the private doors at the edge of the room, taking us into a dim, elegant chamber decorated with more framed pictures of Bennytown's history, a glowing Wurlitzer jukebox, and a hardwood table in the center. Beautifully etched into the table is a take on da Vinci's Vitruvian Man, replacing the man with his arms and legs spread out with an artistic rendering of Benny the Bunny in the same pose.

The three waiters standing at attention stare at us and smile politely.

The hostess explains, "Ms. Dorian asked me to personally relay her apologies for being late, assuring you that she will be here soon. Until then she has asked that you make yourselves comfortable and feel free to order."

"With pleasure," Olivia says, making for the table. The instant she moves, one of the waiters pulls out a chair for her, while another puts a menu into her hands. I take a seat next to her, only for the waiters to do the same for me.

One asks, "Could we start you with drinks?"

"You check ID here?" Olivia asks.

Shamefaced, the waiter says, "Lamentably, madame, we must."

"Coke, then," she says.

"Me too," I say.

"Very well. Could I interest you in some appetizers, or would you prefer a few minutes to review the menu?"

The menu is enormous, with very small print. I say, "I could use a few minutes."

"Very well, sir," the waiter says, ushering the other three out.

Olivia looks the menu up and down, eyes wide. "You say this is on Dorian, right?"

"Yeah, why?" I ask.

"There's no prices listed. And if I'm not paying…"

"You're looking at the lobster, aren't you?"

"For starters," Olivia says. For a slim girl, Olivia's always has an admirable appetite.

Now that we've got some privacy, and some minutes before company arrives, maybe we can indulge in some other appetites.

I pull her chair closer to mine. For a moment, she looks surprised, but when I pull her close and kiss her, the surprise turns to a smile.

"Hi," I say.

"Hey," she says, kissing me back. "How long do you think it'll be before they're back with drinks?"

"Probably a few minutes."

"I can live with a few minutes."

She kisses me again, and for the first time in a very long time, we make out. We trade soft kisses at first, then deeper, more passionate ones, getting lost in the moment as we pull closer to each other.

"I've missed you," I say.

"I've missed you too," she says.

"You know, I love you. More than anything."

"More than anything?"

"More than *anything*." I'm pretty sure that's true.

She shudders.

"What's wrong?" I ask.

"This… place. I feel like I just walked over a grave. It's like I'm not wanted here."

"*I* want you here."

"I know, but I don't know if that's enough."

"Let me show you some places here where you can be wanted and feel at home. Hidden surprises I can share with you. I know spots here where we can just be ourselves and have some private time," I say.

She looks at me, hesitant. "Noel, I—"

The door's opening.

"Shit," she says, straightening herself out.

Elle Dorian, completely stunning, walks in. Her dress is provocative, short enough that it shows a lot of leg accentuated by her heels, low enough that her impressive cleavage is highlighted, and tight enough that you can't miss everything that she clearly wants you to see.

The dress is a slightly richer shade of green than Olivia's.

"So sorry I'm late, that meeting went way longer than expected," she says, walking over to us. I stand up to greet her, and she pulls me tightly into a hug, kissing me on each cheek. She's so close, pressing against me so tightly. I'm still a little geared up from making out with Olivia, so I try to back off so she won't notice, but she looks down and smiles mischievously.

She turns her attention to Olivia. "And you must be his girlfriend, Olivia, right?"

Politely, she shakes Olivia's hand. Much less politely, Olivia says, "Charmed."

Thankfully, Olivia's annoyed enough with her that she can't see me blush.

"I'm glad you could make it, since it's not every day someone saves my life," Elle says.

"Well, it's not like he couldn't show. Your name *is* on his checks," Olivia says.

I try changing the subject. "Nothing bad in the meeting, I hope?"

"Only tedious. Lots of bigwigs and Bengineers putting together the final details for the new land announcement we're revealing at the Sixtieth Birthday celebration," she says.

"New land? That's really happening?" I ask, excited. Pretty much everyone in Bennytown's got their own rumors of the legendary eighth land being added.

"Yeah. You want a preview?" Elle asks, guiding us to an old framed park map on the wall. She pulls me gently by the wrist.

She points to the east half of the Upper Park on the old map, beyond Journey through Americana and Primordial World.

From her purse she pulls a card with a stylized logo of the words "NEW SPARTA."

"Welcome to New Sparta, Bennytown's new high-tech, superhero-themed expansion. It will recreate the most famous location from the Superhero City franchise that Dorian Studios recently acquired," Elle says proudly.

"Wow," I say.

"You don't think the whole superhero thing's played out?" Olivia asks.

"Our investors certainly don't think so, and neither does the moviegoing public. If you'd like some convincing, how about I give you a sneak peek?" Elle continues, smiling. She goes into further details, equal parts trying to win over Olivia and impress me. Normally I'd kill to hear something like this about a new land, but something about this map seems off.

There's something in Happy Hollow.

I spot an igloo covered in icicles with a happy walrus waving out of its front door. This map is definitely old and features a walrus artifact that nobody's caught. Before I know it, I'm planning something. It may be something, it may be nothing, but I think I've got a lead no one else has ever tried.

Then Olivia finds her way of bringing me back to earth.

"So, what exactly do you do at these *business meetings*?" Olivia says, only nice enough to not actually put air quotes around the words.

I start, "Olivia—"

Elle laughs. "Don't worry about it, Noel. I get this all the time."

She guides us back to the table. "I may only be eighteen, but with a name like Dorian I have to be more than that. I've been learning the ropes since I was twelve, and once I get my MBA, I'll take my rightful place within the company until it's my turn to embrace my destiny."

"Sounds like a heckuva plan," I say, cutting off Olivia before she can make any other snide comments.

"It's not much, but I mean to take my role in the family seriously. For now, I don't know about you two, but I'm starving," she says, smiling her movie star smile.

As if on cue and probably at Elle's pre-arranged instruction, waiters come by with some fancy, dripping garlic bread and calamari then take our orders. I can't help but pick Elle's brain on New Sparta. I have to know absolutely everything that's going to be in this land. Rides. Shows. Shops and restaurants. Since this is the first new land that's been added in my lifetime, it's a big deal.

Elle plays coy, at first, and she tries to stall with eating when the main courses come. Over the course of the meal, she hands out tidbits a little at a time, ultimately giving me every amazing detail.

Elle's easy to talk to. If it weren't for our wildly different backgrounds, I could see us being friends easily. She's more laid-back than you'd think someone looking like her and with her money would be, and she knows more about Bennytown's history and goings-on than pretty much anyone.

I want to ask her about the walrus, that map, and what it all means, but I have to be cautious. I know that inquiry is enough of a minefield that I don't want to chance it.

Before I know it, we're through with our food and the waiter's asking us if we want any dessert.

"All of it is delicious, but I recommend the chocolate mousse, it's to *die* for," Elle says.

"Sounds good to me," I say, smiling.

For what feels like the first time in a long time, I turn to Olivia.

"Yeah, whatever," she says, pulling a pack of cigarettes from her purse. "Got a place I can light up?"

"Anywhere's fine," Elle says. "But most tend to smoke in the lounge."

"Cool," she says, getting up and looking down at me.

"I'm good," I say, sitting back in my chair and enjoying being full.

"Sure," Olivia says, rolling her eyes and leaving the room.

Elle and I are alone now, and suddenly I've got nothing to say. No questions, no talk of New Sparta, just her looking incredibly hot, and me sitting here being me.

Elle must sense the awkwardness. "I'm sorry."

"Sorry? About what?" I ask.

"When I came in here, I interrupted a private moment," she says.

"It's fine, we were just talking about—"

She places a reassuring hand on mine. "Don't worry about it. If you want a few minutes of alone time in here, that can be arranged. The staff here is very discreet, believe me."

I do believe her. I honestly don't doubt anything Elle Dorian has to say.

The door opens, and Olivia reenters. Elle removes her hand from mine, but I don't know if it was quickly enough. She stands up, pulling her phone from her purse.

"I have to make a call!" she says dramatically, making her way to the door. "It'll take a little while, so I think you two should get a head start on dessert."

She tips me a conspiratorial wink and leaves, ignoring Olivia's scowl.

Slowly, Olivia starts back for the table. I get up to meet her.

A blind, confused desperation sweeps over me. I have to do this now. *We* have to do this now. I need her now more than I've needed her at any other moment of my life. I just need to do this to get Elle and Jolene and every other distraction out of my head.

Instead of sitting, Olivia walks up to the old map and stares at it. I walk up behind her, putting my hands on her waist.

"That was a fast cigarette," I say, breathing into her hair.

"Yeah, well, the lounge's ambiance left a lot to be desired," she says.

"Mhm," I say, nuzzling her neck.

"Do you know what they have in there? A wall of pictures of dead people. Accident victims. Crime scene photos. All underneath a plaque that says, 'THE NEED FOR ORDER: LEST WE FORGET.' How fucked is that?"

"You know, Elle told me these rooms are pretty private," I whisper into her ear.

She pushes away, disgusted. "Have you listened to a word I've said? Have you even noticed me since she entered the room?"

"What?" I ask.

"Oh, don't *what* me; you know damn well what I'm talking about. Yeah, we might've gotten a little hot and heavy, but when she walks in, it's like I don't even exist."

"It's not like that," I say.

"Yeah, it is, and it's not just her. It's this place. I get that Bennytown used to be your crutch. Ever since you took this job, you've changed. You said you'd choose me, but you chose this place. This *fucking* place," she says.

"Olivia," I try to come up with the right words and fumble, "It's not like that. I did this, today, because I wanted it to be special. For us."

"For *you*. You want to fuck her? Fine, enjoy. You want to fuck Bennytown? Go for it! I think you'll be happy together," she hisses, storming away.

"Olivia!" I yell, grabbing her wrist. I want to break something. I want to break a lot of somethings. I want… I want… *what do I want right now?*

"Noel!" she shoots back, looking at her wrist. "You're… you're hurting me."

"I did this for us! I did this for *you*! I thought this was supposed to be special!" I yell.

She looks at me with a look that might very well be terror.

"What have they done to you, Noel?" she asks.

I want to tell her, to make her understand what they've done for me, for *us*.

I take a deep breath and say, *"I believe in Bennytown."*

BOBBI
1993

"I can't see a bloody thing in this damn mask," Bobbi Zimbardo said, struggling to adjust her wooden Green Door Society mask.

"Hush now, dear," her mother whispered fussily, pushing Bobbi's hands away from her mask. "It's not polite to complain during the procedure."

Bobbi crossed her arms across her chest petulantly.

There had been a time when she thought it was the greatest thing in the world to be the daughter of one of Bennytown's creators. Growing up, the park had been her playground and Bobbi enjoyed the life of privilege that being the child of a Bengineer provided. Even when her mother spoke of great responsibilities to come.

Everything changed around the time she turned twenty. Her mother dragged her to a lot of boring meetings with other Bengineers, where they'd lecture her about the secret true history of Bennytown. They told her that as the daughter of a founder, she was expected to live up to a great legacy. Since that normally didn't mean much but being bored a couple hours a week, Bobbi didn't mind the responsibility.

The rituals where she had to put on a mask were just the worst.

The man tied to the table stopped screaming after the doctors removed his tongue and muzzled him. Bobbi hated to admit that she was grateful for the silence. She could now hear Mother's whispers in case a quiz came later, like it inevitably would.

Mother narrated, "After the doctors complete the glossectomy and gonadectomy, tubes are inserted into the subject for the purposes of feeding, hydration, waste removal and a steady feed of our special, proprietary cocktail of drugs that make sleep unnecessary while keeping them in peak condition."

The subject didn't care too much for this part of the procedure. Bobbi felt more concern for the hardwood table beneath the patient. Bobbie hoped the elaborate etching of Benny the Bunny as the Vitruvian Man on its surface wouldn't get ruined. At least, she hoped that it was a problem the cleaning staff could fix.

The surgeons installed the tubes quickly compared to the more invasive procedures. Mother gripped her shoulder.

"Now the fun begins." Mother was unable to keep the glee from her voice since the Redeemer suits always had been one of her favorite inventions.

"I'm sure," Bobbi said.

A piece at a time, the suit came together around the subject. At a glance, it looked almost like one of Bennytown's character suits, but cruder and thicker. The suit appeared better suited to fighting fires than entertaining children. By Mother's descriptions, fighting fires was much closer to the Redeemer's actual job description. Per one of her lengthy speeches, the costume was thick due to a complex array of servo-mechanisms and radiation shielding that would make the wearer stronger, more durable, and more capable of maintaining Bennytown's peace.

During the day, they patrolled the borders and made sure the salt line was kept whole. At night, they performed the same duties and were the only "family members" allowed inside Bennytown during the dark hours.

Better them than someone useful or important.

At Mother's instructions, the subject tested the flexibility of the hands and feet as they were slowly transformed into Stumbles.

Curious, Bobbi asked, "What did this one do?"

"Chronic tardiness, alcoholism, and violent outbursts. We've cut him slack for eight years after he witnessed his partner die on the escalators. Our patience has run out. For more details, you'll have to talk to human resources," Mother offered grimly.

"That's not necessary," Bobbi replied.

When nothing but the man's pained, fearful head stuck out of the Stumbles body, the doors to the room swung open.

Nicolas Dorian, twenty-nine-year-old son of Fletcher Dorian and heir to the Dorian fortune, stood solemnly in the doorway. He was as well dressed and masked as any other member of the Green Door Society. Pushing a wheelchair containing a skeleton covered in pale skin, he delivered a special guest.

Fletcher Dorian had seen better days, but the mask covered what had become of his face. For once, Bobbi was glad for the masks because that meant she didn't have to kiss his withered cheek.

Mr. Dorian was wheeled around for the final stage of redemption. While everyone was distracted, Nicolas slipped in next to Bobbi the moment he was on his own, running a hand through her fiery red hair in anticipation.

"I missed you last night," she whispered.

He glanced to see if they'd been overheard. "I missed you too."

"Where were you?"

"Board meeting," he said. Ever since his father's health had taken a turn, there had been more of these "board meetings" to attend. Bobbi wondered, idly, how many of these meetings were real and how many were engineered to keep her and Nicolas apart.

For close to three years now, they had been seeing each other since she had that brief internship with him at Mother's insistence. He was so hot and well connected. Although he wasn't terribly bright, there was only glorious fire between them. A night didn't pass that she didn't dream of their fairytale ending.

On the other hand, their parents couldn't have disagreed with the match more. Time and again, Mother speechified about how seeing Nicolas was a bad idea, and he was getting even more of the same from his father. Over time, the star-crossed part of their romance had become an inconvenience. She was hoping to get past it, so she could have that happily ever after.

Somehow, she'd prove how right they were together.

Fletcher Dorian cleared his ancient throat and began the invocation.

"Redemption is a hard-fought path that few earn and fewer seek. Those who don't seek it can become something more, with sacrifice. Bless you, my poor boy, and know that what you are becoming will be far greater than you ever were," Fletcher Dorian said. There was a wooden mallet in his weak, warped hands. With great difficulty, he held it above his head.

The now crying subject stared at the mallet, a difficult task considering the metal probe aimed at the corner of his eye socket by one of the surgeons.

Dorian swung the mallet.

He missed, hitting the side of the subject's face and drawing blood.

Given the mallet again, he took another swing. This time he hit the table, the mallet falling from his hands.

Something wasn't right. Monitors on the side of his chair started beeping. Dorian doubled over.

The doctors, Mother, and Nicolas ran to him, while Dorian said weakly, "The ritual! Complete… the ritual!"

Nodding, Bobbi picked the mallet off the ground, approached the doctor still holding the spike to the corner of the subject's eye, and pounded the probe into the subject's brain.

"Is that all?" she asked the doctor.

"One more, in the other eye," he said, pulling out another probe and lining it up. With another powerful swing, she pounded it into the subject's head.

The doctor looked at the subject briefly, then nodded to Bobbi.

The lobotomy was complete.

Fletcher Dorian lay on the floor, slipping away a breath at a time.

Bobbi comforted Nicolas, who had taken his mask off and was now weeping openly.

"Nicolas, Bobbi, come closer," Dorian said.

They did as they were told, kneeling beside him. With one weak hand, he pushed his son's hand into Bobbi's.

"Keep the family alive. I will protect Bennytown, but it's up to you two to keep the family alive. Caroline… Caroline… won't you show yourself even now?"

At that, his eyes closed. Instead of beeping, his monitors now just held a single, long, high tone.

Fletcher Dorian was dead.

Bobbi was sad, but only just barely. Fletcher Dorian had always been like a father to her, but she just saw his death as an obstacle being removed for her happily ever after. When Nicolas squeezed her hand and buried his face in her shoulder, she felt a momentary twinge of sadness. She watched blandly when the Bengineers put Stumbles' head on the Redeemer with the understanding that it would never come off.

It was time to start working on that happily ever after.

NOEL
2019

Olivia's gone. It's my fault. I drove her away. She didn't understand, and nothing I said could make her understand. I shouldn't have started a... *ruckus*, not at the Green Door Society, not when I was invited there by Elle. This special day was ruined by my mistake.

Somehow, I'll make it up to both of them.

While I take a minute to compose myself, I stand outside of the Green Door Society, wondering how exactly I got here and what happens next.

I'm not alone.

There are three Sack Head Kids waiting when I exit the building. They stand on a bench, hunched over, cocking their faceless heads at me, moving jerkily like nervous birds.

Vultures.

I want to scatter them and force them to take the bags off their heads. Honestly, they'll die if they don't, but they scuttle away before I can move. One of them even looks back at me, and I feel something like pity coming off of them.

I don't want pity.

I don't *need* pity.

I don't...

Olivia's gone.

Great.

We've fought before, and while this one seems worse than most, it's not the actual worst by my recollection. Just because it isn't the worst doesn't make my current situation any less infuriating.

I could call Dad, but I don't want him to know this happened, not yet at least.

I could take an Uber or the bus. But I don't feel like dealing with weirdos today.

There's only one option left, though I'm dreading the strings that'll come attached to it.

I pull the card from my pocket and punch in the number.

She picks up on the third ring.

"Hey, Kathleen? Yeah, you said to call if I needed help…"

HER CAR'S A lot nicer than I would've expected, but I guess a few decades at Bennytown can afford you perks like a new hybrid SUV with an "I Love My Chow Chow" bumper sticker. Staying oddly quiet since meeting me after her evening shift, she answers with only the shortest quips to the most basic pleasantries, even as we enter the car.

The moment we hit the freeway, all the tension leaves her body, like letting the air out of a balloon.

"Are you okay?" I ask.

"Maybe. Probably. Just glad to be away from their ears so I can tell you what you need to hear," she says, adjusting her hair.

"What do I need to hear?" I ask.

"Your life's in danger," she says bluntly.

I wait for a punch line, but one doesn't come.

"What?"

"Quit. Quit now, and you might still have a chance. I'd fire you if I could, but there's people above my pay grade who want to keep you around. I don't know how many hooks Benny-town's got in you already. If you leave now, it may lose interest."

(*ruckus*)

I don't have time for this shit after the day that I've had. "Can we not?"

"Not what?"

"Look, I'm sick and tired of everybody telling me what I should and shouldn't do about Bennytown!" I exclaim, letting out my pent-up frustration.

"Noel, look at me," she says.

I don't feel like it, but I ultimately look since I respect Kathleen. She tugs on her hair, and soon it's a wig she's pulling from her bald scalp and tossing onto the backseat. Only… only she's not bald. Her scalp is a patchwork quilt of scar tissue that's so horrifying I want to look away, yet so captivating I can't.

"Are you done?" she asks.

"Yeah," I say, entranced.

"You want answers?"

"Answers for what?"

"The strange shit I know you've seen around Bennytown. What happened that night you got stuck in the Sky Bucket. Everything that might make you reconsider not quitting, if my little accident here doesn't convince you?" she says, cocking a thumb at her scalp.

Though I'm still horrified with what happened to her, I can't stop myself from saying, "Say your piece."

After a long moment's consideration, she asks, "How much do you know about Fletcher Dorian?"

Easily, I answer, "He was a genius at whatever he put his mind to, a classic rags-to-riches self-made billionaire, died a tragic death from a strange disease…"

I could go on, but I let it hang there.

She nods softly. "And all that's true, but not the full picture. Did I ever tell you I used to know him?"

Okay, didn't see that one coming.

"No," I say. Though I want to ask a million questions about what he was like, I figure it's more polite to let her finish before I start pestering her.

"I used to work as a show hostess in Creepy Corner's old Frankenstein's Lab Experience. It was before your time, but do you know anything about it?"

"A little," I say.

It closed down a few years before I was born, but I've read about it. In one of Fletcher Dorian's first ideas for Creepy Corner, guests were strapped into chairs in the middle of Frankenstein's lab. From there, they watched him bring his creation to life. When the lights went out, scared guests got the impression that the monster was stomping around them with the help of speakers in their chairs. Shifting wall facades combined with flashes of light made it seem as if the lab was being torn apart. Although it sounded cool, the ride was closed when they broke ground for Escape from Briarthorne Manor.

She continues, "Back then, I was a cute, perky thing full of smiles. I had a beautiful blond ponytail that made me look a shade more American than apple pie, and I was *damn* good at my job. I could get folk to smile even when they didn't want to. Like any Bennytown family member, I'd already seen some strange shit, but I just brushed it off since I had my own problems to deal with."

"*You* had problems?" I ask, skeptical. With the possible exception of her thinking my life's in danger and the reveal of what's beneath her wig, she's always appeared to be one of the most together people I've ever met.

"It was the '70s. If you didn't have some problems, you weren't havin' a good time. Like I was sayin', I could excuse a lot of what I thought I saw because I believed in Bennytown."

Instinctively, I say, *"I believe in Bennytown."*

Kathleen winces. "One day, everything changed. That beautiful blond ponytail of mine got stuck in the lab's moving walls in the middle of a show and ripped my scalp clean off. I never screamed so loud or saw so much blood in my life. The worst part was some folk just saw me and laughed, thinking it was all part of the show."

The image makes me sick.

Kathleen continues, "They said I must've stepped off my platform the wrong way, but that's bull. That wasn't *no* accident. Someone tugged my tail, put it in the shifting walls. The doctors offered skin grafts and pleasantries. Park lawyers and investigators tried explaining to me how I caused this accident but said they'd have my back. I was in a bad place, wonderin' if I'd made the wrong move leaving Tennessee, wonderin' if I'd be best off making good with my mom after our last fight that made me run off and join this circus in the first place. I even thought about just climbing the stairs to the hospital roof and steppin' off. And then, *he* came to visit."

She sighs, half-pained, half-nostalgic. "We'd all seen the pictures, but he was more handsome than I'd ever imagined. Just being near him, filled me with a wonderful feeling. I felt like what he was saying was right and that anyone who didn't believe it was a damn fool. He apologized, covered my medical bills and told me that if I was discreet about my little accident, then I was welcome to a fund with my name on it. I took the hush money 'cause I didn't wanna go back home with my tail between my legs. He convinced me that staying on would prove my bravery, and that I'd be an inspiration for the Bennytown family. Like the starry-eyed twenty-year-old I was, I listened. I took on a job at the Safari Lodge, and I've been there ever since. You know why?"

"Loyalty?" I suggest.

"At first, yes. And sometimes, he'd come by to check on me and see how I was doing. Like a stupid little schoolgirl with a crush I encouraged it, because he was handsome and nice, and I was so fucking lonely. And then, for a little while, we were something else."

I can't tell if she's crazy or if this is just the craziest thing I've ever heard.

All I can stammer is, "I never… I never…"

She laughs. "You're not the only one. It's a pretty well-kept secret that Fletcher Dorian was a horndog for Bennytown's young women and men. His wife accepted it since he had no qualms with her doing the same. I knew what it was when it happened, but I had my fun. He was a good man. For him it wasn't all about foolin' around, either. About half the time he just wanted someone to listen, and I was fine with listenin' if it meant I got to be around him more. Right up until I didn't want to hear any more of what he had to say."

I don't want to listen to this. She's breaking, no, actually *hurting* Bennytown with every word.

(not as bad as you hurt Olivia)

This can't be real. This isn't the world I know, the world I want, but I can't stop now, no matter how much I want to.

"What'd he say?" I ask.

"How proud he was of the Bengineers. How he let them explore their ideas without oversight, letting them push the limits of creation without morality. How they were so grateful for this freedom they formed a cult of sorts around him. How they helped him create not just a place that'd be fun for the whole family, but a place so shiny and subconsciously comforting that people wouldn't notice the darkness. 'Cause you see, it wasn't just to confuse the guests. It was also to confuse *them*."

"Who?"

"The ghosts," she says, without any hint of drama or irony.

Again, I wait for a punch line that doesn't come.

Like the ghost of Wallace Vickers?

"Fletcher Dorian became obsessed with the occult after his daughter died, and he built Bennytown as a conduit to bring her back. Everything, from the layout of the streets, the Rabbit Holes, and the great hidden machines inside of Candy Mountain, was designed to maintain a great doorway between this world and the next. It worked much better than he meant it to. After tapping into forces beyond his control, *evil* forces, he had to transform Bennytown from a conduit to a prison, capable of holding in everything he unleashed. Once the dark energies got trapped inside by Fletcher's workings and his Redeemers, they got bored and started fucking around. Getting into folk's heads, making them hurt themselves or each other. Causing accidents. Building a family of their own of spirits bound to Bennytown. Accidentally creating the Dark Park—an evil, twisted version of Bennytown, a place between worlds, not quite for the living, not quite for the dead, a place of blackness and terror we weren't meant to comprehend."

I want to tell her she's insane, that this is all just some insane shit she's bought into out of bitterness from a long life in Bennytown that didn't pan out the way she wanted it to. But blackness and monsters…

(allinmyhead)

"Every so often, I think Bennytown picks someone it wants. Someone it'll break and twist to its grotesque whims. It'll make them do bad things, make 'em destroy everything they love, and it'll absorb them into the Dark Park to make itself stronger. You ever heard of Wallace Vickers?" she asks.

"Of course," I say.

"He was one of 'em. I was almost one too, but I fought it off, and eventually, it lost interest and moved on. Now Bennytown wants *you*," she says.

I'm not sure what's crazier, what she just said, or that I'm actually kind of flattered that in whatever crazy alternate universe her head is stuck in, Bennytown actually wants me.

"I've stayed all these years trying to protect everyone in Bennytown from these forces, but until today I haven't had a real chance to do anything big. But this time I heard the Voice of the Park. There're plans for you. They know you're weak, and they'll come for you. Listen to me. Quit. Quit *now*."

"I'm not weak," I say.

"Yeah, you are, son. You're a sweet kid. As far as Benny-town's concerned, you're the sick gazelle just waitin' to be taken down by a hungry lion."

"I'm *not* weak!" I exclaim. I want to pound on something, maybe her dash, for emphasis. Since I don't want to damage her car, I force myself back into the seat.

I won't be violent, but I can be mean.

"And why are you telling me this *now*? Because I'm friends with Elle? Do you think I might run away to bigger and better things than Pedro Parrot's Safari Lodge? Are you mad I might do more with my life in Bennytown than you've been able to?"

I meant to hurt her, but she's unfazed.

"See, that's Bennytown talkin'. Tell me you'd have said that before working here," she says.

I say nothing.

"My point exactly," she says. "Quit. Go back to school. To your family. To your friends. Your *girlfriend*. Run while you can and never come back, and maybe you might still have your-self a life."

A life. Right. What life?

Olivia ran off.

Dad won't respect me for fleeing this commitment.

If I leave, I won't have Garcia, or any of my other friends. If I never come back, I won't have Bennytown.

She might as well ask me to cut off my arm.

I don't have to listen to this. "Just take me—"

(to Bennytown!)

"—home."

"I just wanna help you, Noel," she says.

Not taking my eyes off the road, I say, "I don't need any help. I know exactly what I'm doing."

The passing glow of a streetlamp makes her eyes look espe-cially haunted as she considers what she wants to say. Finally, she just settles on sighing and turning up the radio.

I smile at this modest victory.

DEWEY
1990

As Dewey Farmer dropped the needle on his record player, he relaxed. He might not be able to stop what was about to happen, but the soft music let him fall into memories. In this moment those reminiscences had a leg up on the violent certainty of what came next.

The Voice of the Park hadn't spoken to him for three days. Or had it been four? It was hard to tell sometimes.

It didn't matter. Successfully, he added another sack on his wall. It would please the Voice, especially please it this time because this was lucky number seven.

Numbers never mattered before. Back before Bennytown, he'd only ever taken four children in three states. It was the greatest thrill in life, but there was always great fear associated with it.

What if this was the one time he got caught?

What if this was the one time the police knew what they were doing?

At Bennytown, there was none of that. Every day he walked the grounds, he became a new man.

Energetic.

Confident.

The kind of guy who had real friends.

The Voice of the Park told him what he had to do. It even let him know that, as long as he was in Bennytown, he had nothing to worry about. Heck, Bennytown wanted him to take playmates and send them to a place where they could be kids forever without any of that growing up nastiness.

Bennytown made it easy too, hypnotizing people, making it so those briefest of brief moments when a person could be taken without anyone noticing lasted longer, at least longer to an eye as trained as Dewey's.

With the Voice silent, Dewey knew his fun was at an end.

Today, he had worn a smart suit to work for the occasion. Eight years ago, he'd worn it to his father's funeral. It still fit, even if it was tighter around the belly. The one new embellishment he purchased was the bowtie.

Light purple, just like Wilbur the Walrus.

Closing his eyes, he swayed along to the music from his record player. Kim Carnes's "Bette Davis Eyes" was playing. Her voice was silky smooth and easy to get lost in. It was a fine song to play at his end. He danced along with it for a few moments, imagining each of his seven children as his partner. Tears formed at the corners of his eyes.

Finally ready for what happened next, he opened his eyes. Checking himself in his dressing room mirror, he saw a dapper, balding, middle-aged man. Meticulously, he checked his fingernails, then his teeth, and cleaned his glasses with his sleeve.

Well, it was time.

Fondly, he touched the plastic bag containing the Wilbur Walrus costume, remembering the joy he'd brought so many children in his igloo. With a hand shaking with the memories from his last dance, he drifted his fingers through each of the seven sacks he'd nailed to the walls, savoring the memories.

Walking to the door, he flicked off the light switch, exited, and locked his dressing room.

Turning around, he said, "I understand why you're doing this."

The fire extinguisher came down on the back of the head.

WHEN DEWEY CAME to, he was aware of three simple facts.

First, he was naked except for his glasses.

Second, he was tied standing to a lamppost in Creepy Corner.

And finally, he was surrounded.

There were perhaps forty of them, some in full character costume like Brutus the Bear, Terry Tortoise, Stumbles the Clown Dog and even Benny himself. Others stood with bandannas covering their faces like old west outlaws.

Benny stepped forward and spoke in the heavy, muffled voice of Jeanine.

"Dewey Farmer. You've been charged with the kidnapping, murder, and violation of numerous children, and of repeatedly and unrepentantly violating the sanctity of Bennytown and its family. How do you plead?"

She must've been getting a special kick out of this one. Despite her grave words and the tone of a judge, she had a smirk in her voice.

Well, best not disappoint the lady, Dewey thought.

"GUILTY!" he cried.

The crowd jeered and hissed, until Jeanine raised one of her great green paws.

"Guilty? That's all you have to say for yourself?"

"What do you want? Should I beg? Want me to tinkle myself like a little baby girl? What's the point? We all know how tonight ends. I've spilled blood, and now you'll spill mine. Come on, family! I BELIEVE IN BENNYTOWN! FEED ME TO THE DARK PARK!"

Jeanine took half a step back in disgust. She dropped her paw. "Skinners. Do what you do best," she said, turning away.

Nearly half a dozen Skinners, including Oren and Erin, stepped forward armed with straight razors and knives. If they had any hesitation or fear, they didn't show it.

Dewey chuckled.

While they thought they were doing justice, they were doing exactly what he wanted.

And they weren't alone. There were other watchers this night, living and dead alike, standing around the edges and observing the horror show. The living wore green wooden masks and were dressed for a ball. He knew they wouldn't leave the shadows or dirty their hands like the vigilante mob. But they'd watch and silently cheer among themselves.

The dead, who actually lived in the shadows and communed with the Voice of the Park, were the ones who mattered most. Before the night was over, he'd be part of their ranks forever.

Along with his children.

Dewey howled with laughter and didn't stop, not even when they began to peel the skin from his body.

NOEL
2019

Everything changes today.

I'm going to work, and I'm gonna kick ass.

I'm gonna fix things with Olivia, and we'll be better than ever. I know it feels like this is beyond fixing, but I *know* that I'll make this right to her. Bennytown can fix anything.

If my theory holds water, I'm also gonna find the walrus.

Kathleen told me a lot about Bennytown but didn't offer anything new on the walrus.

I feel bad for her, really.

She's one of the best people I know, but it's clear that she's had some bad experiences that have left her with a less than perfect grip on reality.

I can relate.

There's no way I'm going to quit. If I decide to be more honest about what happened in my own past, then she'll open up about hers. Maybe we can become friends and figure our shit out together, form our own Bennytown support group.

Yeah, I know it's ambitious, but it's not impossible.

The Olivia issue is proving far more difficult.

She still won't respond to my texts. Although I don't blame her, it's getting annoying. Our fight at the Green Door Society becomes blurrier with each passing moment, but I know it wasn't that bad. She's blowing everything out of proportion. When I find the walrus and get rich, she'll want to be back in my arms, and she'll never leave me again.

Once I find the walrus, I'll have the money. The car. The respect.

Olivia begging me to take her back.

Everything I need to get my life back on track.

As I walk downstairs, I'm smiling, maybe even whistling. Dad looks up at me, amused.

"Someone's in a good mood today," he says.

I laugh. "It's gonna be a *great* day. Isn't that exciting?"

THAT *GREAT* DAY lasts right until I reach the Safari Lodge.

The mood in the rest of Bennytown is electric. Decorations for the Sixtieth Birthday were put up overnight, and a sense of excitement permeates the air. Tomorrow marks a new chapter in Bennytown history, and everyone knows it.

On the other hand, Pedro Parrot's Safari Lodge feels like a funeral parlor. Most family members are looking grim, some even crying.

"What's up?" I ask.

One of the older Leads, Ben, responds, "Kathleen's dead."

I can always tell something really important is happening when my ears start to ring. My heart's pounding with something like fear… more than just regular fear, but a truly inescapable, primal terror.

And maybe it's that ringing in my ears that makes me miss the next few things he says, because the first word out of my mouth is, "What?"

"Car accident," Ben says, hand shaking as he fills a plastic cup with water from the soda machine. "Don't have many details yet, but they say someone sideswiped her into a freeway divider. It was bad."

"Was it—"

Was it what? Was it ugly? Did she burn?

Did she burn like Mom? Did she scream your name?

I can't finish the question. Not today. Not when everything is going so well, when everything is finally being sorted out.

Carla, one of the Assistant Leads, wipes ineffectively at her smeared mascara. "Everyone on the morning shift is gonna have a get-together to remember Kathleen at the Bennytown Plaza Applebee's. Why don't you join us? I know Kathleen really liked you."

I'm honestly torn by the sweet offer. It hasn't sunk in that Kathleen's dead. This tragedy will feel more real if I join them. Listening to people talk about my mom helped me cope after her death. I know it will help me deal with the loss of Kathleen.

At the same time, I have plans after work today. Dad knows to pick me up an hour after my shift to compensate.

Plans can wait, can't they? I can search for the walrus tomorrow night, can't I?

Why should I have to postpone my search when I got my best clue so far? I want to do this now, because I know it *will* make everything better.

Why did you have to die today, Kathleen?

IN THE END, the choice is easy: I'm hunting for the walrus.

I'm pretty sure that Kathleen would understand what I'm doing. It's what I have to do to secure my future, especially when I've got a lead like this.

Well, it's more an idea than a lead, but that's more than nothing.

The rest of my shift goes by at a snail's pace. I have to appear cheerful when I feel the opposite, though my co-workers are having a harder time of it.

When it's over, I leave behind the bright, albeit temporarily depressing, confines of Pedro Parrot's Safari Lodge. I try to look forward to descending into the dark corridors of the Rabbit Holes.

I don't know the full layout of the tunnels and couldn't find a map of the abandoned ones in the Lower Park. I'm trusting on my memory to get me there. Taking the mausoleum Rabbit Hole entrance Garcia showed me, I improvise from there.

The totality of the inky darkness still surprises me.

I pull out my phone and turn on the flashlight.

For a moment, it flickers *(Vickers Flickers?)*, and for half a second it cuts out entirely. Soon it's bright enough to get me to the bottom of the twisting metal staircase, bright enough to help me find and light the lantern that Garcia left behind.

I shut off my phone's light, get my bearings, and follow the tunnels to Happy Hollow.

According to the map I saw in The Green Door Society, there was a time when the walrus had a house in Happy Hollow between Dare the Hare's and Flora Fox's abodes. Now there's a restroom there.

Since everything in Bennytown is connected by Rabbit Holes, it makes sense that each of the houses used to be connected as well. I come to the conclusion that each house probably had its own underground changing room for the characters. So, I predict that if the costume is anywhere, that'd be the place.

I could be wrong, but I have a feeling it's in here. And I know I'll find it.

The tunnel feeds on light, the lantern barely penetrates the darkness. Every sound, every shadow is the ghost of Wallace Vickers or those dark forces that Kathleen was talking about, or maybe—

(allinmyhead)

Stop it.

"Eyes on the prize," I whisper.

Most of the hallway toward Happy Hollow is intact with some heavy cracks and roots breaking through. I can feel the massive flow of people rumbling above me, shaking down dust.

Passing a sign with an arrow stating "HAPPY HOLLOW CHANGING ROOMS" only solidifies my resolve, even as my path becomes more obstructed.

The walls and ceiling ahead are buckled, piles of earth pouring in and I barely squeeze past. Farther on, the ceiling bends lower than it should, concrete slabs cracked and held up by gnarls of roots and rebar that looks inadequate to hold them back.

How many people have walked over that spot without knowing what's down here? How many would it take to make this all tumble down onto me?

I keep moving, even as the tunnel tightens around me. As I pass by dressing rooms, some have collapsed completely while others sit empty except for odd bits of rotted furniture. In one room, there's a big fluffy glove writhing with the rat's nest that calls it home.

The stretch of hallway up ahead is the worst. The spider-webbed ceiling bows down almost two feet, while the earth from the shattered walls piles up almost to within a foot of it. It's going to be a tight squeeze, and I realize I'm going to do some digging before I can pass through.

Setting the lantern down in a small crook of earth, I dig at the pile in front of me. At first, I'm timid but when I think of the bounty ahead, I start digging like an animal, eager and vicious. I take down the mound of dirt a few handfuls at a time. I hear a hiss.

And there's a rattlesnake, right there, staring at me.

It barely moves and hasn't gotten into the strike position. It patiently looks at me, flicking its tongue. From its crevice, it waits, not even rattling.

I'm torn between being deathly afraid of it and pissed at it for being in my way.

"Please move," I say, stupidly, knowing it won't do anything.

Cautiously, I reach for the lantern. The snake doesn't move.

Turn back. Turn back now. This isn't worth it.

The voice of common sense. It sounds a lot like Kathleen. If I let it keep talking, soon she'll convince me to quit.

But maybe this time she's right. Why am I doing this? I can leave now. Leave the snake. Go home. Beg to make things right with Olivia and…

And what? Give up on an opportunity for greatness when it falls into my lap?

I can't turn back.

The snake won't turn back.

What choice do I have?

I'm left here with a lantern in my hand. A heavy metal lantern, its light bouncing off the walls, glimmering in the snake's focused eyes.

It happens before I know it.

I raise the lantern high, then swing it down on the snake's head. It tries to move, but I don't think it expected this attack. The corner of the lantern crushes its head. Afterwards, its primitive reptile brain keeps its now lopsided jaws working, trying to strike but too badly broken. I bring the lantern down again.

And again.

And again.

Somewhere, far-off, I hear Kathleen screaming for me to stop, but I don't listen.

The snake's body hitches and shudders in a pitiful, mechanical dance, while the twisted gore that was once its tiny head looks like a squashed piece of fruit.

Using a chunk of rebar from the floor, I scoop the snake's remains out of the way. There's blood and guts all over my shirt. The wardrobe people might assume it's just food, thankfully.

Squeezing through the gap is a piece of cake.

The hallway beyond is almost intact and ends in another curving metal staircase. The roof looks more stable here. Hallways and rooms branch off around me. One at a time, I check each door, finding abandoned and dingy dressing rooms and storage. Most have been cleaned out, but I still see traces of long-expired supplies.

When I see the door with a faint sign reading "Dare the Hare," I know I'm going in the right direction. The next door says, "Flora Fox," and I'm confused.

The walrus is supposed to be between them.

There's a long stretch of concrete wall with the usual water stains. When I look closely, I notice one section of wall that's a different shade of gray, barely visible in the lantern light. I move the lantern closer, examining the narrow, inconsistent patch.

It's narrow enough to have covered a door.

Experimentally, I tap my short length of rebar against this section of wall.

It sounds hollow. I bet the concrete is no more than half an inch thick. Hastily put up, its uneven appearance makes me think they were trying to cover up a mistake.

Isn't this what they did at Chernobyl? Are you sure you want to go digging through that?

Setting the lantern down, I grab the rebar in both hands and swing it at the wall like a baseball bat.

A small hole forms in the concrete. Behind it, I can see the faint green wood that makes up the changing room doors. Harder and harder, I slam rebar into concrete, carving away more chunks that rain down around my feet. The harder I hit, the more rotten wood comes out with the concrete. The feeling of certainty about what I'm doing grows stronger with each blow.

This is it. This is it!

Soon I've knocked enough concrete away that I've created a hole large enough to crawl through. Once I start pounding at the door, weakened from decades of decay and wet, I'm quickly able to cut a hole into the room beyond.

With the lantern back in hand, I stretch my arm inside. No creepy crawlies. Nothing moving. This room has been untouched for ages.

Gingerly, I climb inside.

The room is a mess, even by the standards of these dressing rooms. The walls are covered in graffiti in dozens of languages, Latin being the most common. The words repeat over and over. The only English I find is in big, erratic red letters on a closet door.

SHIFT'S OVER
ON TO THE DARK PARK!
ISN'T THAT EXCITING?

A brief chill hits me as I recall Kathleen's story, but it's not enough to distract me.

An ancient big-screen TV is built into one wall. Its screen is broken outward, almost like something crawled out from the inside. To the right of it, a bulletin board has seven nails driven into it, each bearing an old plastic Bennytown shopping bag. Beneath each bag, an index card is pinned with a name neatly printed on it.

ADAM
BRENDA
CARLOS
SUSIE
BOBBY
BRUCE
AMANDA

Idly, I touch one of the bags. Its plastic dissolves as if it were made from cotton candy.

Turning to the other side of the room, I see a tarp wrapped around something sitting vertically in front of a vanity mirror. Hands trembling, knowing what I'm about to see, I pull it off.

Hidden beneath the tarp, sitting in the chair, is the walrus. Plastic eyes underneath a cockeyed pair of sunglasses look back at me in the mirror as I stand over its shoulder. A face kept in a permanent grin with a bushy mustache and a bulging stomach barely hidden by a Hawaiian shirt. Floppy arms meant for wrapping around kids and hugging.

The costume smells even worse than the rest of the room. Like death, no doubt from years of wet and darkness. I wouldn't be surprised to find something living or dead inside it. Snakes or rats or something worse.

It's so big. It has to be lighter than it looks since someone used to wear it all day. I know there's a lot of metal inside forming supports and air conditioning units. If you add the radios and tracking devices on top of all the fur and fabric, I know I won't be able to move it on my own. I could probably get Garcia to help me carry it out, but I don't want to share the glory.

I'll let Elle Dorian know since I still have her contact information. She'll make everything right as rain, and when she makes everything right, everything *will* be right.

Especially with Olivia.

I'm walking on air. Heck, I'm whooping as I jump up and down.

During this moment of joy, everything almost goes awry. Maybe it's my cheering or one step too many above me, but there's a rumbling in the hall outside. Instinctively fearing an earthquake, I duck down as I hear the crackling roar of concrete shattering and collapsing heavily outside the room. A plume of dust shoots around me and sends me coughing and screaming more in fear than delight.

When the rumbling stops, I'm surprised that I'm in one piece. I breathe a sigh of relief when I find the walrus costume is also untouched.

Then I glance at the doorway.

A slab of concrete and jagged rebar blocks the hole I carved. I press my hand against it, but it won't budge. Holding the lantern up to the hole, I see a sliver about six inches wide leading into the hallway.

I'm trapped.

I'm in Bennytown. Nobody can be trapped in Bennytown.

My ears are ringing again and my heart pounds with fear.

No, I'm not trapped.

With shaking hands, I check my phone.

No reception. Of course, there's no reception, I'm underground.

(Vickers Flickers.)

I'm trapped underground in Bennytown with only a six-inch-wide hole to escape through.

It's not very long before I start screaming.

MY VOICE GAVE out after twenty minutes of screaming, and it took about an hour after that before I realized no one was coming. I battered at the thin layer of concrete that had been used to hide the doorway, but beyond it are only massive slabs of collapsed ceiling that still block my way. The air duct above me is too narrow, and there's no doubt that I'm truly, completely trapped.

I'm gonna die down here, aren't I?

No, no, no. There's no dying in Bennytown. this is a place of miracles, something will come along, something will save you.

(It's alright, sweetie. Benny will take care of you.)

After two hours, the lantern died. I hunch over the light of my phone, but there's not a lot of battery. I need to save it for when I'll really need it.

The darkness becomes my enemy, because in the darkness, it's easy to let what's *allinmyhead* take over.

I keep hearing voices in the dark.

The walrus chuckles behind me, a rotten sound.

Olivia screams obscenities at me.

Kathleen calls for help, but I know she's dead. I'm just imagining her because I'm trapped.

(allinmyhead)

I'm trapped underground with Wilbur Walrus, and I don't know why.

I don't know how long I've been here. It feels like days, though I know it hasn't been that long. Hours, surely, I'm damn hungry, but not days, not yet.

I bet Olivia would have some snide remarks about it. She'd say that this is the sort of thing I get for working at Bennytown. Dad. Oh, God, I can't even think what he'd say. It feels like a million years since I've really talked to him.

And Mom…

(Benny will take care of you)

No, I can't think like that. I got into this, I can get out of this, somehow. I'm not buried alive at Bennytown, because people aren't buried alive here.

Footsteps. High heels on concrete. I can't be sure it's not *allinmyhead*, but I want them to be real. When I see the light illuminate the six-inch sliver of the real world beyond the collapsed concrete, I know it's real.

"Hello?" I call out, voice hoarse.

"Hello, Noel."

I know that voice well.

"Elle!" I call back, scrambling up to peer through the hole. "Thank God!"

"God? I don't think you'll want thank him just yet."

Looking through the bright sliver is a green, carved Benny mask, one like in all the pictures at the Green Door Society.

"What's going on? Is this a rescue party?"

She raises a finger to the lips of her mask in a shushing gesture. "Not like you think. Not yet, but soon you will be saved."

I'm having a hard time believing anything I'm seeing right now, so I say nothing.

She continues, "On behalf of Dorian Studios, I want to thank you for finding Wilbur Walrus. It is an unfortunate reminder of a time best forgotten, when our ambitions got away from us. It was a PR nightmare that your discovery will finally put to rest."

I hear her rifling through her purse. In my confusion, I almost expect her to pull out a check for the $40,000 and slip it through the gap. Instead she drops something else inside. Grabbing it, I see it's a small digital travel clock.

Its red numbers read 11:22.

Elle asked, "As I understand it, you've entered the Dark Park twice already."

The Dark Park.

I know that phrase. Wallace Vickers. The Walrus. Kathleen's warning.

"For Bennytown to continue on, we'll need to send you in one final time."

"What?" I ask.

She continues, "I wasn't sure you were right for this, and I did not want to listen to the Voice of the Park. After what I saw in you at the Green Door Society, I was happy to be proven wrong."

"What's going on?" I ask.

She ignores me. "Bennytown has faced terrible problems lately that you can't possibly understand, not yet at least. With the Sixtieth Birthday celebrations tomorrow, we *need* tonight more than ever. It probably won't be pleasant, for there are many harsh truths to face, but by the end you'll understand it's all for the best. If you love Bennytown as much as I know you do, you'll know what you must do after this moment."

She walks away with the light. The gravity of what she's saying hasn't sunk in yet.

"It was fun knowing you, Noel. I look forward to seeing what you become after tonight."

Finally, my voice works. I yell after her, begging for her to get me out of here, but my voice falls on deaf ears. Soon I can't even hear her footsteps.

11:26.

I pull out my phone, turn on the light. After a few seconds it goes out, completely dead.

"FLIP!" I yell.

11:27.

I pace around the dark chamber, yelling, pounding at the collapsed doorway, kicking it in some futile hope of getting free.

11:28.

11:29.

This can't happen. The Dark Park's just a myth, a scary story they made up to haze the newcomers. Everyone's gotta go through this at one point or another, right? It's not like they chose me to be some sort of sacrificial lamb to save Bennytown. The park won't drink my blood. Will it?

This is *Bennytown*.

Heart pounding, I watch the clock like my life depends on it. The seconds drag longer and longer until they feel like hours. I both dread and need the clock to change over.

Any second now.

Any second now.

Any second—

11:30.

I close my eyes tightly, fearing the worst, fearing that everyone's bad words about Bennytown are true.

But nothing happens. I'm still here in this chamber, all by my lonesome. No terrible Dark Park is coming to eat me. I'm fine.

I'm fine.

Really.

11:31.

11:32.

I start laughing like a loon. Lock me up and send me to an asylum because I just about had a meltdown.

The clock flickers. The numbers have been replaced with that harsh digital 88:88 that means error.

Its vague red glow means I'm still in this world. Maybe things still operate like they should. Until I hear the sound of shuffling feet in the hallway. That shuffling sounds like Wilbur moving in the corner.

Get a grip, get a grip, it's all in your head, it's all in your head.

All in your head.

all in your head

allinyourhead

(allinyourhead)

There's a rustling sound behind me, and a sick stench of rot that strengthens as it approaches me.

I try to scream, but it's hard to get a sound out when you're being choked unconscious by a walrus costume.

PART 3
THE DARK PARK

NOEL

A rusty wheel echoes off concrete walls.
Dull laughter.
Music, far-off, cheerful but out of tune.
Screams. Moans.

My hearing comes back before anything else.

Pain follows shortly thereafter. I'm sitting up with my neck lolling to the side. There are sharp pains in my temple, but the rest of my head feels dull. Hot, wet blood drips down the side of my face. I want to wipe it away, to try and clear my head, but I can't.

I can't move my arms. Or my legs.

I can't move anything.

I struggle, thrashing around limply in the heavy metal chair I'm tied to. My wrists, ankles and waist are bound tightly with thin cord, while strips of cloth cover my eyes and gag my mouth. I try to scream for help through the foul-tasting gag, to fight my way free, but all I get is more pain and sounds too piti- ful to register in my ears.

A light turns on above me. Even through the rough fabric of my blindfold, I can see it's fluorescent, faint blue and buzzing.

I'm fully conscious now, and I want to cry. I want to scream. I want to run home to Mom and Dad and have them tell me it's all going to be all right. I want Olivia to wrap her arms around me, so I can tell her she was right. I don't know if I believe it fully, even now, but I know it's what she wants to hear, and I want to make her happy.

I want to go back to Bennytown, but I know I never left.

I shouldn't be punished since I did everything right. I shouldn't be here.

I don't wanna die.

I don't wanna die.

I'm not gonna die. I'm gonna get out of here and—

Footsteps.

Behind me. Not shoes. Heavy, padded.

I moan in fear. The footsteps continue to approach until they are standing over me. Breathing heavily, it just stands there, waiting.

I cry out again.

Big, fluffy hands forcefully grab the top of my chair. Thick, furred fingers with short-clawed ends press into my shoulders painfully.

Then my chair starts to move with the sound of rusty wheels squealing.

I'm in a wheelchair.

I'm propelled forward. It wheels me into *(or farther down?)* a hallway. Water splashes around my feet. I can hear it dripping from the ceiling in streams.

The sounds of screams and moans are louder on either side of me. Periodically I see flashes of light beside me through doorways. The terrible sounds that come from these doorways, each worse than the last, make me glad I can't see what's happening.

Whatever is pushing me grips tightly to the top, claws digging into my shoulders through my uniform shirt. Now I'm being propelled forward as it sprints ahead.

I hear its heavy footsteps splashing in the now ankle-deep water as it jerks me violently around one corner, then another, then down a straightaway. Sprays of water shoot up around us, soaking the chair.

At one point it takes a corner too hard and spills me onto my side, my face scraping against the concrete wall. The side I land on hits the ground so hard the armrest of the chair almost pops out of place. I just want it to leave me here, but it lifts me and keeps pushing me along.

After taking a soft curve through a narrow doorway that scrapes the sides of my chair, it finally stops running. Taking me forward a few steps, it spins the chair around so I'm now facing in its direction. Gently, it raises its massive, stinking paws to my face. Its claws work delicately at the edges of my blindfold until I can see what is around me.

I wish I couldn't.

This small, concrete room must be from a Lower Park Rabbit Hole, but it's in terrible condition. Large patches of mold cover the walls, weeping water and other fluids in stinking rivers that make the walls almost pure black and putrid yellow. A single lamp hangs above me, the faded yellow light blasts my face and hides the rest of the room in shadows.

The light illuminates what is before me.

Standing in front of me is a foul perversion of a Doctor Dare character costume.

Its fur is burnt black and rotten under its stained doctor's scrubs, stinking from years of decay. The costume is thinning and falling apart in places so I can see what looks like a weird combination of chicken wire and raw, charred flesh beneath. The fur on its face is almost completely gone, exposing the metal framework and strips of rotten, black flesh. The dripping flesh wraps around the frame and work the jaw.

It cocks its head one way, then the other. Then, it lets out a joyful giggle as it raises a paw to my chest and points to my nametag, then back at itself like a terrible introduction.

It raises both of its paws comfortingly, then steps out of view. It drags over a couple rolling metal tables covered with medical implements, none of which have been cleaned in a very long time. One at a time, it shows them off for me, even demonstrating a very rusty, very loud old power drill inches from my eyes, unmindful of my screams.

Finally finished, it strokes its chin with a big paw. Pulling away with a finger raised in a cartoonish gesture that feels like it should have a light bulb going off over its head and a *ding* sound effect, it runs through the doorway in front of me, slamming the door.

Where am I? What is this? Why?

You know you're in the Dark Park.

You're here because you didn't listen.

And now you're gonna pay, if you don't do something about this predicament.

But I can't. I can't fight, not after what they did to me.

You can fight, or you can wait for Doctor Dare to come back and gain an intimate understanding of what some of those tools really sound like going into a human body.

The trays are just inches from my hands. With one of those I could maybe…

I can't reach, no matter how far I stretch my wrists. I can't reach.

As I attempt to stretch my right arm fully, I feel the loosened armrest from when I was dropped. I struggle to loosen the armrest an inch, then two inches until I break free. I grab a large, serrated blade from the table and start hacking at the cable around my other wrist. Though the cable is tough, the blade is even tougher.

With one hand completely free, I release myself from the rest of the cabling, rip out my disgusting gag and tear the broken armrest from my right wrist. Triumphant, I stand up proudly and almost cheer.

Then I remember where I am. Or more precisely that I don't know where I am.

Or what I'm going to do.

Escape, obviously.

Obviously.

I can't wait for Doctor Dare to come back. I can't fight him. The closest I've ever come to being in a fight is…

(ruckus)

The door isn't locked. I inch it open and peer out. The hallway is dark, lit only intermittently by flashes of light accompanied by screams. I inch my head out, looking both ways. Either seems just as likely to offer escape.

Another flash of light reveals a figure rounding the corner. Big, backlit, floppy ears. Dragging something heavy through the puddles.

I run in the opposite direction down the hall. My footsteps are loud, but I don't hear pursuit.

I get the faint feeling that the floor is sloping upward. I am relieved that the water is getting shallower and the dank, fetid air getting gradually fresher.

When I round another corner, I see her.

Or it. I can't tell what, for sure.

It's Terry Tortoise. Her costume is worn and fleshy, like Doctor Dare, but bent over in great pain. Her moaning sobs subside as rolling gouts of steam pour from her mouth. I feel cold just being around her. I feel like I just walked into a giant refrigerator, her presence actually causing the water at her feet to solidify and frost over.

Frozen Terry cranes her neck toward me, her rotting lower jaw falling open as she croaks, "NOEL!"

I know that voice.

She shambles to her feet, the walls freezing in great patches where she touches them. Slow as her namesake, she ambles toward me. Turning on my heels, I run back to where I came from. Right around the corner, I open the first door I see and force myself inside.

I find a room that is mercifully black and empty. Frozen Terry moves around outside the door, her stomping footsteps displace water, crackling and freezing everything around her.

She stops right outside my door. I know she can't hear me or see me. I hope she forgets about me and keeps going. Instead, she's trying the handle and slams her weight against the door. I hold it closed as hard as I can. Grabbing the handle, I don't let it move and ignore the cold burning my hand. She feels so much stronger than me.

Please go. Please just go. This door's locked. Nobody's in here. Just keep moving.

As if hearing my thoughts, she continues down the hallway until I can't hear her at all.

When I pull my hand away from the handle, my skin sticks to the icy metal. In the darkness I feel strips tearing off as I pull away. I hiss through my teeth, cradling my burning hand.

I wanna go home.

I close my eyes tightly, trying to will reality back. None of this is real. Everything that has happened has to be in my head.

After my eyes have adjusted to the darkness, I make out some shapes in front of me. It might be furniture, but better yet, it might be a door.

I grope blindly along the walls for a light switch, but I recoil before I can test it out. Light switches aren't supposed to throb.

In the darkness, I find a leather belt suspended on the wall. It's the kind of belt a police officer or a security guard would wear. Pulling it off its hook, I feel around until I find a long, heavy flashlight.

When I click it on, its brilliant light illuminates a whiteboard. Someone has hastily scrawled, "REMEMBER WHAT U DID."

Lifting the belt off the hook, I angle the beam down over a security room. It's as rotten as the rest of this Rabbit Hole, though shag carpeting seems to have absorbed much of the marshy, moldy water. I try not to notice all that seems to be wriggling around my feet and try to find an exit.

My flashlight comes across a sign on the ceiling that reads "EMERGENCY EXIT," with an arrow pointing farther into the office. Ignoring the squelching, sucking sounds at my feet, I follow it hurriedly.

Fighting back the urge to vomit as the sucking at my feet intensifies, I barge through the exit and don't stop running. I follow all the signs with arrows along the walls. I just want to get out of here, get away from this, get out of here and…

And I've reached the end of the line.

The hallway ends in the dark, gaping maw of an empty elevator shaft.

Wheezing and pained from my mad sprint, I approach the empty, black hole. There is light a few stories up, and I think I hear Bennytown's incidental background music.

Down leads to blackness. The kind of blackness where squirming things with sharp teeth and long bony fingers live, a blackness so complete it swallows the beam of my flashlight.

Something down there laughs.

(The Voice of the Park)

I need to get out of her now. But how? There are no stairs nearby, and it won't take long for my pursuers to find me.

There are rusted ladder rungs built into the opposite side of the elevator shaft, but I'd have to jump to reach them. It's not a long jump, but I don't trust my frostbitten hand.

I can't fall. Not with what's down there.

Would you rather stay put? Let the things down here catch up and have their way with you like

(Jolene)

monsters from a fairy tale? Monsters that aren't just allinmyhead anymore?

Footsteps behind me. I'm out of time.

Strapping the security officer's belt around my waist, I take a few good steps back down the hall.

"I'm not gonna die, I'm not gonna die," I whisper.

I can hear claws scraping against the concrete of the hall behind me.

I run.

"I'm not going to die, I'M NOT GONNA DIE!" I yell as I leap with hands outstretched into the elevator shaft's darkness.

THE LADDER SEEMS to be shifting away from me.

The Rabbit Hole, the elevator shaft, and the ladder rungs can read my mind. They know what scares me and want to drive me completely insane. I bet they'll laugh as they pull the ladder from my grasp and watch as I scream and tumble down the elevator shaft. They will chuckle as I bounce off the iron and concrete into the waiting claws and teeth of whatever lurks down in the darkness of the pit.

I want to scream about the unfairness of it all.

Instead, I hit the opposite wall, grabbing frantically onto the ladder rungs. My burned hand stings so fiercely that my eyes water. As my feet scrabble for purchase, I break a rusted ladder rung and nearly plummet to the bottom of the shaft, but I manage to find footing on a sturdier rung.

I made it.

I laugh, a harsh, cheerless sound in the darkness.

I clutch the ladder and take steadying breaths as I realize that I'm safe for the first time since I woke up in that chair.

But I have to keep moving.

Hand over hand, I climb. The ladder rungs strain and protest, some bending and creaking as I put my full weight on them. They hold as I ascend toward the dim light of the open door above.

A light touch grazes past me. The shock of it raises my gooseflesh. But then I recognize the bunny ears balloon they sell throughout Bennytown.

As another one falls past me, the latex grazes my face and the static makes it cling to my back. I brush it off and keep climbing.

But another one hits me.

Then another.

I hear hundreds of balloons falling down the elevator shaft, squeaking against each other as they force their way past me. The shaft fills so quickly that I have to fight against the tide. The balloons start popping as they press into bits of twisted metal and the sound like gunshots startles me, nearly making me fall.

The light above me grows brighter, while a waterfall of balloons keeps pouring through the hole. More balloons pop right beside me. Above me. Below me, right next to my ear.

Squeaking. Rubber on rubber, everywhere.

The squeaking is enough to drive me mad. It sounds like nails on a chalkboard behind my eyes.

I've reached the top. The shaft's open door is right behind me, faint light beyond it. The light is tinted by the color of balloons in shades of red, blue, green and yellow.

It's time to jump to get out of the elevator shaft, and it's not going to be easy with the balloons filling every available space.

They'll move around me, and I can cut through them just like a knife.

It'll be easy.

Awkwardly, I turn around on the ladder, holding onto it behind me. I brace my legs. I ready myself to jump away from this madness.

One...

Two...

THREE!

I jump. The balloons squeak and press around me, but I cut through them. The balloons wrap around me like they're grabbing me or slowing my jump.

I almost make it. My stomach smashes against the bottom edge of the open elevator doorway, knocking the wind out of me. My hands scrabble for purchase, finding nothing but cracked concrete as I start to slip slowly into the elevator shaft.

Not like this. I made it this far, so I can't fall, can't lose it, can't fall into darkness. Oh God, no, no, no!

My fingertips are barely keeping me on the edge. I wail as my grip slips. I'm falling and there's nothing I can do about it. Maybe I should have tried harder in gym.

Powerful hands grab me by the wrists and pull me up to the landing.

Backlit and surrounded by balloons, the figure is dark and threatening. I mean to scream, to fight, but before I can, it speaks.

"Hey," she says.

"Hey back," I instinctively respond. "Garcia?"

She's harried and as worse for wear as anything else in the Dark Park, but it's undeniably her. Garcia smiles at me sardonically, cocking her head down the hallway.

"Come on. You're ahead of them, but they'll catch up soon," she says, pulling me by the wrist down a hallway through the torrent of balloons.

Without any better options, and welcoming a familiar face, I follow.

NOEL

"Fucking balloons," Garcia says, leading me down the hall.

The balloons pop and squeak as we force our way past. Only in the light can I see that they aren't the Benny balloons I know. The normally cheerful, smiling Benny face has been replaced by twisted, anguished human faces. Some of the balloons have extra ears, some of them seem to move of their own free will using ears as flagella, and some are only partially inflated, looking like they're feebly holding onto some pale imitation of life.

I try not to notice these grotesque details but find it impossible as Garcia guides me down the hallway. One catches on my shoulder and sticks there. It's pitiful to watch it flailing and deflating after getting caught on something. Its mouth slowly opens and closes as if wheezing for air. As it deflates and one of its cartoonishly exaggerated ears starts to drape against my neck, I'm suddenly aware that it's made not of latex, but of human skin.

I grab it with my free hand and tear it away, throwing that terrible face into the teeming mass.

"Come on!" Garcia exclaims, pulling me around a corner.

"Where are we going?"

"Away from this!" She's led me to a doorway, forces the door open, flings me inside, and closes it behind us.

We're in a break room somewhere inside one of the Rabbit Holes. It's as grotesque as any on the lower levels, but drier and better lit. Since it doesn't have any of those terrible balloons, it's probably the best place in the Dark Park I've seen so far.

Maybe since it's less awful than the rest, that makes it so much worse. A reprieve from the horrors lets them sink in. All at once the crushing nightmare of this place hits me, surrounds me like an over-tight blanket, and I find it hard to breathe. I'm dizzy and brace my hands on my knees to stay standing.

I see blood that's not there, hear people screaming, it's…
(allinmyhead)
Garcia slaps me back to my senses.

"What the flip was that for?" I ask.

She shakes her head. "You're really worried about the Poison Words now?"

"Force of habit." I rub my cheek.

"Yeah, well if you wanna make it through tonight you're gonna have to ditch everything you think you know, Noel. Shit don't work the way you think it should in the Dark Park. If you don't adjust, you're gonna die real quick, you hear?"

I've never seen Garcia act like this before. Even during serious moments, she's always had a hint of a smartass grin hiding somewhere. She's always been quick with a joke, but now she's deadly serious.

As I look her up and down, I can tell she's been through some hard times as well. While still wearing her janitorial uniform, all of her clothes from her ribcage down are horribly tattered and stained with what looks like dried blood or oil.

"I hear," I say.

"Good, now help me move this." She gets behind a nearby rusted box that might've once been a vending machine and braces to push it in front of the door. I help her push it, even though I'd rather ask her one of the few million questions swimming around my head.

"That'll hold 'em for a little while," she says.

I settle on a simple question. "What's… what's happening to us?"

"Not us, *you*," she clarifies.

"Me?"

"Yeah. The Dark Park's got its hooks in *you*. It'll take everything *you* love, everything *you* fear, everything *you* know and twist it until it gets what it wants," she says.

My heart lurches. "Everything?"

"*Everything*. When Wallace Vickers went on his crowbar frenzy, he had visions of his wife and daughters dancing before his eyes. They were begging for his protection even though he'd already murdered them. They guided him, sometimes even protecting him, until he was ready to do what the Dark Park needed. You can't trust *anything* you see or hear, no matter how much sense it makes, how good it makes you feel, or even how much it scares you. *Never* let your guard down."

"If it's after me, what're you doing here?" I ask.

She considers this question. "How much do you know about the Dark Park?"

I tell her everything Kathleen told me about Dorian's designs to make Bennytown a conduit to the afterlife. Also, I explain what I know about the Dark Park being a repository for dark spirits, the people it chooses, and the writing I saw in Wilbur Walrus' dressing room.

Garcia remains silent throughout this description, only speaking after considering everything I've said carefully. Finally, she says, "Kathleen picked up a lot of the truth, but not all of it. Or she only told you some of it, I dunno. I really kinda wish she'd died here. She'd be a good person to help explain a lot of this."

"I wish she was here now," I say, missing Kathleen tremendously.

Garcia sighs and adjusts her hat. "All right, let's get you some Dark Park 101."

She guides me down a hallway branching off the break room.

"Thanks to a variety of dark rituals and the unholy machines inside Candy Mountain, Bennytown isn't just a conduit to the afterlife, but a ghost magnet. Anyone that dies in here, even the cats and the rats, stays here thanks to the Redeemers' salt line. Ghosts can show themselves when they want, or they can be seen by folk with the sight, like you and Kathleen," she explains.

"The sight?"

"Psychic powers, whatever you wanna call it. Before you get too excited, understand that a lot of people have got it but don't know it. There's nothing special the sight can do for you here anyway. These ghosts usually aren't half bad, 'cept for the revenants."

"Revenants?"

"The ghosts of killers: Wallace Vickers, Doctor Dare, Clifford Tally, The Heartbreaker, Wilbur Walrus. All of them are real dangerous sonsofbitches. The kinds of guys who weren't sweethearts in life and are even worse now that there ain't no consequences for 'em. The day park usually keeps them in line, but that doesn't keep 'em from claiming the odd victim here and there. At night, though…"

I'm pretty sure I've got a fair idea what comes at night, since we're in the middle of it, but I'm too lost to do anything but let her continue.

"At night, between the safety hours the signs warn you about, the Dark Park comes out. These are the hours when Bennytown's deep into the space between the worlds of the living and the dead. What you see during that time are the vague spirits trapped between worlds. They aren't quite solid like your daytime ghosts. Full of confused energy and anger, they want to live but don't know how. They'll latch onto anyone alive in Bennytown and twist reality to their darkest, most twisted nightmares. Then, they lick your blood from their fingers."

I wish I didn't have an overactive imagination. God, if she's right, I must be like a buffet to the Dark Park.

"How do you know all this?" I ask.

"Well—"

A gray, jerking figure darts out of the corner, tossing Garcia aside. This is no sheet ghost, but a gaunt, mangled figure in an Island of Legends ride operator uniform. Its head is missing and in its place is a ragged stump of dark flesh with a shock of dull yellow-white of spinal material. Black, tarlike blood coats the front of this ghost's uniform as it flails toward me.

I tumble backwards and try to shuffle away as this thing starts climbing onto the wall, then the ceiling above me. A spout of its thick, dark blood sprays me.

I scream as the foul, greasy fluid fills my mouth.

"Jimmy, damn it, we're not playing it like that tonight!" Garcia screams.

"We're not?" The quavering, unnatural voice comes from the headless ghost. I gag, spitting out mouthfuls of chunky slime.

"No. We're friends tonight!"

"Oh," the ghost says, dropping from the ceiling and landing beside me. No longer moving jerkily, it bends over and offers me a hand.

For what I like to think are understandable reasons, I don't take it.

"Oh, come on, Noel. This isn't a trick this time," he says. I know the voice even though I don't want to remember. I want to hold onto that denial for as long as I can because it might be the only thing keeping me sane right now.

"What the *flip*?" I say, backing against the wall and forcing myself to my feet.

"Relax, Noel, it's just Jimmy," Garcia says.

"This is like you said, the Dark Park getting in my head?" I ask because I want it to be true and not because I actually believe it.

"No, Jimmy's a ghost. Me too, if you're wondering," Garcia says, casual.

My ears are ringing again. "What?"

I don't want to believe it. I can't believe it. Garcia's been the one thing that's been constant at Bennytown since I started working here. I *felt* that something was odd about her for the longest time, but I wrote that off as the general oddity of everyone who works here. This revelation makes terrible sense, but I can't accept it. I don't want to accept it.

Garcia must see my disbelief, because the lower half of her body fades into a mangled mess of blood and tattered flesh. Her usually sardonic face is replaced with a look of agony and fear. In the back of my mind, I can hear her screams over the clank of the great gears beneath the escalators. The sound of grinding into flesh and bone chills me to the core.

I'm rooted in place by this, even when she becomes her usual self again.

"I'm sorry you had to see that, Noel, but… Noel, are you okay?"

I answer her by doubling over and vomiting onto her shoes.

GARCIA AND JIMMY lock their arms under my shoulders and help me to the end of the Rabbit Hole tunnel. There's a sign by the door.

REMEMBER!
PAST THIS POINT YOU REPRESENT BENNYTOWN!
STAY IN CHARACTER!
ISN'T THAT EXCITING?

The bloody three-fingered handprint right beneath it does little to comfort me.

They lead me into a large room that seems to be Pedro Parrot's Safari Lodge's Dark Park twin. The animatronics have undergone years of decay and look like leering, rusty skeletons. The trophy heads in each booth are no longer cutesy robots, but real animal heads, freshly removed and crudely nailed to their boards. None of them are nearly dead enough to my tastes.

A mannequin from one of the shops on the Road to Adventure, dressed like a Secret Service officer, falls from the upper floor and clatters in front of us, making me yelp.

"Save your screams. You'll need 'em later," Garcia says.

The stage is dark and curtained, and Garcia and Jimmy tell me we need to wait for the show to begin before we can move on. Until then, I'm sitting in a booth with them, listening to the laments of the damned.

"I bit it in the summer of '97," Jimmy says. Unlike Garcia, he hasn't felt it necessary to take on his living form and sits opposite me, headless and checking his nails. "I was being a dumbass, trying to speed through the end of my shift because I had a couple of tickets for a showing of *Batman & Robin* up at Bennytown Plaza burning a hole in my pocket. There's all sorts of procedures we're supposed to follow when someone drops something, but, hey, I thought I was young and bulletproof and that I knew the ride better than anyone else."

He snaps his fingers, and the sound of a roller coaster passing fills the air. People scream, first from fun, then from pain and horror as there's a sound of brutal impact and the tearing of flesh. A dark, severed head flies across the room in front of my eyes before fading into nothingness.

"Now I'm young and bulletproof forever, and from what I'm told about *Batman & Robin*, I probably dodged a bullet there," he finishes.

For the first time in what feels like a long time, words find me. "This... this can't be real."

"Oh, it's real," Jimmy says.

"Yeah. We kinda expected you'd have figured this out earlier," Garcia says.

"You did?" I ask.

"Oh, yeah," Garcia says, both of them nodding. At least, if Jimmy had a head, I'm sure he'd be nodding.

"I mean, we didn't want to rub it in your face. Do you really think people have orgies in stinking underground chambers all the time?" Jimmy asks.

"Thinking people are ghosts is not normal," I say.

"True," Jimmy concedes. "As much as the living want to believe in us as proof of an afterlife, few seem capable of handling the truth. Noel, you seem like the kind of guy who might've believed once upon a time in a great beyond, and yet take a look at yourself now. Calling you a deer in headlights would be charitable."

He's not wrong. About any of that.

In my rare moments of clarity after Mom died, I often wondered what'd happened to her. I knew that she was dead, but I knew that couldn't be the end. It felt like just her body died in that flaming car, but her mind, her soul, the *spark of life* continued forever. Dad never raised me to be religious, so I had to make up a lot of this for myself. I liked to believe that if you were good, you got to go someplace safe and peaceful for all time.

For close to a year, I think that's why I thought that Mom had gone to Bennytown.

With age, I realized that if there was a heaven, Bennytown wasn't it.

Seeing with new eyes, I can't reconcile how the real Bennytown lines up with that childish fantasy. I lean over the table to hyperventilate.

Garcia smacks Jimmy on the shoulder. "Nice one, asshat."

"Sorry," he says.

Garcia puts an arm around my shoulder. I almost pull away, repulsed, but I don't, because it's Garcia. She may have lied about being alive, but she's still my friend.

"Look, Noel, I know this is a lot to take in, but it's not the end of the world. We can't escape Bennytown, but you can. If you leave the park's boundaries, you'll be back in the real world. And we can get you there," Garcia promises.

"You can?" I ask.

"Well, we can try," Jimmy says.

"Shut up," Garcia growls.

"Why's he gotta shut up?" I ask.

Garcia sighs. "Because I was gonna try to break it easy to you about how dangerous it is out there. On your own, you'll be little more than a target for every dark energy and revenant that wants to see what your insides look like."

I feel like I'm gonna be sick again.

"But! But it's not gonna be like that. If we can get enough of us together, we can help you escape, I promise," Garcia says.

I shouldn't trust this. All the time I've known these two, they were lying to me. Lying to me about Bennytown, and about who they were. How do you lie to someone about being alive? If they're willing to lie to me about that, why should I believe them now?

The answer's as simple as it is brutal: I don't have any other choice. I don't know where I am and what I'm up against, and these two are all I've got. I have to believe them, because I don't know what else I can believe in.

So, I believe her. God help me, but I believe her.

Ancient speakers within the Lodge crackle to life with garbled music as a few working floodlights illuminate the moldy stage curtain, making Garcia smile.

"And if I'm not mistaken, the next member of our merry band has come to join us."

The curtain parts to reveal a twisted perversion of the Lodge's band. It looks as if a fire has melted all the robots together. The group jerkily play their fake instruments with sickening, squelching noises. In the arms of what used to be Brutus the Bear playing a saxophone is the twisted body of Lance. He's wearing a Safari Lodge uniform from the '70s. His back is broken at a ninety-degree angle, and his face is a twisted grimace of agony, but when he sees the others, he smiles.

"Hey guys, what's happenin'?"

LIKE JIMMY, LANCE isn't too concerned with my comfort and joins us with his back still horribly broken as Garcia lays out the plan.

"We're going for the Lower Gate. You know the one, Noel?" Garcia asks.

I do. It's a decorative iron gate behind Creepy Corner that's more a photography spot than an actual entrance. I've heard it leads to an alternate parking area for family members on especially busy days.

It's also a long walk from where we are now.

"Yeah," I say.

"There's usually a Redeemer guarding it. If two of us keep them distracted, the other can help you climb over the fence," Garcia says.

It's not much, but for the first time since I've entered the Dark Park, I feel something close to hope.

"Thank you," I whisper.

"No problem," Lance says.

"Yeah, what are friends for?" Garcia asks, sliding out of the booth and offering a hand to help me to my feet.

The moment I stand up, I know what I did wrong.

I let my guard down.

I let the camaraderie and friendship distract me because I was desperate for something to hold onto. That's why I don't see the arm shooting out of the adjacent booth and why I don't dart away fast enough to avoid the beefy, purple hand grabbing my belt.

I'm pulled closer to Fritz's crying, purple face.

Through sobs, he whispers desperately, *"Vertraue ihnen nicht! Sie führen dich nur zur Gefahr! Überleben bis morgen und du wirst entkommen können!"*

As I struggle to get away, Garcia, Lance and Jimmy grab my belt and hit my attacker. Fritz is stronger than all of us as he repeats the same warning over and over again.

As the belt slips slightly, the radio touches Fritz's hand and roars to life with a blast of static. This startles Fritz enough that he lets go, the four of us falling to the ground in a heap.

"Fucking Fritz!" Lance shouts back. Still crying, Fritz fades back into his booth. His mournful eyes leave my face and disappear into the shadows.

"Sorry about him. Heart attack victims tend to get pretty melodramatic. There's a handful around Bennytown, but you don't gotta worry about them," Garcia explains.

"Old Fritzy's more annoying than the rest since he died in front of his wife and kids," Lance says, turning back to the booth angrily. "Do you know what the rest of us would've given to see our families one last time, you Kraut fuck? You should be grateful you're so lucky. Why do you have to start shit like this?"

Vaguely, I follow what they're saying. At the same time, I'm listening to the faint voices that are coming through the static of the radio. They seem far away, but very familiar.

It's the sound of real voices from outside Bennytown. It's the little bit of hope that I need to make it through the rest of the night.

"Let's just get the heck out of here, all right?" I say.

"Couldn't have said it better myself," Garcia says. "Boys, let's get this show on the road!"

NOEL

Some of my fondest memories are in Bennytown's Lower Park with Dad.

After Mom died and I disappeared into my head for a while, we'd spend almost half our time in Happy Hollow. I loved being surrounded by the characters and the cartoon wonder. He reasoned that Happy Hollow had to be a better place to spend my days than in my head, and he was right. After a time, I got better, and I had Happy Hollow to thank for much of it.

At that age, I was vaguely aware of Happy Hollow's dark neighbor, but Dad steered me away from Creepy Corner whenever my curiosity drifted. He told me he didn't want me having nightmares, but I've come to understand that's not entirely accurate. Dad was always protective, but I'm sure he's the one who's really scared by Creepy Corner since he's always had an aversion to horror movies.

When I was nine, I bugged Dad for an hour and he finally let me explore Creepy Corner. If I promised not to be scared, we could go inside and go on some rides if I met the height requirements. Being a kid who really wanted to prove himself, I ran up to the baddest ride in the world, Escape from Briarthorne Manor. I knew I could prove it to Dad right then and there that I was ready to grow up and visit Creepy Corner.

I ran right up to the wooden cutout of a ghostly-looking Benny the Bunny holding out a hand, a speech bubble above him saying, "You must be this tall to ride this ride!" Promptly, I conked myself on the head with Benny's hand.

I came to half an hour later in a Bennytown nurse's office with a bump that lasted almost a week, but I got to ride.

That story comes to me unbidden the moment we stepped out of Pedro Parrot's Safari Lodge. I thought the story would bring comfort, remembering the way Dad always tells it in a slightly too loud voice because he always speaks that way. I could almost hear the way he laughs at the *clonk* sound when he gets to the part where I hit my head. I hoped an embarrassing "Dad story" would take me out of the Dark Park for a moment or two, but now every time I think of Dad, I find myself getting irrationally sad, and I hate myself for it.

The Dark Park has begun to twist any sense of comfort and familiarity into fear and sorrow.

I have to fix this.

I *will* fix this.

I just have to escape first.

As I look upon the Dark Park's Happy Hollow, my first thought is about how much Dad would hate this.

It looks like Happy Hollow's been to war and lost. Buildings are crumbled ruins, populated only by rats and choking, black vines under a blood-red sky. Each of the characters' mailboxes has been replaced by sharpened posts with character heads bloodily skewered to them. I tell myself that the heads must be empty, even though I know it can't be true, not in the Dark Park. The street is cracked and full of garbage and dying weeds that fight one another for survival. The winning vegetation appears to be on their last legs, growing to chest height and ending in sickly flowers that sway like they're gasping for air.

Instead of people, the road is lined with the still and silent forms of thousands of fully dressed Road to Adventure mannequins. They are decked out with Benny ears hats and balloons and it looks like a normal day in the park. The blank faces with carved in smiles make Happy Hollow look like one of those fake towns designed for nuclear tests back in the '50s. I'm stuck staring at them in mute horror before Garcia prods me onward towards Creepy Corner.

She explains, "They're harmless, mostly. Don't touch them or look at them if you hear any movement. Especially don't do anything else that might upset them, and you'll be fine."

"Anything that might upset them?" I repeat.

"Yeah. It's not like they'll kill you or anything, but…"

I barely acknowledge the warnings until I realize they mean to take me through that mob. I'd hoped some shortcut or magical ghost trick would save me the horror of having to go through them. Once again I find the only choice I have in the Dark Park is a terrible one.

As if to echo this thought, my radio hisses another long string of static and muted voices.

(It's all right, sweetie. Benny will take care of you.)

Garcia takes the lead, grabbing me by the hand. While Jimmy grabs my other, Lance takes up the rear of our chain, making us look like a field trip of the damned as we snake our way through the sea of mannequins.

Rustling sounds fill the air behind us, and I know that Garcia was telling the truth about the mannequins moving. I hear soft shuffling sounds followed by what might be low groans or chuckles. It feels like a crowd of people are staring at me and whispering about me behind my back. I listen to the warning to not look back. If I keep my eyes on the ones that haven't moved yet, then they can't sneak up on me, and if they can't sneak up on me, they can't—

(allinmyhead)

As I keep my eyes ahead and to the sides, I run as fast as my legs will carry me.

"YEAH, WOO! GO, SACRIFICE BOY, GO!" a voice calls from my side. A teenage girl dressed in a gold and white cheerleader's outfit jumps in the air while her blond hair frizzes around her head with sparks of electricity. Like some of the ghosts I've seen tonight, her flesh is dark and decayed. The stench emanating off her is more burnt flesh than rot.

"Cool it, Jill, he's with us," Garcia says.

"Hey guys, are we still on for statue garden croquet on Thursday?" Jill asks casually. She smiles broadly, and her bright white teeth shine under her burnt lips.

"You know it!" Jimmy shoots back.

"New guy gonna join us?" Jill asks.

"Not if we can help it," Garcia says.

"YEAH!" Jill exclaims, tossing one of her pom-poms into the air.

Garcia shakes her head, muttering, "Cheerleaders."

I eye Garcia questioningly.

Garcia explains, "Not often do we get a living human here. It tends to gather an audience."

She's not lying. The further we go, the more ghosts I see. Dark shapes hide behind the wreckage of buildings, too frightened or timid to fully come out. These ghosts are different from the spirits of Bennytown and seem older and more faded. Without anyone telling me, I know they're different because they've been bound to this land since before Bennytown was even a dream of Fletcher Dorian's. Hollow, black eyes on pale faces stare at me with mixed looks of sadness and boredom.

Before the gates of Creepy Corner, I see the spot where Wilbur Walrus's igloo used to be, and where a bathroom should be now.

In the Dark Park, Wilbur has retaken it.

Sitting on his throne of twisted metal and bone surrounded by flaming torches and low groans of agony and ecstasy, he is unquestionably the most horrible thing I've seen in the Dark Park so far. No longer the friendly character I spotted on the folder, he has become the stench of death and corruption from when his costume came to life in the tunnels. With worn fur exposing flesh and rusted metal and eyes that pierce through me, one flipper strokes a writhing, rotten, vertical tear in his belly. The other flipper holds leashes attached to the necks of seven sad-looking Sack Head Kids.

When we're as close to him as I ever wish to be, he waves the flipper that had been stroking his slimy belly at me and calls out in a high, taunting voice, "See you soon, new meat!"

Just close your eyes, close your eyes and focus, focus on something else, anything else, something better…

"So where are the others? Monica? Lorraine?" I ask, finding the question as good a distraction as any.

"Most nights Monica gets depressed and loves stalking the Rabbit Holes in her old Terry suit," Lance answers, the burned patch in the palm of my hand twinging with the thought. "Lorraine mostly keeps her eye on the animals, and Jolene—"

"I don't need to hear about Jolene," I interrupt.

"You don't? I thought you two really hit it off," Lance says.

"We didn't hit it off." I don't want to think about her because I don't want to give the Dark Park any more fuel.

"That's not how she tells it."

"I don't care about what she says; that's not what happened," I say.

"Well, your loss." Lance shrugs as something unseen crawls over my foot.

"Break the chain, guys, we're crossing into Creepy Corner," Garcia says.

I don't want to break the chain. If I'm in the chain, I don't have to open my eyes. I can follow them without having to worry about anything until I've escaped. If I let go of them, we can all move faster and escape sooner.

At least, *I* can escape sooner.

Opening my eyes, I let go of the others and wipe my hands on my shirt to remove all traces of my dead friends. The archway leading into Creepy Corner is about as intact as anything I've seen in the Dark Park so far, so now I'm convinced they actually are made of stone and rusted iron. The gate is open slightly, enough for each of us to squeeze through one at a time. Garcia takes the lead, followed quickly by Jimmy. Lance, soft and floppy from his shattered back, doesn't even need to use the gap and just squeezes between two of the bars.

That just leaves me.

I'm not supposed to look back. I know it's a bad idea. Mannequins shuffle and groan and whisper behind me. I shouldn't look, but I have to. Not knowing what horror is behind me would be worse than not looking. I'm afraid I'll be forever tormented by the idea of what's behind me.

So, I do it. Against all my better judgment, I look back.

The crowd of mannequins has parted like the Red Sea, all of them kneeling as if in prayer. Standing at the end of this opening is Benny the Bunny. He's untouched by the Dark Park, looking like he just stepped from his Happy Hollow home. His fur is vibrant and green, his eyes polished, and his gloves are almost blindingly white under this dark red sky.

He just stands there, silent and smiling.

Then he raises a hand and waves to me.

(It's all right, sweetie. Benny will take care of you.)

That voice, Mom's voice, is in my head. I know this.

The voice I'm hearing now is very, very real and echoing with static over the radio on my hip. After the first shock, I hope that I've just imagined it. There's no way I could've heard that voice, but it's there. It's there, and it's real.

"What have they done—"

Static breaks the call off, and then her scream is loud and clear.

"OH GOD, NOEL! STOP IT! STOP IT! PLEASE, HELP!"

Olivia.

The calls are too clear, too close.

Olivia is in the Dark Park.

THERE AREN'T NEARLY as many mannequins in Creepy Corner as there were in Happy Hollow, and they allow us to jog backstage to the Lower Park's main gate.

"You must've imagined it," Garcia says.

"I didn't imagine it. She's here," I say.

"Well, what is she doing here?" Garcia replies.

"I don't know. Following me, maybe? What if she was kidnapped like I was, or—"

"Do you have any idea how crazy that sounds?" Jimmy asks.

"*Don't* call me crazy," I threaten, which makes me sound crazy.

I haven't heard anything on the radio since that first message, and I don't have the faintest idea where she might be. I want to tear through Bennytown to find her, but I know that won't be a good idea.

I'll stick with the plan. Get out and find some way to call for help. I don't know how exactly to do that or how I can make them believe what's going on, but I'll figure out something.

When we finally reach the gate, I don't think I've ever felt more relieved. It's a dark gate, an ugly gate, as terrible on this side as it is on the outside any other time, but right now I couldn't care less for how it looks, just for what it means.

I can be free of this cursed place.

And maybe, just maybe with what I know, I might be able to do something to save Bennytown from the Dark Park.

Maybe.

I know I should want to cut all ties with Bennytown after what I've seen, but I can't do that. Bennytown is a place of hope and wonder, and this Dark Park is a terrible perversion of all that. I can't imagine Fletcher Dorian doing any of this on purpose. He would never want Bennytown to lose its innocence. After everything, I think I might be qualified enough to do something about saving it.

Just as soon as I've escaped. And rescued Olivia.

(PLEASE, HELP!)

I have to focus, something that's damn hard in here and getting harder by the minute.

I need to get out of here.

The real world past the gate is a murky, dark fog. Blurry and indistinct shapes move beyond it. Two smaller shapes approach us, shadowy and gaining form.

"Shit," Garcia says.

"What?" I ask.

"There's never two. One we could distract, but not two," Garcia says.

"Stumbles is probably just breaking in new meat. If that's the case, Lance and I can distract him, while you help Noel over the fence," Jimmy suggests.

"I can swing that," Lance says.

"Only if we have to. Lemme try something first," Garcia says.

"Two what? A new *what*?" I ask.

"Redeemers," Garcia reminds me.

The bulky radiation suit perversions of Stumbles the Clown Dog and Pedro Parrot come out of the fog. Garcia, Lance, and Jimmy keep a respectful distance from the gate.

Cautiously, Garcia takes a step toward them.

"Hi, Stumbles, it's been a while. Pedro. You're new here, right?" Garcia says, amiable.

Redeemer Pedro nods and takes a step toward the gate, but Redeemer Stumbles places a hand on his chest to hold him back.

"Well, welcome to the family! Look, I just need to talk to you guys. You see our friend here? He's not like us."

Redeemer Stumbles whips a cattle prod from behind his back and sparks it against the bars. Garcia leaps backward, yelping.

"Listen, assholes, we've got a real human being! He doesn't belong in here!" Garcia protests. She pokes me. "Say something. Tear at their fucking heartstrings if you have to."

I panic and grope for the right words.

"Please. I have a girlfriend and family that are gonna miss me. I love them, and I just want to see them again. Please, just let me go?" I plead.

Redeemer Stumbles is unmoved by our arguments.

Redeemer Pedro takes another step forward, wrapping both of his great hands around the bars of the gate.

"OEL?" its voice bellows, horribly mutilated and terribly familiar.

"You know this guy?" Garcia asks.

"I don't know," I say, even though I'm becoming increasingly certain I do know.

"ALL YOUR FAUL!" it continues.

The voice is slower, duller, but I know the pain in those exact words. I've heard them before on one of the recent days that changed my life.

"JK?" I say.

When he pounds the bars with his great gloved hands, they dent. He attacks the gate with the ferocity of a caged animal. Redeemer Stumbles grabs him and tries to pull him back, but JK knocks him away.

I never thought I'd see him again. I figured Bennytown would be done with him, either kicking him to the curb or sending him to jail.

Instead, they turned him into a monster out for my blood.

"We need another plan," I say.

"Clearly," Garcia says.

Jimmy suggests, "We can try the Family Member Building in the Upper Park. It's still within the salt line, and we should be able to—"

"Well, well, well, looky what we have here!" a high, taunting voice calls.

A greasy-looking madman wearing ratty jeans, a black leather jacket, and a t-shirt with a bright red heart in the center stands behind us. Though not physically imposing, when compared to the Redeemers, the way he carries himself and the baseball bat at his side scares me.

"The Heartbreaker. Just what we need," Garcia mutters.

Standing slightly behind this Heartbreaker is another familiar face, though she doesn't look nearly as happy.

"Bogart, sweetie, we don't gotta do this!" Jolene pleads.

The Heartbreaker backhands her across the face. In spite of the sick feeling I get at the sight of her, I still feel a hot spike of anger in me.

(ruckus)

"Shut up, Jolene. I'll tell you what we need and don't need. And what I need is *him*." The Heartbreaker points his bat at me.

"Me?" I say.

"Yeah, you've been touching my girl! *My* girl! Not your girl, but mine!" he yells.

"That's not what happened," I say.

"He-said, she-said, none of that fucking matters. This bitch ain't yours, and you touched her girl parts. And for that there's gonna be a reckoning!" the Heartbreaker announces.

Jolene, having recovered her feet, says, "Do you even know what *reckoning* means, you fuck?"

"It means I'm gonna kick his ass!" he proclaims.

"No, *this* is kicking someone's ass!" Jolene shoots back, punching him in the head.

He takes it pretty hard.

"You whore! I love you!" he yells, swinging his bat at her head. It connects with a sickening *thock*, and for a moment, she switches to a mangled corpse with brains spilling out from underneath her cowboy hat.

"Asshole! We've been dead damn near twenty years; I can do whatever I want!" Jolene says, slowly reverting to her normal self.

"We're not having this conversation now," the Heartbreaker says, stalking toward us.

"You got this, you got this, you got this," Jimmy whispers to himself, before prodding Lance. Nervously, Lance nods.

You got what?

Yelling pitiful war cries, Lance and Jimmy charge the Heartbreaker. They are neither as strong nor as fast as him, but they have spirit, taking his blows and kicking him.

"Hey, stop it! You're embarrassing me!" Jolene yells, grabbing Jimmy and ripping him off the Heartbreaker. Garcia joins the fray, punching Jolene in the gut and knocking her down.

I'm stuck watching this melee of the dead, watching as blows distort them, transforming them from corpses to people and back again. The mannequins, the eyes in the dark, watch this fight as if it were the greatest entertainment in the whole world.

And that's before the strangled screaming from the other side of the gate starts.

JK impaled the Stumbles Redeemer on a cattle prod. Stumbles grabs at the prod in his chest, then tries to strangle JK, but soon collapses from his wound.

JK turns to me. I can't see his face, but I can feel the hate behind his mask.

He wants me dead. No matter what happened to him, whatever made him a Redeemer, whatever binds him to Bennytown now, he'll do whatever needs to be done to make sure I don't escape with my life.

He crouches down, and in one move jumps higher than a man in a suit that bulky ought to be able to jump. He clears the gate, then lands heavily inside the Dark Park. Too heavily.

His suit wasn't made for this kind of landing, and he's stunned in a heap at the base of the gate. I feel a thrill at this development. If I run at him, I can use his prone body to boost myself high enough on the gate to get up and over. The spikes up top might hurt, but I can make it.

I can escape the Dark Park.

"FUCK!"

The Heartbreaker holds his bat against Garcia's throat. Jimmy and Lance are down, Jolene kicking them and shrieking about how they ruined everything. Garcia's eyes tell me to run. I should listen to her. I *have* to listen to her. I don't know if I'll ever have another chance like this.

The Heartbreaker twists his body, tauntingly showing off Garcia to Jolene.

Looking from JK to Garcia, I weigh my options. I know what I have to do.

I charge at the Heartbreaker's exposed back and hit him with everything I have. He curses as he falls to the ground, and then he lets go of Garcia.

I help her to her feet.

"Thanks," she says.

"You're sure you can get me out through the Upper Park?" I ask her.

"No. But I'll do my best," she says.

JK's regaining his feet, but so have Jimmy and Lance.

"You guys go on ahead. We'll give you a head start," Lance says.

"We got this," Jimmy confirms.

They may be dead, and they may like to mess with me, but it's hard not to appreciate the friendship. This park may have turned them into twisted reflections of who they once were, but right here and now they're good people.

Maybe, if I can save Bennytown, I can save them too.

With that dim light of hope to hold onto, Garcia and I run back to Happy Hollow.

NOEL

"**O**H GOD, NOEL! STOP IT! STOP IT! PLEASE, HELP!"

Not long after Garcia and I started climbing the stairs beside the Stairway to Heaven, I hear Olivia's voice over the radio again. The same words repeat over and over, but it doesn't sound like a recording. Garcia heard them this time, so I know they're not *(allinmyhead)*. The message comes in clearer than ever.

She's in the Dark Park, and we're getting closer.

I'm coming, Olivia.

"Aren't you wishing we took the Sky Buckets now?" Garcia asks, panting.

"Don't remind me," I reply.

"We could still double back and see if we can get them running. They are faster than hoofing these steps," she says.

"No!" I say, too quickly. "No, this'll do."

Taking the stairs was our compromise. I didn't want to take the Sky Buckets, she didn't want to take the escalators, and neither of us wanted to navigate our way up the hill through the Rabbit Holes. So, we were left with the stairs.

This would be difficult going if I were in peak condition, but I'm hurt and tired from all the running, so they're excruciating.

The Dark Park's efforts to twist them against me aren't helping either. The stairs are as crumbled and worn as everything else in Happy Hollow. Often rusted metal or empty air opens beneath them, meaning one wrong step could lead to a drop into inky darkness. Garbage and broken glass litters them as well as a few mannequins, which makes the going slow. Every time I look behind us, I remember why slowing down would be a bad idea.

JK is slow and lumbering in his suit. His oversized feet clearly weren't meant for narrow steps, but he's implacable in his pursuit. Despite being a good distance ahead of him, he's catching up as the stairs becoming an obstacle course.

Longingly, I look at the wall to our left. It's only neck high and topped with an easy to grab railing. Just beyond it are the escalators of the Stairway to Heaven.

A gravelly voice echoes from the speakers by the escalators.

"Benny the Bunny would like to remind you that a wide variety of lethal weapons can be found at any one of our many gift shops. Isn't that exciting? Benito el Conejito quisiera recordarles que una gran variedad de armas letales se pueden encontrar en cualquiera de nuestras muchas tiendas de regalos. ¿No es emocionante?"

"That isn't Benny," I say.

"It's Wallace Vickers," Garcia confirms. "After night falls, anything electronic belongs to him. He's crazy, but he can be persuaded to be helpful if you remind him of who he used to be before the park broke him. Were you expecting Benny?"

Cautiously, I say, "I saw him."

"When?"

"After everyone went through the Creepy Corner gate. When I got my first call from her, he just stood there, watching me. He waved."

"Huh," Garcia says, noncommittally.

"Someone you know?" I suggest.

"Sort of. Of the many things here that are hard to explain, he's probably the hardest to explain of all." Garcia says inches past a mannequin that's trying to force a baby stroller full of writhing insects up the stairs.

"Is he your god or something?" I ask.

Her hint of a smile disappears. "Don't joke about that."

JK roars in frustration behind us.

"Come on, we should pick up the pace. He's getting closer," she says.

"That's all I get?" I ask.

"What?"

"Come on, you know things. Things I need to know if I want to get out of here alive, and you're only telling me bits and pieces." She's my friend, and I don't want to hurt her, but I'm getting frustrated with only bits and scraps from people who clearly have the answers.

And there's something more to it, isn't there? As the anger grows, the clearer my head becomes, *especially* if I'm angry with someone I like.

"I can't say," she says.

"Can't, or won't?"

"Call it a little of both," she says, without meeting my eyes.

"What does that mean?"

She sighs. "You don't know what it's like, bein' dead in Bennytown."

"Then why don't you tell me? Please? I have to know. I'm already half-crazy as is, and not knowing is only making it easier to fall off the edge."

She pauses for a moment to offer me a hand and help me over a particularly empty patch of rusted rebar. The ground beneath us seems too far away, almost as far away as the real world.

"PLEASE, HELP!" I can hear Olivia's voice in my head if we stop talking.

"I have been dead thirty-four years this October," Garcia explains. "Bennytown didn't want me like it wants you. I was just an accident thanks to lazy maintenance men. The settlement from Bennytown was enough to set my family up for life and send my son to college. He brings my granddaughter by at least once a year, which is definitely the highlight for me."

When she doesn't meet my eyes, I can tell it's not as nice as she says. Her voice tries to sound light to hide the sadness there.

"But bein' a ghost here ain't like bein' a ghost anywhere else. I don't know if you've noticed that we've never stopped working for Bennytown. We're not slaves, since it can't make us do anything we don't want to, but it can limit us. If I wanted to tell you something it doesn't want you to know, my words will start to trail off. I have no control over what the park wants to share with anyone. Since I don't get to be with my family ever again, I gotta make the best of what I got here. It's not much, but it could be worse. A *lot* worse."

I want to ask her more, but I don't. If she can't tell me, she can't tell me. Garcia's one of my best friends. If I've got no choice but to navigate my way through the Dark Park to escape, I don't think I'd want anyone else by my side.

Especially when things don't go to plan like when you find a gap where there ought to be stairs.

We come across it so quickly I nearly fall into it. Pinwheeling my arms, I scream in surprise. In answer to my pitiful cry, there's a deep mechanical roar from the Upper Park, one so loud it shakes the entire hill. It nearly pitches me into the abyss, but Garcia grabs me by the shoulder and pulls me back at the last second.

Heart pounding, I ask, "What… what was that sound?"

Garcia shrugs. "It's your Dark Park, man. I just live here."

I look down into the space where there ought to be stairs, and the news isn't good. The crumbling damage has opened up a gap about fifteen feet wide and ten feet vertically. There's only a smattering of rusted, twisted rebar filling the space.

There's no way to edge around this. If I tried to jump but missed, the fall would kill me just as assuredly as JK would.

For some reason, the situation makes me laugh.

"What's so funny?" Garcia asks.

"I don't know," I lie.

From the start, this misadventure has felt like a punishment. I told myself that I didn't deserve this and that I'm not a monster like JK or any of the other dark spirits here, but then I remember how I treated Olivia in the Green Door Society. I know this punishment has merit. I'd neglected her for so long after taking this job, and I let this place convince me that it was more important than her.

I believe in Bennytown. I want to *save* Bennytown. To do that, I need to get my own life in order first. To do that, I need to save Olivia and make things right with her.

At this moment, I need to deal with these stairs.

As if on cue, JK cries out, "OEL!"

"Carp, carp, carp," I whisper, running a hand through my hair.

"We should've taken the Sky Buckets," Garcia says.

"It's a little late for that!" I exclaim.

"I'm sorry, Noel," she says.

"Me too," I say, though I don't fully mean it. Sorry is something you say when you know you're gonna die, but I don't know that yet. I push away the fear and remind myself that I'm not gonna be killed by JK.

The escalators!

An idea hits that is so plain and clear I've no idea why I didn't think of it the second we came to the gap.

"Follow me!" I exclaim, grabbing onto the railing on the top of the wall and pulling myself up. The escalators, though squealing and carting hundreds of mannequins, seem to be in working order. I pull myself up onto the wall, then reach down for Garcia.

"Come on!" I urge.

Garcia shakes her head with eyes as big as saucers. JK's within throwing distance and has picked up his pace. He barrels his way through the mannequins, unmindful of the frothy, yellow slime that leaks from them. And he doesn't notice the way they flop about like dying fish when they hit the ground.

"Come on, darn it, he's almost here!" I yell.

"I can't!" Garcia whimpers.

I didn't know Garcia was capable of whimpering—it's a sound that's just so completely alien to her confident image. And all at once, I know why.

Even though she's dead, she's still afraid of the escalators. Perhaps it's some trick of Bennytown to remind her of her place or it's just some trauma like PTSD. I want to comfort her and then laugh about this later over drinks, but there's no time. I need to move.

"Garcia, I know you're scared. I'm more scared than you know. The escalators are my only chance to escape, *to save Bennytown*, but I can't make it without you. Please. Help me, and I'll help you. We can make it through this together," I say.

Through tears streaking her face, she gives me a disbelieving look. Her face switches to a withered, mangled corpse that was drawn into the gears of this escalator more than thirty years ago. I force myself to look at the gruesome sight because she's my friend.

I reach out to her as JK gets within a few steps of her. She grabs for me, back to her normal self.

Awkwardly, I pull her towards an escalator heading up. The device screams and protests at our added weight, though not as much as JK screams at our escape. I'm stepping on something painful, and I swear the mannequins are staring at us, scandalized. Still, the escalator holds as it brings us to the Upper Park.

I shift my foot to see what I'm stepping on.

It's an emergency fire ax, with a wide, rusted chopping blade on one side and a sharpened pick on the other. Its wooden handle is carved with ancient text and crude depictions of Benny & Friends characters. At once, I feel compelled to pick it up despite being repelled by it. Some primal part of me burns at its touch.

When you pick up a weapon, you mean to use it to fight. Is Bennytown something you want to fight?

I roll the ax over in my hands, admiring the Benny face carved into the dark wood of the handle's base, similar to the masks of the Green Door Society.

Is this aid or a threat?

Before I can wrap my head around that thought, I'm brought back to earth when Garcia buries her head in my shoulder. Tears are streaming from her tightly closed eyes.

"Tell me when it's over," she whispers. Her freezing body shudders so fiercely enough to shake herself apart. In a gesture that reminds me of comforting Olivia, I hold Garcia close and stroke her hair.

"It's okay, it'll be over soon," I whisper back.

Still pinching her eyes closed, she says, "I'm sorry I lied to you about being alive."

I smile, slightly. "I'm sorry you died. I think I would've liked you alive."

She laughs a pure, spontaneous bark of a laugh. It's contagious and makes us both laugh. I enjoy this moment of hope, a brightness swelling within me that lets me know that this *is* going to be all right.

Suddenly, my hair stands on end, not just the hairs on the back of my neck and arms, but on my head. The fillings in my teeth ache, and there's a buzzing sensation in my stomach.

Floating above us with arms outstretched is a man-shaped shadow surrounded by a glowing blue aura. Only two things pierce this absolute darkness: a pair of glowing blue eyes and the sound of someone whistling "I'm Your Boogie Man."

At once, the whistling stops and the blue eyes circle down and lock onto me.

A growling voice full of the pops of electrical sparks scrapes its way out of his ancient mouth and throat.

"Howdy, Noel," Wallace Vickers says.

"We don't have time for this!" Garcia yells, eyes still shut tight.

I shut my eyes like her, trying to will him away. I beg for the feeling of electricity to disappear, but it doesn't.

"Just because you don't got time for this don't mean I don't!" Wallace Vickers declares.

"We don't want to fight you!" Garcia calls out.

"Lucky for you, I'm on orders not to touch ya, but I can have *some* fun, can't I?" Wallace Vickers says, filling the air with sparks that burn and sizzle on my skin.

They sting and bring the radio in my belt to life. I hear Olivia's voice again, screaming and crying for help. She's calling for *me*, with such pain in her voice that I nearly collapse with the feeling of her agony.

Another familiar voice interrupts her. The new voice is neither pained nor scared, and cackles with confidence.

As this voice mixes with Olivia's, I consider the ax in my hand with its ornately carved handle. My thoughts are now clearer than they've been since I entered the Dark Park.

I know where I have to go.

NOEL

I've known two Kingdoms of the Robots in my life.

When I was younger, the Kingdom of the Robots had been the same since opening day, a land of gleaming, steel roller coasters and building-sized robots straight from the '50s B-movie era. It was cheesy fun, and the roller coasters were pretty fantastic for a kid.

About six years ago, Bennytown updated the land with a steampunk-inspired look. While most of the rides remained the same, the gleaming silvers were replaced by faded bronzes, and all the details featured gears that worked in sync to keep the land going. Everything from robots to decorations had this new look. While I enjoyed some of the new rides, the changed aesthetic didn't have the same charm of the old land. I had gone on at length to Dad and Olivia about how I didn't think anything could be worse than this reboot.

Seeing it under the influence of the Dark Park, I change my mind.

The turning gears run with the help of thick, black grease. The sounds of bones being ground to dust fill the air. The towering robots look upon us with corroding leers. Their stoic faces dotted with blinking lights are almost entirely rusted through, showing gleaming chrome skulls beneath. As we pass one, its stomach breaks open to rain down clear hoses that throb with dark, viscous liquid, tangles of dirty Christmas tree lights, and thousands upon thousands of cockroaches. The mess reeks of burning metal and rotting meat, and I try not to throw up again.

We dodge out of the way of this greasy torrent, keeping our eyes low and our conversation on topic as we make our way through the land.

"Elle Dorian?" Garcia asks skeptically.

"I heard her voice with Olivia, and I know they are in the Green Door Society. The rest of those people in the Benny masks have trapped Olivia inside it. If we get there, and I get her out, then the two of us escape. I'll tell everyone about what's going on here. And I think I might be able to save Bennytown." I grip the ax with all my might.

Garcia looks skeptical.

"What?"

Choosing her words carefully, she says, "It's an interesting idea, but…"

"But what?"

"Don't get your hopes up. I've been stuck in Bennytown for thirty-four years and even I have a hard time believing what happens here. You tell anyone what you saw here, and they'll think you're-"

"Crazy?" I finish for her. Garcia nods.

I know she doesn't believe I can do this, and I don't blame her. I've made a real mess of things lately. When I break things, they tend to stay broken. If I were her, I don't think I'd have faith in me either. More than ever, I have this overpowering certainty that I'm right. If I can make it to the Green Door Society, I can save Bennytown.

I don't say it out loud because I know she won't believe me. Instead, I intend to prove it. When we make it to the Green Door Society, I'll show Garcia what I can do for Bennytown.

After another earth-shattering roar nearly tosses me off my feet, I double over and cover my ears. The sound came from ahead of us near Candy Mountain or Primordial World. The noise shakes Kingdom of the Robots with the power of an earthquake, toppling one of the great robots and spilling the mechanical, writhing guts of another on the ground. Dark birds take flight, cawing and chittering, while stray cats and other crawling things run away like rats from a sinking ship.

As the roar fades, I realize it wasn't just the animals it stirred up.

The Sack Head Kid wearing the Thundercats t-shirt stalks out of the Kingdom's ruins. A leash hangs around his neck, dragging behind him like a tail. Even though I can't see his face, everything about him feels terribly pitiful.

"Damn it, Adam, what are you doing here?" Garcia asks.

The Sack Head Kid only cocks his head.

Garcia sounds terrified.

"Is this bad?" I ask.

"You could say that, yeah," Garcia says.

"Why?"

"ADAM?" a shrill voice calls. "COME OUT, COME OUT WHEREVER YOU ARE, MY SPECIAL FRIEND!"

"Wilbur Walrus, that's why," Garcia says.

The Sack Head Kid, *Adam*, hides behind us, shuddering. He cocks his bag-covered head in every direction in a frantic attempt to find his pursuer. I can guess why he's so scared of the Walrus.

"Can we help him?" I ask.

Garcia considers this. "Not in the long run. We might be able to hide him for tonight, but it would slow us down. Your call, man."

I examine the shaking boy behind me and know any little help would be a relief for him.

(PLEASE, HELP!)

"YOOHOO! ADAM! OLLY-OLLY-OXEN-FREE!" The Walrus cries out with a hint of desperation sneaking into his voice.

I take one of Adam's hands. The boy looks up at me.

"Come on, I know a place you can hide," I say.

I NEVER THOUGHT I'd see the inside of Ice Cream Villa again, but desperate times calls for desperate measures. If Bennytown is warping itself to my memories and fears, I think Ice Cream Villa may be one of the safest places here. I haven't had any good experiences here, nor have I had any terrible experiences. Ice Cream Villa was just a dull, laborious job, and I'm hoping that'll be enough to keep Adam safe.

Getting a look inside gives me hope that no one, living or dead, would ever choose to be in here.

The air is not cold enough to keep anything frozen, like a freezer that's been left to thaw. The air is wet and smells of stagnant water and sour milk. Long, melting icicles hang from the ceiling, while nearly every surface is covered in paper-thin ice and patches of mold. The floor is covered in an inch-thick layer of water, curdled ice cream mix, and bright, multicolored sprinkles. This slurry sucks at my shoes with every squelching step, soaking through my socks and pants. The smell is unspeakable, even by Dark Park standards.

It feels positively homey compared to the rest of the Dark Park.

Adam doesn't let go of my hand as I show him the various hiding spots in the storage rooms behind Ice Cream Villa or in Miners' Favorite Pizza. When I try to lead Adam into Miners' Favorite, he balks, shaking his head and pointing inside in a gesture that's all too familiar.

When I was little, I used to do it all the time when I wanted Dad and Mom to look under my bed for monsters.

"Has anything terrible ever happened in Miners' Favorite Pizza?" I ask.

"No, but that doesn't mean you shouldn't be afraid," Garcia says.

"Thanks." I hoped to find comfort in her words, but I'm out of luck.

Another great roar comes from Candy Mountain (no, from *within* Candy Mountain). I let go of Adam and dodge into a low cabinet full of moldy hot fudge. Loose icicles rain down from the ceiling like clear daggers.

I'm tempted to just run, leave Adam and take Garcia and make a break for the front gate. I'm not a hero and dreaming of saving Olivia and Bennytown was stupid.

Before I can act on that instinct, I stop myself.

That's the old you. The you that overthinks things, the you that hasn't felt empowerment by being part of the Bennytown family. Instead, I need to focus and remember my goal to save Bennytown and save Olivia. Don't let anything else get in my head. You know what's real and what's not.

I can control this.

When the roar subsides, Garcia offers me a hand. "You all right, Noel?"

I let her help me up. "Fine. Yeah."

"Now that the is kid safe, let's make tracks to get out of here," Garcia says.

"Not yet," I say. "Let me check Miners' Favorite and make sure it's clear, then we'll go. Let's make sure it doesn't have any bogeymen before we leave."

I tip a shaky wink at Adam, which makes him cock his head.

"You get one minute. Any longer, and I'm coming after you," Garcia says.

"Fine by me." I rub a hand through my hair to push some of the nervousness aside and get a handful of what I hope is moldy hot fudge for my trouble.

Hesitantly, I hand Garcia the ax, hoping that might be enough to defend Adam against the walrus. Cracking a slight smile, she nods back at the gesture.

Do this but make it quick. The longer you're here, the more power it gets over you.

The kitchen of Miners' Favorite Pizza is down a short hallway from the backroom of Ice Cream Villa, but the difference in lighting is like stepping into a dark cave.

Not as dark as the Rabbit Holes.

I still can't get the flashlight out of my belt, but I can turn it on. Its beam shoots straight into the ceiling, illuminating the dark, wet, rusty kitchen. The equipment is silent, and the pizza ovens are as cold as anything in Ice Cream Villa. I have only ever had to put a tray of churros on the conveyor belts that pass through the pizza oven, but it always had a different feel from Ice Cream Villa.

Now it feels like an ungainly, vestigial limb that should've been cut off ages ago. The layer of rotten ice cream mix on the floor is deeper here, almost deep enough to swallow my shoes whole. The drip, drip, drip of the melting icicles gets into my mind more than the monstrous roars. In the silence, I feel sneaking, slithering things preparing to pounce and take me.

Safety was an illusion. There might be safety from the walrus, safety for Adam, but no safety for me. Ice Cream Villa, Miners' Favorite Pizza are no safer than anywhere else in Bennytown, and I need to get out of here right now.

If the sucking layer of fetid muck on the floor wasn't pulling at my shoes, I'd run. It feels like quicksand dragging me in deeper the harder I try to flee. I tell myself that the floor is only a couple inches beneath my feet, but the suction seems to increase the more I walk.

Wet, rasping sounds fill the air. And then I hear the wails of damned souls. Suddenly, there is more than the swamp pulling at my feet. Strong, bony hands, hands that shouldn't be, but they're here all right *(allinmyhead)*.

Skeletal figures emerge from the muck. Gaunt figures composed of bones and rotten lumps of ice cream mix slump out of the stagnant water. Sprinkles melt within their murky flesh, drawing streaks of bright orange, green, red, yellow into rivers that mix into a dull brown. The forms are little more than heads and arms at first. Soon, ribcages, spines and legs form as they claw their way toward me. They scream wet, raspy hisses while they grab onto my legs and pull me deeper into the mire, their eyeless sockets offering little mercy or pity.

I fight and thrash and scream, but hands grab at my wrists. Another hooks into my mouth, and I'm pulled down face-first into the disgusting darkness.

Rotten dairy sludge fills my mouth, nose, eyes, and I start to choke. They're pulling me deeper, deep enough to *see* into the past.

A construction site that would be Bennytown, bathed in the blood of its workers.

The World War II prison camp, with cruel guards battering the Japanese prisoners.

The Spanish mission that committed atrocities on the local population. Whippings. Torture. Crucifixions.

The cruel history of this place unfolds before me. Monsters, both human and beastly, have ruled this land and drawn power from it for millennia. I see the great hidden beams of light buried deep within the earth that connect this land to other places of great power on this planet. These rotten milk demons force me to watch, and they want to warn me. I know they don't mean to hurt me, but if I watch this for one second longer, I'll lose my mind.

Great, strong hands grab my legs and pull me from the swamp. With a scream, I'm pulled away from this world of terrible truths, and brought back into the reality of the Dark Park. Anything is better than that ancient subterranean truth.

With my first breath of air, I cough violently and then vomit what little is still in my stomach. I'm not frightened when the giant hands fling me through the air, and I land painfully on some piece of kitchen equipment. In point of fact, I'm laughing uncontrollably. Compared to those hidden beams of light and what they mean, there's little in this world or beyond that can scare me right now.

The giddiness fades when the great hands pull me from the industrial sink I landed in to throw me back down the hallway leading into Ice Cream Villa.

That's when I realize that I'm being tossed around by flippers. My burning eyes focus on my rescuer, Wilbur Walrus.

Up close, he looks more grotesque than any nightmare. His whole body is rotten and swollen, mouths *(mouths inside of mouths)* hide behind his cartoony smile with the broken tusk, while his plastic eyes don't look nearly plastic enough the more I look at him. The vertical slit in his stomach oozes a pink, frothy pus laced with fat and writhing grubs, making it impossible for the myriad squirming fingers trying to escape from it to find purchase. These fingers are attached to small, children's hands. Wilbur strokes this horrible opening and the scrambling fingers that will never truly find escape luxuriantly. Behind him cower six of the Sack Head Kids, still on leashes.

"You're supposed to be joining the family, not taking my special friends. You've been a very bad boy. You know what I do to bad boys around here, don't you?" He cheerfully rubs the slit in his stomach.

In a corner of the Ice Cream Villa, Garcia and Adam cower while Garcia holds the ax defensively. The walrus, the Sack Head Kids, and I are between them and the door. There's no way to escape.

"Cat got your tongue? That's not very nice, is it? When you're one of Wilbur's special friends, that won't be a problem. Sure, they all got plans for you. If I getcha first, then they'll make plans for someone else." He chuckles.

The Sack Head Kids flinch, which makes the walrus snort.

"Ah well. If you're gonna be a bunch of Gloomy Guses, we might as well skip the foreplay and get down to business," he says. The mouth of his suit splits open vertically to reveal a rotten, skinless human face. The slit in his stomach widens, and the small, delicate hands pour out, each attached to a pulsing tentacle. They are made from some terrible melding of sticky, pale white, foul-smelling flesh and costume fur. They crawl towards me, squealing and slipping over one another with frantic intensity as each tries to be the first to touch me. The walrus coos and groans with glee.

"Hey!" Garcia shouts, sliding the ax across the floor. The tip of the handle grazes my finger. I feel that that dark rage that tells me I can do anything, at least not when I'm doing something so righteous. Energy flows through the ax into me, and I grab the weapon and swing outward.

I strike first at the tentacles. The ax cuts through easily, severing them to the floor and spilling dark black slime. The tentacles scream and squeal as they writhe on the floor, dying.

The walrus looks down at them and puts both flippers onto his split-open stomach.

"No fair, no fair, no fair!" he wails.

I don't care what some undead monster *freak* in a walrus costume thinks about fairness.

I want what's right for Bennytown, and what's right for Bennytown is spilling the walrus's blood all over Ice Cream Villa.

"FLIP! YOU!" I roar, chopping at him over and over. He fights me, but with every chop he gets weaker and weaker. His squeal loses steam until his flippers lose all strength.

Soon, save for the writhing larvae that live within him, he's motionless.

Panting, covered in his gore, and feeling more alive than I have since I stepped into the Dark Park, I glance at his Sack Head Kids and Adam. Curiously, they watch me, cocking their heads like birds.

"It's all right, kids. I've taken care of you." I try to echo Mom's calming words. One at a time, they nod, and then run for the exits. Before leaving with the rest, Adam considers me briefly, gives me a hug, and then runs off.

Garcia approaches me warily, one hand held in front of her.

"You okay, Noel?" she asks.

(PLEASE, HELP!)

"I'm fine," I reply.

(Benny will take care of you)

"I'm fine." I shake my head.

(allinmyhead)

"Why?"

(ruckus)

"Just wanted to make sure. I'll take the ax back," she says, slowly approaching.

When we were on the Stairway to Heaven, I was wary of the weapon. Drawn to it but repulsed by it. *Scared* by it. Being around it filled me with a dark certainty that I didn't trust.

After wielding it against Wilbur, I like what it promises. I might even need it. With it, I might be able to save Bennytown and Olivia. Maybe finally show everyone that I'm strong. That I'm *right*.

(I've taken care of you)

Reluctantly, I hand it back to Garcia. Wordlessly, she accepts it and leads me through the door and back out into the Dark Park.

The crowd of mannequins changed positions while we were inside. They have arranged themselves like they did in the Lower Park, parting to opposite sides of the street. Benny waits at the end of this path, waving.

Garcia's saying something I can't hear over the roaring in my ears. When Benny points, my eyes follow his guidance.

Something's happening to Candy Mountain.

Its surface is splitting down the middle, much like the walrus's stomach. Large pieces of fiberglass candy break off and rain down the side. The ride tracks split and crack while great fingers of twisted metal, plastic, and rubber rip through its brightly painted face.

Over the sound of breaking, I can hear a deep growl that rattles the ground beneath us and breaks a couple streetlights.

A single, glowing eye is visible through the split. It seems to both malevolent and familiar, alarming and comforting.

I hear a great intake of air that sounds like a badly maintained jet engine as this new monster lets out another of its ear-splitting, mechanical roars.

When its finished, there is a different kind of roar behind me.

"YOU!" JK yells, running toward us like a bull.

NOEL

Bennytown was the reason that Olivia and I got together. Don't get me wrong, I'd have always loved her, but if it hadn't been for Bennytown, I'd have never been crazy enough to consider making it a more-than-friends sort of situation.

About a week after she broke up with Tommy, I helped both of them through the sadness. Tommy was my best friend, so we spent a lot of time hanging out and talking about other hot girls. Olivia snuck over to my place whenever Tommy wasn't there to cry on my shoulder. Often, she'd ask if she should get back together with him. I was in a strange place trying to figure out who deserved my loyalty.

I decided that I needed to lavish Olivia with more attention since she was suffering the most. I knew one surefire way to cheer people up, so I convinced Dad to take Olivia to Bennytown with us.

Dad left us to our own devices, but not without a sly wink and a few jokes about the two of us enjoying our first date. I kept telling him that this wasn't a date, a protest that made both Dad and Olivia laugh to no end. I didn't want to make those kind of moves on my best friend's ex. This trip to Bennytown was meant to cheer up a friend and nothing more.

Still, there was an undeniable tension in the air. She wasn't a thrill seeker, so we ignored the rides and focused on the slower things. I enjoyed every quiet moment with her. While I wanted to impress her, I didn't feel that overwhelming *need* to impress her.

Maybe that lack of urgency is how it all started. Sitting close on rides or at shows and being crammed in tight quarters in the crowded lines ignited a spark between us. As the day went on, she began flashing me warm smiles I hadn't seen in a while. These smiles made me feel good to be alive.

By noon, she was holding my hand so we wouldn't get separated by the crowds. There was a certain soft strength to that grip that made my stomach feel strange in a not entirely unpleasant way.

By two, she was finding other excuses to touch me. We tried on items in shop windows and continued playfully flirting. My resolve to not do anything because of Tommy was waning, and I was starting to make excuses to myself.

Those last shreds of my resolve held until our final picture of the day.

Olivia took tons of pictures, and she made a special effort to get photos of us with each of the nine main members of Benny & Friends. By day's end, we'd gotten pictures with eight of them. In each one, we stood closer and closer to each other.

Pedro Parrot had eluded us.

We searched Bennytown high and low, but we couldn't find him. Olivia kept telling me that it didn't matter if we never found him. She thought eight was still pretty damn good and that she'd still had a really fun day. By that point, it had become an obsession, more like a *quest,* to complete the set and finish off our perfect day.

When the sun started to set, we finally found Pedro Parrot. He was standing for photo ops by Candy Mountain. Olivia practically cheered at the sight of him, and we sprinted to get our final selfie of the day.

Olivia and I squeezed in tightly together and Pedro posed behind us. I was so wrapped up in my feeling of victory that it took me a few moments to notice Olivia trying to get my attention.

Before I knew what was happening, I was looking into her eyes, staring straight into the soul of one of the happiest, kindest, and most wonderful people I'd ever known. Seconds later, looking turned into kissing. I was kissing a girl for the first time, and it was awesome.

To this day, I call it one of the greatest moments of my life. It may have been the last time Olivia was happy about Bennytown, but it's a day I've treasured whenever I'm feeling down.

THE DARK PARK enjoys perverting this memory.

Ahead of us, Candy Mountain is a dark monument that roars and crackles from the great beast slowly digging its way out.

The friend I'm with is the ghost of a woman who's been dead for twice as many years as I've been alive, ripped in half by a malfunctioning escalator.

Pedro Parrot's still here but is now a hulking Redeemer. The man inside doesn't mean to make us laugh or goad us into kissing, but he certainly wants me dead.

Memories of what happened melt into what's happening now, and I have a hard time telling the difference between the two. Suddenly, JK knocks me to the ground with one powerful backhand. Rolling ten feet, I scrape skin and hit my head hard enough to see stars. With an audible snap and a gush of blood down my face, I know my nose is broken.

"Hey!" Garcia screams. I don't see him hit her, but I hear her groan of pain and the sound of her flying through the air, roughly landing nearby.

Head still spinning, I manage to get up onto all fours, only to get a heavy boot to the gut for my trouble. Heavy kicks and punches rain down on me. Any hint of the jackass who showed me the ropes on my first day and tried to get me to buy his rap album is gone.

He shocks me with a cattle prod, searing my body with agony greater than I'd ever known was possible. My own screams mix in my ears with Mom's dying cries.

When I come to, I'm on my back while his heavy foot digs into my chest. My eyes are blurry and losing focus with every extra bit of pressure he puts on me. I look up at him hatefully, because I don't want him to see how afraid I am in this moment.

It's not fair.

I believe in Bennytown.

He raises his foot, preparing to crush the life out of me like a bug. He's going to crush me and make me a permanent resident of the park. Olivia will be doomed. And Bennytown—

With an animalistic howl, JK falls onto his side, wailing and holding his leg. Garcia stands behind him, shaking the blood off the end of the ax. She offers me a hand.

"Come on! That won't stop him for long!" she says.

Weakly, I reach toward her, but my arm feels like it weighs several tons and is full of broken glass. Somehow, she manages to pull me to my feet and wraps my arm around her shoulders, awkwardly holding onto both me and the ax.

"Gimme that," I say miserably.

She looks uncertain but passes it to my free hand. Although I'm exhausted, I still get a boost of hot, violent energy that it's imbued with. I shamble along with Garcia using the ax as a cane as she leads me away from JK.

She guides me into the overgrown Primordial World. Mutilated rubber duckies hang from trees. We can barely walk, let alone run through the choking foliage. I hold out hope that JK will be slower than us.

Garcia slows, then stops, her eyes conflicted.

"What are you doing?" I ask, frantic.

"I can't do this," Garcia says.

"I'm sorry. I should've been stronger."

"No, it's not that, it's…" She freezes up, stuck on words she isn't meant to share. "I lied."

"Lied? About what?"

I'm afraid that JK is catching up to us. In this vegetation it's impossible to tell where he might be.

"I was told to befriend you, all right? I've been doing what I'm told to get you in an agreeable state for their plan. But you… damn you, you made me doubt this, 'cause I like you. Nobody who'd have helped me on the escalator like you. I can't let them keep doing this to you," she says.

Her words sink in dully. While every part of my being doesn't want to believe her betrayal, I know she's telling the truth. Even more, her remorse feels real, and I can't feel angry at her for too long.

"I understand," I say.

"You—wait, what?"

"I understand. When Bennytown tells you to jump, it's really hard to not ask how high."

"So, you're not angry?"

"A little. But you're still my friend?"

"Of course."

"And you're not lying to me this time?"

"I'd cross my heart if it still beat, but I'm not lying."

"Then get me to the Green Door Society and we can fight about this later," I say.

The thick vegetation hides us from the animals that snuffle and growl as they move through the jungle.

Garcia laughs, letting out a heavy sigh. "While I wanna thank you for being so forgiving, I can't let you go to the Green Door Society."

If she didn't want to anger me, she's not doing a very good job of it.

"I have to."

"No, you don't," she says.

"It's the only way. I have to save—"

"It's not what you think. Haven't you stopped to think that you are heading right where they want you to go? Where they've been leading you all this time?" she asks.

"Of course, I have! I know the Dark Park is in my head and that it's leading me to some*thing*. If I want to save Olivia and Bennytown, I need to get there. If I get into the Green Door Society, I can make things right again, because *I believe in Bennytown*."

Garcia looks at me skeptically but says nothing. She starts moving again, guiding me to Journey through Americana.

"If you do this, you know you're probably gonna get yourself killed, right?"

"I feel pretty dead already," I joke, though she doesn't laugh.

"Since I'm bound to this park, I can't stop you. If you get some sense, head to Teddy Roosevelt's Wildlife Adventures; Lorraine used to be a trainer there, and it's her usual Dark Park haunt. Most of the animal spirits are loyal to her, and with an army like that, none of the other spirits fuck with her. I'll be waiting there. The three of us can wait until morning, when all this will feel like a bad dream. You'll have to be strong for what happens next, but I believe in you."

It's a tempting fantasy, but I can't just stop now. Not when Bennytown's salvation is almost within my grasp.

Soon we're passing through the gates to Journey through Americana.

"I have to do this. But if it goes to heck, I'll find you," I say.

"That's all I'm asking," Garcia says, relieved.

"YOU!" JK roars behind us. Garcia picks up the pace, and we're half running, half hobbling through the mannequins in the streets of Journey through Americana as JK barrels out of the jungle behind us.

We cross the road and find the alley leading to the Green Door Society. Garcia lets go of my shoulders.

"I can't go any further," she says.

"Thank you for getting me this far," I say.

"Sure," she replies. "Now, don't fuck up."

The words hit me hard when I recall the words that Dad told me on my first day here. They were echoed by Kathleen on my first day working at the Safari Lodge. I'm reminded of the real reason why I'm here and the true weight of what I have to do.

Overcome with love for her, I wrap Garcia in a quick hug, then force my way down the alley. Looking back over my shoulder, I'm sad to see she's already disappeared.

"YOU!" JK is limping badly, while a small river of blood pours down his leg. Relentlessly, he pushes his way through the mannequins. I almost surrender to the futility of running away from a *monster* who just won't stop.

Then my radio crackles to life one final time. "PLEASE, HELP!"

Bennytown needs me.

Thank God the red door is in sight. I stumble for it, gather up enough energy to pull together a hopping run, and then grab for the door handle.

I grip the handle tightly in my wounded hand and try to turn it.

It won't budge.

Frantic, I rattle the handle, grip it harder, but it won't move. I pound on the door, kick it, scream, but nothing makes any difference.

I can't get into the Green Door Society.

Bennytown has rejected me.

After everything I've done.

(PLEASE, HELP!)

(Benny will take care of you)

After everything I'm willing to do, Bennytown has rejected me.

"Why? Why, WHY, WHY?!? I did everything you ever asked! Why? Just tell me, darn it, tell me!" I yell, pounding on the door with the ax's handle, but it doesn't budge.

And then I know I'm not alone. JK stands at the mouth of the alley, cocking his giant head, not charging because he knows he has me cornered.

I close my eyes, trying to find power from Dad and Olivia, hoping they'll give me what I need to fight off JK, but they offer nothing but anger and sadness.

They can't help me here.

Only one thing can.

I whisper rapidly, hoping beyond all hope that Bennytown, the *good* in Bennytown, is listening. "Please, please, please, if I did something wrong, I apologize. Save me now, let me do what I have to do, and I'll do whatever you want. You know that I believe in Bennytown."

With those words, the ground rumbles slightly, unsettling JK.

That's where the power is.

"I believe in Bennytown," I say with confidence. I grip the ax tightly, enjoying the feeling of fire it gives me as the ground rumbles even more heavily. JK is almost shaken off his feet, while I'm holding firm.

"I believe in Bennytown. I believe in Bennytown! I BE-LIEVE IN BENNYTOWN!"

An explosion lights up the sky, shattering windows and raining metal and chunks of fiberglass all around us. The mechanical roar is louder, now free of Candy Mountain. Heavy, swift footsteps approach, shaking the world around us. Although I know I should be afraid, I realize that I have nothing to fear.

Perhaps sensing this, JK charges. Before he can get more than three steps, a great hand reaches down from the sky and grabs him. JK squeals indignantly, batting at it with his one free arm.

Even in his current state, he's no match for the Candy Troll.

Balding and dragging a club in one hand, it's the same towering Candy Troll that used to scare me when I was little. Now, it's every bit as horrible-looking as anything else in the Dark Park. Its normally bright colors are faded, its flesh corroded with bits of metal and hydraulic tubing exposed, and its mouth is filled with candy-rotted teeth sharpened to points. The ground-shaking roars were the sound of its frustration at digging out of Candy Mountain.

It wanted to protect me.

The Candy Troll holds up JK to its snarling face and roars. JK thrashes around frantically, as the monster shoves him into its mouth and bites him in half. The Candy Troll chomps down on what's left of JK and swallows dramatically, wiping gore from its animatronic lips with the back of its hand.

I look up at this great beast who haunted my childhood nightmares, and I see nothing to fear. Its terrible face is now kind and familiar. I sense *love* in those giant, glowing eyes.

Turning to head back to its lair, it stops to look back at me longingly.

"It's all right, sweetie. Benny will take care of you," it says in its rumbling, ghastly voice, disappearing around the corner with heavy footsteps that fade into the distance.

I want to follow her to reaffirm my faith in Bennytown, but I can't.

Not when I'm surrounded in light.

The Green Door Society is open, brilliant white light spilling out all around me.

Olivia and Bennytown's salvation lie beyond this portal.

Garcia's warning echoes in my ears, so I tighten my grip on the ax and step into the light.

The Green Door Society is cleaner than I remember, like it must've been in the early days of Bennytown. The wood shines with polish, while the linens are crisp and smell freshly laundered. People in tuxedos and gowns wearing wooden Benny masks sit at the tables. They celebrate as a masked woman in a sparkly dress croons Roy Orbison's "Cryin'" accompanied by a big band. The room is decorated with streamers and latex bunny-ears balloons, while a large banner spans the entire room. It states says proudly, "CONGRATULATIONS ON 60 GREAT YEARS!" When the partygoers notice me, they stand up and clap, some of them raising flutes of champagne, cheering my name or shaking my hand as I pass.

These are unmistakably members of the Green Door Society, and the people I mean to destroy. At a glance, they look glamorous but on closer inspection I can see through them. I see their age and decay, and that their clothes are cheap attempts for the dead to look alive.

A large man dressed in what looks like Bennytown branded riot gear opens the door to Dorian's private dining room. White light pours from the chamber, beckoning me. I can't see Elle or Olivia in here, but if they're anywhere, that's where they'd be.

I stride purposefully toward the open door, trying not to focus too much on Garcia's warnings.

I can do this.

I have to do this.

When the doors close behind me, I'm certain I'm alone for a second. As my eyes adjust to the dimming light, I know this isn't true.

Sitting at the head of the Vitruvian Benny table is Benny himself.

Not quite. Just an empty character costume.

"Now isn't *that* exciting."

I'd know that voice anywhere, and despite every instinct telling me it should be comforting, my blood chills at the sound.

Stepping out of the room's only dark corner, he's a burly, vibrant man dressed in overalls and a checked flannel shirt with the sleeves rolled up to his elbows. His hair and magnificent beard blaze red, while his eyes and smile twinkle with kindness.

Holy flip, it's Fletcher Dorian.

"I've been expecting you, Noel. Want a root beer?"

NOEL

A finely dressed masked waiter enters the room carrying a tray with two open bottles of root beer. He sets the tray down on the table and leaves without looking at us. Wanting something to do with my hands other than worry about wiping any of the grime of the Dark Park from myself onto this very nice room, I take one of the bottles and sip on it.

This is the greatest root beer I've ever tasted.

Remember why you're here. This isn't right. They led you here, they've done something to Olivia, they've defiled Bennytown, you need to keep a clear head, or they'll distract you.

"Do you like the band, Three Dog Night?" Mr. Dorian asks, punching numbers into the jukebox. It stutters for a second, but then catches and begins to play.

"Uh, sure," I answer. Until this moment, I've never had a firm opinion one way or another on the musical stylings of Three Dog Night. As the lead singer sings about his good friend Jeremiah, Mr. Dorian grabs the other bottle of root beer and sits next to me.

"Rock and roll is one of mankind's greatest creations. People from my generation hated it. They just didn't have an eye for the future. Do you think a lot about the future, Noel?" Mr. Dorian asks.

"I try to," I admit.

He laughs, clapping me on the back with one of his strong hands. But when it touches me, it's the gnarled hand of a dying, skeletal man, from Fletcher Dorian's final years. The sensation is brief but frightening enough that I flinch. And then I feel bad for flinching. After everything I've seen that resides within Bennytown, I can't stop gawking at the fact that I'm sitting here, drinking root beer and listening to music with Fletcher Dorian.

That's not Fletcher Dorian, just a ghost. A leftover attached to Bennytown like any of the other spirits you met tonight.

Stop it, that's just doubt talking.

(allinmyhead)

"Tell me something, Noel," he says.

"What?"

"Did you see Kathleen at all tonight?"

"No. Why?" I ask as a sick feeling grows in my stomach.

"Her spirit should be here, but I had to engage some of my Bengineers to keep her out of your way for tonight. I'm happy to hear that was successful," Dorian admits gravely.

The question I want to ask is almost too painful to consider, but I need to know. "She didn't die in a car accident, did she?"

Mr. Dorian strokes his beard. "No. After she drove you home, she came back with a mind to start trouble. I wager she was trying to save you. She got violent, so park security intervened. She gave them no choice."

This is my fault. It's always my fault.

He continues, "We had to stage her accident to not raise suspicions, but now she'll remain forever a part of the Bennytown family."

Though I still have concerns, this relieves me more than expected. "Good. I don't think it'd be Bennytown without her."

"No, it wouldn't, would it?" He laughs. "You know, I like you, Noel. Always have."

"You do?" I'm not sure if I'm supposed to be flattered or scared by this, but Kathleen's fate no longer worries me.

"Yes. At your core you're everything we look for in a Bennytown family member. You're hardworking, believe in keeping Bennytown great, and fundamentally want to do the right thing. You do believe in Bennytown, don't you, Noel?"

"Of course, I do!" I say, defensive.

"Excellent. Because on this eve of triumph, Bennytown is facing its greatest crisis, and I believe that you're the only one who can avert it," Mr. Dorian's voice is low and full of warning. He speaks with conviction, like just saying the words should make perfect sense. Somehow, it makes me feel worse.

Perhaps sensing my confusion, he walks over to the map on the wall.

I feel stronger when he's not looking at me, strong enough to form my own questions. There are a million things I want to ask. Things I need to say, but I can't find the right words. I spy the ax out of the corner of my eye, still dripping with gore from attacking the walrus and JK and put on a placemat at Mr. Dorian's insistence, so it won't dirty the table. Not even that gives me the strength I need. In his presence, I'm too tongue tied to ask where he's keeping Olivia. I'm a child, and he's the greatest adult who ever lived.

I came here to kick butt, and I'm paralyzed, entirely at his mercy.

He looks at me with one eye, and self-consciously I wipe my hands on my uniform shirt, which does nothing to clean them.

He turns back to the map. "I apologize for any inconvenience you may have suffered tonight. The Dark Park was never in my designs, but it has proven to be surprisingly useful. It has become a crucible for testing the worthiness of those with potential, and for punishing the guilty."

Finally feeling as if my tongue has become unlocked, I ask, "Which one am I?"

My voice is barely a squeak.

I can't see it, but I know he's smiling.

"I brought you here because you're ready to understand certain truths. They won't all be pleasant, but you need to hear them so you might *understand*. I want you to understand why we do what we do and how *important* you are. When we're done talking, you'll be given a choice that will shape your future and Bennytown's. If you're as strong as I believe, I know you'll make the right decision. Are you ready to hear the true history of Bennytown?"

No, no, God no. Run out of here and never come back. You know this is wrong. Something bad has already happened even if you don't understand it, but something even worse will happen if you stay here. Just get out and head to Garcia. For the love of all that's good and holy don't stay here another moment and get out of here now!

"Yes," I croak.

He looks at me, seriously considering me with a look I might call pity. I'm about to protest that I'm a loyal enough Bennytown family member and I can take anything. I'm torn between that or running away screaming. I want to save everyone and free Bennytown from the darkness that holds it, but I'm not sure if I've got the strength to do it.

I'm no longer paralyzed. I know that the door's unlocked and that I wouldn't be stopped if I walked through it.

But I stay put. God help me, I stay put.

Mr. Dorian has made up his mind to tell me everything. "It started during the Second World War. My unique aptitudes landed me into a special unit with the singular goal of interfering with Adolf Hitler's research into the supernatural."

He traces his fingers over the map in deliberate, diagonal lines, and I shudder when I see the map glow faintly along those exact paths.

"His interests were fairly limited to utter nonsense and fairy tales. While I worked to undermine him, I learned of true ancient powers that laugh in the face of what most call God."

The map of Bennytown glows even brighter and begins to move.

All the pictures in the room have been brought to life. They seem to be windows to bygone eras full of long-dead people now watching over us.

"After the war, I started the Dorian Studios empire with hard work and gumption. With Benny & Friends, I could have taken over the world with more efficiency than old Adolf ever could have dreamed about. I could have accomplished that without a single death, but I wanted to entertain the children of the world. Childhood is a dark period for so many, and I only wanted to remind the most innocent that life is full of wonders. In this period, I began sketching out the ideas for Bennytown. I kept this *seed* of an idea in the back of my mind. And then life stepped in to intervene." He takes a framed picture and slides it across the table to me.

It's black and white but moving with life. A beautiful woman dressed in '50s clothing is holding a baby and rocking it gently.

"My wife, Juliette, gave birth to Caroline on July 17th, 1950. I've had many children with many women over the years. Caroline was my first, and I was so proud of her. She was a bright, *bright* girl, always smiling, always laughing. Have you ever had someone who just made your life better simply by being in it? Have you ever known that kind of love, Noel?"

"Yes," I say, thinking of Olivia. The thought that she's hidden somewhere within this club fades to the back of my mind with every passing second. My memories of her are being pulled away to be replaced with anger and revulsion.

What's happening to me?

Mr. Dorian smiles and takes a sip of root beer. "Consider yourself fortunate then. A lot of people are never so lucky, or, like us, have their blessings taken away from them too soon."

How does he know about my mother?

He's Fletcher Dorian, of course he knows about my mother.

"As you know, cancer took my Caroline from me too early. There was nothing the doctors could do except make her comfortable. 'No' wasn't an answer I was accustomed to, so I put all my resources into saving her, to no avail. I couldn't imagine living in a world without her, so I entered a year-long spiral of self-destruction. I tried to dull the pain with cheap pleasures and self-delusion, telling myself that it was better to live in a world of imagination than one where anything could hurt me."

The picture in front of me changes to the time when Dad and I visited after Mom's death. I look like a zombie, and it startles me for a moment. I'm drawn to it anyway, and my gore-soaked fingers leaving a smudge on the glass. My heart aches when I look at my optimistic Dad that just wanted to give me the best when he was going through one of the worst periods of his life.

I can't imagine how he managed that kind of strength.

"Soon, imagination wasn't enough. I knew that a mind like mine was wasted on self-pity, and that if I truly wanted Caroline back, I would have to do it myself. I vowed that I'd do whatever it took to bring her back. And *that* is when I decided to use what I had learned and brought back from the war to make Bennytown a reality."

Tapping the map of Bennytown again, golden lines spread out from his touch.

"There are lines of natural power that run beneath the earth, and the locations where they converge contain great power. Power, if harnessed, that could break the barriers between worlds. I scoured the world for a suitable location and found one to have greater power than nearly any on earth."

"Here?" I ask.

He nods. "This place was a nearly empty plot of land with a dark history, but it also had *power*. I turned Bennytown into a great machine that would allow me to breach the silence separating life and death. Its fuel would be the emotions of the guests who walked through her doors. The protectors of that great power would be the Bennytown family, lost souls bound together by a greater purpose. They would keep the machine running because they believed in Bennytown. It'd be a place where innocence and creativity could run free and unbidden by the evils of the outside world. Some people called me crazy, but I didn't care, not so long as it brought Caroline back. That was my first mistake."

The room dims and fills with dark voices. Malevolent whispers make my skin crawl.

"Early tests revealed that while we'd opened a rift between worlds, it wasn't one that could easily be controlled. Instead of a window, we'd created a gaping hole. Darkness flooded through and claimed the lives of many responsible for building Bennytown. The salt line and the Redeemers were able to contain them for a time, but something more would need to be done to control them. A sacrifice would need to be made."

He faces me now with a large, leather bound tome in his hands.

Flipping open its pages, he reads, *"For restfulness of the land, the sacrifice of a broken person with no connection to the world who has spilled blood of the living on this sacred spot will be needed."*

He snaps the book shut and sets it down on the table. "Latin's never been one of my best languages, so the passage loses a little zest in translation. Bennytown is a repository for spirits, not only those from the rift, but for anyone who has died within its borders. The Redeemers police them as best they can, and when things get truly rambunctious, I'll don the Benny costume and step in myself to keep the peace. With the ever-increasing number of spirits in Bennytown, there is a great restlessness. So, every decade, we've had to cultivate a broken soul for the greater good of Bennytown."

The lights flicker on, one at a time, and illuminate black-and-white pictures of dead, mutilated bodies with brass plaques beneath them.

<u>Dr. Randolph Ziegler – 1959</u>
<u>Clifford Tally - 1970</u>
<u>Wallace Vickers – 1977</u>
<u>Dewey Farmer – 1990</u>
<u>Bogart Dwyer – 1998</u>

Dorian continues, "Most of these men were the worst of the worst. Murderers, pedophiles, and drunks became Bennytown revenants. The need for them to spill blood within the park's confines for the ritual to succeed are unfortunate evils. Over time we may have gone too far or pushed people too hard. For instance, the Dewey Farmer murders led to seven children getting killed. We tried to erase his existence, but as you've seen, the walrus is awfully persistent."

"For almost twenty years, we've tried to cultivate a perfectly broken soul, but none have worked out. They've been too… weak. In their failures, Bennytown has weakened, and the Dark Park has only grown in power."

As if on cue, the ground quakes beneath us, shaking dust from the ceiling and sending the chandelier swaying back and forth.

"Bennytown celebrates its Sixtieth Birthday tomorrow, Noel, and it's on the verge of being torn apart. There will be no more joy, no more innocence, no more Bennytown. Not without sacrifice," he says.

He lets these words hang in the air. I get what he's saying right away, no matter how much I don't want to.

Finally, I find my strength. I can see everything wrong with what he's proposing, and I find my voice. I'm no longer grasping for words, and I'm filled with fiery resolve.

"No," I whisper.

Not quite the powerful response you were expecting, but it's a start.

"Come again, Noel?" Mr. Dorian says.

"I won't be your sacrifice," I say firmly, but still shaking.

He starts to say something, but I interrupt. "What's happening here, what you're doing, is wrong. I appreciate what you created, and your reasons for doing it, but I won't—"

"Noel, the Bennytown family—"

I interrupt again, stronger. "I love being a part of the Bennytown family, but I'd be a terrible sacrifice. Not just because I haven't spilled the blood of the living in Bennytown and never will, but because *I'm not broken!* I have a *real* family, people who love me. I know you've got my girlfriend somewhere, and I'm here to save her."

"Is that what you think?" Dorian asks, stroking his beard.

"I know you do. I've heard Olivia on the radio," I say.

He's got no response to this. I continue, "I just want them back. Free Olivia, let me take her with me, and you'll never have to see us again. I won't anything do against Bennytown. I still love it, and I would never hurt it, but I just want my girlfriend back."

There's no way he can know that I still mean to save Bennytown *and* Olivia, and that I still mean to tear down everything that's dark and twisted about the park so I can help restore its true glory. I know it won't be simple, but I'll find a way. I'll call the press and the to tell them the truth about Bennytown's horrors.

Why is Fletcher Dorian laughing? Not big, maniacal, supervillain laughing like you'd expect at a moment, but an amused chuckle. He flashes to the pale dying skeleton in his wheelchair and his voice is no longer joyful and booming, but a hiss escaping from an open tomb.

"You really don't remember what happened, do you?" he says.

"I…"

I don't remember because I blacked out. Did something bad happen? My mind is tickled by unwelcome images and feelings.
(allinmyhead)

Dorian flips to his younger self again. "Noel, despite what you tell yourself, you're truly a broken young man."

"You took something from me, didn't you?" This sounds like a feeble accusation even to me.

"Noel, we did nothing to you. Like it or not, what happened here was all your own doing. Take my hand, and I'll show you," he says.

When he holds his hand out to me, I see no malice in the gesture. Still, I can't take it.

I dread the touch of that gnarled, ancient claw.

"No," I whisper.

"You know what they say, Noel: the truth shall set you free. The truth *will* catch up to you. Would you rather stumble into it blindly, or be guided into it by *family*?" Mr. Dorian proposes, his hand still out.

I don't take it. I won't take it. It's not real if I don't see it, don't hear it. I haven't done anything wrong, at least nothing that can't be fixed. All I want to do is work hard, do good, come home, be a good boyfriend, a good son, and nothing bad'll ever happen to me or anyone else I love.

If I don't touch him, I can still live in a world where this is possible for a while longer.

Sighing, Mr. Dorian says, "This is for your own good."

He darts for me and clamps his onto my shoulder.

OLIVIA STORMS AWAY from me.

"Olivia!" I yell, grabbing her by the wrist.

I want to let her know that I mean business.

If she's scared, she'll understand.

"Noel!" she exclaims. The look in her eyes isn't fear, but anger. "You're... you're hurting me!"

She looks like she wants to hurt me. She's pushing me away when all I wanted to do was something nice for her.

I yell, "I did this for us! I did this for you! I thought this was supposed to be special!"

I catch a glimmer of fear in her eyes. I like it.

"What have they done to you, Noel?" she asks.

She just doesn't get it. She'll never get it. She'll never get it because she doesn't know what Bennytown really means to me. If she doesn't get that, how can we ever work?

I'll make her understand. Somehow, I'll make her understand.

I take a deep breath, and say, "I believe in Bennytown."

She doesn't like that answer.

She doesn't like what she sees in my eyes.

She tries to twist away, but I grab her arm and pull her towards me, making her yelp in pain.

"Let go of me, Noel!" she says.

I don't. I need to make her understand.

I pull her close.

She swings a slap at me but misses, and her wrist collides with the side of my head.

This only makes me angrier.

I yank her by the arm until she stumbles and slips from my grasp.

With a loud, wet sound, her head hits the side of the jukebox.

She looks at me sadly, her bloodied lip quivering.

"What did you do?" she asks.

I approach her.

She holds up one of her hands. "Please, don't. I'm sorry, I'm sorry, please..."

She says she's sorry, but she's not. She still hates this place, and that angers me more.

I grab a handful of her beautiful, chestnut hair, the hair I've always loved running my fingers through. I grab it tight.

Now she's screaming.

"OH GOD, NOEL! STOP IT! STOP IT! PLEASE, HELP!"

I swing her head into the jukebox once. Twice.
I don't need to swing it a third time.

WHEN THE PRESENT materializes around me yet again, I feel sick. I begin to shake all over.

I'm a monster. I killed *her*. I killed Olivia.

I can't come back from this or fix it.

All I have left now is Bennytown.

Mr. Dorian was right. He was always right.

"Kinda rough, huh?" he asks, clapping me on the back. "I know you think everything's over, but it's all uphill from here, I swear."

I look up at him with tears pouring from my eyes. How does he expect this to get better? I've destroyed everything, and he expects this to get better.

He pulls me to my feet, guides me to the wall with the map.

"You've got two options, Noel. First, you can escape the Dark Park and get picked up by the police to get prosecuted. Feel free to tell them whatever you want about Bennytown and the Dark Park. Maybe they'll believe you, or maybe they'll think it's just the psychotic ravings of a person of interest in the disappearance of Olivia Verne with a documented history of mental illness."

He waits for me to ask about the second option. It feels like a very long time. When I don't, he just shrugs and continues.

"Or, there is a second option: you can become Benny," he says.

I croak, "What?"

"Be the sacrifice Bennytown needs. Spill blood tomorrow, during the Sixtieth Birthday celebrations and make sure to spill a lot of it because Bennytown is thirsty. Then find a way to die, because Bennytown is hungry. For your sacrifice, you'll be forever bound to the park, and I'll turn you into the new Benny.

I'm tired, Noel, and I can't police Bennytown anymore. I want to dedicate more time searching for Caroline. Become Benny, and you will become the symbol the revenants fear. You will keep Bennytown pure. And if that isn't enough incentive…"

He taps the wall which opens to reveal a hidden hospital room.

Lying in a bed, Olivia is heavily bandaged and hooked to numerous pieces of machinery. A respirator hisses with each breath she takes.

I run to her, crying and grabbing her hand. The spark is gone, and her hand is weak. Oh, my poor, sweet Olivia.

"Elle found her after your attack, almost brain-dead. Then, she found you in a fugue state and cleaned everything up rather efficiently. If you do what we need, we'll let Olivia die in Bennytown. She'll be bound to the place with you, so you two can be together forever."

I stare at Fletcher Dorian, trying to reconcile everything I've ever believed about him with everything I've seen tonight.

I weep when I look at Olivia, seeing the horrors I've brought to life.

Then I look to the dinner table where the ax rests, and then glance at the Benny the Bunny suit. Benny's plastic, staring eyes bore into me.

(It's alright, sweetie. Benny will take care of you.)

This is wrong. *Beyond* wrong. I started working at Bennytown because I love it and because it *saved* me when I was most vulnerable. I barely wanted the job. Dad talked me into it and made me get up early on my birthday to apply. It wasn't even a great job, not when I went home every night stinking and tired.

It shouldn't have led to this.

(allinmyhead)

I should tell the cops everything and take my punishment. Part of taking this job was accepting responsibility. Wouldn't that mean owning up to what I've done? I wanted people to see me as a man, as someone capable and strong. People would notice me. This kind of thing never goes unnoticed by the media. I'll have a platform to shout to the world about what's happening at Bennytown. Most people will think I'm crazy, but maybe someone will listen.

But… what if I did what Mr. Dorian wants? What if I became the sacrifice Bennytown *needs*? I'd never have to leave again. I'd be with friends, and I'd get to help make Bennytown into exactly what I want. With the powers that Mr. Dorian's promising, I could try to save it from within. Maybe with the power of Benny, I can fight the darkness and make Bennytown everything it should be.

And I'd get to be with Olivia. We'd be together forever with no more worries.

"What's it going to be, Noel? Will you run, or are you ready to join the real Bennytown family?" Mr. Dorian asks.

I consider the choices for a long time, but in the end, my answer is pretty obvious.

GARETH
2019

There was a Pony Party at Candy Mountain. Not a drill.

"Perfect. Just flipping perfect," Gareth Jenkins said. There were warnings from Management that they expected something big to go down on the day of the Sixtieth Birthday, so all available security personnel were stationed around Bennytown. Spread thin, they planned for one armed guard to pop out of a Rabbit Hole anywhere in the park within fifteen seconds of a call.

This decision, combined with the heightened Daywalker presence, let Gareth relax his guard. Since he was content with the limited possibility of danger in his quadrant, he hoped for a light day doing Sudoku.

Gareth tapped his earpiece. "Gareth here. Specify, inside the Mountain, or in the land? Over."

"Inside the Mountain," Cassidy responded. "The Mine Carts have broken down. All vehicles stopped in their tracks, but there are reports of screaming in the Candy Troll room. Cameras don't have an angle on the action, but someone is definitely inside causing trouble. Over."

"Is this our VIP? Over."

"Possibly, or it could just be another Vickers wannabe. Either way—"

"I'm en route. Ned, Dara, Violet, fall in behind me, I might need backup. Over and out." Gareth took off running down the Rabbit Hole as the others followed suit.

There was at least one minute before any of them showed up.

If this was just a Vickers wannabe, or, even worse, their VIP, a minute could be the difference between life and death.

Nevertheless, he raced to the pathway that led directly into the chamber of the Candy Troll.

He entered the fray inside a large rock candy geode. Though the ride was stopped dead, the ride operators hadn't turned off the animatronics or music. The candy miners still sang their frightened song and cowered from the giant Candy Troll, who swung his club in an arc above the track, roaring with each laborious swing.

Three ride vehicles were stuck in the chamber, and each one normally held up to eight people. The first vehicle was no more than three feet away from the Rabbit Hole exit.

Gareth didn't need to look long to know that all the people in it were either dead or dying. Unable to move due to their lap and over the shoulder restraints, each of them had been chopped open with a large weapon. Gareth had done three tours in Iraq with the SEALs, and even he wasn't sure he'd ever seen anything as horrible as the blood and viscera-drenched ride vehicle.

A fourteen-year-old girl looked up at him with pitiful, pleading eyes while staunching the blood pouring from her neck.

The second ride vehicle wasn't any better, and the riders had been stabbed and mutilated horribly. There were a strange number of empty seats. Restraints were pried open, and the occupants were nowhere to be found. The attacker was not in his line of sight.

"HOSTAGE SITUATION! SPOTTERS REPORT HOSTAGES ON TOP OF CANDY MOUNTAIN!"

The call was so loud, Gareth almost tore his earpiece out. He sprinted for the stairwell that went to the top of Candy Mountain. Skipping the steps two at a time, he found the hidden break room with its jai alai court. Two Candy Mountain maintenance people lay on the ground, torn apart with similar wounds from a heavy blade.

One of the men was still alive. "OH GOD, THEY'RE KIDS, HE'S MAKING THEM—"

"Darn," Gareth cursed, running for the ladder. Carefully, he climbed the ladder to the landing above. Stepping onto the great red-and-white mint landing, he saw something peculiar.

Benny?

Benny the Bunny stood at the edge of the mint, covered in blood and wielding an ax. Eight children were with him. Each of them covered their eyes and waited for a surprise with wide, expectant smiles on their faces.

Benny guided one of the kids to the edge of the mint. Although the little girl looked a little worried, she still smiled when Benny patted her on the head with one of his big, bloody gloves.

"It's all right, sweetie. Benny will take care of you," he said.

Smiling broadly, the little girl took one great step and fell from the edge of the mint.

Gareth didn't know what unsettled him more: that it was Benny doing this, or that the little girl didn't scream.

Gareth unholstered the Desert Eagle from inside his jacket and trained it on Benny.

"Drop your weapon and put your hands in the air. RIGHT! NOW!" Gareth commanded.

Benny turned toward Gareth, awkward, as if the costume wasn't something he was used to. The bright green of his fur was drenched with blood, staining it a dull brown. He didn't move to raise his ax, merely cocking his head.

"I SAVED BENNYTOWN!" Benny shrieked in a high, mad voice. "ISN'T THAT EXCITING?"

As one, the seven remaining kids cheered, "YAAAAYY!!"

Benny shifted his weight forward slightly. That was the only opening Gareth needed. He pulled the trigger three times, each bullet hitting Benny center mass. Blood sprayed all over the children. Benny collapsed into a heap, while the ax slid out of his hands and over the edge of the fiberglass mint.

At the sound, the kids removed their hands from their eyes, looking at Gareth and Benny.

"Why'd you shoot Benny!" a girl who couldn't have been more than four asked.

"He said we could stay here forever!" a young boy angrily declared.

Unmindful of the kids, Gareth put two more shots into Benny's body, then one where his head should've been in the costume. Through this, Benny didn't move, even as the kids continued to scream and cry.

With some effort, Gareth rolled Benny onto his back.

"What's going on? We heard gunshots."

Violet and Dara climbed out of the ladder hatch, their own guns drawn.

"Violet, call in ride operations. Get them to release restraints and evacuate. Initiate Walrus Protocol, cancel the Pony Party, and get these kids to safety," Gareth commanded.

"On it." Violet tapped her earpiece and issued a few harsh commands before gathering the children. Even when she guided them back to the ladder expertly, they kept staring at Gareth accusingly.

Gareth tore his eyes away from the children.

"Dara, I need to see who's inside. Keep your weapon on him," he said.

"I won't miss," she said, smirking.

"I know you won't," Gareth replied gravely. Dara was former IDF and always dominated Bennytown Security's yearly shooting competitions. If there was someone he'd want watching his back when things really hit the fan, it was Dara.

It took a few fumbling moments before he found the seam, then another to unlock the mechanism. With one final twist, the head popped off easily.

The right side of the boy's head was almost completely blown off by Gareth's final shot. Somehow, the kid was still alive, his one remaining eye studying Gareth, the side of his mouth that still had skin curling into a smile.

Before anyone could move, the boy used the last of his strength to pull himself to the edge, plummeting over the side of Candy Mountain. Looking down, Gareth watched in mute horror as his bright green, blood-stained body splattered against every decoration and Swirler track that dotted the outside of the Mountain. The corpse landed next to the bodies of five children who hadn't been as lucky as those Gareth saved.

Gareth never forgot this particular face after that one fateful day in Pedro Parrot's Safari Lodge, despite it being wrecked and broken.

"Was it him?" Dara asked.

Gareth tapped his earpiece. "This is a general call: the VIP is down. Repeat, the VIP is down. Bennytown is saved!"

Instead of cheering like all the other voices on the line were doing, he reholstered his gun and pulled Dara into a hug.

EPILOGUE
THOUGHTS AND PRAYERS

NOEL
2019

I have a better understanding of fear since the Sixtieth Birthday than I ever did before. The one thing I learned is that fear held me back from success. If I hadn't let fear rule my life, I could've been a better person, a stronger person, the kind of person that I'd always dreamed of being.

I thought I was saving Bennytown, but in the end Bennytown saved me.

Isn't that exciting?

"She's gonna be late," Monica repeats as we walk backstage toward the Family Member Building.

"She won't be late," I say.

"You don't know her like we do," Jimmy says.

"I've heard the way she's been talking about this all week, so I know she's not gonna miss out," I say.

"You wanna bet on that?" Lance suggests.

"I'll win," I say.

"I'll take that chance," he says. We shake hands. I'm gonna win, and I'm going to enjoy rubbing it in for a while.

"I'm on Noel's side this go 'round, I'd say," Lorraine says.

"You're always on Noel's side," Monica says.

"Because it's always best to be on Benny's side," Lorraine replies.

"Hey, hey, hey, I'm just a part-time Benny. And I'm still the new guy. Aren't you gonna at least haze me a little?" I say.

"The new guy who's shared root beers with Fletcher Dorian. Most of us have never seen the man's face," Jimmy says.

I shrug, trying to maintain some modesty, even though I don't really have to.

When Mr. Dorian asked me to be the new Benny, I didn't realize it is mostly a night job. Keeping the other revenants in line and the Dark Park peaceful, I like to think I've used the title to do some good too. I've kept the Sack Head Kids and the other child ghosts safe from Dewey, spent some time with Wallace Vickers so he's not so grumpy and murderous, and given Bogart and Jolene relationship advice.

Benny can't fix everything, but what he can fix makes Bennytown a better place.

When I'm not Benny, I still keep busy. I spend a lot of time in my old Pedro Parrot's uniform helping clean up around the restaurants. God knows I've saved more than a few living family members from nasty accidents. They never see me but still look relieved if a little unsettled, like they just walked over a grave. A little gratitude would be nice from time to time, but they're usually busy so I don't trouble them.

When Bennytown is open, there's nothing I love more than watching people having magical days. I've been known to take misplaced items to Lost & Found or bring any lost child to Guest Services at the front of the park. If I see someone who needs directions, I have no trouble making myself visible and guiding them where they need to go. When they thank me, a few have given me an extra-long second glance like they know me from somewhere. None of them believe it is me, so on their merry way with a little less spring in their step.

Finally, we reach the Family Member Building's entrance. There's a good-sized crowd of other spirits already gathered here, waiting eagerly to see the show. I recognize a few familiar faces like Wallace Vickers, Jill, Jolene and Bogart, and even JK who's become a lot less of a jerk after the Candy Troll bit him in half.

A few spirits run off after we arrive, probably because I killed them. I hope that'll change eventually, since I hope to be friends with as many of Bennytown's ghosts as I can.

Admittedly, these ones might take a little longer to befriend.

In saving Bennytown, I killed eighteen people, grievously wounding several more. Except for the kids who leaped before me, the other new members of the Bennytown family haven't adjusted to an eternity here. My goal is to help them get over it in time, so we can all be one big happy family. Since time is on my side, I'm optimistic.

If only they could heal as fast as Bennytown.

While attendance dipped for a brief period after my so called "Bennytown Sixtieth Birthday Massacre," it recovered swiftly. All it took was a turbulent news cycle of presidential politics and rumblings of viruses from across the sea before people forgot and moved on with their lives. Bennytown's handling of the crisis, especially by the brave security team who subdued me, has been widely praised. While the media is still trying to assign blame for my killing spree to whatever flavor of the month evil they're on right now, Bennytown has publicly called for a compassionate review of mental health laws, since I was clearly a deeply troubled young man.

Their attentiveness and call for thoughts and prayers has actually marked a record increase in ticket sales.

All because I saved Bennytown.

Looking from the small crowd of spirits back into the park, I see a familiar head of black hair bouncing over to us.

"Told ya," I say.

"Yeah, yeah," Lance says. "Lemme guess, I'm distracting Dewey tonight?"

"You read my mind," I say as Lance scowls.

Garcia runs up to us, beaming.

"Were they here?" I ask.

"In the flesh," she says, pulling someone's no doubt "lost" phone from her pocket.

She shows us a few pictures of a handsome, man in his mid-thirties next to a slightly overweight man wearing glasses. The couple are standing by a young girl around the age of six. They're taken at a distance, but Garcia took enough pictures to show off her family well.

"My son, Diego, his husband, Miles, and my granddaughter, Lucy," Garcia says with a sense of pride and longing. Monica and Lorraine coo appropriately, while Jimmy and Lance just clap her on the back.

Seeing her family leaves a bittersweet taste in my mouth. I'd kill for news about Dad, since he's avoided Bennytown like the plague. If he ever decided to visit, I'd find a way to explain myself to him. Part of me doubts he'll ever come here, but I have my hopes.

"You have a beautiful family, Garcia," I say, holding back the sadness in my voice.

"I know," she says. "I even got to talk to him a little. I took a crumpled old map from my trash can and asked him if he dropped it. He said it wasn't his but thanked me for trying to help." She sniffles, a little. "My little man, so polite."

"No surprise. He's got an awesome mom," I say. She smiles back, softly.

Things between us were awkward right after the Sixtieth Birthday. Garcia was ticked that I didn't listen to her and wound up killing all those people. When she realized we had an eternity to spend together, she got over it and things are like old times.

If only things were so easy with the rest of the spirits here.

"Incoming," Lorraine says as she watches a family member approaching us.

"I got this," I say.

I break apart from the group and jog down the path toward the park, intercepting Kathleen before she can join the audience.

"I'm gonna have to ask you to turn around," I say, firm.

"And why the hell's that?" Kathleen asks.

"You know why, though your language certainly isn't helping your case," I say.

"Seriously, Noel?" Kathleen asks.

"Seriously. Mr. Dorian recognizes your contributions to the Bennytown family and is pleased to have you here full time, but we can't abide by what you're planning. Until you've renounced your plans and vowed allegiance to the family, we can't have you potentially interfering with any family events," I say, lying only a little. I haven't seen Mr. Dorian since the night before the Sixtieth Birthday, but I like to think I've got a handle on his feelings.

I'm pretty sure he'd be deeply disappointed in Kathleen right about now.

From what I've heard, Mr. Dorian personally freed her from his Bengineers and apologized for the inconvenience. What did he get for his kindness? A slap in the face followed by Kathleen gathering forces for some kind of spectral insurrection. She's already won over the hippies and a number of my victims. I won't let it escalate, but it has been disrupting the peace lately.

"You disappoint me, Noel," Kathleen says.

"I'm really sorry for that, Kathleen, but you're the greater disappointment. I have hope for you, though. If JK can come around to an understanding, I know you can too!"

"It'll take more than an ice pick in the eye to make me come around. Come hell or high water, we're gonna burn this park to the fucking ground," Kathleen says.

"WAIT!" I yell, before they can get too far away.

With body language declaring that she's doing this against her better judgment, Kathleen stops.

"Is Olivia happy?" I ask.

"No. She was murdered by her fucking boyfriend, and then her soul got trapped in America's favorite theme park by a corporate conspiracy. I'd say she's pretty fucking unhappy," Kathleen says.

"Can you tell her I'm sorry? I never meant to hurt her. I never meant this for her. Can you tell her that?"

Kathleen sighs. "Of course."

"Thank you," I say.

She walks away again. "Stop drinking the Kool-Aid, kid. If you want her back, that's what you need to do."

I wave to her, waiting until she gets out of sight before dropping the act.

Kathleen wants me to turn my back on Bennytown, something I can never do.

Olivia will see the light. I believe in her.

I'll do whatever I have to do to get into her good graces again. It might take some years, but I'll win her over to me, to Bennytown, and then everything will be right with the world again.

And that, I think, is the most beautiful part of Bennytown. It's got its problems, but nothing that can't be fixed with hard work and gumption. Believe in Bennytown enough and all your dreams can come true. They may not come true the way you imagine, and the path to getting those dreams may not always be pleasant, but things will work out if you believe enough.

I join the others when Garcia beckons to me.

"They're coming, they're coming!"

I hop into my hiding spot with the rest of the Cool Kids Club as the new winter hires parade by us. On their orientation day, watching them enter the park as first-time employees is the greatest entertainment in the world. We take bets on who'll make it to full time and who's going to crack under pressure and everything in between.

Garcia, in particular, has her own ideas.

"We need another girl for the Cool Kids Club. No offense, Noel, but you're throwing off my preferred chick-to-dude ratio," she scoffs.

"None taken," I say. "Any particulars you got in mind?"

"Not bad to look at, but not too heavy on the makeup. Someone who looks like she can have a good time," Garcia says.

"I'm tired of being the token blonde," Lorraine says.

"Dancers are always fun!" Monica says.

"You won't hear any complaints from me on any of those," Lance says.

"Ditto," Jimmy replies.

While they debate, I scan the orientation group as they file toward Bennytown, keeping an eye out for any who fit the bill.

One likely possibility pops up right at the end of the group.

She's sporting pixie cut blond hair, hipster glasses, and the petite body and graceful walk of someone with dance training. With an innocent face, she seems fresh out of high school. She keeps tugs at the long sleeve of her shirt to cover up a butterfly tattoo on her wrist. With sharp eyes, she's taking in the details of her surroundings.

Her nametag reads ALEXIS.

Something tugs at my senses that the others don't seem to notice. I try a little experiment.

I make myself visible, but only barely, and not as myself, as Benny. If she's like all the others, she won't see me, but if she has the sight, I'll stand out, maybe not as clear as day in the shadows like I am, but clear enough.

Her scanning eyes go past me, then lock onto me.

She smiles.

I wave at her.

She waves back, shyly, then runs to catch up with the rest of her orientation group.

Smiling myself, I say, "Well, isn't that exciting?"

ACKNOWLEDGMENTS

This book has been a labor of love that's off and on taken about five years of my life. I've picked it up and set it down more times than I can count, nearly lost it and threw it away almost as many, but at the end of the day I kept going thanks to the help and encouragement of a lot of great people. So here, I thank them.

As always, the first thanks must go to my wonderful agent, Fran Black, at Literary Counsel, for everything she has done, will do, and is always doing for me. Thank you for taking on a project that I know was outside of your comfort zone, and for believing in *Bennytown* when I had difficulty doing so.

Thank you to everyone at Owl Hollow Press who took a chance on me and helped sculpt my raw words into something even remotely readable, especially my editors Olivia Swenson and Hannah Smith, who really helped the material take on a new life, and helped me deal with my many, many written verbal tics.

Thank you, Dad, for taking me to Universal Studios so many times when I was a kid and encouraging me to apply there for my first job. And more than that, for teaching me the value of a good story and character development. I wish you could've lived to see this book; I think you'd have had fun with it.

A special thanks to everyone working in the theme park industry for working your butts off creating magic in a world that is frequently in desperate need of some. I know this book comes across harsh, but you're some of the hardest working people I've ever known and had the privilege to work alongside, and you deserve all the praise you can get.

And finally, of course, thanks must go to my amazing wife, Fiona. You are my inspiration always, and the greatest partner in both life and writing that anyone could ever ask for. Thank you for your belief, your encouragement, and patience. I don't think Bennytown could have happened without you. Also, thank you for acting as my human shield whenever we go to Halloween Horror Nights; I couldn't do those mazes without you!

MATT CARTER

is an author of Horror, Sci-Fi, and Superhero fiction. He has used his lifelong love for writing, history and the bizarre to bring novels like *Almost Infamous: A Supervillain Novel, Pinnacle City: A Superhero Noir* (co-authored by his wife, Fiona J.R. Titchenell) and the *Prospero Chronicles* young adult horror series (also co-authored by Titchenell) to life.

He is represented by Fran Black of Literary Counsel and lives in the usually sunny town of San Gabriel, CA with his wife, their pet king snake Mica, and the myriad of strange fictional characters and worlds that live in his head.

#BENNYTOWN